the fall

claire mcgowan
the fall

headline

First published in Great Britain in 2012 by
HEADLINE PUBLISHING GROUP

1

Cataloguing in Publication Data is available from the British Library

Hardback ISBN 978 0 7553 8633 8
Trade paperback ISBN 978 0 7553 8634 5

Typeset in Sabon by Avon DataSet Ltd,
Bidford-on-Avon, Warwickshire

Printed and bound by CPI Group (UK) Ltd, Croydon, CR0 4YY

Headline's policy is to use papers that are natural, renewable and
recyclable products and made from wood grown in sustainable forests.
The logging and manufacturing processes are expected to conform to
the environmental regulations of the country of origin.

HEADLINE PUBLISHING GROUP
An Hachette UK Company
338 Euston Road
London NW1 3BH

www.headline.co.uk
www.hachette.co.uk

For my parents, who gave the books, told the stories,
and held us all together.

Prologue

Monday

This is it. Her head was strangely clear despite the blood filling up her nose and mouth. An inch from her eye, the floor of the toilet was that kind of speckled plastic you got in public buildings, the dots like islands marooned in a sea of blue. Funny how she'd never looked at it properly before. But yes, that was it – little islands, on a vast blue sea, and every one filled with small people, somewhere a million miles from here. She heard distant sounds, like someone talking far, far away, a voice on a crossed phone line. It was a whimpering, like an animal in pain. It was coming from somewhere inside her.

This is it. She was bleeding from her mouth and she couldn't get up; something had happened to her legs – they'd given way or they wouldn't work or . . . something. Maybe she would lie here for ever. Maybe if she just stayed here and closed her eyes she could go back and none of it would have happened.

This is it. Through the roaring in her ears, she had the thought very clearly, as if looking down on herself crumpled up on the floor. This was what it felt like when you hit rock bottom, when you'd lost everything that mattered. Rock bottom, and it smelled of bleach and tasted like the sour, metallic tang of blood.

Part One

Three days earlier – Friday

Keisha

The social-worker woman was really fucking Keisha off. It was the way she sat there, dull as shit in this awful cardie from BHS or somewhere, and the short grey hair and the glasses on a string, like a granny, for fuck's sake. But mostly it was the way she talked, all soft and gentle, like she'd been on a course to deal with fucking retards.

Keisha slumped down in the plastic seat, squeaking her Dunlop trainers over the floor, and her mum gave her a look. Of course *she* was nodding along with every word Sandra said, like it was the Lord's own gospel. Yes, Keisha, you *are* too unstable to have your own bloody kid living with you, even though you've got a flat and a job and a man. What fucking more did they want?

'But I don't get it, right?' She folded her arms in her new denim jacket – one of *his* presents, trying to make up for yet another crappy thing he'd done. 'I did what you said, yeah? I got her room sorted, and her bed, wardrobe, all that shit. In bloody pink ruffles.'

Keisha's mum glared at her. 'Language,' she muttered, her thick voice pure Kingston even after thirty years in England. 'Manners of a field hand.'

Sandra was staring between them probably thinking she

3

couldn't get enough of all this juicy *unresolved conflict*, as she would call it. If she loved it so fucking much, she should go and work on *Trisha* or something.

'The thing is, Keisha,' Sandra said, setting her pen down carefully. 'The thing is, we're still a bit concerned about the relationship you're in.'

'He's her fucking dad!'

'Don't you be effin' and blindin' before the lady!' her mother bellowed. If Keisha had been just a few years younger, Mercy would have belted her round the ear.

'That's OK, Mercy,' said Sandra earnestly. 'I understand it must be hard for Keisha, when Christopher is, as she says, Ruby's father. But after what happened, you must see he needs to change. He's never even come to meet with me, in all this time.'

'He's busy.' She'd begged him to come, much fucking use it was. Sat at home in his pants and Arsenal top, playing on the Xbox – *me time*, he called it. While she had to trudge up to this depressing shithole, smelled just like her old school, same echoing corridors, and Sandra talking at her in that *you-are-a-loony* voice.

Her mum was nodding along again, meaty arms folded over her vast boobs. 'Good for nothin', that boy. Only good thing he ever do's make that baby.'

Keisha slumped further. It wasn't fair, these two spinster bitches telling her to leave the man she loved – *her* man. When everyone knew how lucky she was to even be allowed to breathe near Chris Dean. They didn't understand a thing.

'OK, Keisha,' Sandra said, blinking rapidly. 'We'll see if Christopher will come next time. Until then my hands are tied, I'm afraid. He has to show he won't let it happen again, what he did.'

'He won't.' He'd promised her, when she screamed in his face. She'd even slapped him – now, months later, she wasn't sure how she'd been able to do that, or why he hadn't slapped her back harder.

'I'll let you out.' Sandra got up, huffing. She wasn't as fat as Mercy, but she still had rolls of flab jiggling under her chin. Gross.

In the crappy waiting room, all dirty windows and bent plastic seats, Ruby was playing. She had a colouring book and a tatty old Barbie doll Mercy'd bought her in the pound shop. It wasn't even a real Barbie, just a white plastic doll with blonde hair. Didn't look much like Ruby, with her kinky hair tied up in bunches. The kid's big dark eyes were nervous behind her glasses. The cast was off now, thank God. Keisha had hardly been able to look at the thing. She hovered in the doorway, looking at her daughter.

Sandra obviously thought she was good with kids; probably she'd been on a course for that too. She stuck her fat face down to Ruby's. 'Hello, precious. Is that your dolly? Isn't she pretty?' Ruby ducked her head, and you could see her going in on herself. She was shy, and who could blame her after what her own dad did to her? Ruby looked from the social worker to Keisha. Then she shuffled close to Mercy, clutching hold of her cheap dolly, hiding in against her granny's fat body.

'Well, you're a shy one.' Sandra laughed but Keisha could see she was hurt. She understood how that was – it'd taken her a while not to expect Ruby to come over and hug her like she used to. She stuck her hands under her arms so she wouldn't try to hold the kid.

'Come on, my sweetypie, home time.' Keisha's mum folded her granddaughter into her chest, and it was right,

Keisha had to admit. You would see the two of them, and even though they were both light-skinned enough, you'd say, oh yeah, black granny, black grandkid. It looked right. That was the problem. That was when everything had started to go wrong.

'We'll get sweets, eh? Fruit Pastilles, ice lolly?' Puffing, Mercy let the girl slide down. Ruby's face puckered, thinking about what sweets to have, no doubt, and for a moment Keisha wished it was her going home with her mum, the safeness of it, eating sweets in front of Friday cartoons. Or even that she was the one buying, saying to Ruby, *You have to brush your teeth after*.

She wanted to say something to Ruby. It was the first time she'd seen her in weeks; Chris didn't like her going to visit. She wanted to say something, but what was there? Nothing. Fuck all. She waited till Mercy and her granddaughter had wobbled far enough down the corridor, and then set off fast in the opposite direction.

Charlotte

'So, Charlotte – keeping busy? Not long now, eh?'

Charlotte was by now an expert at minimising one computer window while beaming a large smile at her boss and calling up a document on the branding of a new rice-cake snack. 'A week tomorrow.'

'So we shouldn't count on seeing you down the boozer after work?' He leaned over the partition, so close she was breathing his aftershave.

She managed to look regretful. 'Oh, sorry, no. We just have so much to do – you know how it is.'

He waved his empty coffee cup. 'How about I make you a cup of the hard stuff, at least, before you abandon us?'

'I'll do it, Simon, you must be swamped,' she said, as she knew he expected.

Filling the kettle at the tiny sink area, Charlotte sneaked a look at the clock. 4.06 p.m. She would be out of here soon, for an increasingly rare free weekend with Dan. It was a lie that they had plans. For the past month Dan had crashed into bed at nine, worn out from fourteen-hour days, and she'd sat up poring over wedding magazines and stationery designs. It felt like they'd been passing in the corridor for so long. But not tonight. It was going to be a proper romantic evening in, talking, being together. She'd make sure of it.

As she brought him his coffee, Simon was standing over the new girl – what was her name again? Tory, that was it – his crotch pressed into the back of her ergonomic chair as he pointed to something on the screen. Charlotte remembered it – she remembered that part of Simon a bit better than she wished.

'Coffee,' she said brightly, passing him the mug he always had to have, the one with the crest of his Oxford college on it, to remind everyone he was an intellectual, even if he wrote copy for cereal ads.

'Oh, Tory,' she said. 'I wanted a quick chat with you, about the Snax rebrand?' Like every woman in the office, all Charlotte's statements were questions, rising up at the end. It showed friendliness, a willingness to be contradicted. She didn't notice she did it any more.

Simon withdrew. 'You've got it now, Tory. I'll leave you ladies to it.' He strutted off in his Prada cardigan, drips of coffee catching in his beard.

Tory looked worried. 'God, it's a bit dodge, isn't it? His you-know-what was, like, millimetres from my armpit.'

Charlotte pushed back her curly hair, the colour of very good old gold, and imparted some wisdom. 'It's mostly harmless. But listen, if he asks you for a drink, make sure there's other people there too. Like, seriously.'

The other girl laughed uncertainly and Charlotte felt pleased with herself, how she knew her way round this office, how she could handle Simon like a little lamb, after hard-learned lessons. She'd done it now, and she wouldn't have to go back and be like this Tory, clueless. 'It'll be OK. Don't worry.'

4.15 p.m. Surreptitiously she opened her table-planning software. Yes, the rebranding of seventy-calorie snack bags was a big deal, and she would definitely buy them herself when they came out, but the wedding was just a week away and her bloody cousin Mary and that drip of a husband of hers still hadn't RSVPed. Unbelievable! And what about Dan's rowdy college group, which would include at least one broken-up couple and an ex of his? She pursed her lips, moving little names round the screen, like some very organised goddess.

Keisha

Chris hadn't believed her at first, when Ruby arrived. 'She's fucking black, that kid,' he'd said, when the baby was just days old, when you could see her eyes turning all these shades of brown, like stones drowned under water. It was the most gorgeous thing Keisha'd ever seen.

'I dunno how,' Keisha had said over and over, her eyes leaking as much as her stupid pregnancy boobs, like a tap she couldn't turn off. 'She's yours. I swear to God, she's yours.'

Of course the kid was his. There'd been no one else, not since Keisha was twelve and sitting in History and saw him standing in the door with a fag hanging down from that mouth of his. She'd heard it could happen sometimes. And it must have. Only a quarter black in this baby – less, maybe, if Mercy had any white in her – but you could see it in Ruby's hair, in her nose, in the dark almonds of her eyes. And there was Keisha, nothing like either of them. White, you would say, unless you looked closely.

'People be sayin' I stole you,' Keisha's mum used to say when they went to mother and toddler group, years ago. But whose fault was that? It was Mercy who'd had it off with some random white guy, got knocked up, and dropped out of her college course. Keisha had spent most of her life wondering about every white guy she saw of the right age; dudes with briefcases and umbrellas, drunks hanging round tube stations. It could be anyone. Mercy had never told her a thing.

Walking away from Sandra's office in West Hampstead, she decided. She would bring Chris home some nice dinner out of Waitrose, that shiny new Waitrose on Finchley Road, and if he was in a good mood she'd ask him again to help her get their kid back. But when she took out her purse she realised the money from her wages was gone again. 'You fucker,' she said out loud, and set off walking home.

Charlotte

With just a week to go to the wedding, Charlotte's mother's phone calls were up to four a day. Did she get the message that Auntie Jan was gluten- and dairy-free now? Had she found out the surname of Cousin Lucy's new boyfriend? Because you couldn't just put someone's first name on the place-tag, imagine. And what if the roses weren't the right shade of pink? They'd clash with the table linens. And now, right at the checkout in Waitrose on Finchley Road, as Charlotte was struggling with her basket of Friday-night groceries, her phone rang.

'Mum?'

'Hello? Hello? Goodness, I can hardly hear you.' Charlotte's mother only used the phone if she was seated at her special phone table, the message pad and pen at the ready. She didn't understand that her daughter might pick up while at work, or in the gym, or crossing a busy road.

'Hang on, Mum, I'm just paying.'

'Pardon? Oh, you're in a *shop*.' Gail considered it extremely impolite to be on the telephone whilst being served in a shop.

Charlotte heaped her groceries up, balancing the phone while stacking the olives, the ciabatta, the good bottle of Prosecco.

'Hello? Hello? I just had another thought, darling – what if someone's lactose-intolerant?'

She scrabbled for her debit card. 'What if someone's *what*?'

'The chicken, Charlotte, it's cooked in cream. Some people don't eat that. That's why I wanted to get the salmon. Chicken's so – well, it's ordinary, darling, for a wedding.'

Charlotte took a deep breath, as Dan had urged her to do when her mother went off on one. 'It's fine. It's the Mandarin Oriental, Mum. They'll handle it.'

The girl was waiting for her to pay, and Charlotte heard an impatient sigh behind her from another shopper. She flashed an apologetic smile at the cashier, keyed in her pin, and started dumping the groceries into her eco-friendly cotton bag. 'Sorry, Mum, can I call you later?' She hung up with no intention at all of ringing again.

From the Waitrose on Finchley Road it was just two streets to Charlotte and Dan's flat, the second floor of one of the square, solid Belsize Park townhouses. She fumbled with the keys and shopping, but someone had left the front door ajar again, it was so annoying. She suspected the weird guy from the basement flat.

She bent to pick up the scattered post from the shared hallway – again, no one ever lifted it – flyers, a catalogue from Mothercare (Dan would raise his eyebrows and throw it straight in the recycling), an acceptance card from Tom and Julie. She blanked on the names for a minute, mentally scanning the endless guest list her mother was insisting on. Tom was a friend of Dan's from Oxford, she thought. Who would RSVP with only a week to go? It was so rude. Dan always shrugged and said, 'Who cares?' but he didn't have a retired mother breathing down his neck every day, and an endless source of worry about everything from bridesmaids' hair accessories to the ribbon on the favour boxes.

Her phone rang again, as she hefted the shopping up the two flights of stairs to their flat, and she rolled her eyes – *Please, not another Mum call.*

'Charlotte, it's Sarah.'

'Yes, I can see that.' She juggled her key into the lock of the flat door.

'What?'

'I mean, your name comes up – never mind.'

'Has Gail spoken to you about this shoe issue?'

'She called before, but not about shoes. I thought it was sorted.'

'It's not sorted! I can't actually *wear* the shoes. I've told her again and again, my toe's broken. I can't wear strappy sandals when I have a splint on.'

Charlotte vaguely remembered her mother saying something about Sarah breaking her toe on a dry-ski slope, but she'd screened it out.

'I don't want to get Dad involved, but really, I know she's your mum and all, but I really think she's lost it on this one.'

Charlotte was in the flat now, registering with distant surprise that the lights were on and Dan was home already, standing at the window looking out at the view of Parliament Hill. She tried to focus on her step-sister. 'Well, I don't know, can you get a different pair in the same colour?'

Sarah laughed bitterly. 'You'd think so, but no, that would be far too easy.'

Dan hadn't turned round as she crab-walked into the kitchen with the bags and started putting things in the fridge, all the while struggling with the phone. 'Look, I'll talk to Mum. I'm sorry about your toe. Call you tomorrow maybe?'

'I'm going to Bangladesh for a week, remember?'

Wondering how she could still travel with a broken toe, Charlotte said goodbye and hung up. Her step-sister Sarah, tall and square, a journalist who skied at weekends, hadn't responded well to being decked out in Charlotte's mum's vision of pink frills.

'Finally,' she said to Dan, who still hadn't turned round. 'I'm switching this phone off.' She bustled round the kitchen, looking for the nice plates to put the food on. 'I got us some little tapas-y bits, I thought we both needed a relaxing night . . .'

Finally he spoke. 'Can you come here?'

'Just a sec.'

'Charlotte – come here.'

She had a tub of olives in one hand and one of marinated anchovies in the other. That was what she remembered afterwards. That for just a moment before he told her, choosing between olives and anchovies was the most difficult thing she thought she'd have to do that night.

Keisha

It took Keisha a while to trudge back to her flat, down Finchley Road to the Swiss Cottage junction, under the underpass, to one of the grey concrete blocks overlooking the busy road. She could hear their TV three floors below, the stone stairs echoing with it – he was home, watching *The Simpsons* on Sky. He could always find the cash to pay for things he wanted.

The flat was cold when she went in, and it smelled greasy, like an empty McDonald's wrapper, and no surprise there was a heap of them on the coffee table, scarred with tea-rings and fag burns. He never thought to put the heat or lights on, but he was there, in front of the telly with a joint, a two-litre bottle of Coke open at his feet. The kitchen was a tip. It was so bad she didn't even notice anything was gone for a while, clearing the dirty dishes and takeaway boxes and fag-ends.

Lifting a crushed can of Carlsberg, she stopped. 'Where's the microwave?'

'Eh?'

'The microwave – it's gone.' Was it? She turned round in the cramped space, thinking maybe she was losing it. But it wouldn't be the first time she came home and something was gone, like the CD player. Or her GHD hair-straighteners.

Both easily found by walking down the road to Cash Converters in Kentish Town.

He didn't even look round when she went in. 'You hocked it,' she said.

'Needed to pay the Sky. Anyway, it's mine, isn't it?'

'Yeah, but . . .'

'But?' He tapped out his joint into an empty beer can, still not looking up from the TV.

'What're we going to eat?' There were only ready-meals in the freezer. 'I was gonna go to the shops, but . . .' She decided not to mention the cash.

'Who needs to eat? C'mere.' He jerked his head at her and, encouraged, she sat down and ran her hand over his shaved hair – like rough velvet.

'Leave off,' he said, but not nastily.

'So I saw her,' she risked. 'Earlier.'

'Who?' He scratched his eyebrow, where the new ring was still red and swollen.

'You know. Ruby.'

He said nothing, and she lost her nerve. 'Yeah, she was OK. They said maybe, soon, if everything's OK, we can have her back.'

He flicked ash delicately, waiting for her to say more. She didn't. It was the right thing to do. His arm snaked round her and under her jacket, under her T-shirt. His breath in her ear was of ash and sugar. 'How's about we head out, babes? If there's no dinner. You can get those sexy legs out for me.' He ran a hand over her thighs.

'Where?' She was so knackered. After a week on nights, she'd gotten up early to see Sandra. She was so worried about Ruby. The last thing she wanted to do was go out with high heels blistering her feet and R 'n' B pounding her head.

'Well, there's this guy, yeah, and he's got this club down in Camden, so I thought I'd do, like, a bit of a business visit . . . What? What's that fucking look for?'

'Oh! Nothing.' What his business was exactly she didn't ask any more. When Chris got fired from his security job in the recession, he said he wasn't going crawling to some twat, he'd set up on his own. She wasn't sure what his work was but it meant going to bars and clubs a lot, never the same one twice, shaking hands with men in cheap suits, ordering bottles of vodka.

His mouth came down on hers, as he threw the spent joint on the table. 'You and your looks. Drive me mad, them looks.'

She tried one last time, as his hands reached into her jeans. 'Will you come with me, next time? Maybe?'

'Maybe.'

Charlotte

Dan said, 'Did you not even see it? How could you miss it?' He turned round from the window, still in his crumpled suit, and she saw his face. She should have known something was wrong, because he always took the suit off right away when he came in. It had cost over five grand.

'Did I see what?' she said stupidly, still holding the tubs of food in both hands. But when he said it, she knew. She had seen it, yes, on the paper-stand at Waitrose, but flustered and rushed, she hadn't taken it in. 'Oh, God. It was your place – your bank.' HAUSSMANN'S AT THE BRINK. That was where Dan worked. 'What does it mean? Are you . . . ?'

'No.' He collapsed down on the sofa, running his hands through his hair. 'Not yet. They sent us home. People were walking out with boxes. You know, in case we don't open next week.'

'Christ. Is it really that bad?' She couldn't take it in.

'I don't know.' He looked shell-shocked. 'They won't tell us if there's a buyer or not. I swear, people were walking round like a bomb went off. I saw one of the partners crying. Fuck. It's a mess.'

She sat the olives and anchovies on the table and went over to him. 'But there could be a buyer?'

'Maybe. There was talk – I don't know.' He was staring at the blank eye of the TV, shoulders rigid with shock.

'But that's crazy,' she soothed, rubbing down his hair. 'They'd hardly let a whole bank go under, come on. All they've done is send you home. I'm sure there's loads of buyers. It's a good asset, isn't it?'

He just shook his head. 'If anyone goes, it'll be me.'

'What? You're one of the best, aren't you? Dan? Didn't you make them tons of money last year?'

She looked at him, all the muscles in his solid back stiff, and a jolt of fear went through her. 'Dan? Oh God. It can't be true. The wedding – what will we do?'

He let out a long shaky breath. 'No, you're probably right. It'll be OK.'

Relief flooded her. 'You're sure?'

'Course. I'll look after you.' His hand scrabbled for hers, the one with the ring, and pressed it to the side of his face. 'I've been going mad. Why's your phone always busy?'

'Well.' She got up to change. 'That's because my mother is crazy. Did you know you were marrying into a family of nutters?'

'Yeah.' He put on his wedding look, unsure and slightly afraid, as if he didn't quite know what of.

'So you can't lose your job,' she said, saying the words out loud, to make them true. 'We've got two hundred people coming for dinner next week – we need that bonus!'

Keisha

After they did it on the sofa, Chris had a sort of gleam in his eyes. He slapped her on the arse as she cleaned her teeth. 'Get your kit on, then.'

He was different from most blokes. He noticed what she wore, bought her things. Could be a cheap print dress from the market, and the colour would bleed out in the wash, or could be brand-new Kurt Geiger shoes, fresh from the box. She didn't ask questions any more.

'Put on the purple dress,' he said, leaning on the doorframe. When they went out like this, aftershave rolling off him, his tie tight to his raw shaved throat, his eyes so cool, so blue – well, she was proud. She always hoped they'd bump into someone she knew, one of those bitches from school who looked down on her for being not white, not black. *Look, it's my fella*, she'd want to say. *He's sexy. He's mine.*

'Wear heels with it.'

'But I'm too tall! And they're so sore.' Keisha was five-ten, and the heels made her taller than him, but he wanted her like those other girls, plucked and tweezed and squished. So long as it wasn't comfy it would do. Had he always been this way, wanting her squeezed into things, so other men could see? Or was it the gangs, the clubs, the scabby men and tarty women he hung out with? She'd rather wear her jeans and trainers, but she took out the untouched box from the bottom of the wardrobe and limped into the stupid high shoes, like he wanted.

Charlotte

Secretly, Charlotte had always fancied Dan more when he was in a bad mood. His eyes would go flinty, his mouth set firm. When she saw him so shocked, so beaten, she felt the weakness in her, that her world was built all around him like a fragile plant on a trellis, and if he pulled away it would tear her up. Let's go somewhere, he'd said, rifling through their untouched copy of *Time Out*, and even though she was so tired and she wanted to watch a DVD, she knew she would say yes, just because of that look on his face.

'I suppose we could. Is anything on?'

'What about this? Kingston Town – a Jamaican club. That'd be good, wouldn't it, get us in the mood for the honeymoon?'

She'd never been anywhere like that in her life. 'Where is it?'

'Just down the road. Camden.'

'Oh.' She didn't say it, but Camden on a Friday night . . . Well, Dan would keep her safe if anything happened. 'Are you sure . . . Do you think we'll like that sort of thing?'

'I don't know. I just want to try something new. Don't you?' Restlessly, he got up and came to stand in the bedroom doorway. 'You should wear that thingy. You know, that lacy thing.'

He didn't know much about clothes, but liked her to have expensive ones. Charlotte earned enough at the PR company, more than lots of people, she knew that, but it was Dan's money that had floated them up to this level, like boats in a lock.

'What thing?' Charlotte's French Connection wrap dress puddled on the bedroom floor, and she was glad she'd put on vaguely matching underwear that morning.

He pointed. 'That one.'

She looked at it doubtfully, a slip dress he had once brought back from Hong Kong for her. She would never normally have worn it, never had before, but her body was winnowed out with the wedding diet – she would be her thinnest when she walked down that aisle if it killed her.

'I've got something for you.' Dan had something in his hand, a small plastic baggy. 'Guess what Alex wanted out of his desk in a hurry?'

'What's that?'

'Charlie, Charlotte. It's Charlie.' He laughed, sounding not like himself, and she understood what it was, and that he had already taken some.

'Oh. But you know I've never . . .'

'Come on, sweetheart. I really need something. My head's fucked. Everyone there'll be on something, I bet.'

'But – is it safe?' She hesitated as he chopped the powder up on the dresser and held out a tenner. He put up his hand, stroked her face. She was still in her underwear.

'You're so sweet, you know that? The only person I know still just saying no. Was it *Grange Hill* that did it?'

She pushed him gently; so strong, so solid. If she could lean on him, things would be OK. 'As long as you look after me.' She bent and inhaled and felt it fizz up her nose. 'I don't feel anything. Is it working?'

'It'll work. Take some more.'

Keisha

Keisha was pissed off. He'd made her walk all the way down from Swiss Cottage to Camden, too tight to pay two pounds for the bus, so when they got to the club her ankles were red-raw. It was May, but she was still fucking freezing in just her denim jacket. He spoke to the doorman in that annoying cool-dude way of his, and they breezed in past the queue of people. Some white guy standing with his girlfriend shouted out in a posh voice, 'Oi, mate! We were here first!'

That felt good, she'd admit. But now they'd been in the club ages and he was still 'doing business' in the VIP section – two crappy roped-off booths. Chris was acting like P bloody Diddy or someone. That was when she spotted the girl, the blonde one from the queue coming in, saying loudly to her boyfriend that she wanted a *mo-hi-to*, saying it with an annoying accent. She'd a lovely dress on, all silk and lace, not like the cheap knock-offs Keisha could afford to buy. Some people got all the luck.

The two other girls in the VIP bit were getting right on her tits, too. This ho with the 'fro, the tall pretty bitch in the silver dress, was flirting with Chris so blatantly, even touching his arm. He bought her a Bacardi Breezer, green colour, the twat. The other girl – shorter, skankier – had an over-relaxed 'do' and no self-respect, you could tell. When the owner of the club came out he squeezed the shorter girl's arse, and gave Keisha a look-over. Probably thinking she could do with a boob job and a hair weave. She thought somehow this boss was pissed off with Chris being there, though he was all smiles. The two men pulled their chairs away from the girls, and talked, leaning in close. Anthony, they'd called the owner. The girls didn't talk to her and the stupid shoes hurt, so Keisha was already in a pretty bad mood when the white guy from the queue came over shouting at Anthony about something. When it started getting loud she decided to go to the loo. Stay out of trouble, that was the way. She had to if she wanted Ruby back.

Charlotte

The drug was definitely working by the time they got on the tube at Belsize Park. She giggled, clutching at the yellow pole in the carriage, wobbling on the Louboutin shoes he'd bought her for her birthday. They were so high, it was lucky she couldn't feel her feet any more. 'It's working,' she'd said, too loudly. 'This must be why people do it.'

'*Shh*, you cokehead.' He stroked the metallic blusher from her cheek and kissed her hard. Charlotte felt dizzy, his muscles solid against her. How long since he last kissed her this way? Everyone was watching. The carriage was packed with people struggling home, dead-eyed with exhaustion like Dan usually was on a Friday. The cocaine, the fright of earlier, the unexpected night out, it cast a glow over everything, transforming the trundling tube, littered with free papers, into something magical.

Charlotte was feeling the effects even more now they were in the Kingston Town club. It had crept up like a fine mist over her brain, like one minute you felt the same, wondering what all the fuss was about, and then suddenly, pow! Your brain moved at light speed, and your voice was loud and fast; it was like you could do anything. *Warp speed*, she thought, reaching out for him, but although he was dancing close to her, the drug was making them all alone in the haze. The music was fast and loud, ringing with steel drums, and she thought about the honeymoon they'd be on soon, the warm sand under her feet, looking at him through the dark of the sea. She motioned to him, as if already underwater. 'Just going . . . ladies'.' She wasn't sure he noticed.

Charlotte stumbled to the toilets, feeling clumsier than ever. She hadn't noticed it before, but this was a very *black* club, a mostly West Indian crowd. Probably that was why they called it Kingston Town. Maybe they thought she shouldn't be here, with her blonde hair. Charlotte felt inside the first stab of bad feeling. *Paranoia*, she said to herself, running water over her hands. It was why she didn't normally take drugs.

There was no soap or paper towels – dirty and wet underfoot as the toilets were, there was an attendant. Christ, they made her feel awkward. The woman had probably hidden the soap so she could scrape up more wet coins for herself.

'Fuck off,' someone was saying. 'I'm not paying to wash my bloody hands, you dirty cow. This is London, not fucking Nigeria or wherever you've come from.'

Charlotte was about to be virtuously shocked by the racism, but as the face of the speaker wavered in and out, she saw the girl was black too, or at least half-black or something. Her skin was pale but you could tell from her eyes, the shape of her face. 'It's fucking disgusting,' the girl was saying.

Privately, Charlotte agreed – it *was* disgusting, but still feeling the sharp chafing of panic, she scrabbled in her Radley purse for money. Crap, she only had notes.

The girl turned on her. 'What're *you* looking at?'

'Oh. Nothing.' Charlotte was swaying so much she could hardly get the money out. 'It's kind of a pain, I know, I agree, but yeah – bet it's not much fun, is it, sitting here? No – right?' She gave a slightly dazed smile to the angry girl and the blank-faced toilet attendant, and crumpled a fiver down in the dish, embarrassed. 'Anyway, thanks.' She wobbled out.

Keisha

The bitch! The fucking bitch! She'd been trying to make a point – it *was* fucking horrible to steal all the soap and charge people a pound for it. It was like begging, it was shameful, sitting there with your cheap market perfumes and sad little lollies. Who'd want a lolly when there was wee all over the floor? She hated clubs like this, tired black women in the toilets, your drink on a little napkin so you had to leave the change just for pouring it.

Keisha liked to know the price of things, pounds and pence, not tips and VAT and all that shit. Just a haircut, a drink, a fucking *piss*, for Christ's sake. She hated it when Chris hid tenners in his hand and palmed them to doormen and waitresses. *There you go, mate, darling, love.* Since she had Ruby she could only see those tenners as nappies that weren't going on her baby, shoes not on her kid's feet.

And then this rich bitch from the queue, chucking down her fiver, making Keisha look like a tight-arse. She would get what was coming to her, this one. You couldn't walk around for ever with lovely wavy hair and loads of money in your purse that was real designer and not off a market stall. Keisha was sure of it – things had to come back around again sometime.

She was so annoyed she went in and sat on the toilet seat for a while, just to calm down. She wondered was the white guy still going off on one outside. She had to watch herself. Chris was in a funny mood, she was in a funny mood. It was times like this that things happened, and not good things. She knew that now.

Charlotte

The first Charlotte knew anything was wrong was when the music stopped. She stood in the middle of the dance floor, like someone caught out in musical chairs – *quick, run* – dazzled by the lights.

It was Dan who was shouting. When they'd first met he never shouted, not even when shares dipped and he lost millions of pounds at work, or when she drove his Alfa Romeo into the gatepost.

'It's not fucking cancelled,' he was yelling – bellowing. 'That's a twenty-grand expense account, *mate*. Your machines are buggered up.'

Dan was over in the so-called VIP section of the club, not much to look at, and having an argument with a short dapper black man in a shiny suit, diamonds winking in his ears. Or diamanté, at least. There was another white guy there too, walking quickly away from the group, his back to them, and a short girl with flat fake hair and fake boobs was screaming in Dan's face, 'Don't you fucking speak to him like that!' Another girl with an afro and a silver dress, a tall pretty girl, was crying.

Dan shouted again – she couldn't hear what the black guy was saying to him. 'Just run it through again! There's thousands on there.'

She remembered it suddenly. Dan two months ago, in that restaurant. The long wait, the waiter rude, the food cold. Then the crash, the broken glass. Afterwards, Dan looked surprised more than anything, like he didn't understand what had happened. *It slipped.* It must have slipped.

'Maybe they stopped the card,' she said out loud, but no one would have understood her thickened voice, and anyway, she was too far away. Dan had a company credit card, but half the time he used it for himself to get the air miles that built up, and it got taken back from his salary. He was holding a beer in his hand, which she guessed he'd been trying to pay for.

Across the stilled dance floor, where people were starting to murmur and stare, Charlotte saw the black man smile. It was as if he said, 'Let's step into my office and sort this out.' That was more or less what he did say, she would later learn. When everything that happened in the next ten minutes would be repeated and endlessly rehashed in court.

She saw Dan sag, as if ashamed of what he'd said, and walk off with the man to a little door by the bar. They disappeared through it, and the music started up again.

Two days earlier – Saturday

Hegarty

DC Matthew Hegarty still, on balance, preferred London to the heaving metropolis of Barrow-in-Furness, where he'd grown up. For all its mountainous beauty, the Lake District was one of the most deprived areas in the country, and London had shops, theatres, and beautiful sexy women you hadn't gone to school with since you were four.

But it had other things too, like Jamaican men lying in sticky pools of blood, and shrieking girls in upmarket flats.

'You need to calm down, miss,' he said, unsticking his shoe from the cream carpet. Ah, crap. There was a bit of blood on the sole. The crime scene had been full of blood, awash with it as if someone had tipped out a bucket of the stuff. Footprints tracked all over it where people had tried to help. He'd burst in when he got the call, and tramped all through the blood himself, but it had been clear to see the guy was already dead. No one could lose that much blood and survive.

Remembering that, he hardened his heart against the hysterical blonde girl who was spilling out of her little silk nightie. 'Miss, we're here to arrest him,' he tried again, raising his voice over her sobs. 'He left his credit card, easy to trace. We have to detain him.'

'But everyone does it,' she was babbling. 'I don't even do drugs. It was the first time, I swear.'

Hegarty raised an eyebrow at DC Jones, the partnering officer, and made a note in his book. 'I'm not sure you've understood, miss. It's nothing to do with drugs.' Although he would certainly put that in his report, the silly bint.

The boyfriend, by contrast, hadn't said a word. He'd been naked when they came to the door, the bedroom a tumble of sheets, a thick hungover fug in the air.

The girl was all legs and curves straining out of silk. She looked like that actress, what was her name? Scarlett What's-her-name. Her full mouth was hanging open. 'But – you can't do this! You can't just arrest him!'

'Afraid we can, miss, according to the PACE codes – a reasonable belief that the suspect has been involved in a serious crime. Don't need a warrant.' He placed a card on the table. 'We'll be wanting to talk to you too, miss, if you can present yourself at the station. It's not far – Mornington Crescent. You can attend voluntarily for now. You aren't under arrest.'

Still she just stood there, staring. Her nightie was hanging very low over her breasts.

'Miss? Do you understand? You might want to get dressed, there's a search team on its way.'

She swelled with anger, which made the nightie droop even lower. 'I know you need a warrant to search the flat, for God's sake!'

'No, not if a suspect's been arrested – PACE codes again. And he will be in about two seconds.'

The boyfriend had dressed now, methodically, in jeans and a leather coat, sheepskin-lined. He looked expectantly at Hegarty. 'Well, I'm ready.'

'Daniel Stockbridge, I am arresting you in connection with the murder of one Anthony Johnson at the Kingston Town nightclub, Camden, in the early hours of May tenth this year. You do not have to say anything, but it may harm your defence if you fail to mention when questioned something that you later rely on in court. Anything you do say will be given in evidence.' He rattled through it; Matthew Hegarty knew the PACE codes inside out and upside down. 'Do you understand the caution?'

The man gritted his teeth.

'Do you understand?'

'Of course I bloody understand.'

The girl could hardly speak. 'Who the *hell* is Anthony Johnson?'

The boyfriend said, 'The guy from the club. That's who it is.'

Hegarty made another note. It would be quite significant later that Stockbridge knew this, that he wasn't even surprised. *Fatalistically calm* was how Hegarty would put it in his report, causing great amusement down at the station.

The man turned to the girl, who seemed to be rooted to the spot, tears coursing over her face, and he kissed her hard on her full mouth. Hegarty saw DC Susan Jones turn her eyes away.

'It'll be OK,' Stockbridge said to the girlfriend. 'I'll be back soon.'

Hegarty, with the dead man's blood drying on his shoes, wasn't so sure.

Charlotte

As Dan was being bundled down the stairs, Charlotte stood still in the middle of the living room until she realised she was shivering. She had on her skimpiest nightie, and the policeman had probably seen the side of her breasts. She didn't even remember putting it on. Snapping out of her frozen calm, she went to the bedroom for a jumper.

The woman officer was at the door. 'Miss? You have to stay still. We'll be doing a search.'

She could hardly speak for a moment. 'But . . . can I at least get a jumper?'

The woman watched her like a hawk as she pulled on Dan's old college sweater, drawing the hood tight about her face. Then Charlotte went through to sit on the sofa in her tiny nightdress. It was all a mistake, of course, it had to be. Maybe they'd sue and be able to upgrade to the private villa in Jamaica.

What did she even remember about last night? They were in the club, and everything was fuzzy and light, and she was laughing and talking very fast. There was that girl in the toilets, that angry girl, and she'd put down the fiver, too much, but she had no change, and she was embarrassed and she'd wobbled out and there was Dan, and he was shouting at that man in the shiny suit. Was that who they meant? Anthony Johnson – was he the club owner? She couldn't think. Her head felt huge, like a planet turning slowly in orbit, as if it was getting bigger and bigger until it would bounce off the ceiling like a balloon.

But Dan hadn't been gone that long with the Johnson man, she was sure. She'd been standing outside in the street; somehow she'd got the coats and was waiting with her bare legs, and she wanted to go home. She was there, how long? A few minutes? And then someone pushed past her – was that right? She couldn't remember anything, just the push and a smell of something sweet, a muttered curse. Had that happened? When was it – in the club, or outside?

Christ, if only she remembered! There must have been a taxi, there usually was. She'd fallen asleep, or more likely passed out, until the insistent hammering on the door, and the police, the woman very plain with a Birmingham accent, the man nervy, wiry, and they'd said, *Daniel Stockbridge?* And then, well, then Dan had gone. Her mouth still stung from his last hard kiss. She stood listening to the quiet of the Saturday-morning flat, the hum of the fridge and the tick of the retro *Happy Days* clock they'd bought in Spitalfields Market. What was she supposed to do now?

That was when she heard the voices and heavy feet on the stairs, and thought, *Crap*. Mrs Busybody downstairs would have a fit about all this noise.

Hegarty

Back at the station, Hegarty leaned on the front desk to do his notes while Daniel Stockbridge cooled his heels in the interview room. It was a little trick he'd learned from his dad, a forty-year Force man – leaving them just long enough that they'd get angry and talk more. 'What's he said then?' He was busy noting down the blood he'd walked in. That was going to be a right nightmare to explain away, but at least they had Stockbridge in custody.

'It's weird, right?' Susan Jones had a thick Brummie

accent. 'He's confessed straight up, says he did it, but not a word about the bottle.'

'Did it all get recorded?'

'Yeah – well, most.'

'Most?'

'He just started talking. All calm, like.'

Hegarty had noticed the calm, too. 'Let me speak to him, before you go traipsing all over the case.' *My* case, was what he wanted to say. This was the one, he could feel it. He'd be a DS, running his own teams. He already had his Part 1, aced the Q&A, and now this. He could almost taste it. 'You coming in for the interview?'

Susan seemed a bit more interested in the Double Decker she'd just bought out of the vending machine. 'You're doing it?' She sprayed chocolate over the case-notes she was carrying.

Hegarty winced. 'No one else here, is there? Come on.'

'I didn't mean to hurt him.' Daniel Stockbridge did seem almost robotically calm. His clothes looked too good for the grimy interview room, expensive leather, things Hegarty only saw on the pages of *Esquire*.

He started his tape recorder, saying, 'Interview with Daniel Stockbridge, DC Matthew Hegarty and DC Susan Jones. Daniel Stockbridge, you have been arrested on suspicion of the murder of Anthony Johnson. You do not have to say anything, but it may harm your defence if you fail to mention when questioned something that you later rely on in court. Anything you do say will be given in evidence. Do you understand the caution?'

'You already asked me that.'

'Do you have anything to say to the charge?'

The man looked away. 'This is ridiculous.'

Hegarty continued. 'You understand you have a right to legal counsel?'

'Look, just get on with it. I want to go home.'

Hegarty glanced at Susan. 'OK. Can you repeat what you said just before, sir, for the tape?'

Stockbridge flexed his hand. 'I hit him. Look, my knuckles are cracked. But it wasn't that hard. I missed the first time.'

'You went for him twice?'

'But not hard. He seemed OK.'

'What do you mean by "OK"?'

'I mean, he staggered back. Didn't fall over.' Stockbridge frowned, as if struggling to remember. 'Then, well, I left. I was ashamed – it's not like me.'

'And why did you hit him?'

'I was annoyed.'

Hegarty raised his eyebrows. 'Annoyed?'

'Angry.' Stockbridge folded his bruised hands on the chipboard table. 'He said my card was stopped, but I'm not— I mean, that would never happen.'

'Ah yes, your card.' The platinum Haussmann's Master-card, abandoned in the blood-stained office, had easily led them to Stockbridge. The bank had been more than willing to give out their employee's address. Strangely willing. 'But it *had* been cancelled, as it happens. Your employer blocked all expense accounts over the weekend. To stop abuse, I gather.'

For the first time Stockbridge showed some emotion. 'It's not like that, for Christ's sake. I use it all the time. It's interchangeable with my personal account.'

'Interchangeable.'

'Yes.'

Hegarty had to get a full receipt in triplicate if he bought so much as a packet of Hob-Nobs out of petty cash. 'But not working. Maybe that's why you were so *annoyed*, as you put it.'

The man was granite. 'Maybe. There was also the fact that my bank was collapsing.'

'Hmm. Do you know why you're here, Mr Stockbridge?' Remind the cool bastard that he'd spilled someone's blood all over the floor just hours before.

Stockbridge put his head in his hands. 'You said he's dead. And I don't know, that's terrible . . . But I'm telling you, he was fine when I left.'

'When you were arrested, you said . . . Can you remind us, DC Jones?'

Susan read out in her flat Midlands tones, ' "It's the guy from the club." '

'Right. Now how did you know that, Mr Stockbridge?'

'I saw his name on his desk, when he took me to the office. He had one of those silly little plaques.'

'You remembered that?'

'I have a good memory, it goes with the job.'

'But you said earlier, when your prints were taken . . . DC Jones?'

' "I think I just hit him. I don't know." '

Stockbridge shrugged. 'Yeah – well, OK, it's a bit hazy. I'd been drinking. But I remember the name.'

'I see.' Hegarty leaned back in his chair. 'And what about your ladyfriend – she was there?' *Ladyfriend.* It was a mystery why these old-fashioned phrases came out during interviews.

'Charlotte? Yes, she was there.' Stockbridge's eyes narrowed.

Hegarty tried not to look like he was picturing the curve of the girl's breast. 'Your wife?'

'Fiancée. The wedding's next week.'

I wouldn't be too sure about that, thought Hegarty, with a certain satisfaction.

Keisha

Keisha would never forget the first time she saw Chris Dean. She still had the scar to remind her, after all, the little raised lump on the side of her knee.

It was her first day in big school, the posh school she'd got into after doing the exam in that funny echoey room up in Hampstead, and her mum had cried and cried, she was so happy. 'Just like me, an A student. I was top of my class in Jamaica. Everyone said, That girl will go far.' Until she'd had Keisha, of course, and gone no further than wiping arses in the nursing home. Still, Mercy thought education was right up there with God Himself.

So it was Keisha's first day, the navy uniform cutting into her, stiff and new, and there were Asian kids and white kids and black kids, but she was the only one nobody was sure of. What was she? She was crouching her head down to the desk, her History book open to a picture of a Norman castle, when the door opened.

'Well, thanks for joining us. Christopher, is it?' The teacher, Mrs Allen, had that special sarky voice they all did. She was a fat woman who spilled over the sides of her chair.

'No worries,' he said, in the half-Irish, half-London voice, and she looked up, and as she saw him she did something spastic with her leg so it banged into the desk and started to bleed.

'Shit!' she'd shouted before she could stop herself, and

laughter spread out round her like a Mexican wave. Mrs Allen said, 'Watch your language, and do try not to break the school on your first day.'

Keisha had looked up at the boy, too cool to laugh. His eyes were the kind of blue she didn't think eyes could be in real life, a blue like the sirens on police cars. He had a pierced ear, unlit cig in his mouth – in school! He was Irish-white, pale as milk, and at thirteen, a year older than her. And that was it for her, sort of like Game Over. Even when they both got kicked out of the school the year after and her mum wouldn't speak to her for weeks, Keisha didn't care 'cos Chris was with her. It was her and him against the lot of them. Like Romeo and Juliet. Or at least, she thought so. She'd been too busy snogging him behind the bike sheds to actually pay attention in English. Course, things hadn't turned out so great for Romeo and Juliet, as it happened. So why should they for Chris and Keisha? She'd been daft to ever expect it.

After the club on Friday night, Keisha couldn't believe he'd left without her. The bastard. What a twat he was, really. When she came out of the toilets he was gone. Eventually she got fed up and took the smelly night bus home, only to find him there already, in bed.

'You left me!'

He'd mumbled under the covers, a hump in the darkness. 'Felt sick.'

'How did you— You got a cab, didn't you?' It was the only way he could have got back so soon. She couldn't believe it – that was twenty quid down the drain.

'Give over.'

'Fine, whatever.' She went to pee, easing off the shoes of death, and saw that the floor was wet from the shower.

Weirder than that, there was a tied-up plastic bag in the corridor, with what looked like clothes in it. Maybe he'd been sick. Or pissed himself. She almost laughed, then stopped herself. He went mental when she laughed at him.

Keisha squinted at the old pink bath mat – soaked of course, silly bugger. And there was something on it. Pulling up her knickers, she leaned over. It looked like he'd vomited up a Jägerbomb, like she had a few months back (bad memory). Dampening a bit of toilet paper, she dabbed at the stain. She went back into the hall and there were his new Adidas Classics, standing on a sheet of newspaper, red stains round the bottom. She went into the room. 'What happened to your shoes?'

'Stepped in a kebab. Now leave it.' He was buried in the duvet.

Exhausted, nerves jangling, she'd fitted herself into bed so she wasn't touching him, and went to sleep.

Chris had always been it for her. Back in 1997 when they'd met in school, Keisha knew for sure she would never look at another boy, not ever in a million years. That nothing could ever come between them. And this was nearly true, until what he did to Ruby, of course.

Hegarty

When Hegarty went back to the interview room, Stockbridge was looking less cool, rumpled and tired. The remains of a soggy ham sandwich sat on the table, along with the dregs of the worst cup of coffee the police station could summon up – and that was pretty bad. 'What now?'

Hegarty threw the pictures down on the table. 'Look.'

The man's face only tightened a fraction. Cold bastard. 'Why are you showing me these?'

'So you can see what you did.' See if this would break the guy's calm.

The man frowned. 'I'm confused here. Is this that Johnson guy?'

'Why don't you tell us?'

He looked away impatiently. 'I wouldn't be asking if I knew.' He pushed the pictures from him – a crumpled body, a foot sprawling in a blood-soaked office. 'And you think it was me, because I – I hit him. But I told you, Christ, it was just a light punch. He laughed at me.' Stockbridge ran his hands through his hair. 'He said something like, "Look, Mr Banker, your card ain't working. Just like the rest of us tossers now, eh?" And I was so – I was out of it. You know that. So I swung at him – I didn't even hit him the first time. His nose was bleeding. But he just kept laughing. That's what I'm telling you. He was fine. I swear he was fine.'

Anthony Johnson's nose had been lightly contused, true. But that wasn't exactly the end of it. 'Then what?'

'I went home. Charlotte will confirm that.'

'Were you carrying anything when you went into his office?'

Stockbridge looked confused. 'I don't remember. I had a drink, I think.'

'A drink in a glass, or in a bottle?'

'Does it matter? A bottle, probably. Beer. I don't drink spirits.'

Hegarty pushed another picture across the table. 'Anthony Johnson's throat was slashed with a broken beer bottle. Bled to death in three minutes, they tell me.'

All the blood drained from Stockbridge's face, too.

Charlotte

They came in the open door, a team of three men in boiler-suits. The woman officer conferred with them in low mutters, pointing out something on the carpet that Charlotte was sure hadn't been there before. Or had it? One immediately started taking photos and Charlotte backed away, arms over her chest.

'Morning, miss,' said one, the bald one. 'Gotta search the place. You'll have to stay in the hall.'

'But I need to get dressed.' Crap, the first policeman had been right.

The officers exchanged looks. 'All right. You'll have to leave the door open.'

This was mad. This was just too much. With one policeman watching her, Charlotte got some clothes from her dresser, then waited while the other two rifled through her bathroom in plastic gloves. At least it was clean in there.

They had questions. Had Dan showered since last night? What was he wearing? Where were his shoes? They lifted strange things – the towel, Dan's toothbrush, the soap dispenser from the sink. She was asked to witness each one being bagged up, and soon there were gaps in the room like missing teeth, and she was allowed to dress with the door ajar. She did it very, very quickly, tying back her smelly hair, and when she came out it was so strange, like having a plumber round. Should she offer them tea?

'Er – what do I do now? They said go to the station.'

The bald one was turning over her sofa cushions with gloved hands. 'We'll give you a lift, love, if you hang about.'

So polite! The other two were in the messy bedroom, and

she saw the Asian one pick up her discarded nightie and put it in a plastic bag.

'That's mine!'

He turned patiently. 'We need to take anything he might have touched, miss. Sorry.'

'Don't worry, miss, you'll get it back.'

What could she say? 'Er – OK. Thanks.'

When they'd finished they took her down to Camden, to the station. Baldy thrummed his fingers on the steering wheel as they waited in traffic on Chalk Farm Road. 'God love us, traffic's bloody murder round here on weekends now.'

The little one eyed Charlotte almost flirtatiously. 'Ever been in a police car, miss? See, in the West End on a weekend, mobbed by ladies, we are. Them hen dos, they all want to get inside. Like firemen, innit?'

'Sometimes we let them in right enough – if they're puking on the pavement or decking each other with stilettos.' Baldy chuckled.

Charlotte stared out of the window at the clean, gleaming morning. It was still only 10 a.m. 'That happens?'

'Just as much as you like, love. You'd be shocked.'

Baldy was being kind, assuming Charlotte would never puke or fight in public, but seeing as she had only the haziest of memories of the night before, she kept quiet until they pulled up near Mornington Crescent.

'That's the station, love. Out you get.'

What were they going to do to her in there? Suddenly she felt like throwing up too, and bent over, taking deep breaths until she felt she could go in.

*

'But I don't understand,' Charlotte said later, for the hundredth time that day. 'Wouldn't he get, like, released on bail?' It was surreal to hear those words tripping off her own tongue.

The duty lawyer from the police station was about ninety years old. Bits of the skin round his nose were white and flaky; Charlotte couldn't stop staring. He explained the procedure to her over and over from tatty laminated handouts, but she couldn't seem to understand. 'I'm sorry, dear. It's unusual to get bail in murder cases, you see.'

'So he's here till Monday? Is that allowed?'

'Yes, dear. They need to take him before a judge. But as I said, it's unlikely bail will be granted.'

Her mind was like wood; nothing went in. 'What does that mean?'

'It means he must stay in custody until there's a trial, I'm afraid.'

'Custody?'

'Prison,' he explained, shuffling his papers together.

Charlotte's brain was moving with the speed of geology. 'So, even though he didn't do it, he can't come home?' She said it hopefully. As if it would make the lawyer laugh and say, 'Of course not, dear. You can't send someone to jail when they didn't do anything. This is England!'

But instead he said, 'Until there's a trial, no. That could be a while.'

'A while? What – like, weeks?' *Oh, Christ*, she thought. *The wedding*. But surely not.

'Oh no, dear.'

Thank God. She smiled in relief.

'We could hope for maybe five, six months, if it was fast.'

She gaped at him. 'Six *months*? But – but people are always out on bail on TV.'

'Well.' He blew his nose with an old-man honk. 'I'm afraid the television-makers aren't always accurate. And, my dear, the evidence at this stage does look rather compelling. Your barrister may advise a guilty plea.'

Charlotte looked at her huge, flashy engagement ring. 'We're getting married next week,' she heard herself say. 'It's all planned.'

The lawyer looked alarmed. 'Oh. I hope you took out insurance?'

Only the glacial speed of her mind stopped Charlotte from slapping him across his flaky face with the splinter of rock on her hand.

One day earlier – Sunday

Keisha

The weekend had been fucked up. When she woke up on Saturday after the club he was gone, the bed empty and cold. The bag of clothes in the hall had disappeared – weird – and he'd even tried cleaning his trainers. The kitchen bin was full of red-stained kitchen roll; he'd used the whole roll up, so she'd have to buy more. She went into the bathroom and saw again the red drop on the pink mat.

Keisha wasn't thick, even if she'd got kicked out of the posh school. She'd washed blood off the bathroom floor before from his dripping nose or knuckles. But he'd hardly had time to get in a fight the night before, and why would he lie to her if he had? Usually he was proud when he'd 'sorted people out'.

He hadn't done a good job of cleaning the shoes, despite the whole roll of paper, so she filled a basin and let them stand. She shoved the bath mat into a bag, yet another thing to drag down the laundrette. There was still only frozen food and no microwave, so she ate a few handfuls of Choco Pops without milk. They were for Ruby really, if she was ever allowed home again.

Work at the old folk's home, two miles up Finchley Road, was the usual crap. Mr Smith, a big fat man who ate everything put near him, filled the commode up so high it touched his old white bum, and he just sat on top of it smiling away, ignored by the nurses. The bastard owner Barry called in all the night staff at the end of her shift and bitched about food costs. No special diets, he said, even if someone was literally wasting away. Keisha wasn't about to fight with him – like all the girls she was off the books and grateful for work.

She walked home as it got light, passing the shut-up shops, the O_2 centre, still and empty, no one up. As she drew near home she started to wonder. Would he be there? The sick feeling was back, that kind of anxiety about unlocking your own front door. He could be gone days, it'd happened before.

He wasn't there. She turned on the telly for a while and it was playing weird religious stuff, Sunday-morning programmes, but somehow she couldn't sleep. She kept thinking. The shoes. The mat. Where the hell was he? Where had he gone when he'd left her at the club?

She must have slept a while, because she woke up when the door slammed. Her face was creased from the nubbly sofa. 'You back?'

She heard him moving about in the hall, and then suddenly he was in the room. 'Where's the fucking bath mat?'

'Eh?' She dug her fists into her eyes. 'Oh, I was gonna wash it. It was dirty.'

There was something wrong with his face. His eyes were too wide.

'What's the matter?'

'Don't fucking touch my stuff, OK? What else did you move?'

'Nothing!' She felt it rising up in her, so tired, so pissed off. God, she was sick of this. 'All I did was clean up some of that mess you left. You ruined your shoes.'

He froze. His blue eyes fixed her across the room. 'What did you do with them?' His voice was very soft.

She started to get up; she could tell from the light it was late afternoon. 'I didn't do nothing, they're in the kitchen. Don't walk that mess over the carpet.'

'You cleaned them.' He hadn't moved.

'Well, yeah. They was dirty, yeah? I mean . . . you said, you said you stepped in a keba—'

Suddenly Chris was across the room and holding her round the waist. His face was very close, like he might kiss her. He smelled like he'd slept out all night – cold, greasy. 'That's right. I stepped in a kebab, yeah?'

'That's what you said. But—' She stopped herself. She knew the difference between blood and ketchup, but maybe he had his reasons. She'd given up trying to understand. 'Look, babe, it's fine. I'll clean 'em again if you want.'

He let go. 'Just leave them. Leave them, OK?'

'OK.' She started moving to the door.

'Er, where the fuck are you going?'

She turned to look at him, in his dirty T-shirt, his face like he hadn't slept at all. 'I'm going to work. It's Sunday. I have to work.' She held her breath – maybe he'd take that as a dig, that she was saying he didn't have a job. But he just nodded slowly, looking confused. He raked his hands over the skin of his eyes. 'All right. All right. What time are you back?'

'Usual. Five-ish. Will you . . . you'll be in?'

'Yeah,' he said, but she didn't think he was listening at all.

Hegarty

Yawning, Hegarty finished his dry Danish pastry and brushed the crumbs off his tie. He'd been worried about yesterday's ID parade, he had to admit. The sister, Rachel Johnson, and the other girl, Melanie Taylor, had been a problem from the start. They didn't want to go to the station, didn't want to do the ID parade, didn't want to look at the other men paid to appear alongside Daniel Stockbridge.

'What if I'm not sure, like?' asked the Mel one.

'That's the idea,' he'd explained as patiently as he could. 'It's just another way to see if we got the right guy.'

'How comes I can't do it with Rach?' She annoyed him, her narrow suspicious face smeared in last night's make-up. Both girls had come in wearing their club clothes, cheap and shiny. He didn't like the holes in their stories either.

'He was saying racist shit,' Mel maintained. 'That posh guy.'

'Like what?'

'You nigger. That sort of thing.'

He'd written it down, wondering if her over-confident tone meant she remembered or she was making it up. The other girl, Rachel, seemed less certain.

'Just, like, racist stuff.'

'Like what?'

'Dunno.' She'd picked at her silver nail polish, matched to her dress. Her eyes were red and he reminded himself that her brother was dead. Both girls seemed anxious he'd caught 'that racist fucker'.

'They should hang 'em, bastards like him,' was Mel's opinion.

'Well, we don't actually have capital punishment in the UK.'

'Eh?'

Rachel, tall and beautiful, had used up tissue after tissue in her interview. 'Why'd he kill our Anthony? He'd never done nothing to no one, never hurt a fly.'

Hegarty, who'd been looking up Anthony Johnson's long and dodgy gang-related record, wasn't so sure. 'I'm sorry for your loss.'

Pain twisted up her pretty face. 'Mum's devastated. Heart-broke. Doctor had to sedate her, and Tanika, that's our Anthony's missus, her and the kids are just sort of, like, in shock. Won't even remember their dad, will they.'

A wife, then – that was interesting, given the discussion Hegarty'd just had with Mel about her relationship with the deceased. 'Is there any other family to inform?'

She dabbed her eyes. 'Our Ronald's still in Jamaica. Not sure when he'll make it back. Don't even know when we'll get Anthony home – his body.' She was crying again, clear tears rolling out of her dark eyes. She hardly seemed to notice.

'I'll make sure the Family Liaison Officer keeps you up to date,' Hegarty said. He felt as usual how pathetic those words were – the only comfort he could offer to the raped and knifed and bereaved. All he could do was try his best to catch the bad guy, so they could at least see who was responsible. Justice, some people called it. And if he was right, and he hoped he was, he'd got the guy for this one sweating in the cells.

Rachel sniffed loudly. 'You not got any balm tissues? My nose's getting chapped.'

'Sorry. Can't get the public to pay for them.'

'I got a picture of him,' she said suddenly. 'On my phone. I was doing a pic of me and Mel when he come over.' She'd whipped out her Nokia and shown him a blurred shot of the two girls in the foreground, and in the background a white man approaching. Could have been Stockbridge.

'Can I?' A phone picture wouldn't be much use in court, but he took it and flipped through. The picture before was of Rachel with a different white man, adopting a cool gun-finger gangster pose. 'This guy with the shaved head – who's that?'

She went cagey. 'Dunno. Some fella at the club.'

'Would he have seen anything?'

'Dunno. Dunno who he was.'

Rachel Johnson was pretty, yes, but he was fairly sure she wasn't telling him the truth. In the end, though, both girls identified Stockbridge at once in the parade. In the past, Hegarty'd seen white witnesses fail to identify black suspects, since 'they all look the same, don't they?' But both black girls knew Stockbridge at once.

'That's him,' Mel had said, giving the man the finger through the reflective glass. 'That's the bastard. Hope he rots.'

Heading down to the interview room, Hegarty spotted one of the search guys he'd sent round to Stockbridge's flat yesterday. 'You get the shoes?' The bald guy nodded. It was all round the station that whoever knocked off Anthony Johnson had also stamped on his hand, breaking the fingers. It was the kind of thing that made the officers really want to nail someone for the crime. They'd have blood all over them for sure, the shoes of whoever did it. If there was still any doubt about that.

Charlotte

Eventually, on that endless Saturday, Charlotte had fallen asleep across the orange plastic chairs. When she woke she had no idea what time it was, but they had definitely missed *Britain's Got Talent*. The strip-lighting fractured on her tired eyes.

There were voices in the corridor, behind the shatter-proof glass with the posters about legal aid and benefit fraud and not slapping your wife about. Charlotte sat up, feeling sweat under her armpits.

'Leave off, I can walk meself.' A woman's voice, and in the corridor, a girl walking tall and proud, her hair like a gold and bronze halo about her face. Charlotte recognised the girls from the club, the one with the afro, still in her shimmering silver dress from the night before. Her legs went on about a mile, and behind her, slinking against the wall, was the shorter one who'd shouted at Dan, her hair flat with over-straightening. That girl looked like she'd been crying. It was what Charlotte's own face looked like in the yellowing glass, ravaged, screwed up like a dam against the tears inside. Their eyes met, and the other girl looked away.

Charlotte tried to put her thoughts in order. The guy at the club was dead. Murder, the policeman had said. God, it was so hard to remember – everything was slipping out of her head soapy-slick. So, what – Dan got in a fight with him? But he'd been away such a short time, just a few minutes. And he was fine, wasn't he? No bruises, no blood. Wouldn't she have known if Dan had been in a fight?

She had another memory. Dan, a few weeks ago, shouting at her: *I don't give a fuck what kind of flowers we have!*

He'd been at the table surrounded by spreadsheets,

49

working on a Saturday again. She was trying to get him to finalise the wedding details, take an interest in it.

'I'm sorry,' he'd said, after two hours of her hurt silence.

'It's our wedding. Excuse me if I thought you might care.'

Running hands through his hair, his face haggard. 'I'm sorry. Sometimes I just feel like there's no way out.'

The waiting-room TV, set on news, scrolled on and on as the hours dragged forward. Eventually she slept again across the hard chairs, the ridges digging into her spine, woken by the noise of people coming in as much as by her own creeping, rising panic. It would be OK. Of course it would. But why were they still here, hours later?

All night long people had been brought in, drunks with blood streaming from their heads, women shrieking, sirens going. The TV was showing BBC news, and on it a rolling story about Haussmann's Bank. *Bailed out by government loan*, it said. Then in the scrolling ticker she saw: *Man arrested over London club death*. The irony of it didn't escape her, that the very catastrophe which had sent Dan falling into this mess hadn't even happened in the end. Instead he'd made his own private disaster, now joining the bank on the news. But it would be OK. It had to be.

'Miss Miller?' It was the flat-shoed Brummie woman. A thin morning light was coming in the high windows.

Charlotte's mouth tasted dry and sour, her eyes felt gritty. All she'd eaten was half a disgusting corner-shop sandwich, washed down with the worst cup of coffee she'd ever tasted, so bad she'd almost spat it back out into the polystyrene cup. But there was nothing else, so she drank it, and afterwards she had sat and picked the cup to pieces with nerves.

She stood up, dizzy, sure that what she was about to be told was going to change everything in a way she didn't yet see. She had an urge to squeeze her eyes shut and hope it would all go away.

'Can you come with me, miss?'

'Sorry. Coming.'

Hegarty

'But I don't understand!' Stockbridge's girlfriend was wearing old jeans now, a baggy sweatshirt with the name of some Oxford college on it. Her face looked tired and confused, but she was still sexy. Very sexy.

'I'll try to explain again. We've charged your fiancé with the murder of Anthony Johnson, owner of the Kingston Town nightclub.'

The crosser she got, the rougher her voice became. Was that a northern accent creeping into her posh tones? 'It's ridiculous.' She folded her arms. 'To say that Dan might have killed someone – well, you don't have a clue, obviously. Listen, I know he can seem kind of – sort of closed up, but I promise you he's not, he's just under so much pressure, and that's how he goes when . . . It doesn't mean anything.'

Hegarty bit back the urge to tell her about the mothers he'd interviewed, tearful and loving except for the dead toddler in the morgue, the favourite teacher and what you found on their laptop. You never knew. That was what he'd learned, if anything, from being in the police. 'Let me ask you again, miss. When you came out of the ladies', your fiancé was arguing with Mr Johnson?'

'I didn't say arguing!' She sighed and rubbed her face. 'Oh, I suppose they were. But it doesn't mean—'

'Then you saw the two men go into his office, yes? You

waited outside the club, you say for just a few minutes, and then you went home? Did you get a taxi?'

'Yes.' Her eyes flicked away.

'You're sure?'

'I – we must have. I don't remember.'

He made a note. 'You've already told us you took drugs that night. Is that correct?'

She nodded slowly, staring at her feet. 'I wouldn't normally.'

'Where did he get the drugs?'

'How would I know?' She sat up suddenly. 'Look, am I under arrest?'

'No, miss. Not at the moment.'

'Well then, I've already told you everything. I really don't know any more.'

Hegarty clicked his pen. 'Does Daniel have a problem with black people?'

She gaped. 'What?'

'It's just a question, miss.'

'Are you trying to say he's a racist or something? Just because the guy was— Dan's not racist, for God's sake. He was the one who wanted to go to the bloody club in the first place. It's so stupid.' He thought she was about to say they even had black friends, but she seemed to think better of it.

'There were a number of witnesses to the argument. You say you saw a group of people, possibly two black girls. Anyone else?'

'I don't know.'

'Recognise this man?' He slid over a printout of the picture from Rachel Johnson's phone, the mystery white man. She stared at it with a hunted look on her face. 'Any idea who he could be?'

'Of course not. This is all crazy.' Her face was pale.

'Hmm. OK, I suggest you go home, Miss Miller. You look tired.' He saw her bristle. 'I meant, you might like to have a rest. Nothing will happen today. The hearing will be at ten at the Magistrates' Court. It's on Holloway Road – they'll give you the address outside.'

She tried to take this in. 'So, tomorrow he can come home? That's the bail hearing thing, is it?'

'You should talk to the duty lawyer about it. Do you have your own lawyer, you and Mr Stockbridge?'

'Of course not, why would we?'

'Best get one soon. They'll give you some numbers at the desk.'

'He was a judge, you know.' She got up with admirable poise. 'Dan's father. High court, for twenty years.'

Hegarty forced a smile. 'Then I'm sure he'd advise you to get a lawyer as soon as you can.'

Charlotte

When Charlotte could finally leave, it was getting dark. She emerged into a quiet, rain-washed Camden, the May skies darkening with clouds. After waiting twenty minutes for a bus, shivering with tiredness, she got home to the ransacked flat and washed her hair free of the smell of the police station, immediately feeling better. Then she picked up the phone and listened to the dial tone. Imagined the cut-glass tones of Dan's mother, Elaine: 'Good afternoon, 54372.' Saying *hello* wasn't polite, apparently. Or his father, Justice Edward Stockbridge QC: 'Pardon? *Pardon?* Speak up, will you, Charlotte.'

Charlotte knew she should get a lawyer, of course, but the

thought of ringing the Stockbridges made her feel even more sick than before. Wouldn't it all blow over after the hearing? Dan had only been gone a few minutes, not long enough to kill someone, for God's sake, even if he was capable of it. Which he wasn't.

Slowly she put the receiver down. After all, what could his parents do today? Maybe they would never need to find out.

There was no food in the fridge except for what she'd bought on Friday, a lifetime ago. She ate three olives, making her stomach churn. The clock kept up its insistent tick, stringing out her nerves, so she got up and turned on the stereo, but it was playing the last CD she'd had on, the song for their first wedding dance. She turned it off, resisting the urge to chew on her nails. No point in spoiling months of careful maintenance. Tomorrow it would be over and she could forget all about those head-spinning facts.

The witnesses. The row. The drugs . . . All of it was true, but she'd kept opening her mouth to say, 'Yes, but . . .' There was always an explanation when it was you they were accusing. Meanwhile that young policeman, the one who'd seen her boobs, kept whipping out more and more evidence. Like Paul bloody Daniels.

Charlotte hated that policeman. He had an answer for everything. And he'd left a large footprint on her cream carpet. Red-brown and sticky, she knew what it was. It was blood, that Johnson guy's blood, smeared on her living-room floor.

Charlotte went to the hall cupboard where their cleaning lady kept supplies, and rooted about until she found a cloth. She never did her own cleaning, so she wasn't sure what they had.

She scrubbed it until just a red tidemark was left, then

poured away the bloody, brackish water. Her hands smelled of old metal pipes. Tomorrow she would get up, fix her hair, go to court and bring Dan home, then put this behind her as one of the worst weekends of her life. And maybe by the time their first anniversary came round she'd be ready to think of it as a funny occurrence in the past, but she doubted it.

Monday

Keisha

'Jesus! You scared me.'

He was sitting on the pile of dirty clothes by the bed, watching her. She sat up, head and heart pounding, and felt for her bottle of Coke. 'What you doing up? It's what – eight? Christ, are you sick still? I only got in at four.'

He said, 'We're going to court.'

'Court?' She pushed down her hair; that bloody woman had diddled her on the chemical straightener, lasted two months her *arse*.

'That's what I said. Come on, shift it.' He tugged the duvet off her and she gathered up her gangly limbs.

'Fuck! It's cold. Is the heating not on?'

'Meter's run out.' He was leaving the room. That meant he hadn't put the money in, spent it all on booze for some club owner. And why were they going to court? Must be one of his loser mates in trouble again. For fuck's sake.

When Keisha had come home before light earlier that morning, Chris was bedded down on the sofa with his coat over him. The microwave was back, she'd noticed. Trying not to wake him she'd brushed her teeth and got into bed in the almost-dark, and next thing she knew he was shaking her awake.

She rubbed her face, trying to wake up. 'Why are you going to court? Fucking hell, I got, like, three hours' sleep.' She looked at the clock on the newly returned microwave. 'Is that right? Jesus, why'd you wake me up so early?'

''Cos you're coming with me. So get dressed.'

'But . . .' She tried to catch his eye but he looked away and made a sort of jerking movement.

'Stop asking questions. You're just coming, OK?'

'Why?'

He turned, met her with a hard stare. ''Cos I don't trust you here on your own.'

Keisha's mouth fell open. What could you even say to that? She just stood there, saying nothing.

Chris pulled his jacket off the chair. 'Get a move on. I'm leaving.'

Keisha didn't look at the papers or go online, and if she watched TV it was only E4 or MTV. They didn't show the news in the old folks' home in case it upset them. So it wasn't until they went to court that morning that she even knew Anthony Johnson was dead.

Charlotte

Charlotte had dressed carefully for the hearing. Somehow she was expecting it to be like courtroom dramas she'd seen on TV, with a judge and jury and a last-minute bit of evidence to change the whole thing.

The rain had let up overnight, leaving the sky washed-out, the colour of nothing. She'd carefully checked the route to the court, terrified of being late, and taken the Northern Line to Euston, changing on to the Victoria to get there.

She sat in the third row of the public gallery, boxed in by windowless walls and veneer benches. She was the only person there who wasn't a reporter, by the looks of it. It had come at the perfect time for them, a banker lashing out at a black man. Most were middle-aged women, slightly harried. One even had M&S shopping bags under the bench. Then, just as it was about to start, a group of people came in late and noisy – all black. '*Where's the bastard?*' she heard someone hiss. She didn't look round.

Charlotte looked straight ahead, twisting the band of her engagement ring. She wouldn't meet their eyes. It would all be over soon. The court doors opened and then everything was moving. There were three judges, not one – magistrates, was what Mr Crusty, as she called the duty solicitor, had tried to explain. There was Mr Crusty and some prosecution lawyer, a young woman with glasses and a sharp nose. Then there was Dan, dragged out by officers, pale and blinking, unshaven. She suddenly couldn't look at him and stared hard at her feet. Around her, the reporters were scribbling so fast she thought their notebooks might catch fire.

It all seemed to be over so quickly.

First the clerk read out something to Dan, and he mumbled back, 'Yes.' She couldn't hear what was going on, the CPS woman spoke so quietly. 'Your worships, we are here to consider bail in the matter of Regina versus Daniel Stockbridge. Mr Stockbridge was arrested on Saturday morning for the murder of Anthony Johnson, owner of the Kingston Town nightclub in Camden. The arresting officer, DC Matthew Hegarty, is present and willing to answer questions on the evidence if the court requires.'

She paused, adjusting her glasses, which gleamed in the dull strip-lighting. Charlotte found she was squeezing her hands together so tightly it was cutting off the blood. There was more murmuring. 'The court calls DC Matthew Hegarty.'

Then the policeman was leaping up to the stand. He couldn't have slept much at the weekend either, but he seemed perky as could be, whereas Charlotte felt like she'd been hit by a truck.

He took the affirmation with loud northern tones and the lawyer said, 'Officer Hegarty, can you connect the defendant with this case?'

The officer smiled, leaned forward. 'We believe so, yes.'

'Will you be recommending bail in this case?'

The policeman leaned forward further. 'Your worships, this is a serious case of brutal and possibly racially motivated murder. The defendant has shown signs of violent and unstable behaviour, which may pose a risk to the public.' He paused to take a breath. Murmurs went round the courtroom; Charlotte tried to block her ears. She wanted to turn to them, shout, say, *I'm sorry he's dead, but Dan didn't do it! You've got the wrong person!*

'Furthermore, the defendant has access to considerable resources, and therefore, represents a high likelihood of absconding. There has also been a large degree of public interest in the case, and as such, bail could represent a danger to the defendant's own safety.' The policeman smiled. So he was saying Dan had to be in prison for his *wellbeing*? Charlotte gaped.

More chat, and the lawyer sat down, rearranging her papers neatly. The three magistrates, a woman in the middle and two men on either side – one Asian, one white – scribbled furiously.

Dan's lawyer, Mr Crusty, got slowly to his feet and at this point Charlotte got lost in his wavering tones, interrupted by loud sneezes into his cotton hankie. He asked various questions of the policeman. Had Dan said he was innocent? Did he deny the charges? Did he waive his right to have a lawyer present? Was it true Dan did not fully remember the incident? The policeman answered them all with the same confident smile.

It dragged on. Mr Crusty was citing point after point of procedure and kept saying, 'Your worships, the evidence is highly circumstantial.' He didn't even bring up what Charlotte thought was the most obvious point, that Dan had no blood on him when they'd left the club that night. Wouldn't he have blood on him, if he'd stabbed someone?

After a while, Charlotte stopped listening. Her knuckles were white from gripping her hands together, trying not to leap up and shout how stupid it all was. Of course Dan didn't do it. He was a banker, for God's sake. He bought his ties on Savile Row. In a few years he'd be softening in the middle and losing his hair. He didn't go around getting in bar fights over declined credit cards.

The facts were like a crossword puzzle she couldn't make fit. The club. The row. The arrest. Even with the drugs, which had seemed to change them both, she knew Dan just wouldn't do this. No. No. He wouldn't. It was like some awful dream, like one of those nightmares where she forgot her bouquet or no one turned up at the wedding. But even if it took a while to explain all these damning facts, he'd still go home on bail, still be able to marry her. Wouldn't he? Maybe he wouldn't be allowed to leave the country, maybe they'd lose the honeymoon. Would travel insurance cover it? But still, even if they couldn't go to Jamaica, she would try to be good and brave about it. She would rise to the occasion, so long as he could come out from behind that screen and grip her hand in his strong one, so long as she could breathe his smell over the varnish and lino reek of this place. She tried to shut her ears to the calls and whistles. *'Ra-cist! Ra-cist!'* The guards made half-hearted attempts to shush the gallery. She sat there with her head down and in the dock Dan did the same.

They were coming to an end, the judges and lawyers talking in low voices. One of the reporters coughed loudly. Dan had a strange look on his face, as if he was about to cry.

'Fucking send him down! Bastard!'

Dan was trying to speak. Again the courtroom exploded with murmurs and she heard herself say out loud, 'What? What?'

'Order, please.' The lead judge was irritable. 'Mr Stockbridge? Do you have a statement to make? Please be aware that anything you say now may be admissible in your later trial.'

Dan stood up slowly, his height filling the dock. The metal on the jacket he wore rattled against the glass walls. He stared right ahead, looking anywhere but at Charlotte, it seemed. His throat moved.

'Mr Stockbridge? Please proceed. Could the guards please silence the gallery?'

'Ra-cist! Fuck him!'

'I'm sorry,' Dan said, over the din. 'God, I'm so sorry. I just don't remember. I don't remember what happened.' And then he burst into tears, sobs rasping like sandpaper. He tried to put his hands over his face but the guard held his arm, so he hung his head, tears running unchecked to the floor.

Charlotte's mouth fell open among the racket. What the *fuck*? Did he have some kind of plan?

Mr Crusty was talking over the noise. 'Mr Stockbridge

has been provoked, your worships, and so anything he has said cannot be taken as an admissible confession of guilt . . .'

A woman was screaming, 'Racist! Fucking racist!' Charlotte couldn't see who it was. A volley of murmurs swelled and rose. *'Send him down! Send him down!'*

The head judge called out over it: 'Order, order, please! Bail is denied in the case of Regina versus Stockbridge. Case committed to the Crown Court for trial. Please remand the defendant into custody.'

Charlotte was going to be sick.

Over the chaos of the judge calling order, and the bailiffs trying to quieten the screaming woman, she ran out, hands over her mouth, searching for the ladies' sign. She leaned over a basin, her stomach heaving, and choked up a small bit of bile. There was nothing else in her stomach to throw up. That was when she saw the faces in the mirror, blurred through a lens of tears.

The first kick came as such a shock she couldn't even cry out. She might have even said, *oh sorry*, assuming they'd bumped into her by accident. It took her a few seconds to understand that people were behind her, hitting. Girls, two girls, with the heels of their shoes and points of their nails, a smell of hairspray in the air. Black girls, she could see, through her tears. One had a purple scarf over her face. The blows were coming from all over. A kick to her legs. A scratch at her face. *Fucking bitch*, one said.

She felt one tug at her bag as the other pulled her hair. Her things clattered onto the plastic floor; her head jerked back.

Then the door opened, and someone was saying, *For fuck's sake, leave it*. And then something hit her, heavy and swinging, her own bag maybe, and she stumbled and the sink was coming at her teeth, and then the endless blue of the lino and she just had time to think of Jamaica in the turquoise sea, that they would never get there now, and then she was going under. This was it. This was rock bottom, she knew it for sure.

Part Two

Hegarty

Hegarty had been seated near the back of the courtroom when Daniel Stockbridge was remanded into custody, and saw the girl slip out past him, hands over her mouth like she was going to throw up. He was just checking his watch to see if he could make it back to the station for the weekly meeting, when he heard all the shouting and, like everyone else, spilled out to see what was happening. In the crowd he saw a face he thought he recognised. A white man, with a shaved head. But there was no time to stop, and in that second the face was gone.

From the door of the ladies' toilets came a sound like an animal wailing, and then two black girls burst out, one tall and one shorter, sprinting past the security guards and into the street. 'Leave off, Grandpa,' one shouted back. They'd pulled scarves over their faces and by the time he'd followed outside they were long gone, slipped into one of the side streets and vanished. The only witness left was a third girl, the skinny mixed-race one who'd run out of the toilets shouting for someone to call an ambulance. A female security guard went in and led out Charlotte Miller, her mouth and eye streaming with blood. Her hand was clutched in front of her and when it leaked blood all over the guard's white shirt it was found to be her own tooth she held, knocked out when the girls had attacked her.

Hegarty took control of the situation – it was his job. He gave Charlotte Miller some basic first aid, and through the gushing blood his clean hankie failed to stem, she recognised him. 'Offisher.'

'Don't try to talk, miss.'

When the victim was carted off to hospital – yet more blood leaking all over Hegarty – it was left to him to interview the witness. 'Your name?'

The skinny girl folded her arms. 'I didn't do nothing. I just went in and they was hitting her.'

'Who were the girls?'

'How'm I meant to know?'

'Do you know the victim at all?'

'Who, the blondie? Nah.'

'Well, what are you doing at court, then?' He tapped his pen off the notebook cover and she narrowed her eyes.

'Anyone can come in court, can't they? S'a free country.'

He sighed. 'So, you're just an innocent bystander.' They always were.

'Eh? I just went in, s'all. Them two girls was hitting her, and I must of scared them off, so they scarpered.'

He unpeeled the printout of Rachel Johnson's phone picture from his pocket. 'You know who this is? The white guy?'

She looked at it just a bit too long. 'Course not.'

'Was he here today?'

'Dunno, OK? I got nothing to do with it. I don't even know what the case is.'

'I'll still need your name, miss. And your address too.'

'How come?'

He was losing patience. 'You want me to arrest you?'

'Fine.' She scowled. 'Keisha Collins. Live up in Swiss Cottage – here, I'll write it. There. Can I go now?'

As she stormed out he followed her to the door and saw her walk off to the bus stop. Hegarty had very good eyesight. He saw a white man emerge from behind the sign and leave with the girl, both of them waving their arms like they were having a fight. What were the chances this was the white guy from Rachel Johnson's phone, and that the fleeing girls were Rachel herself and her mate Mel, taking out their grief on the girlfriend of the accused? He sighed and put his notebook away. What were the chances he'd ever be able to prove it?

Keisha

By the time Keisha and Chris left the court it was past lunch-time and she was starving. She was also raging mad.

Chris got into the flat and switched on the TV, which was showing reels of Daniel Stockbridge being led away to a police van. He fiddled with the remote and turned on Sky Sports. He didn't look at her. He'd barely spoken all the way home. Now, still without looking at her, he said, 'Get us some lunch, will you.'

She was still furious as she went into the kitchen. Weird enough to be woken and made to go down there, but that had been nothing compared with seeing Chris nod to Rachel and Mel as they went into the court coffee bar. What were they doing there, the girls from the club? For a moment she'd seen white with anger – was that slut Rachel out to get her claws into Chris?

Chris had spoken to them. 'After,' he'd said. 'In the bogs, if she goes, or outside. Get the purse, remember?'

They'd nodded, all grim, and when Keisha said, 'What's going on?' they'd just looked at each other like they were Charlie's fucking Angels, and no one was telling her a thing. They'd waited in the lobby while the hearing went on, and when the blonde girl from the club came rushing out all crying and choking, Rachel and Mel followed her to the loos.

Chris had nudged Keisha. 'You. Go in the court, see what they said.'

'What? What're you on about?' She couldn't understand why they were all here, the posh blonde girl from the club, Rachel and Mel, her and Chris . . .

He shoved her, quite hard. 'Just fucking go. I wanna know did he get sent down.'

Keisha started walking to the door of the court. She had a wobbly lurching feeling in her stomach. There was a noise from the toilet, a squealing frightened sound. She looked back at Chris but then she was veering away from the court, into the toilets. By the time she'd got in there, the blonde girl was on the floor, and the noise – it was pathetic. They were kicking her and she couldn't fight back to a fly, anyone could see it. And the blood . . .

She snapped back to their kitchen. Chris was saying, 'Oi, did you hear? What's up with you?'

'Why did we go there?' She was standing in the kitchen holding the sleeve of the macaroni cheese meal, ninety-nine pee from Sainsbury's. The returned microwave whirred round. It had been cleaned of its spaghetti hoop stains and she hardly recognised it. 'I don't get it – is he dead, that club guy? The guy we saw?'

Chris came in and looked in the fridge, took out a beer. 'You need to do some shopping, there's only one left.'

'What? No, listen. Why did we go there, to that court?'

He cracked the bottle open on the table. 'Friend of the family, aren't I? Pay my respects, see the fella get done for it.'

'Since when? I thought you went to get money out of that Anthony. Is that not why you went down to the club?'

'He was a business colleague, right.'

Keisha felt a slow volcano of rage erupt in her stomach. 'Your fucking business – what's that? Beating up some clueless blonde girl? I know you told them to do it, that Rachel and her mate.'

He shrugged. 'Fella tapped her brother, stands to reason they'd be upset with his missus.'

'That girl – fuck, I mean – her tooth got knocked out.' Keisha'd seen fights, of course, been in plenty too, but not where one person was crying and groping on the floor like that, blood rushing out of their mouth like a fucking tap. She didn't think anyone had ever hit the white girl in her life before. Why else would she look so damn surprised? Like she was actually shocked anyone would hurt her. Did she not see it coming? And then there was the tooth in the pool of blood, and those two girls had scarpered and guess who was left to face the music with that nosy-parker policeman. And he'd showed her a picture of Chris (with that slut Rachel)! Why did he have a picture of Chris?

She thought about the shoes, and the stain on the bathroom rug. 'What's going on, Chris? You said you didn't trust me – why'd you make me go?'

Chris opened the last beer on the side of the table, where the veneer was all chipped away. They'd lose that off their deposit but he never gave a shit. The microwave pinged. 'You getting that?'

'Why'd you want her purse?'

Suddenly his calm was thrown off like a coat. 'Did you get it? Give it to me.'

'No, I—'

'You got it. Don't fucking lie to me.'

She couldn't. 'Well, she dropped it when I went in – Johnson's sister, fucking idiot she is – but it's just library cards and shit like that—'

He snatched Keisha's bag off the counter and emptied it all on the table, bus tickets, bits of old crisps, tissues falling out everywhere.

'Hey!'

'Where is it? I mean it, fucking give it to me.'

'For fuck's sake.' She had tears in her eyes. 'Your food's done.'

He grabbed her arm.

'Oh, all right. Fucking hell. I'll get it.'

'Tell me where.' His grip tightened.

'Ow! In my jacket, OK?'

He went and was back in seconds, emptying the purse over the table. The blonde girl's Oyster card fell out, twenty pounds cash, video and gym cards. Coins bounced tinnily across the small kitchen; one hit the door of the microwave. Keisha felt weak. 'See? Nothing there.'

'Fuck.' Suddenly his arm was on her throat and she was backed up against the fridge. It was such a fucking small kitchen, she always said that. 'You take something out?'

'No. For Christ's – sake!' She choked in air.

'Nothing with her address?'

'You're hurting me!'

'Fuck.' He let her go.

'She's just a dumb white girl, she didn't even see them coming. Why do you want her address? Why did you really go? I know you didn't want to pay your respects, whatever shit you said to that Rachel.'

'Shut up.' He turned round in a circle, rubbing his chin.

'You want to find out where she lives, is that it? But why? *Why*, Chris? It's not 'cos you liked him, Anthony – you said he was a jumped-up tosser. He wouldn't pay you, would he, was that it?' The words were tumbling out of her like a train in that bit of a film where you can't stop it and it goes falling over the cliff. 'You went back to the club? Is that where you went? I know it wasn't ketchup on your shoes, I'm not fucking stupid.' She couldn't stop talking.

Chris was pacing in the small kitchen. One two three, one two three. 'I said fucking shut it, Keisha. I'm warning you.'

But she never could control her mouth. 'Did you see him dead, is that it? You didn't want the police to know you went back? But you wouldn't get in trouble if you just tried to help—' She felt an odd surge of something, like her stomach was doing somersaults. 'Were you afraid? Fuck, Chris, fucking hell – is that why you went today? Why won't you tell me? *What did you do?*'

There was a crash – Chris had snatched the bottle off the table and smashed it. The air smelled of beer and he turned, screaming. 'I told you to shut it! You never learn!'

'Stop fucking shouting at me, I'm trying to help! We could just tell someone—'

And there was her, smart-arse Keisha Collins, who sneered at the poor white girl for not seeing her beating coming, who really should have known better. She was still surprised somehow when his hand came up and his ring connected with her cheekbone, and his foot with her knee.

'You stupid cow,' he swore, as his fist came down. 'You're going nowhere.' The jagged edge of the table came up and flew at her face with shocking speed. 'You're talking to no one.'

Really, you could never see it coming, however much you should know.

Charlotte

By the time Charlotte had been taken away to have her face stitched up, a young reporter from the local paper, twenty-four years old and fresh from City Journalism School, had finished typing up his routine court reports and, with an eye out for a good story, the one that would lift his career out of the court circulars and car boot sales and into the big time, decided to place a call to the newsdesk of *Metro*. Doing a search for other bankers sent into meltdown by the recession – suicides, shoot-outs, murders – he started to draft a story on the Banker Butchers, playing with alliteration in the margins of his notebook.

Calls were made, names Googled. While Charlotte was queuing to have her lip stitched, it was all over the news – *London banker charged with murder*. Soon Charlotte's phone had started to ring, and ring, and ring. But it was still on silent in her bag, and she was sitting in the Royal Free waiting to have her face sewn back together.

It was after eight when Charlotte finally left the hospital, having waited for hours with an ice pack held to her face that smelled strongly of dirty old freezers. A locum doctor from India jabbed her mouth with a local anaesthetic and then pulled the thread through her lip, for Christ's sake, her actual *mouth*. One of her bottom teeth had been knocked out by the fall on to the sink, and Charlotte had carried it to the hospital in a gummy pool of blood. It was too late to reattach, they said. She could have an implant when her mouth healed.

It was the idea of being toothless that made her cry most, more than the bruises to her ribs that left her struggling for breath, more than the split lip or black eye she was squinting out of. She was missing a tooth, like an old bag lady on the street! She'd always been a baby about injections, but she was so dazed she sat silently, tears welling up until the doctor had to wipe them away with a piece of gauze. It would never heal if she kept crying on it, he said.

By nine Charlotte had walked the few streets from the hospital to her house, and just wanted to sleep and sleep for ever and not wake up.

There was, in her head, a list of things she would have to deal with soon. Knocking on her skull. Like that Dan was in prison, right now, this second. That he wasn't getting out. And the worst – the absolute worst . . . But she couldn't think about the wedding. It was too big to think about, like looking at the sun. Getting a lawyer, a decent one this time. Explaining to Simon why she hadn't turned up today. Somehow, she'd thought that when Dan was released, they'd both go merrily off to work.

But she'd barely got home when there was an almighty buzzing from the door and her name was being yelled up from the street loud enough to rouse the whole building. 'Charlotte! Charlotte! Are you there? Right, that's it, Phil, call the police.'

Oh, crap. It was her mother.

*

Charlotte's mother was short, like her daughter, and had greying fair hair in a sensible feather cut. She burst out crying as soon as she saw Charlotte. 'Why didn't you answer your phone? I thought you were dead!'

Phil, Charlotte's step-father, was trying to get his wife inside. 'Come on, Gail, let's not make a scene.'

'Why shouldn't I make a scene? To see it on the news like that! I just don't know what to tell everyone. They were looking forward to the wedding so much!'

Charlotte's stomach flipped; she wasn't ready to think about that. 'How did you get here?'

Phil was settling her mum on the sofa, coaxing her out of her M&S suede jacket. 'Came down the M6. Easy run, at this time. Stopped at the services for a bite.'

Charlotte felt slightly hysterical; in a minute he'd be telling her what route the SatNav had taken them on. 'I mean, what are you doing here? It's a Monday evening.' In normal circumstances her mother wouldn't make the drive south without a six-month detailed planning period.

'Well, what else could we do?' Gail started up noisy sobs. 'It's just not fair, Charlotte. I've been working so hard on this wedding, and now who knows what's happening!'

Charlotte shut her eyes. 'Mum, will you just – I don't know, OK? I don't know what'll happen now.'

'But why didn't you call us?'

She snapped. 'Because I got beaten up, OK? I've been in hospital all day.'

'Where are my glasses, Phil?' Gail peered at her daughter and pressed a hand to her own chest. 'Oh my goodness, your face!'

Charlotte sank down at the kitchen table. 'I was in the toilets, after the – at the hearing. Some girls hit me.'

Gail's face said that everything she'd always believed about London had come true.

Phil cleared his throat. 'Shall I make us a brew?'

'What? If you want. Mum, I didn't tell you because it was all so fast. I just never thought it'd go like this. I honestly thought it would all be fine after this morning.' As she said it, Charlotte realised it hadn't been fine – so now what? How was she going to think about what was next?

'But they said he – he killed a man!'

'I know, I was there, all right? But he didn't. I know he didn't.' Her voice wavered.

'But we saw it, didn't we, Phil – right there on the lunchtime news! And a picture of him! Where in the world did they get it from? Did you give them that?'

'For God's sake, Mum, I didn't even see it. I've been waiting in Casualty all day.'

'It's the cuts, isn't it,' said Phil, rummaging in her cupboards.

Gail fretted at the hankie she was holding. 'I just didn't know what to do. We'll have to get in the car, I said, didn't I, Phil? I didn't even put the video on for *Holby City*.'

'Any milk, love?' Phil was still pottering.

'Oh – no. I didn't exactly get time to go shopping.' She bit her lip, wincing at the pain.

'There's no milk, Gail. Would you take it without milk? Have you a shop nearby?'

Charlotte nearly screamed at him. What good was tea at a time like this? But Phil was already getting back into his beige jacket. 'Think I saw a foreign shop round the corner. Always open, aren't they?'

When he left, the silence settled round Charlotte and her mother like a heavy cloak. The clock ticked. Gail sniffed and looked about her, bewildered. 'I was supposed to be seeing the florist tomorrow. What'll I do? Will we have to postpone it? Charlotte?'

Charlotte gazed at her immaculate nails, buffed and shaped to perfection, ready for what she had thought would be the best day of her life. 'They said there won't be a trial for months.'

Her mother stared at her. 'We'll have to postpone it then. Good God, and I just put down the deposit on the cake. And what about that band *he* insisted on?'

Charlotte flared up. 'You can say his name, you know. *Dan*. Remember? He's the one who fixes your computer for you. Walks your bloody dog. Do you really think he would just kill someone? Wise up.'

'I don't like your tone, Charlotte. They've charged him, haven't they? You never know, do you?'

'You do sometimes.' No one was going to convince her that she was engaged to a killer. It just wasn't possible.

The door opened and they both jumped. Phil came rustling in with a bulging carrier bag. 'Did you see that scrum outside?'

Gail was peering out of the window. 'Darling, he's right. There are *press* out there.'

'What? Don't be silly.' But Charlotte looked out and saw three people gathered at her gate, a man with a camera and one with a sound mike, and a woman with a microphone. *Sky News*, it said. She turned back, thinking, *This isn't happening*. It was as if her life had turned into a film.

'Very rude of them,' said Gail crossly. 'What if someone's having renovations done and the house doesn't look its best?'

Phil was opening cupboards as if he owned the place. 'Got a few bits,' he said placidly. 'Your mam and I like Bran Flakes in the morning. Keeps us regular.'

From this charming piece of information, Charlotte gathered that they were planning to stay with her for some time.

Keisha

This was it, then. When it all cracked off in your hands, like some crappy old saucepan you thought you'd get one more use out of, but really you knew it was just a matter of time before it all fell to bits. And now it had. In one day she'd gone from patching things up with Chris, maybe getting Ruby back soon, to not knowing who he was at all. A man who'd do what he did to his own baby. A man who'd knock his girlfriend out in her own poky kitchen.

She'd woken up on the floor when the door slammed. At first Keisha felt like she was on a roller coaster, going so fast her feelings were a few seconds behind. For a moment it was like floating, weightless. Then it was coming, it was coming – oh, the fucking pain. The head. The ankle. He'd fucking stomped on her leg – she could see the imprint of his shoe on the unshaven skin. Her nose was pressed to the floor, beside a spaghetti hoop. It was fucking filthy, this kitchen. You would think it'd have been dirtier when Ruby was there, but Keisha had scrubbed it every day with that Dettol stuff, like her mum said. Now though – bits of fag ash, breadcrumbs, a frozen chip under the fridge. The floor felt gritty under her cheek.

She tried to see if she could get up. Pulled up one arm, one leg. Well fucking done, Keisha Collins. Have a GNVQ in sitting up. The blonde girl's wallet was still on the table, the cards spilled out. For a minute she imagined they could go back: they'd never seen this girl or her bloody boyfriend, Chris had never knocked her out. Imagine.

Something splashed onto the soft leather of the purse – red, warm. Her nose was bleeding.

Keisha had no idea when Chris might be back. It took her five minutes to stuff things in a bag. Pants. The bit of money she'd hidden inside a pair of socks. Jumper. Picture of Ruby – no time to pull down all the ones she'd tacked up to the cupboards, so she just took one. She couldn't find her keys, had he taken them? The last thing she did was feel in her jeans pocket for Charlotte Miller's driving licence, the address printed bright and clear on the pink background. It was still there where Keisha had hidden it, as soon as she left the court. Why? She'd no idea. Was it worth getting knocked out for? No idea.

Keisha stood in her hallway with her pathetic little bag of stuff. Shit. Was she really going? Where to?

She heard a noise from downstairs and, heart going like a train, reached out to turn the handle. Nothing. He'd locked her in. And someone was coming up the stairs.

Charlotte

After her mother had arrived to stay – and on *Holby City* night – Charlotte fell into her bed, and slept for two solid days. She woke in the darkened room from time to time but, hearing a murmur of voices about buying the *Mail* and calling to check the cat was OK, let herself slip back into oblivion. It was easier than having to think what she would do next. When she had to pee she went through the room trying not to look at them, ignoring them when they said, You really ought to get up now, darling. Don't you think you should have a nice wash? Invariably there'd be a paper lying about, and they would try to whisk it away but not before she saw Dan's face staring out at her. The arrest had triggered an avalanche of anti-City stories. BANKER BUTCHERS, she saw on the cover of the *Mail*, before they could hide it.

She woke to a memory. When had it been? A month before That Night, maybe. Saturday morning, and Dan awake before her. That was no surprise, he often got up early on weekends, unable to stop his brain whirring with work. This time he was sitting on the bed fully dressed, staring at her.

She'd yawned. 'You OK?'

Still he stared. 'How much does it matter to you?'

'What?'

'The money. Big wedding, big house.'

'What are you asking?' She'd rubbed her eyes.

'Hypothetically, I suppose, if you'd stand by me without the money. If I did something. If we lost it all somehow.'

She'd laughed. She thought it was a joke. 'It's not the money I care about. I suppose it's just hard to go back, once you're used to a certain . . . lifestyle. And I thought you wanted to get a bigger place soon?'

'Yeah. Never mind.'

Now she wondered what he'd really been asking.

Outside she heard her mother's voice. A thin pale light was coming in through the curtains. 'Phil, there's more of those people outside.'

'Shall I chuck the water again?'

'They started shouting about the police last time. The nerve! She's in no fit state to give interviews, for goodness sake. It's all over my *Telegraph* as well, this racism malarkey.

Apparently there was some coloured girl in his work, and she had to leave because they called her a Paki b-i-t-c-h. I'd just never have thought it.'

'Bad business, love.'

'Well, between you and me, this is Charlotte all over. She's never had the best judgement. I always thought there was something odd about him, something held back.'

Charlotte put her head under the pillow. She wasn't going to think about any of it. She had no strength to do anything but fall back into the dark.

Hegarty

'Bad business, Matthew.' Hegarty's boss, Detective Inspector Bill Barton, shook his head as he put down the paper. 'Banker Butchers, indeed. You'd think they'd never heard of contempt of court.' A career policeman who was widely rumoured to wear some kind of holding-in corset under his shirt, DI Bill Barton was pretty dull. He didn't listen to opera or do crosswords, he didn't have colourful nicknames for his staff or a maverick way of getting things done. He'd got where he was through playing by the rules, absorbing pressure from 'up above', and being nice to everyone. Everyone apart from wrongdoers that is, and there was no one he hated so much as a journalist. 'These bally reporters, they don't seem to realise people can walk free if they plaster this all over the headlines.'

'Will it affect the case, sir?'

'Never worry, lad, you did sterling work, bringing him in. Very good for our PR, they tell me. White man kills a black fellow, it's a powder-keg. Your actions put a lid on that sharpish. Now we just have to build the case and he'll be in the slammer where he belongs. Excellent job.'

Hegarty nodded, but somehow this wasn't as rewarding as it should have been. What was the matter with him? He'd been hungry for this: success, promotion. 'Sir – you know Stockbridge's fiancée was attacked at the hearing?'

The DI sighed. 'Another bad business. Goes to show how high feelings can run.'

'Yeah. Thing is . . .' He didn't know how to explain what was on his mind. He wasn't even sure himself what it was. Like something you'd seen in the corner of your vision and then it was gone. 'We haven't found that other witness yet. The other white guy. Got his picture off a phone, though.'

Bill Barton winced. 'Phone pictures – it's dodgy, Matthew. Be careful with that. It was easier in the old days, I'm telling you. Now where've you got with the investigation?'

'Spoke to Stockbridge's bank – they were very helpful, I must say. Didn't even ask for a court order. Just handed it all over, his HR records, the lot.' In fact, he'd been wondering about how helpful they'd been. A woman called Kerry Hall had sent over a packet of documents on Dan Stockbridge, his medicals, disciplinary record, appraisal notes, the lot. Interesting reading.

The boss prodded the paper again. 'Is it true then, this story about bullying black staff?'

'Looks like it. They've had to pay a few people off over the years. All that City boy stuff, sir. You know how it is.'

'I do. But I wonder how the papers got hold of it.'

Same place Hegarty had, he shouldn't wonder – from Haussmann's themselves. And that was a strange thing to do to your own employee. 'Sir, I'd like to keep looking for this other witness, if I can. I might have a lead.'

'Hmm. Be mindful of resources, lad. We're all watching the pennies now.' DI Barton jabbed a finger at the paper. 'Main thing is to get that fellow behind bars, safe and sound.'

Keisha

So, odd choice. The last place she'd thought she'd end up that Monday, in fact. When she'd realised that Chris had locked her in, and obviously didn't want her out of his sight, Keisha had panicked. Could you rattle a brain? If so, hers was going round like a coin in a washing-machine. Oh fuck. She had to get out. Thank God all the ex-council flats had to have fire escapes. It was a tight squeeze, but she'd made it out of the window in the bedroom and down the iron stairs. Then she was down on the road and running as fast as she could, trainers pounding, her little bag bouncing on her back. But where to? She couldn't go to her mum's; she'd never get Ruby back if they knew what Chris had done. Again. He hadn't changed a bit, the fucker.

Desperate to go somewhere he wouldn't know, she'd ended up in Swiss Cottage library. Her mother used to take her there sometimes for story groups, Keisha as a kid already ashamed of how her mum nodded and um-hummed her way through the lady's stories. She wished Mercy understood you didn't join in with things in this country.

It was hushed in the library, and she liked how it smelled of clean, of books. You could go in without ID or some twat of a bouncer up in your face. Best of all she liked how she could be about ninety-five per cent sure Chris would never find her here. Still, she crept in with her hood up, paranoid.

The lady behind the desk was really quite glam, not like a

librarian. She had on glasses, but they were kind of funky, and purple knee-boots. 'All right there?'

Keisha flushed. 'Er – is it OK to come in? D'you have to pay?'

The woman laughed a bit – nicely. 'Nope. You pay for it in your taxes.'

No need to say she didn't think she paid taxes out of the brown envelopes she got at the nursing home.

Keisha stayed in the library until it was getting dark and the lights from cars on the ring road started to sweep in the long narrow windows. It was so nice there, all the books on their shelves, all the people working so quiet you knew someone would say *shhh* if a phone rang or you rustled the page. In the toilets she washed the blood off her face, carefully, like a bruised piece of fruit.

There was even a café, and she bought the cheapest thing off the grumpy girl there so she didn't have to go outside. She wondered what her mum would say if she knew they charged four pounds fifty for a bowl of broccoli and Stilton soup. *You make it from gold, this soup?* Mercy would say, misting the glass cover with her hot breath, wanting to poke and prod the ciabattas and haggle them down. *Two pound fifty, OK?*

There was a dish by the counter that said TIPS, with a little heart over the 'i'. A tip for passing you a bowl of soup! Some bits of London were mad.

The day passed in a bubble. So long as she stayed there, she'd be safe. Keisha got a whole pile of books, so she looked busy. You could even go on the internet, so she put her name down for it – not her real one, she gave the name of a girl she'd been at school with, Shondra Potts, right bitch. When it was her turn she didn't know what to look for but her fingers twitched, taking her to news websites. There were a few bits about the Johnson case. Everyone was saying about how the banker's office was racist and they all bullied people and got stressed, so no wonder he'd done it. It was over, as far as everyone was concerned. So why did she care, what did she owe them, this white couple, when they had everything, and she had nothing, less than nothing, nowhere to live now, not even – not even her own kid.

Thinking the words *nothing, less than nothing* in her head made her want to cry, but she snuffled the tears back inside, pulling her hood up so no one could see. Eventually it was ten to six, and she realised she'd have to do something. Could she risk going back, would he have calmed down? No. This Chris was someone she didn't know any more. He might do anything. Had done.

She sat hunched at her desk for as long as she could, pretending she didn't see them pulling the blinds and turning off the lights. But eventually someone was standing over her. It was the librarian – Julie, her badge said. 'You know we're closing now.'

'Are you?' She pretended to be surprised. 'I was – studying.' The book in front of her was Jordan's autobiography.

Julie laughed again. 'It's Shondra, is it? You put down Shondra for the computer.'

She hesitated. 'Yeah.'

'Well, whatever your name is, here's what I think. I think you've nowhere to go, because whoever did that to your face is there.'

Keisha's hand went up to her eye before she could stop it. 'I'm all right.'

'That's good. How about a cup of tea, at least? Save you paying two pounds, or whatever they charge in that café.' That was better. They were talking the same language.

Julie unlocked a little door beside the toilets and they went into the tiniest kitchen, with a smell of going-off food. 'See the glamour behind the scenes here, Shondra. You wouldn't believe it, would you?'

Keisha smiled nervously. She had to put her hood down to drink the weak tea, but she knew Julie had already seen her face so it didn't really matter. 'Ta.' She hadn't drunk anything since she'd managed to beg a glass of water off the café bitch.

Julie crossed her legs, sipping on the tea like she was the Queen. 'Foul,' she said. 'So, Shondra, do you know what the thing is about being a librarian?'

'Er – nah.'

'Well, it means you're a public servant. Like a doctor. Or the police.'

Keisha stiffened.

'So you see, *Shondra*, we have a bit of a duty to help people when they come here. Not just to find the new Jackie Collins – but sometimes with other things.' She sipped the horrible tea. 'You'd be surprised who we get in. Drug addicts, battered women, homeless people . . .'

'I'm not homeless.' Keisha set the cup down angrily. 'I got a home.'

'But you can't go there, is that right? Because of – can I?' Gently, she touched Keisha's forehead. Her nails were painted candy-pink. 'That needs cleaning, you know. I can do it, I'm the first-aider. It was a good way to get a week off work.'

Keisha hated to be touched by strangers, but what could she say? She'd barely opened her mouth before Julie had whipped out the white box with the cross on it and was dabbing at the cuts with something that stung like fuck. 'Ow!'

'Come on, I bet you've had worse. Try giving birth!'

'I have,' she said, surprising herself. 'I got a kid.'

Julie's copper eyebrows went up. 'And where's he or she?'

'Away,' she said quickly. She didn't want this woman to think she'd left her kid with someone violent. Although she had of, course, in the past, hadn't she? Never mind that.

Julie snipped the gauze. 'You don't have to tell me. Listen, there's a hostel I sometimes send people to. It's not free, though.'

'I got money.' She was so pleased she had those five tenners from her wages. A getaway. Dignity. It was everything.

Julie took out an A-Z and made a little ring on the page where the hostel was. 'You'll go there, promise?'

'S'pose.' Keisha made it sound like she had millions of other options. That was called *keeping your head held high*. She stood up. She was crap at saying thanks. 'Er, I know you didn't have to do all this, so . . .'

Julie laughed. 'All part of the job. Sometimes I pretend I'm in *Grey's Anatomy*, you know? Then I remember I'm a librarian. Take care, now.'

Keisha paused. 'Your boots are cool,' she said. 'Are they, like, designer?'

'These? Forty quid from New Look. I work in a *library*, mate.'

Charlotte

On the third day after Dan went to prison, she woke up at her normal time – eight – and shuffled into the kitchen in her pyjamas. Her mother and step-father were up, bright-eyed, sitting at the table eating Bran Flakes. Gail had on her usual weekday outfit of jeans, padded gilet, immaculate hair and make-up, while Charlotte had creases across her face from the pillow.

'There you are. I thought you were coming down with the flu!' Her mother's tone suggested she'd have woken Charlotte at dawn; of all the things Gail and Phil didn't believe in, sleeping late was high up the list. 'You missed the news coverage. It showed this house!'

'Front wall needs painting,' Phil grunted. 'You want to have someone look at that.'

She shuffled in. 'You're still here, then.'

'Someone has to look after you, darling. Have some Bran Flakes.' Gail waggled the bright blue box, the descending milk like a stream, frozen mid-splash. Was it real, Charlotte had always wondered. Was it just an illusion?

'I don't like them.' Feeling like a petulant child, she rummaged for Nutella and made toast.

Her mother tutted but said nothing. 'I called your work for you. Explained you were in shock. Quite a nice man I spoke to. Simon, was it? Educated, you could tell. Is he your boss?'

Oh God. 'Did they – had they heard?'

'Everyone's heard.' Gail sniffed. 'It'll be all round the village like wildfire, you can be sure of that.'

There was nothing to say to that but sorry, and why should she? It wasn't her fault. It wasn't Dan's fault either.

'You really must speak to them. *His* parents. They even rang up – sounded as if they'd never used a phone before in their life.'

She winced. 'Er, Mum, what's happened about – you know? Will we tell everyone it's postponed? What about the suppliers?'

Gail's face dissolved into little flurries of frowns and tears.

'It's been so *hard*. Most of them won't give the deposits back.'

'But weddings must get moved, surely? I mean, lots could go wrong.'

Phil crunched his cereal. 'Wedding insurance. We did say.'

'But you wouldn't be told, would you, darling?' They were a double act. 'I'm afraid you'll be rather out of pocket on this.'

Charlotte took a brave breath. 'Look, we just have to try to forget the wedding for now. It'll happen. I just need to sort all this out first. It can't be that long till a trial, surely?'

'Can be years,' said Phil helpfully, from behind the *Daily Mail*.

'And all the invitations went out. Such a shame. You'll need to call your friends, darling. Your phone was going and going, such a racket.'

Why had she been sleeping when there was so much to do? She mustered herself. 'Mum, it was really good of you to come, but I'm OK now. I can manage.'

'You haven't eaten a square meal in days!'

'No, but I'm better now. Wouldn't you like to get home to your own nice house?'

They glanced at each other; they loved nothing better than being at home in their own nice house. 'But Charlotte, you've been such a wreck. It's such a terrible, terrible thing. We can't just leave you on your own. You need to get a lawyer, cancel things. What about money? You can't afford to live here on your own, can you?'

She blocked her ears. No time to deal with that now. 'Sarah could come over, if you think I need someone.'

'Hmm, I suppose. Where is she now?' Her mother turned to Phil, who although he was Sarah's father was nothing like her, except in a certain inflexibility of spirit.

'Some foreign place – Bangladesh? Meant to be back for the wedding, isn't she?'

'Oh yes, and she wouldn't be told to come back sooner, would she? Well, if you think she can help . . .' Gail's tone expressed severe doubts that Sarah would help anyone.

Charlotte said, 'You'll beat the traffic if you set off soon. I wouldn't want you stuck on the M6.' It was the right thing to say – beating the traffic was practically part of Phil's religion, and within an hour they were gone, leaving her in the dubious peace of the empty flat. As soon as the door shut she was in the recycling box, pulling out dirty crumpled paper until she found the article she wanted. She sat back on her heels and read about Dan, and his work, and the things they had done. *Institutional racism. Psychological torture. City-boy bullies.* And for hours the sound of the ticking clock was all she could hear.

Keisha

The hostel was a bizarro place. Weirder than weirdsville. Half the people were like her – *between homes* might be the nice way to say it. Ex-prisoners, single mums with nowhere to go. Most had skin so ruined from smoking it was stretched back over their faces like a mask. Keisha wasn't the only one with a battered face, either.

The other half of the guests were normal, people who thought it was just a hostel that didn't allow men. There were Asian girls taking pictures of everything on their camera phones, and once a bunch of middle-aged ladies from Bradford who just wanted to see *Billy Elliot*. She could hear them long before they came down the corridor, muttering over and over things they weren't happy about. 'And there's never any pastries left at breakfast. The ad said pastries – and the noise, Margaret!'

'I know, Sue, we should complain.'

'We should. We absolutely should complain.'

There weren't any pastries because the other half, the in-between women, got up at six and grabbed them – it was free food, after all. One morning Keisha was in the canteen, killing time reading *Metro*, when a wrinkle-faced woman nodded to her.

'You want that?' There was a small sticky Danish on Keisha's plate, and she'd been going to save it in a napkin for lunch, but she said, 'Nah.' In a nanosecond the woman's middle kid, a boy, had scoffed it. There were two other kids, a boy fiddling miserably with a mobile phone, and a girl about Ruby's age, squirming to get off her mum's lap. 'Lemme go, Mam!'

Ruby'd never have been so loud or so cheeky. The woman had ratty dyed blonde hair and glared at Keisha, who quickly snapped her eyes away from the kid. 'I got a girl,' she explained. 'Five, she is.'

The woman narrowed her heavily mascaraed eyes. 'How old're you then?'

'Twenty-five.'

'Same. Ta for the bun. Tyler, Kian, Jade, get a fucking move on!'

Twenty-five, and the oldest kid was ten at least, maybe eleven. Christ, there was always someone worse off.

At twelve she went out before the Irish cleaning lady, Brenda, came with her fug of floral air freshener, gassing them out like wasps. Then it was the library all day, reading book after book and all the papers and magazines in the place. She'd never known so much about the news. The name of that bank kept coming up again and again. Haussmann's, a German-sounding name. That was where the blonde girl's fella worked, or did before. Maybe not now. And it hadn't collapsed in the end, the government had bought it after the owners lost ten billion pounds.

Keisha had to squint down at that figure, then lay the paper on the table to look at it properly, and an old biddy gave her evils because it rustled the teeniest fucking amount. Was that *right*? If you were rich already, and you lost billions – from dodgy stuff, this paper seemed to be saying, although she couldn't work out what – then the government would just say, oh, no worries, we'll cover it? While if she lost a tenner, say 'cos she was stupid and dropped it out of her purse paying a bus fare, and it was all she had to spend in Tesco's for a week, that was just tough shit?

She saw Julie a few times at the library, but ducked her head down into her hood. She was grateful and all, but sometimes it just hurt more when people were being nice. She didn't know why, it just did.

At night Keisha lay awake to the constant comings and goings, Asian girls drying their hair at 5 a.m., babies screeching, women shouting all night in the corridor. Her mind raced with worries. She should call the nursing home, explain why she'd not been in. She should ring Sandra, tell her she'd left Chris. She should tell her mum, check on the kid. But she didn't do any of it.

She thought about Ruby and her face the last time she saw her. Sometimes, however she tried, she thought about what he'd done to the kid, and how she'd just stood there and watched and couldn't move to stop him until it was too late. Her hands clenched up in her sleep, dreaming about it. She kept thinking about that blonde girl – what did she know? It must be something, or Chris wouldn't have gone after her at the court. If she could find out what the blonde girl knew, would it keep him away? But, stricken with fear, that was as far as she got.

After three days she was down to her last tenner, and her corner-shop Polish noodles had all run out. It was time to go crawling back.

Charlotte

Charlotte sat still at the table, staring at the huge pile of post. However many times she closed her eyes, it wouldn't go away. For the first time there was no one else to tackle it with her, and unless she slit open the innumerable window envelopes, money would not jump from one virtual pile to another, and soon the lights would go off and she'd be sitting in the dark without even endless re-runs of *Friends* to dull her into numbness.

Three piles, she decided. Wedding stuff – invoices, gifts still coming in from the slow or the uninformed, condolences – they were all going, there was no point in any of it. Then the dross – flyers, credit-card offers, takeaway menus. Finally, the bills. Some of them had red notices on now when they came in the door and she would have been ashamed for Mike and Susie downstairs to see them if she really cared any more. Dan always paid the bills, so she was hazy on the details, but surely they couldn't be overdue so soon. Weren't they all on direct debits from his account?

She got up and shuffled in her slippers to the little spare room. Dan sometimes worked in there at weekends. She rifled through the papers on the desk – lots and lots of printouts in a messy pile, columns and columns of figures, some ringed in red, stamped over with *confidential*. They meant nothing to her. She opened the top drawer and shoved in there were all the envelopes – gas, water, phone – unopened and, she would guess, unpaid. What did it mean? Had he cancelled the direct payments? Why?

She opened the second drawer and there were packets and packets of pills. Paracetamol, Ibuprofen, Zantac, everything you could think of. She touched the silver packets, the popped-out craters where the tablets had been. What did it mean?

Out loud in the quiet room, she said, 'Why didn't you *talk* to me?' She'd have listened. Wouldn't she?

In the middle of all the post was a heavy embossed envelope, the crest of Dan's bank indented into the paper in resolute black. She ran her fingers over the grooves of his name: *Mr Daniel Stockbridge*. Could there be a name more solid, more sure? She had hoped to hide herself in it, to be equally sure and solid. Mrs Stockbridge. But everything could crumble. Everything could fall apart. She knew that now.

She opened the letter. Normally she never snooped, didn't even check his phone; she knew how much he would hate it. But times had changed. When she finally made herself look at the words, it said what she feared. They were very sorry but they had to terminate his employment on the grounds of gross misconduct. If he had any questions he could pop in and see her, signed *Kerry Hall, HR Officer*. Charlotte flung it down angrily, saying out loud, 'You stupid cow.' He couldn't exactly swing by her office. Dan had worked at Haussman's for eight years and they didn't care enough not to copy and paste.

Overwhelmed, she swept the pile aside, tears pattering down and smudging the ink. Who cared? What did it matter if she didn't pay the credit-card bill? But uncovered by her dramatic gesture was a piece of paper with no envelope, scribbled on A4 fileblock, ripped awkwardly so one side tapered in. Curiously she picked it up and tossed it down again as if the paper had burned her. In the cramped crazy writing, the first phrase she'd seen had been, *kill you racist cunt.*

She was suddenly cold right down to her bones with fear. The words spiralled up and down the page in circles, the way a child might write. It lay on the table like a creeping spider, words scored in deeply with red ink.

Charlotte sat at the table surrounded by the litter of her old life. What was happening to her?

Hegarty

The Kingston Town club was shuttered in daytime, closed against the clatter of traffic and delivery trucks. There were grilles on the windows but the yellow police tape was gone. Were they opening again, then, this place where so many lives had been ruined? The back of a restaurant, flats up above with people's plants and posters; a dry-cleaner's. Not much to the street where Anthony Johnson had breathed his last, choking on his own blood.

It was hard to believe this was the same place where Hegarty had come across that scene of horror, the blood spreading over the floor under the fluorescent light, realising he was standing in it and that it was all over his shoes, the dull shine drying in sticky pools. He noticed the yellow sign on the dry-cleaner's opposite – *CCTV in operation here* – and he tried to remember if they'd requested it. Surely they would have? How long did it take?

He pushed in, noting the flutter of an old bit of police tape. 'The boss here?' he called. Anthony Johnson's brother was back, apparently, and had taken over the place.

The skinny black guy behind the counter squared up to him. 'You the police again? You not catch the guy who did it?'

'Is he here, please? Ronald Johnson – he's in charge now?'

The man was slowly polishing a glass. 'Sorry. He's out.'

'Really?'

He shrugged. 'Not here.'

'Right. Can you ask him to ring me, please?' Hegarty placed his card on the bar, in a puddle of beer.

'I'll ask,' the man said, but it was clear from his tone that Hegarty shouldn't expect a call anytime soon.

On his way out Hegarty paused and saw someone open the back office door and peer out, a tall black man. The door quickly shut again and the guy at the counter said loudly, 'See ya, Officer.'

So Ronald Johnson didn't want to talk to the police who were trying to find his brother's killer. Interesting.

Checking no one was around, Hegarty walked along the wall of the club, the windows blind with shutters. By the side of it was a small alley, easy to miss, blocked up with bins. He slipped into it. It was only a few metres long, and so narrow he couldn't hold his arms out wide in it, but there, set in the brick wall, was the outline of a metal door. *Alarm in use*, it warned. He looked at it for a long time, wondering, and then turned to walk to his home in Kentish Town.

Keisha

She didn't know what she was doing.

She was on her old street, walking towards what was still partly her flat. She paid the bloody rent, didn't she? But when she passed the burger shop and turned into the concrete building, after that she had no clue. Maybe he'd be at home. Of course she wouldn't go in if he was there – would she?

The last time they met he'd beaten her up, yes. She knew that. She wasn't one of these stupid women they always had on episodes of *The Bill*, and they're all like, 'oh no, I walked into a door'. He'd hit her. Yes. But it wasn't *that* bad. She didn't need to go to hospital or anything. They'd just got pissed off with each other – who didn't? Sometimes she'd have liked to slap him round the face, too.

What was she doing? There was no sound in the concrete stairwell, so maybe he wasn't home. Unless he was asleep. She'd just go in and get her clothes, look for more cash, eat something – it was her fucking stuff, after all. Then she'd go – somewhere. Do something. Deffo.

She reached her door, or her old door, feeling like a burglar. She breathed in all the air she could get, cold and smoke-smelling on the draughty stairs, and she knocked. If you pressed your ear up to the door you'd hardly have heard it, so no surprise no one came. She knocked a little bit louder: nothing.

She reached up on her tiptoes and felt along the dusty doorsill for the key she'd stuck up there. After Ruby got taken away, Keisha'd had a run of losing hers when she went out, pissed, trying to forget. But the key wouldn't go in. She was just standing there like a retard, pushing at the door. He'd fucking changed the locks. She was so shocked by this that she just stared for a moment. Then she heard a noise and her heart went crazy – he was here!

But no, it was a woman's voice, raspy with smoke, belting out, 'Liam! Watch the bleeding stairs!' It was Jacinta from upstairs trailing her boy by the hand, while trying to lift her little girl's pushchair down the stairs at the same time. No lift in this building and they put the family on the fourth floor. Sometimes Keisha thought these men who ran things could do with trying to lift a baby and shopping and a kid and a buggy up four flights of stairs. 'Want a hand?'

Jacinta gave her a suspicious look through red-rimmed eyes, then jerked her chin, making her high pony-tail fly up. 'Get the wheels.'

Keisha picked up the spinning bottom wheels, and panting, the little boy all the while about to fall and crack his bloody head, they got downstairs.

'You seen Chris?' she said as she put the buggy down, quickly, ashamed to have to ask.

Jacinta paused to take a packet of Silk Cut out of her pink cropped combats. 'Kicked you out, did he?'

Keisha shrugged. 'Had a row.'

'Me and my Keith, we fight like cats and dogs some nights. But he don't ever do that to me.' She nodded to Keisha's cracked face. 'Listen, love. We all heard the racket – whole building did. Nearly called the boys in blue. So Keith up and asks him next day, Is your missus OK?' She lit the cigarette, inhaling. 'And he turns round and says, Ain't got a missus. Then he comes up real close to Keith, all scary, and he goes, If she comes round, you better fucking tell me. Else I'll come after you too.' She dragged deeply on her fag. 'If I were you, love, I'd get off sharpish. He's bad news, that fella.'

Keisha's stomach was heaving. What was she, thick? He'd

banged her head off the table and she came back for more, thinking they could just go back to Happy Families or whatever it was they'd been.

Keisha turned to leave, almost running to get away, but Jacinta called her back. 'Oi,' she said. 'Where's that little 'un of yours. She safe?' Everyone in the building knew what had happened to Ruby.

Ruby. Suddenly Keisha's feelings sank down to an even worse level, and it felt like something heavy was sitting on her chest. She couldn't breathe for a minute. She'd never thought of it, 'cos he was never interested in the kid. But if he wanted to get back at Keisha . . . What if all the time she'd been hiding in the fucking hostel, he was . . . Oh, fuck.

Setting off at a run to the bus stop, she fumbled for the blonde girl's purse and took out the Oyster card. Surely the girl wouldn't mind her using a bit for the bus. Not when it was this big a fucking deal.

Charlotte

She had to admit she was grateful her mother and Phil had come, if only because they'd left her enough food to eke out for nearly the whole first week. But eventually she'd eaten even the manky Bran Flakes and all the food in the freezer and she'd been having her tea black for days. It suited her mood, dark and bitter.

On the Friday – the day before what would have been her wedding – Charlotte was going crazy. She couldn't sleep, couldn't focus on the stupid burbling TV, hadn't so far dared to pick up the phone or go online. It was only hiding from that onslaught of pity, that tsunami of sorry, that was keeping her on her feet, and she knew it. Her thoughts were sliding back and forth like a low-slung pendulum – eat, TV, sleep – and that was where they needed to stay. But now she was twitching with loneliness, standing up, sitting down, waiting for the kettle to boil, then coming to and realising she'd been there for ages and the water had cooled. To make matters worse she knew there were hundreds of things to do. She had already started four different letters to Dan's parents, asking them to help her find a lawyer, and abandoned them all. They weren't answering the phone.

Charlotte pulled her laptop over to her, the tiny silver case light as a box of chocolates. Desperate for contact, any human contact, she clicked on to Facebook, and the white-and-blue screen came up. Photos, names – *Alison is watching* Britain's Got Talent, *oo-er. Pete thinks lemon cheesecake is yum.* So many words spilled out to say more or less nothing.

She took a deep breath and clicked on her own wall.

Hey Mrs Stockbridge how was the wedding? Someone who hadn't heard, idiot.

Charlotte r u ok? Saw the news honey wtf?

From the rest, some kind of shocked silence. If Dan was dead, messages would pour in, she didn't doubt it. There was no grief so deep as to be wordless any more – *RIP, miss u mate, your a great guy,* the usual misspelled rubbish. But what did you say to this? What did you say when someone you knew fell so far and so irrevocably? Maybe it made you look down at your own feet and see how far you could slip, too.

She clicked on and there it was, what she'd dreaded. Messages from people she didn't know. A different sort of hate mail but just as bad. She clicked feverishly to delete, trying not to see them. *Racist. Bitch. You should die.* Dan didn't have a Facebook page, said it was a waste of time. She was glad, now.

It took Charlotte half an hour to work out how to do it, clicking bewildered from screen to screen, but eventually she turned off her profile, so no one could send her messages. She left her relationship status as *engaged* – it was still true, wasn't it? Alone with the tick of the clock, she slowly turned the diamond ring on her finger. This wasn't right. This wasn't how it was meant to be.

At eight it was growing dusky and she pulled on her trainers and got ready to go to the shops. It took an unbelievably long time to find her keys, run a brush through her hair, and then she had to go back because she'd forgotten her phone and didn't want to provoke another visit down the M6 from her mother thinking she might be dead. She had lost her purse in the attack, but luckily Phil had been on the case and ordered her new cards.

The sun was setting over the rooftops outside, the sky bright but the pavements already darkening to shadow. It was a sad night, woodsmoke on fading bright air, or maybe it wasn't and everything just seemed sad to her.

She trudged towards the shop in the same clothes she'd worn all week. She probably smelled, but still, it was only Finchley Road. There was a shop in Belsize Park 'Village', as people liked to call it, but she needed cash, so she went the other way, down the hill. It was a mistake.

Charlotte only realised afterwards that the man in the shop had been staring at her. Normally they didn't look at customers at all, just carried on talking very loud and very fast in what she assumed was Arabic. She wandered the aisles, desolate with choice. She didn't want any of this, Pot Noodles, Pringles, Diet Coke. What she wanted was not to be here at all. She wanted none of this to have ever happened.

When she went outside there was a gang of teenagers hanging about the station, so she walked past quickly with her head down. As she was waiting to cross the road past Waitrose – going in there would have been too cruel – something hit her softly, and she put up a hand to her head and brought it back, red. For a second she wobbled – not again! But nothing hurt. They'd thrown something at her, and red syrupy filth was all over her blonde hair.

The group was a sea of faces under caps and hoods. Boys, girls, mostly black. All shades, in that nonsense way of describing colour, so some were paler than she would be with a tan. They were staring at her.

'Do you mind?' she said, haughtily, and one of them, a boy, threw another carton, some kind of drink. As it flew at her and she put up her arms, she heard him hiss: '*Fucking Nazi.*'

One of the girls, emboldened, whooped up. 'Yeah, racist bitch. Your fella's a killer, inee?'

Charlotte just stared at them. The carton had bounced off her arms and spattered her face with more red goo. 'But – I . . . I . . .'

'Gonna fucking kill us too?' The boy threw again, this time something harder, green, spinning. It was a beer bottle. Like the one that had killed Anthony Johnson. She ducked, and it shattered on the pavement, and with a high thrill of panic, Charlotte turned and ran, her pathetic dried goods rattling in the thin plastic bag. When she got home she bolted the door fast, and sank down against it, panting. Gloop slid down her face.

It was the hair that did it. She had lovely hair, everyone said so. Now it was the night before what should have been her wedding day, and instead of a conditioning mask, her hair was full of acid-red ooze. It was too much to bear.

Keisha

Keisha's mum had lived in Gospel Oak ever since she got up the duff at the unusual age of thirty-five to a mystery white man. Mercy had arrived from Jamaica with a course booked at London University and big plans for her future, but it hadn't exactly worked out that way. Keisha'd always thought her mum liked the area because of the name, because it made her think of Matthew, Mark, Luke, John and all those fellas. She stood out, Mercy. In the same way a massive ship on the water did, tilting with each slow step. No one had ever walked as slow as Mercy shuffling down the street, pausing at every okra and plantain.

Keisha didn't even try to phone – her mum wouldn't get a landline, never mind a mobile. She went to a phone box if she needed to make calls, holding up half the world as she fiddled round for her change. Keisha just got on the bus and willed it to go as fast as possible, hanging on tight to the orange railing. If she didn't sit down maybe it'd go faster. But lots of people got on and an old man gave her a death-stare. 'Can I get past, please?'

'I dunno, can you?' Keisha had a lip on her. It always got her in trouble, but she never learned.

Finally the bus ground to the slowest stop ever, and she got out, jostling past old ladies and buggies to jog down her mum's street. It was why she always wore trainers – you never knew when you'd have to get out, sharpish.

She rattled the letter box of the little terrace house. 'Mum!

Mum! Are you there?' At this time where would Mercy be? At home watching TV, an open packet of Maryland cookies in reach of her hovering hand, or at church, or at the shops buying more food. Keisha had a key, but she'd left it at the flat, hidden in a mug at the back of a cupboard. He'd never look there, would he? He wouldn't know what it was for. No, he wouldn't.

'Mum!' She rattled even harder. Through the net curtains the house looked the same as always, tidy, dark, stuffed with the smell of old furniture and boiling food.

Keisha heard a click and the door of the house next door opened an inch. Mrs Suntharalingam peered out from the chain. Sri Lankan by birth, she had massive glasses like Deirdre out of *Coronation Street*. 'You here?'

There was no love lost between Keisha and Mrs S – it went way back to one time Keisha had puked blue WKD over the garden wall onto some stupid purple flowers, and apparently they'd died. Mercy was always leaning over the back fence to moan to her neighbour about Keisha, blah blah blah, can't look after her own kid, rubbish boyfriend, got kicked out of the good school, works in a nursing home. Of course the Suntharalingams were all accountants or doctors and living in massive houses in Wandsworth.

'Where's Mum?'

'For days we are calling you. All weekend.' The chain rattled.

'What? No one called me.' She fumbled in her bag, catching her fingers on the ripped bits from where Chris had torn it up. The phone hadn't rung in days.

'Not in service, is saying. Over and over we call.'

'What – oh, shit.' The screen was blank – no network. 'Fucking bastard!' Of course he had, he'd cut her off. Mrs S was making loud sucking noises of disapproval. 'Look, where is she?'

Mrs S took on a great expression of triumph and disgust. 'She at the hoss-pital. Her heart, it just go right out of her body.'

'What? She had a heart attack? Christ, is she OK?'

Mrs S flapped her hands behind the still-chained door. 'Very bad, oh, very bad. We call and call you. After he come round, she cry and cry – then she shout out, she clutch herself – drop her samosa on carpet. Oh, Mrs Suntharalingam, she say.'

'I don't get it. Who came? What are you on about?'

'The boy, you cheeky miss. The *bad* boy. *Your* bad boy.'

'My – oh, shit. Do you mean – you mean Chris? Ruby's dad?'

'Yes, yes, the bad boy. Upset her very much. She cry and cry, then she clutch.'

'Oh, fuck.' Keisha grabbed on very hard to the door handle. 'Where's Ruby? Mrs S, please, please, where is she? Did he take her?' Oh fuck! Oh fuck!

'Lady took her. I cannot keep her here, you see, I have the arthritis.' One gnarled hand came out from the frosted glass.

'You mean the Social took her?' Fuck. Well. That was better than Chris, at least. 'Where's Mum then?'

'Hoss-pital.'

'What hospital?' Daft bitch.

Mrs S sniffed and pointed towards Hampstead. 'That one, Royal Free one.'

Keisha set off again running, until she stopped being able to hear Mrs S muttering, 'Cheeky miss, language she used to me . . .'

Charlotte

Something was going to have to change, that was obvious. It couldn't go on this way. On the morning of what should have been her wedding, Charlotte slept as late as she could, even getting up to rummage in the chest-of-drawers for an old airline sleep mask, stubbing her toe and shouting, 'Fuck!' to the empty air. But the buzzer going over and over woke her, and trailing into the living room she answered it before she remembered what had happened the night before. Four washes seemed to have cleaned out the gunk; her hair was still damp.

'Charlotte? It's Mrs Lyndhurst from number two. You need to come down to the lobby.'

'But . . .'

'Now, please.'

The old biddy! Charlotte stomped downstairs in her pyjamas to where a little crowd had gathered on the front steps. Mrs Busybody, Mike and Susie from downstairs with their immaculate baby in a sling, the odd techie guy who lived in the basement with a million DVDs.

Mike spoke. 'I'm sorry, Charlotte, but we think this is aimed at you.' He was squirming with middle-class discomfort.

'It worries us, you see, for Harry,' said Susie earnestly, arranging the baby. Charlotte remembered that she found her annoying.

On the doorstep, it was etched out in red paint, messily done and misspelled – MUREDER. 'Oh.' Charlotte stood and looked at it, and then without meaning to sank down on the doorstep in her pink pyjamas. Her feet were bare and the ground cold.

Mrs Lyndhurst sighed. 'Really, I was only trying to shop

for supper. This ought to be dealt with.' She departed, and Mike said he and Susie had to take Harry to Baby Movement.

'I'm sorry,' he said wretchedly. 'You should really call the police.'

'Come on,' Susie chided, hurrying her child away from Charlotte's contamination.

Basement Guy slunk away, he'd only come to see what was interrupting his playing of *FIFA 11*.

Charlotte sat on the cold step and wondered if she was going to cry. Was there any point? No. There wasn't. She was in a place beyond, where tears weren't going to make any difference, melt any hearts, remove any paint from stone. She went upstairs, leaving the front door wide open. Charlotte hardly ever looked inside her rammed hallway cupboard, but now, for the second time that week, she went through it half-mad, pulling out dusters and cans of polish and tennis racquets and Dan's hiking boots, all the junk of a shared life, the things that have no real place. There was a chisel in Dan's toolbox – untouched – and a stiff wire brush for cleaning shoes. His shoes were always so lovely, shining like mirrors.

She took the chisel and brush downstairs and began to scrape and pick at the red paint, kneeling in her pyjamas and bed hair as if she wanted everyone to see. *Penance*, that was the word that came to her unreligious mind. But what she was penitent for, she couldn't have said.

Much later, only the ghostly outline of the word stayed. But she would always know it was there, every time she opened the front door. Washing her stained, ruined hands, wincing at the little cuts on her fingers, she thought maybe it was right that she wouldn't forget. Maybe while she was consumed with sorrow for herself and for Dan she should remember that someone else was dead.

You should call the police, Mike had said, the standard middle-class trust in those people to bring justice. He'd said it in a kind way, with a keep-your-mess-away meaning. But she had the number of a policeman on a card in her kitchen. Maybe she would take that kindly but judgemental advice, after all.

Keisha

Everywhere she went there was some bitch of a woman up in her face. 'Look, I'm fucking sick of this,' she shouted in the end, to the black nurse behind the hospital desk, giving it all that with her Sawf London accent. 'S'not visitin' hours, you gotta come back lay-ta, yeah?'

But when Keisha said *fucking* to her, the nurse moved back like someone'd tried to whack her. 'Why'd you say that? Oh!' Keisha saw she was crying.

Keisha could actually see her mum behind a glass partition in the ward beyond, it was why she'd gotten so pissed off. She breathed in. 'Look, I'm sorry. S'just really important, yeah? Like life or death, you know?'

Still with her shoulders heaving, the nurse waved her in. Keisha heard her blow her nose noisily and mutter something about being effing sick of it, too.

Mercy was asleep in the third bed down. There were three other women, two fat and asleep, and the third a wizened Chinese lady like a scrap of bark. The only one awake in the humming quiet, she smiled at Keisha with no teeth. She remembered being here for Ruby, how mental she'd been on the painkillers and adrenaline, how she wanted to talk and talk to everyone and wouldn't put the baby down to get some sleep. 'Christ, give it a rest,' Chris had said when they'd finally found him down the pub.

'Mum,' she whispered. Mercy had a tube up her nose and in her arm, and she was giving out her usual snores, like bloody earthquakes. 'Mum.' Keisha prodded her a bit and Mercy's eyes shot open. She gave a snort. For a second Keisha was afraid, she was so fucking afraid that maybe her mother wouldn't know who she was any more.

But Mercy clicked and gummed with her dry mouth. 'Shush your noise. People sick here.'

'*You're* sick here.'

Mercy rearranged her IV tube, just like when people came to her house and she tidied away her teacups. 'My goodness, such a fuss. I'm in rude health!'

Where she got these words from, Keisha had no idea. 'Are you OK? Like really?' She didn't look OK. Her face was a sort of plum colour, like bits of fruit that ended up on the pavement under the high-street stalls.

Mercy waved her hand. 'Just a little turn.'

'They said you'd had a heart attack. I saw Mrs S. She said . . .' Keisha couldn't say it. 'Mum, was he there?'

Her mother said nothing, but fiddled with the IV tube again.

'Mum!' Keisha couldn't breathe when she realised there was a glassy sheen on her mum's bruised-plum face. In all her life she'd only seen Mercy cry like this one time, and that was when Ruby had her accident. Except it wasn't an accident, was it? 'Mum, please! What happened? Where was Ruby?'

Mercy wiped pathetically at her eyes, but couldn't reach with all the wires.

'Oh, here.' Keisha pulled some tissues out of a box on the bedside and dabbed at her mum's face. 'He came, didn't he? Did he try to take her?'

Slowly, Mercy nodded.

'And you stopped him?'

Mercy blew her nose with a big honk and, disgusted, Keisha chucked the tissue in the bin. She'd probably catch swine flu or something.

'He tried to take her. The baby. I keep the door closed. She's watching what's it called, that programme? Strange name.'

'*Balamory?*'

Mercy nodded. 'She saw him banging on the window. Very bad. I said I will call the police. He went away. But then – well. I had a little upset.'

Keisha said dully, 'I've left him.'

Her mother gave her an I'll-believe-it-when-I-see-it look.

'No, really. Look.' She leaned over so Mercy could see her healing eye. 'That's what he did to me. I swear, Mum, I swear to God – sorry – I just never thought. I didn't think he'd come to you. He never looks near her, does he?' She was so stuck up in shame now there was no point in pretending any more. 'Mum, I'm sorry. You were right.' Saying it was so bitter that tears almost burst out her nose. 'You were right, OK? He's a fucker. I'm sorry for everything. I never meant to get kicked out of school, it was just all those posh kids and— God, Mum, I'm sorry, OK?'

Her mum sucked in air through her dodgy teeth. 'Don't take the good Lord's name in vain.'

'S-sorry.' Keisha sat gulping by her mum's bedside. 'Is she OK? Ruby?' She felt so ashamed to be asking, when she was Ruby's mum. People should be asking that question to her.

Mercy honked again, this time choking on a wad of phlegm. 'The Social lady come. They have to take her, they say, if no one's at home.'

Because Ruby was officially in care, wasn't she? It was called 'kinship caring', and it meant they didn't pay Mercy half as much as a non-related foster carer would get. Not that she ever made a word of complaint.

Keisha felt overwhelmed by it. It was as if they'd both disappeared, her mum into the mouth of this huge hospital, down endless squeaky corridors, and her kid somewhere similar. Was Ruby at someone's house, playing with strange toys, eating different food? She couldn't imagine her at all. It was as if she had vanished completely.

Hegarty

Hegarty didn't often make arrests in homes that had what he could swear was a genuine Eames chair in the corner. He was a secret design freak, a fact kept well-hidden from his station mates. Sometimes on weekends he went to furniture shops, the kind of places where he could never have afforded to buy even an ash tray, and just looked and looked for hours.

'Hello?' The front door to the flats had been left ajar, and now he pushed the unlocked flat door open, too.

Charlotte Miller was crumpled on the sofa, wearing tracksuit bottoms and a sweatshirt that was far too big for her – Stockbridge's, he guessed. Her eyes were red and swollen. He felt a surge of annoyance. Didn't she know, sitting there with the door open, did she not understand about the weeping women he saw all the time, attacked, bruises on their thighs, mascara running down their faces?

'Miss Miller? I'm DC Hegarty – remember?'

She nodded dully.

'Can I come in?' Her face was a mess of bruises. He could hardly look at it.

'You *are* in.' She didn't look up.

'You want to tell me what happened then?' He'd seen the step on the way up.

She sighed. 'Is there any point? Some kids threw stuff at me, and someone painted my step. I guess it doesn't matter that much.'

'What about this court attack? That's an open case, you can make a statement.'

She seemed to think about it, and then shook her head back and forth very slowly. 'I don't remember enough.'

'But if you told me something, we might be able to find them. It was two girls, was it? Can you think of any reason you might have been targeted – maybe something you saw at the club that didn't seem important, or . . .'

Something in her face closed up. 'Please. I can't remember. I don't want to talk about it.' She shuddered, as if remembering. Was she afraid, was that it?

'You have been in the wars, haven't you.' He looked round the flat; a week on, it was dirty and smelled stale. 'I know today must be tough – it was today, wasn't it?'

She still didn't look up, but glassy tears were sliding down her face. 'I just can't believe it, you know. Really can't. I'm in shock, I think.'

He hated seeing women cry. 'Er . . . I'll get you a tissue.' He looked round frantically and she laughed, wiping her sleeve over her lovely, battered face. 'I've used them all. None left.'

He perched awkwardly on the side of her chrome and leather sofa. It was a strange mix, this flat, the minimalist lines you'd expect from a macho twat like Stockbridge, but here and there bowls of pot pourri, flowery cushions, a pink dish on the table. Small traces of this girl in front of him. 'Didn't you want anyone with you, your mam or someone?'

She laughed again. 'God, no. She's doing my head in. I can't stand it, you know, them all looking at me and saying, Oh, it's ten o'clock, we were meant to be in the hair-dresser's; Oh, it's one, you were meant to be walking down the ai-aisle . . .' Fresh tears rolled out of her eyes and down her creamy cheeks. She even looked good when she cried, this girl. 'Sorry. It's the shock, I think. I'm supposed to be perfect today – that's the thing. Do you know how much that dress cost? Four grand. And it won't get wo-o-orn!'

Hegarty was at a loss. What did you say to a girl on what should have been her wedding day? 'Can I make you a cup of tea or something? It's nearly dinnertime.' Crap, he should have said *lunchtime* to her.

To his surprise she wiped her face and said, 'Yes, please. I haven't been able to get up.'

He went to the kitchen and opened various shiny red cupboards, found her expensive tea – cotton bags! There was no tea-pot so he couldn't make it proper; in the cups would have to do. 'Got any milk?'

'Oh, I don't know. Does it matter?'

They'd have to have it black. Any chance of biscuits? In the fridge were Yorkshire teacakes and he couldn't help himself saying, 'You're from the north? Really?'

She didn't look round. 'My mother lives there. In the Peaks.'

'I'm from the Lakes myself. Barrow.' His accent came tripping through, running up like an eager dog. 'God, you never see teacakes in the south.'

'Have one.' She couldn't have been less interested.

He brought her tea and she ignored it, even though he slipped a coaster under it, a floral one he was sure had been her choice. 'Haven't you been eating, then?' She was even thinner than before.

'No. I was desperate to lose weight for today too – didn't realise this would be the best way. To have my life ruined, I mean.'

'You need to eat.' He took out his phone.

'What are you doing?'

'Ordering a pizza.'

'What – no! I don't eat pizza. What—'

He held up his hand. 'Yes, hello? Can I order a pizza – have you got a Hawaiian? Large one, please.' He told them the address and hung up.

'Are you serious?'

'Girls always like Hawaiians.'

She tutted. 'Yeah, because we're all the same. I won't eat it.'

But when it came she picked at one slice, then another, finally eating three, which he suspected was more than she'd had all week. His pineapple bits were lined up along the edge of the box lid, never could stand fruit on savoury food. 'You look less peaky now.'

'Who are you, my mother?'

'Hope not. You said she did your head in.' He whisked away the box and napkins, tidying the mess up efficiently. Once the pizza was finished and he'd taken a few details about the graffiti, Hegarty felt he should go. He wouldn't be able to do much. He picked up his jacket and draped it over his shoulder. 'Have you thought about what you'll do? Are you going back to work?'

She winced. 'I couldn't. This wedding, it's all I've talked about for months.'

'You should go in,' he said gently. 'Try to keep things going.'

'For when he comes back, you mean?' For the first time she looked up.

He made a vague noise. 'He'd want you to look after yourself, wouldn't he?' And she would need a job to pay legal fees.

Charlotte let out a shaky breath. 'Maybe I'll try to go in on Monday.'

'Good.' He resisted the urge to stroke her tousled hair. 'I'll be off. Look after yourself, Miss Miller. And you should really keep your doors locked.'

'Please, don't call me Miss – oooh!' A big sob tore out of her and she put her hands up to her mouth. 'I just realised!' She had turned pale green, and he thought for a moment she might faint. He'd never seen a girl faint before – none of the Barrow locals would ever do something so weak – but Charlotte looked as if a wind could blow her away.

'Easy now, sit back.'

'It's when you said Miss – I realised. It was meant to be Mrs today, wasn't it? I was going to be Mrs Stockbridge.' She barked out a short bitter laugh. 'Everything was going to be different.'

Well, it certainly would be, but not as she'd hoped.

'Officer? Is there any chance . . . Are you still looking into the case?'

He said nothing for a moment. 'We still are, of course. But there's a lot of evidence against him, you know.' That was putting it mildly.

Her face was blank, like she couldn't take it in.

'You take care,' he said again, tearing himself away from her bright hair and bruised face.

As he opened the door to leave, a man was standing in the corridor, staring at an iPhone with a map open on it. His hair was greying, and his suit must have cost more than Hegarty paid for his first car.

'The door was open. I was looking for number three.'

'Yeah, you've found it. I was just leaving.'

The two men sized each other up. Charlotte heard the voices.

'Hello?' Tremulous, she was coming to the door. She stared at the man as if she'd seen a ghost. 'What are *you* doing here?'

The man said, 'Well, the tickets were booked, so I thought I'd do some business, and then— Christ, what happened to your *face*?'

A choking sob rose up in her and her eyes glazed with tears again. 'Oh, Daddy. It's all ruined. Everything's ruined.'

Hegarty shut the door on them and went home, where he played *Pro-Evolution Soccer* and ate an M&S Korma in front of the telly, alone in his small flat with the blare of sirens all night long.

Keisha

Keisha woke up in a strange place – her mum's bed. Ruby had Keisha's old room now, and she didn't think she could stand sleeping in there with the kid's things all round.

Her mother, so prudish, had written down what she needed from home in case anyone overheard 'pants' or 'nightdress'. Mercy was on nil-by-mouth but she still asked for 'a little something sweet'.

'Yeah, right. Doctor said your cholesterol was through the

bloody roof.' Keisha kind of enjoyed scolding her mother like this. It made her feel maybe she was being an OK daughter after all, and it was a nice change from always being the one in the wrong. 'They said you could have a cup of tea tomorrow. Nothing else.'

Mercy sulked. 'So I can die of thirst then.'

'You've got a drip!' Somehow Keisha understood without being told that the drip was for liquids, so they didn't go through your stomach, and you couldn't puke up if you needed surgery. 'I'll need the key, Mum. I didn't bring mine. Oh, shit.' She'd just remembered again – Chris had her key. Or at least it had been in the flat, but maybe he didn't know. If the almighty God her mother believed in existed at all, he didn't know.

Mercy was half-asleep. 'Language . . . In my bag . . . Don't be making a mess now. Get Ruby up for school . . .'

Keisha wanted to say it, but didn't. Ruby wasn't there any more. She'd vanished, who knew where.

Back at the house she bolted the back door and went round to check all the windows. There was no reason he'd come back, was there? Maybe he knew Ruby was in care. Maybe he'd try to find her – but no, that was daft. Chris was far too lazy to try to track down a kid through the foster system, wasn't he? She had to think that even if Ruby was gone, she was safe. She fell asleep thinking of her daughter in a snug room, all the windows locked and a burglar alarm, maybe a huge foster dad who did boxing . . .

The next day she packed up her mum's things, the knickers bigger than T-shirts, the nightie like a sheet, her toothbrush and Bible. Some Tena Lady pads – Keisha threw them into the bag, embarrassed to think about why her mother needed incontinence pads. She was only sixty.

When she left the house to walk the short way up to the hospital, past the fancy cafés of Hampstead, she looked about her and drew up her hood. You never knew who might be around, did you?

Mercy seemed better that day; that is, she was grumpy as fuck. 'Tchuh, this nightie! I will be shamed, so old.'

Keisha sank into the plastic chair. 'How was I meant to know?'

'This nurse, she don't give me a bath today. How can I keep decent for the doctors?' It was true Mercy was giving off a bit of a cheesy whiff.

'They said you could get up today. Didn't they?'

She waved an impatient hand. 'One say this, one say the other ting. I want to go home. Where's my baby?'

'I dunno. I was on hold for, like, an hour yesterday. Couldn't get through to Sandra.' Sandra was probably at a seminar on using people's names a lot when you talked to them, or some shit like that.

'You call them again. She can come home with me.'

'Sure, sure.' It wasn't worth discussing now, what was going to happen with Ruby. Since Keisha had nowhere to live, would they let her move in with her mum and the kid? Then she'd have her back, in a way. But what if *he* came?

Her mother was rustling impatiently through the local paper, which she'd insisted Keisha bring from the gift shop. 'Look, look. Here.' She tapped a small notice in the back.

'So, it's a funeral. What about it?'

'You will go.'

'Me? You're joking.' Keisha hadn't been in a church since she left her mother's.

'They will not let me go, even though I am in good health. But you must go for me – a good church family. Such a terrible thing, ah!' She sucked at her teeth. 'I cry when I hear it. These gangs over here, it is just as bad as Kingston when I left. That poor lady! To lose a son!'

Irritated by the suggestion that losing a son was worse than a daughter, Keisha said, 'Who are you on about?' She peered at the paper. *Funeral service for Anthony Johnson*, it said. The name rang many bells; big, heavy, dull ones. 'You knew him?'

'His mother, from church. Good Christian lady. This boy, not so good, but he would have come round. Ah, God, have mercy!'

Keisha remembered him, his hand halfway up that girl's skirt. 'I can't go.' What if *he* went? He'd gone to the court case.

She was definite: there was nothing she wanted to do less than go to a funeral, in a church, of someone whose death she maybe knew too much about, and possibly have to see the guy who'd beaten her up and given her mother a heart attack. But then Mercy had a big wheezing fit, flapping her arms and turning an even darker shade of plum, and the nurses came rushing over and gave her oxygen, and elbowed Keisha out of the way. She heard mutterings about prepping her mum for theatre.

'What is it? What's happening?' She turned between them, the doctors, the nurses, these people in red and blue entirely focused on wrapping her mother up in tubes and stopping the awful choking noise.

'Please!' She never said please. 'What's going on?'

One of the nurses looked at her quickly, then away to the clipboard. 'She might need surgery. Please, you need to let us work. Wait outside.'

As they whisked her mother's body away down the long

squeaking corridor, Keisha heard herself shouting, 'OK, I'll go! Mum! I'll go to the bloody funeral!'

Charlotte

On the Sunday after the not-wedding day, Charlotte had to make her first visit to Dan in HMP Pentonville, and she was so nervous she almost vomited when she cleaned her teeth. The brandies her father had poured down her at Claridge's the night before didn't help. She had to get a grip. It was only Dan.

Her father hadn't offered to go with her. He couldn't anyway – you had to book. This was just one of many things she hadn't known last week that she now had to. Dan was allowed more visits because he was on remand. Three times a week, they said, as if that was *generous*. It was a strange state to be in, since technically you were innocent, not convicted of any crime. But you were in prison, and your girlfriend – almost your wife! – had to get permission to come and see you.

God, what did you wear to visit your (innocent) fiancé in prison? She tried to put together an outfit that would make her look pretty, but not too tarty and not too well-off – she didn't think they got many bankers in prison.

He was leaving already, her father. Stephanie wanted him back to go to an art fair, he said. He'd taken Charlotte out for dinner on what should have been her wedding night. A fancy meal was the last thing she needed, but that was him all over. Spending his money where it would be most conspicuous. Pretending he enjoyed eating liver and quails' eggs, when she knew his favourite dinner used to be pie and chips.

He'd talked at length about how it was a disgrace that

they hadn't given him a refund on the flight, so he'd decided he might as well come. How it was lucky he'd been able to spend the morning with his broker, not a complete waste of time. Eating her rich, thick *foie gras*, Charlotte was too dulled to be upset. She kept thinking, *Now we'd be sitting down to eat. Now we'd have the speeches.*

Her father had ordered brandies and talked about the financial crisis. 'I always said there was too little discipline in the banks. No wonder they have all these claims for stress at work. Stress! They don't know the meaning of it. Aren't you eating your dinner, Charlotte?'

She should tell him that if he really wanted to pass for posh it was 'supper', not dinner. 'Oh, I am, just slowly.' She tried to take a bite.

'I've been thinking, now all this wedding business is knocked on the head, you might like to think about coming out East. Lots of opportunities there.'

She put down her fork. 'Dan's not even had his trial yet, Dad.'

'Doesn't hurt to plan ahead.'

Dan was always so good with her father, humouring his tetchy opinions, letting himself be lectured about wine and cars.

'Dad, he needs a lawyer. Can you – do you know how I do it? I don't know what to do, and the money—'

He misunderstood. Deliberately? 'Of course he needs a lawyer. Wasn't his father some big-shot judge? They'll be able to help, I'm sure.'

Her dad was supposed to have been making his father-of-the-bride speech now, she thought. She'd only asked him out of tradition, and here he was urging her to leave the country, and her fiancé not a week in jail. 'Excuse me.' She walked through the restaurant as slowly as she could manage, then bolted into the ladies' and threw up the brandy and pigeon and *foie gras* in two choking retches. She wiped her face and looked in the mirror at her swollen lip, the stitches still visible, the black and green eye, the whites bloodshot from tears. Her tongue found the gap where her tooth had been and she thought again: *What's happening to me?*

Why get upset? Dan used to say. People don't change. In so many ways her father, Jonathan Miller, was still the same man who'd shaken her off as she clung to his leg the day he left. She'd been eight, and until yesterday that had been the last time she'd cried in front of him, when he told her twenty years ago that he was moving to some place called Singapore with a Dutch broker called Stephanie, and that no, he wouldn't be back for her birthday party. Up till now, that had been the worst day of her life.

Abandoning her efforts to find the right visiting-your-fiancé-in-prison outfit, she settled on jeans. It wasn't as if any of it mattered.

Her stomach churning with nerves, like a combination of a job interview and performing live on stage, she made her way through the quiet Sunday streets. They had always loved Sundays, the one day where Dan would put away his spreadsheets, at least till the evening. The streets were sunny, people walking past with tennis racquets, babies in slings, the women in huge sunglasses and the men in polo shirts. What crap they talked. Jasper's prep school. Our house is worth less than we paid. Holidays in Sardinia. That was the middle-class enclave she lived in. She'd never felt so left out of it before.

It was a short journey down to King's Cross, then a switch to the Piccadilly Line. It was too short, really, and before long she was coming out of the tube at Caledonian Road, blinking in the bright spring light. She'd been there once before with Dan, to do a coaching session at the tennis centre up the road, but she didn't want to think about that. She set off up the scruffier end of the road, past run-down corner shops and takeaways. How many times would she have to come here in future? Would she be getting to know that Chicken Cottage sign a bit better than she wanted?

Charlotte took deep breaths, putting one foot in front of the other. It was ironic that just a week before, she'd been worrying about the walk down the aisle. It's easy, Dan had said, impatient with wedding talk. Just take a step, then another one. You'll be walking to me, remember.

And now she really was walking to him, but not at all in the way she had planned.

Keisha

Keisha was cringing as she snuck into the porch. The Church of Holy Hope wasn't a pretty stone one like you might see in the countryside, it was a huge white building with banners on the outside saying things like, *Jesus Lives, Let the Lord into Your Heart*, and so on. Stuff that her mother believed as truly as she believed that if you got on the train at Gospel Oak, you'd get off at Stratford. In fact, since God didn't do planned engineering works, the route to Him was probably a lot more reliable.

Still wearing her jeans and hoody, she slid into the back seat and tried to keep her head down. No chance of that.

'Welcome, sister!' It was a jolly black vicar in one of those white collars. 'Your first time joining us?'

'I'm, er, Mercy's daughter. You know, Mercy Collins?'

'Sister Mercy? Ah, welcome. We heard of her illness. We are praying for her.' He smiled wide as a banana, flashing white teeth. She could tell from his accent he was an import, reversing the way white people used to send priests out to the ignorant Africans. Now that the white people preferred to go to the pub on Sundays, they were having to get the Africans over to make up numbers. There wasn't a single white person in the church, and Keisha felt, as usual, totally aware of her own pale skin. Sometimes she wanted to get a T-shirt that said, *Yeah, I'm mixed. Stop fucking staring.*

'Is this the funeral?' She nodded at the host of squawking ladies in hats.

'Yes. Such a sad day. The gangs, sister, they are killing our sons. So many of our worshippers came to London to escape violence. But now see.'

'Oh, but I thought – did he not get into a fight? I mean, Anthony . . .' She jerked her head vaguely at the altar, although the coffin wasn't there yet.

The vicar shook his head from side to side. 'There is talk. His mother, I know her well, she prayed and prayed for him to get out of the gangs, the drugs.' He sighed at the endless waste of human life, the parade of coffins decorated in the various football strips of London. Postcode rivalry, the papers called it.

He patted her with a dry hand, and she saw with horror that he only had one. The sleeve of his other arm was empty up to the elbow. 'Let God into your heart, my dear. Send His love to our sister Mercy.'

'Yeah. Er, I will, yeah.' She tried not to stare.

He bumbled off to the head of the church, and then music struck up – an R 'n' B song, how fucking surreal. And in came the coffin, held up by six black men. After came the women, wearing old-fashioned veils. She recognised Rachel Johnson, who'd stuck the boot into the blonde girl in the toilets. They reached the altar and set down their burden. Inside was Anthony Johnson, last seen groping a girl's arse while wearing a cheap shiny suit. Now he was dead, his life all bled out through his throat. Keisha shuddered as the vicar invited all the 'brothers and sisters' to stand.

Afterwards, Keisha was trudging her way up the hill to the Royal Free again. She'd managed to slip out of the funeral without too many people shaking her hand. The vicar had collared her and made her talk to Anthony Johnson's mother, who spoke in the same rich tones as Keisha's own mum. 'Mercy's child,' she said, pulling Keisha into a huge musty hug. 'Pray for us, my child.'

'Sorry for your loss,' she muttered, thinking of the man with his flashing earring and wide smile.

Bloody hell, that had been embarrassing. All that singing and holding hands and eyes closed, begging for the soul of Anthony Johnson to ascend to heaven. When as far as Keisha could see, he'd been a lying cheating scumbag like most men. She reached the hospital and pushed in the swing doors, as if it was home to her now. She knew exactly which corridor to go down for Female Surgical. She knew exactly what bed her mother would be in, probably snoring, her huge bulk shuddering under the covers.

But she wasn't.

Keisha's head swivelled round and round, like some idiot on TV. Eh? Where was she? The bed was empty, the covers smoothed back as if Mercy had never been there. Her Bible and box of tissues were gone and the bedside locker had been wiped clean. For a few seconds Keisha wondered if she'd gone into the wrong ward, like a div.

A nurse in blue padded into view; it was the Irish motherly one who blessed herself every time she saw a patient. 'Are you right there, deary?'

'Er, where's me mum?'

'What's that now, love?'

'My mum – Mercy Collins. She was here.' For fuck's sake.

The nurse stopped at the desk, huffing a little. She was about to end up on her own ward if she didn't lay off the pies. She shuffled around the stacks of paper. 'Now let me see, deary. Mrs Collins, was it?'

'Yeah.' The Mrs was a lie Mercy allowed herself. God wouldn't want her to face the shame of being a Miss, not with a twenty-five-year-old daughter.

'Ah, right so. She had a wee turn this morning, so they took her down to theatre.'

'She's in surgery? Still?' Keisha had been gone hours.

The nurse kept peering; then she stopped and looked up at Keisha. For a second her endless chatter stopped and she said nothing; Keisha's stomach went down like she was on a roller coaster at Thorpe Park. 'Where is she?'

Chattery Nurse didn't look at her. 'I'll just get the doctor, so.'

She left Keisha standing there in the quiet ward all alone.

Charlotte

After a week indoors, Dan was already sallow, his eyes dry and bloodshot as they brought him out. Although remand prisoners could wear their own clothes, he had on the same grey tracksuit as the other men, the rapists and thieves. The killers.

She swallowed hard.

Dan couldn't meet her eyes. That was the most shocking thing. Unlike Charlotte, who was often shy, he'd always been able to meet anyone's gaze. He said it was what made people trust him with millions and millions of pounds of their money. He'd been biting his nails, she saw, and there was a raw pulsing pimple on his neck. And she was such a fool, such an idiot, that despite all the hundreds of films and TV shows she'd seen with prison scenes, she still tried to jump up and hold him. They were nicer to her than they were in American dramas.

'You'll have to stay seated, miss.' The guard looked like someone's dad, soft round the middle. Charlotte caught up an hysterical shout in her throat; she really would have to calm down.

She'd always thought crime was something done by other people, a different type of person altogether. Never had it occurred to her that you could just stumble and fall, and bang into someone, and without meaning to, send their whole life flying off course. That was why Dan was here under this sickly light – because he'd fallen. That was all it took.

There was a little hutch over to the side of the room where volunteers sold tea and chocolate bars and things. It was the hot, sick smell of the burned coffee that she would never forget when she thought about what he said to her next.

For a moment she didn't understand why he was standing there, just staring at her. 'What the hell happened to your face?'

Of course, he didn't know she'd been beaten up. 'It's nothing. I sort of – well, I sort of got attacked at the court. But it's all right.'

He said nothing for a few seconds. 'Because of me?'

'I don't know. It's nothing, honest. Please, baby, sit down.'

'Didn't think you'd come today,' Dan muttered, once he'd sat down and pushed his chair out.

She reached over the table for his hand. 'Of course! It was the first time I was allowed, they said—'

'I meant because of yesterday.' His face was screwed up. 'I kept thinking about it. It was so mad. I kept waking up, thinking I was going to be late for the church.'

'It wasn't your fault,' she made herself say.

He laughed. It was a horrible sound. 'Whose fault was it then? I'm never going to forgive myself for it. Look at your eye, for God's sake! You look like a fucking battered wife.'

He said it so matter-of-factly, it scared her. 'It'll heal, they said. It's OK.' She took out his post, screened at the door for any staples or sharp edges. 'I'm sorry, baby – this came.'

Dan curled his lip at the embossed paper that announced his sacking. 'Big surprise. They'll want me as far away as possible now.'

'But you worked there for years, you worked all hours. It's not fair.'

'You think they give a shit? They're scared, see. Don't want me shooting off my mouth about the things I had to do this past year, how stressed I was . . . No, they want me well out of the way.' He leaned in close, eyes flicking round the room. 'Listen. I've been expecting this. In the house, there's a drawer.' He was whispering. 'In the desk. Promise me you'll keep that stuff safe. Don't give it to them, even if they ask.'

'What stuff?' She was bewildered.

'Just promise.'

'Well . . . OK, but it doesn't seem fair, what they did. Is there anything we can do? Appeal? Sue them? I looked it up and there's a chance you could even ask for bail again, if—'

'What's the point? I'm in prison, you may have noticed. Or did you think we were in Starbucks?'

She stared at him, hurt. 'I don't understand why you won't at least try.'

'For fuck's sake, there's no point. Can you not see that?'

Charlotte blinked, trying to halt the runaway train of this conversation. 'I know this must be hard for you—'

'You're not listening!' He brought his hand down hard on the table, and the guard looked over warningly. 'There were witnesses, and the CCTV . . . can you not see I must have done it? Everyone else sees it. Look around you.' He was shaking badly now.

'But you said you didn't do it! You said you just hit him – just lightly!'

'Charlotte.' He lowered his voice. 'It's true what I said, in court. I have no fucking idea what happened. It's gone – black. As far as I know, I did it.'

'But if you just tried to remember . . .'

'Are you deaf? Jesus! I had a blackout. I've been having them for months, and nothing ever comes back. Bloody hell, you hadn't a clue what was going on with me.'

She looked at her hands, afraid she might cry. 'You never told me.'

'Would you have listened? If it wasn't about the wedding and wrapped up in a pink bow? All this time you've been in La-La-Land, all dresses and flowers and bloody sugar-coated almonds—'

'Stop it! You could have told me.'

'You'd never have understood. You heard the evidence – I went into the room with the guy and I came out, and next thing you know he's got a bottle in his neck. With my prints on. I don't know why, or how – but I have to accept I'll go down. That evidence – how can you get round it? Ten years at least, I'm looking at.'

She flinched. 'It won't be like that.'

'You want to be thirty-eight, coming up here every week? Jesus, you don't belong here.'

She refused to look round at the room full of squealing kids, their ears pierced, smearing Wotsits on each other, and raddled women in baseball caps. 'I'll come as long as you're here. I don't care.'

He lowered his head into his hands. 'That's the thing. I don't want you to.'

She gaped at him. 'Baby!'

'Charlotte, I . . . I can't even start to say sorry to you for what I did. I ruined your wedding. It meant everything to you, I know.'

'*You* mean everything to me!' But as she said it she wondered how much it was even true. She'd been in a wedding fog for months now.

'Look, I can't understand it either, how this happened . . . I just have to accept it. But *you* don't have to. I won't ruin the next ten years for you too.'

Her eyes were overflowing with tears, stinging. 'It's not up to you. You can't tell me this, you can't *say* this.'

'I'm sorry.' He reached out for her hand; took it gently with his limp one. She felt some remnant of the warmth, the strength that had always seemed to flow out of him. 'A week ago, I thought we'd be married by now . . .'

'*Don't!*'

'. . . And I'd have tried my best, I'd have tried to work less – although the cost of that wedding, Jesus, had you any idea?

Forty grand, Charlotte. You know how much I have to work for that?'

'I didn't know – you never said.' She wiped her face on her sleeve.

'You've had some bills come in already, I bet.'

'Yes – I thought they were done automatically . . .'

'I cancelled them. Cash-flow problems.'

Her mouth fell open. 'But why – Dan, why didn't you tell me?'

'I couldn't. See, I wanted you to have it all – I loved you, you know. I know I'm cold sometimes, and I can't help it, but really I loved you so much.'

Past tense. Why was he using the past tense? The words were spilling out of him. 'But the stress . . . You don't know what it was like, the pressure, working all night, knowing we might go under. Christ, it's almost a relief. At least I can say it now.'

'But – but why didn't you tell me?'

'I couldn't explain. You saw the papers, I suppose? What did you think of me, when you heard what that girl said we called her – a Paki bitch?'

She flinched away. 'I didn't believe it.'

'Well, it's true. I didn't say it to her face, but I sent on the emails, I laughed . . . we bullied her. Because in that place, it's kill or be killed. That's the truth. And I hope you never have to understand that.' He stood up, scraping back the chair.

'Wait! You can't just go! You can't leave me . . . *Dan*!'

He half-turned. 'Listen. I'm sorry, sweetheart. Really I am. But don't come again.'

Hegarty

The woman with the badly bleached hair ground her fag out under her trainer, and Hegarty sighed. 'I'm sorry, Mrs Horton. Let me ask again. When did you last see your neighbour?' The address he had for Keisha Collins, the grumpy girl at the court, was locked up, empty. He wasn't sure what he was doing there anyway. Tidying up loose ends? Following a hunch?

Her neighbour wasn't giving him an inch. 'Why d'you want to know? She's all right, that girl. Had a rough deal.'

'Can you think of anywhere Keisha might have gone?'

Jacinta Horton shrugged. 'He chucked her out, is all I know. Battered her a bit, I shouldn't wonder. Then he went himself and next thing they're in changing the locks.'

'And her boyfriend's name is Chris Dean?' She'd already identified Dean from the blurry photos printed off Rachel Johnson's phone. At least he had a name now, an identity for the mystery white man.

'That's the one. He's a bad lot. That's why the kiddy's in care, you know.'

Hegarty was making notes fast. Luckily the woman was happy to spill about Chris Dean, natural distrust of the police giving way to disgust at the man. 'The child's name is Ruby Dean, yes?' he asked.

'That's right. Lovely little thing, big dark eyes. In care with Keisha's mam, and she lives down Gospel Oak way, s'far as I know.'

'You don't happen to know her name?'

Jacinta screwed up her eyes. 'Met her one time when she came round. Loves kiddies, she does. Mercy, that was it. Mercy Collins, I s'pose she'd be.'

Hegarty shut his notebook. How easy would it be to find a Mercy Collins living in Gospel Oak? He wasn't even supposed to be looking. The case was solved – wasn't it? He rubbed his face wearily. 'Thanks. You've been very helpful, Mrs Horton.'

She bent to adjust the hood on her child's buggy. 'Maybe you'll actually come next time we ring up about them gangs. Always in the park, they are, on their bikes. Can't take the kiddies near it.'

'We'll do our best.' It was all you could ever say, and increasingly, his best was nothing at all.

Keisha

Keisha closed the door on her mother's house and put down the frayed embroidered bag. Into it she had shoved Mercy's glasses, her Bible and, worst of all, the cross they'd taken off her neck when she went down the corridor for surgery. Went down and never came back.

The house was quiet, the panes gently rattling with the constant sound of buses on the high street. Keisha walked into the living room, her trainers making no sound on the grubby old carpet. The fridge started up, making her jump. 'Fuck,' she said, to the still air.

It was so fucking stuffy in this house! Mercy hadn't opened the windows for about twenty years. She thought air was generally bad for you, and maybe in the case of Gospel Oak she was right. But she wasn't here now.

Keisha humped the bag into the kitchen and put it on Mercy's little chipped table. She took out her mum's glasses on the string and put them on absently. Everything blurred away behind the thick lenses. In a way it sort of made her feel better, not being able to see the kitchen clearly, as if she saw it in her head remembered from when she was little. Mercy huffing slowly round the tiny space, thick with frying oil. But no, she wasn't seven, she was twenty-fucking-five and Mercy wasn't here.

Fuck. FUCK. How had this happened? This morning her mum had been grumbling and groaning and spilling tea down her horrible brown wool cardie. Now she was – where? Not in the hospital, not really. Where had she gone? Pastor Samuel from the church would say he knew. Mercy herself thought she knew. Maybe that was why she wasn't afraid of the first heart attack, because she felt for sure her God was waiting for her in a blaze of light up some staircase, a bit like in *Stars in Their Eyes* when they went behind the screen with all the smoke. But Keisha, she didn't know a fucking thing.

'Mum,' she said out loud to the empty kitchen. That felt mental. Inside her head she continued, *What the f— what should I do now? The council said they were taking the house back next week, for a new tenant. They said I had to clean it all out before then. They said Ruby was with a foster family. They said I could talk about getting her back when I had a stable home. I don't have any home at all now. And fucking Chris – sorry, Mum, language – he's out there, somewhere . . . And I don't know what to do. Mum. What should I do?*

But there was no way Mercy could help on this one, could she? Because they said she'd died. She was dead. The second heart attack was always likely, they said. Massive cholesterol, they said. There was nothing they could do.

Keisha took off the glasses, but even without them, the world was never going to look right again.

Charlotte

Something had woken her. The flat was quiet, only the sound of the fridge humming and the clock ticking. Dan's side of the bed was cold.

That noise. It had woken her. Voices outside. She sat up in bed, heart racing. Clutching Dan's jumper round her, she went to the window. At first she couldn't see anything in the orange glow of the streetlight. Then one of the shadows moved – people, dressed in black. Kids. She flinched back from the window as the first stone hit the house.

Oh God, oh no.

They were laughing. They knew she was there, cowering like a frightened mouse. Another stone, rattling off the window this time. *Oh God, don't let them break it.*

Then relief – Mike from downstairs was shouting out through the letter box. 'I'm calling the police if you don't leave right this minute.'

He didn't open the door, Mike wasn't that brave. Gradually the kids started peeling away, doing wheelies on their bikes. One shouted out something about *racist fuckers.* Charlotte saw Mike open the front door, the streetlight glinting off his scalp. She saw him look around and straight up at her window.

Quivering with fear and loneliness, she scrabbled for her phone and dialled her friend Holly's number. It was late, and Monday tomorrow, but it was an emergency. The number rang and rang, then went to voicemail – her friend's voice chirping, *Hi, this is Holly, can't get to the phone . . .*

Charlotte imagined her friend waking up, looking at the phone, seeing who was calling, and ignoring it. She gripped the phone and scrolled through the names. Who else was there? John, Chloe, Tom . . . No. There were dozens of reasons why she couldn't call any of them. There really was no one.

Where had her friends been all weekend, when her phone hadn't rung once? Round at Holly's, or Gemma's, all talking about how awful Charlotte was and how they never wanted to see her again now she was engaged to a racist killer? As the wedding got close she had noticed pictures appearing on Facebook of nights out she hadn't known about – but she'd told herself they knew she was busy with the wedding plans and she did like to spend time with Dan at weekends. He worked eighty-hour weeks, for God's sake. She barely saw him.

But now she was alone and the silence of the flat was all about her, creeping under her skin and nails, filling her up. She went back to bed and another memory surfaced up from the depths. Dan, weeks ago, waking her up, shouting in his sleep. Frightened, she'd switched on the light and he was clammy, his fists clenched and eyes open and staring.

'Dan! Sweetie, what's wrong?' She'd shaken him awake. When his eyes focused on her she felt a thrill of panic, because for a moment, it was as if he didn't even know who she was.

'Bad dream,' he'd said, and then because it was five a.m., he got up to do some work.

Keisha

Within two days Mercy was buried and gone. The Holy Hopers took it all in hand; all Keisha had to do was get dressed and turn up, sit in a room full of people who all believed that Mercy was in heaven now as surely as they believed they'd switch on the telly in the morning and GMTV'd be on.

In the meantime Keisha tried to breathe deep and hard, stand up at the right places, keep going. Pastor Samuel had arranged everything, and Keisha just stood in a daze while a whole line of black ladies came up and hugged her. Anthony Johnson's mother was there, trailing the sulky bitch of a sister, who flicked her eyes away from Keisha as if she didn't want to remember what happened in the toilets with the blonde girl on the floor, holding her own tooth up in her hand all covered in blood.

Mrs Johnson hugged Keisha again. 'Ah, darlin', your poor mother. She's up there now, I tell her to keep an eye on my boy.' She smelled just like Mercy, of skin cream and cooking, and Keisha pulled away. Just focus on each person in front of you, each step you had to take, each next thing to do. Maybe sometime in days or weeks or months she might be able to actually think about what had happened. But not now.

At the graveyard she spotted Sandra the social worker, blinking behind her glasses, in this massive hairy cardigan, even though it was hot.

'Hello, Keisha.' Sandra blew her nose on a tissue – hay fever, Keisha thought. If you were a social worker you probably couldn't cry every time someone you worked with died, or you'd be keeping Kleenex in business for a long time.

'Does Ruby know?' She nodded her head towards Mercy's new grave, where the church mourners were doing some chanty hand-clapping thing. Keisha had hung back; she couldn't face it.

'It's been explained to her in appropriate terms.' Sandra paused. 'You should really come and see her, you know. It's important to keep up contact, if you want to regain custody in future.'

'What, sit in some McDonald's with the bloody social

worker at the next table? *Oh, how's your Happy Meal, Rubes?* How's that fair? She's my bloody kid.' Anyway, how did she know he wasn't still following her, looking for her? She'd lead him right to Ruby.

'I always get the feeling you think you're being punished. But it's just what's best for Ruby, until you're settled.'

'But I'm not allowed her, am I? You said.' She scuffed her shoes in the gravel.

Sandra put on her social worker voice – had she any other one? 'I know you've tried very hard to turn your life around, but until we can be sure Ruby will have a safe stable home – well, you understand, I'm sure.' She spoke so gently it made Keisha want to whack her.

'I'm trying. I dunno what you want me to do.' For a moment she thought to tell Sandra that she'd left Chris, but why should she? Things were even worse now he was after her, and she'd nowhere to live once her mum's tenancy ran out. She was sure Sandra could tell she'd a black eye under all the make-up she'd slapped on.

'You know what to do,' Sandra said in her annoying way. 'A safe and stable place for Ruby. In the meantime, you must keep up contact – or there's a very serious risk you could lose custody permanently. You know what that means, Keisha? It means someone can adopt Ruby. For good.'

Keisha stared hard at the ground. As if it was so easy, to make a safe and stable home. No. She wasn't going to ask for Ruby back until she could take her home, to somewhere good. Easier for now to think of the kid somewhere far away, some place nice, happy, safe. 'Is she OK, like?' Her voice sounded as if it was tangled up. She wasn't going to cry. Not here.

'She's in a nice home,' Sandra said kindly. 'A lovely couple, their own family grown up.'

'Are they black?'

Sandra looked shocked, because you were supposed to pretend race didn't matter, weren't you. 'Well, I don't—'

'Please.'

Sandra nodded tightly. 'We try to place children in their own ethnic groups, yes.'

So that was it, official – Ruby was black. But what did that make Keisha? No one seemed to know, and she sure as hell hadn't a baldy.

Sandra threw her fat arms around Keisha, who flinched. 'I'm so sorry for your loss, Keisha! She was a lovely lady, your mum. Please remember I'm always here for you. Any way I can help.'

Great, that was all she needed – Sandra on tap.

Mrs Suntharalingam came up on the arm of one of her doctor sons, neat and weedy in a black suit and tie. 'How I will miss her. Who will move in now, some refugees with ten children? Ah, I will miss her.'

'Me too.' They stared at each other, old enemies mourning the same loss. But Mrs S had children, nieces, grandkids, a whole Tamil family. Who did Keisha have? Chris was gone, Ruby was gone. The old lady grasped her hand in one dry claw and moved on.

Charlotte

Charlotte woke up on Monday morning with a shock, the alarm shrilling. The flat was so quiet without Dan on the phone already, shaving in the bathroom. In the beginning he used to sing in the shower, pop songs in an off-key baritone that made her laugh. But now that she thought about it, she hadn't heard him singing for ages, not for months, that she could remember. Funny how you didn't notice these things until something made you think.

Today she was supposed to go back to work, and she was moving so slowly she'd be late. She stood with her hand under the shower for five minutes until she realised she'd have to put the immersion on to heat it up. Dan always put it on, because he was always up first. He always left her tea bag in the cup, and her bread in the toaster. She just had to breathe, breathe, keep going, put one foot in front of the other. Remember to go the good way to work, not the bad way. Avoid that street. Then it would all be fine.

As she stood waiting for the kettle to boil (a good two minutes before realising she'd unplugged it), she heard the downstairs front door slam and she jumped, knocking the teaspoon off the counter and onto her bare foot. 'Shit! Ow!'

She had to calm down, it was only the postman, of course. Edging open her door, Charlotte hobbled downstairs to intercept it before the other occupants could see. It could be anything. More hate mail? Brochures from the travel company they were supposed to be on their honeymoon with? She was managing to crush out the thought that she was supposed to be in the Caribbean right that second, not standing in her kitchen with her feet on cold tiles.

Sneaking back upstairs, she saw there wasn't much – her phone bill, which she'd have to pay somehow, a flyer for a pizza takeaway place, and under that, a battered brown envelope with her name on the front in Dan's clear blocky writing. It was postmarked *HMP Pentonville Prison*, just in case anyone didn't know everything that had happened to her.

She was really going to be late for work, but she knew she had to sit down right there, while the kettle cooled, and read what it was Dan couldn't say to her in person.

Charlotte, it started.
I can't think what else I can call you now. I wish I'd never had to write this letter, but I do. There's no way around it.

He had written the rest in bullet points.

• *The mortgage is due on the 25th of the month. I can't access my account, so you will need to go in and set up the direct debit from yours instead. The password to my account is your name. The PIN is in another letter I will send you today, you'll know to destroy it.*

That was typical of Dan, he had to be correct saying PIN and not PIN number like everyone else.

• *As you know, there are bills outstanding. I don't know what you'll do for money. I'll write to my parents and ask them to help you, but I used one of my phone calls to ring them and they wouldn't speak to me.*

Of course, Dan's parents were *Telegraph* readers, anti-immigration, 'life means life' fans. And now their only child was in prison for murder. There was a chance it was even harder for them than it was for her. At least she'd been there, she knew it wasn't true. Dan's father, ex-Justice Stockbridge, didn't entirely believe in miscarriages of justice.

The letter was typically concise, setting out what bills needed to be paid when and how to access their savings account. *Clear out the money*, he said. *You'll need it.*

At the end of the bullet points he'd written, *I must make sure you understand one thing. Please don't put your life on hold 'waiting for me', or some other romantic idea. Don't even wait for the trial. There is no point at all.*

You should keep working, you'll need the money coming in. That flat is large just for you. Think about selling or getting a flatmate.

A flatmate! Charlotte threw the letter down. How dare he! How bloody, bloody dare he send her this letter, as if she was his secretary or something, for God's sake, and tell her to think about leaving her home? Or living with some stranger and measuring out the milk, when she was supposed to be married by now?

She looked back to the letter, a PS: *Remember to hide those things like I said.*

'Piss off, Dan!' she said to the empty kitchen, then felt the burn of the day's first tears behind her eyes. By the time she'd cried and cleaned herself up, she was going to be so late for work they'd think she wasn't coming.

Keisha

Keisha sat back on her heels and groaned. How in the name of fuck had her mum got so much crap? The old box room above the stairs was totally wedged out with junk, the whole place stinking of damp. Her hair was so full of dust it looked like she'd gone grey overnight, and Mercy had never got round to having a proper shower put in. Her mum didn't understand that you had to actually wash white hair regularly. As a teenager Keisha had been greasy enough to fry chips on until she worked that out.

She was totally sick of tidying, but she couldn't let all Mercy's things go to a skip, even if it was all shit, china plates with Princess Diana on them, every issue of the church newsletter since about 1800, a million Tesco bags that fell out every time you opened a cupboard. Mercy had been poor when she was little – eleven kids living in what wasn't much better than a shack – so she saved. She saved everything.

Keisha had nearly finished now, piled all the tat up into bags for the bin, bags for the charity shop down the road, which was going to get a real bonanza of crap. Since she actually had nowhere to go once the house was given up, there was a small black rucksack she was filling with things she just couldn't leave. Like her mum's awful glasses. Who else was going to remember how Mercy had rootled around for them any time she had to read a label in a shop? Then she would take them off to show how shocked she was by the price.

The hardest room to empty was Mercy's bedroom. It was stuffed full of her mum, her smell of talc, her fluffy cardigans and old wrecked shoes that she shuffled down the street in. Keisha was on her knees in front of the wardrobe, and had to drop onto her stomach to get the last shoes out, when she noticed it. There was something pushed under the wardrobe, stuffed against the lime carpet, some sort of folder like you might get at school. She pulled it out, looking for a distraction.

In the folder were essays. Handwritten, of course, her mum'd never been near a computer in her life, and they were about law, it looked like. Things like jurisprudence and legal process. Who'd have thought her fat old mum knew these kinds of things? Smiling a bit to herself at Mercy's hidden depths, Keisha leafed through the folder and found a course booklet: *Introduction to Legal Practice*. She remembered Mercy saying a few times that she could have been a paralegal: 'I could have a good job now, if not for you, cheeky Miss Keisha.'

The start date of the course was 20th September, 1984, the year before Keisha was born. Mercy was always going on and on about education. 'You lost your chance at the good school, miss, now what will you do?' And when Keisha would say cheekily, 'Mum, you wipe people's arses, what do you know?' Mercy would whack her round the head with that big hand and the rings, and say, 'I came to this country to study, you know that? But then you come along and I have to stop.' So it was all Keisha's fault. Like everything.

She was just folding it away again, thinking this would maybe be squeezed into the 'keep' bag, when something caught her eye.

Course Tutor, it said, and beside it the name was typed in bold capitals: IAN STONE. She'd seen that name before somewhere, she was sure of it. She'd seen it typed like this, a long time ago. Where?

Suddenly she knew, and she was running downstairs, slipping in her socks on the worn carpet. 'Stop runnin'!' she could almost hear Mercy shout after her.

In the hallway, under ten huge bin bags, there was the 'keep it' bag, an old Adidas rucksack with fraying straps. Now she stuck her hand into that warm plastic interior and rummaged for a big brown envelope, the sides shored up with tape. It was marked in Mercy's writing: IMPORTANT TINGS. The 'h' had been written in below; it was just a mistake, but it made her hear in her head her mum's voice.

She shook it out – gas bills, savings book, NHS card. And a folded-over bit of green paper that Keisha remembered from the time she had to apply for her provisional driving licence (so she could get into pubs). Her mum had insisted on filling in the form, so Keisha couldn't see her own birth certificate, but she'd prised open the envelope and snuck a quick look, so quick she almost didn't take it in, as if she didn't want to see what it said.

There was her mum's name, and in the grid beside it, it

said, *Occupation: student*. Her mum had called herself a student? Her mum, who wiped people's arses all day? But she didn't have time to be surprised, because then she saw the name. Under *Father*, it said: *Ian Stone. Occupation: Lecturer*.

Hegarty

Hegarty glanced down at the address in his notebook again. Yes, this was the right place. He hadn't expected a thug like Jonny McGivern to be living in this neat West Hampstead terrace. But when he'd looked up Chris Dean's associates on the system, this was the address thrown up.

It took a long time for the door to be answered, and eventually a tall, heavy guy in just his pants came to the door, scratching his head.

'Sorry to wake you, sir,' said Hegarty pointedly. It was nearly two in the afternoon.

The man looked confused, glancing past Hegarty to the quiet street outside. Then he stiffened. 'You the police?'

'Top marks. How about a quick chat – Jonny, is it?'

Once Jonny had reluctantly let him into the living room, Hegarty stood by the door. Every chair was covered in clothes, pillows, an Arsenal duvet bunched up on the sofa. The place stank of weed and booze, and through the door to the kitchen he'd glimpsed plates piled up in the sink. Which reminded him – when had he last done the dishes at his own place? These side-investigations made it hard to get time at home.

Hegarty nodded to the sofa. 'Someone been staying here?'

'Er – nah. Er, I mean, yeah, me. This is my mum's place.'

'And where's she?'

'Eh, she's away. Gone to Spain, like.'

Hegarty decided to ignore the drugs paraphernalia Jonny had stupidly left littered round the room. That wasn't why he was there. 'You seen your mate Chris Dean recently?'

'Who?'

He laughed at this poor attempt at lying. 'Come off it, you and him go way back, don't you? When was it, 1999 that you two got nicked for shoplifting? Literally thick as thieves, eh?'

Jonny looked confused, wrapping the duvet defensively round his bare chest. 'Ain't seen him.'

'I see. Just yourself here, then, if your mam's away?'

'Er – yeah.'

'But you're still kipping on the sofa.'

Again the look of confusion and deep pain, as if trying to lie actually hurt the guy's brain. 'Yeah.'

'Tell me this, Jonny, you know anything about this Kingston Town club murder?'

'Thought you got the fella for that.'

Hegarty wandered round the room, prodding aside take-away cartons with his shoe. 'Wrapped up in gangs, wasn't he, Anthony Johnson? Thought you might know a thing or two about that.' He turned and fixed Jonny with a stare. 'Or are you gonna tell me you don't know nothing about that either? Didn't join the Parky Boys before you cut your teeth?'

Jonny just sat there, and Hegarty sighed. 'Well, if your mate comes back, you tell him DC Matthew Hegarty wants a word. Think you can remember that? It's very important.' On his way out the door he called back, 'Oh, and you better clean your act up, Jonny. You might be getting a visit from the Drugs Squad in a few days, and your mam won't like it if she comes back and her door's kicked in.'

Charlotte

Charlotte stood in front of her office building, taking deep breaths. She'd crumpled Dan's letter into the bin in anger, but she knew she'd pull it out again. The words seemed to have leached into the skin of her hands, as if written in acid.

It was time to go in, she was very late. Going the good way from the tube always took longer, but she definitely couldn't cope with the other way now. She'd dressed up today, in heeled shoe-boots and a plain shift, but thanks to Dan's letter she'd left it far too late to do her hair, which hung round her shoulders in a damp frizz.

She blipped her key card over the door and it slid open as if nothing had changed. Getting into the lift with her head down, and reaching up to press the number four, in that movement she remembered something Dan had said weeks before, when declining a second cup of coffee on his way out: 'Sometimes I have to sit in Costa for twenty minutes before I can push that lift button.'

And she hadn't really listened – had she ever? And now it was her turn to feel terrible, heart-clenching fear, as the lift rose and the doors opened silently onto the hubbub of Floor Four, the sleek red curves of the reception desk.

'Charlotte!' Kelly, the Essex-girl receptionist, stopped filing her nails to stare. 'You're here! Er, just a sec.' Calling Simon, no doubt.

Charlotte pasted on a wavering smile and picked her way across the open-plan office, careful to meet no one's eyes. Except that someone was in her desk, a girl in leggings and a wide tutu skirt. Charlotte couldn't believe how young she looked.

Trying to keep down the up-chuck of anger that was

suddenly in her throat, Charlotte said, 'Oh, sorry, that's my seat?' As if she was on a train, politely moving on the chancer who'd sat down in her reserved place.

The girl looked her up and down. 'Are you Charlotte?' As if she was famous – but not in a good way.

'Yeah, hi.' Charlotte tried to put on her work face, smiling over the snarl.

'I'm, like, covering for you?'

'Charlie!' That plummy voice, pimped with East London vowels, made her wince.

'Hiya, Simon. I'm a bit late, er – tube problems.' An accepted London excuse that could mean anything from *I slept through my alarm* to *I woke up last night in Ealing*.

'Well, here was me thinking we wouldn't see you.' He looked over her frumpy outfit and ravaged face. 'You OK, darling? That's a nasty bruise.'

His *darling* was the camp twist of lime in the Soho man's G&T, and a sore red herring to any girl dumb enough to think he might actually be gay. Far from it, as she knew only too well.

'Oh, I'm all right, I suppose.' The lie of the century, but she suspected he didn't really want to hear about it.

'Good, good. The lovely Fliss here has stepped into the breach with your Snax account –' he flashed a toothy grin at the younger girl – 'so if you'd plonk yourself down somewhere else for today. You can sit in on this meeting later though?'

'Oh, sure.' Meeting? What meeting? She was supposed to be in Jamaica right now, not in the traffic-clogged hell of Central London. She needed to get up to speed, but once set up on the temp's desk, all she could think about was Googling appeals, miscarriages of justice, solicitors – anything that might help Dan. It was a mammoth struggle to remember all the perky little ideas she'd had for the Snax campaign a week ago – forever ago. She'd just have to throw round some buzz words like 'social networking', 'digital viral marketing', 'user-generated content' and the like.

All morning people passed by her desk, rushing on in their towering heels. She saw Tory dart behind the water-cooler to avoid her, and her best work friend Chloe rushing to a 'tampon brainstorm session'. Chloe was thirty-two and single, so usually Charlotte felt pleasantly lucky round her, but today Chloe had on some rocking new harem pants and Charlotte managed to feel both stuffy in her dress, and scruffy with her damp hair round her shoulders.

Nobody offered her coffee all morning; they just left her there. She sat hunched over the screen, her spoiled nails clacking off the keys and reminding her they were supposed to be sporting a perfect wedding manicure right about now. Beside the Snax pitch she was pretending to work on was a website for people who'd been wrongly convicted of crimes. *Innocent*, the banner flashed red and black. *Innocent, innocent, innocent.* A word so powerful it could slay you right through the heart. She did her best to stay away from sites mentioning Dan but the story was everywhere. *Racist murder. Racist.*

'Charlie?'

She jumped a mile, what was wrong with her? She was used to Simon by now, surely. 'Oh, sorry. Is it time?'

'*Cinco minutos*, darling. Better print out the pitches.'

'I'll just go – freshen.' She bolted to the ladies' and into one of the cubicles, suddenly breathless at the smells of toner and people's tuna lunches. Charlotte sat in the cubicle, trying to breathe in and out. It would be OK. It would be OK. She'd been all over those Snax before. Surely it would come back. Crispy, crunchy snacks, just seventy calories a bag . . .

Outside she heard the door open, and Chloe's voice said, 'Oh my GOD, I so totally did not know what to say to her.'

'I know, yah.' Tory. 'I thought she'd be away for ages – she was going on and on about her honeymoon.'

'I'm not being funny, but how can she even come in after that?' She could tell from the slurring of her voice that Chloe was putting on her lipgloss, like she always did before and after lunch. 'I mean, he like, *killed* someone.'

'And Fliss is so totally peed off that Simon's putting her in the Snax pitch meeting. I bet she is so totally not ready.'

'Well.' The tap ran. 'Simon's always had a soft spot for Charlotte, if you get my meaning?'

Tory gave a posh-girl laugh. 'Totally!'

'Anyway, Prêt?'

'Yah, but I'm not eating carbs today, like, at all.'

'I know, I need to lose four pounds . . .'

They went out, banging the door. Going to Prêt à Manger at lunchtime was what Charlotte did with Chloe. Chloe would be small-minded about everyone she knew and Charlotte would say how creepy Simon had been that day (it was easier somehow if she made jokes, that way no one would notice she really meant it) and they'd goad each other into getting a chocolate pot or a flapjack. Though in recent weeks Chloe had seemed a little miffed at the success of Charlotte's wedding diet.

'Maybe I need a big white dress to fit into, too,' she'd said, sucking the sugar off her coffee stirrer instead. 'Maybe that's the motivation I'm after. Skinny bitch!'

There were voices in the corridor, loud noises of welcome,

so the Snax people must have arrived. Charlotte rearranged her dress and ran water over her hands and face. She would have to go back out there.

Keisha

Keisha was meant to be out by noon today, the council said they'd given her enough time. Whatever was left would have to go to landfill.

Finding her father's name hadn't had as much an effect on her as she might have thought. He was still an unknown white guy, a blank, just like he'd always been to her. Now she knew he was smart, not a drunk like Chris's dad, shouting about the IRA all the time. That was something, she supposed. But then she thought, *And what have I ever done? Fucked up my GCSEs and worked in a nursing home?* Yeah, he'd be proud of her – not.

Mercy had been everything – head-wrecker, pain in the arse, source of all food and advice – wanted and unwanted. Mercy had been home, and now she was gone and so was home with her. This guy, this Ian Stone, he was nothing but a bundle of genes. What difference did it make if she knew his name?

Still, she put the contents of the old folder into the 'keep' bag, and closed it up before she humped the rest of Mercy's stuff down the high street to Oxfam, hoping no one thought she looked daft.

'Some stuff,' she muttered, dumping the bags at the old white woman behind the till.

'Oh, thank you, dear.' The crumbling woman peered at it through her glasses. Posh. Keisha waited a second, as if the woman was going to challenge her to prove she owned the stuff, hadn't nicked it. 'It was me mum's,' she said.

'That's kind.'

They believed her. Keisha headed back to the house, light-handed. It was bright and sunny, and everyone seemed to be out on the streets, mums with buggies (she didn't look too closely at the kids, wondering where Ruby was on this nice day), old ladies shuffling along with huge plastic shopping bags, dodgy geezers hanging about with mobile phones. It was when she was passing the fruit and veg shop that she suddenly got a bad feeling. Had someone stopped in the crowd for a minute, and she'd sensed it? Whatever it was, she could feel eyes on her. Someone was watching. On the warm street, Keisha felt a chill run over her, and zipped up her Adidas top. She looked around the street, noisy with voices. Nothing. She walked on faster, and turned into her mum's quieter road.

Behind her she heard footsteps continuing, the soft tread of trainers, a shadow on the bright pavement, and she turned round with her heart racing.

'All right, Keesh?'

'You scared the shit out of me.'

'Just saying hi.' Jonny shrugged. A tall guy, heavy in the arms and legs, signet rings on his beefy hands. He was Chris's mate – his best mate, she supposed. But what was he doing on her mum's street?

She narrowed her eyes at him, stepping back out of his reach. 'And what're you doing here? Last time I checked, you lived in West Hampstead.'

He cracked a knuckle. 'Deano's been looking you. Asked me to keep an eye out.'

So he'd been watching her. She tried not to shudder. 'And

he sent you down here, did he? What's he want me for? He's the one changed the fucking locks.'

'Naw, he got put out, didn't he.'

'He got evicted?' That would explain the locks being changed – if it was true. She zipped her top up tighter. 'Yeah, well, my mum died. Did he know that? After he "visited" her, she fell down dead with a fucking heart attack!'

Jonny dipped his head. 'Yeah. He's sorry. Never meant her no harm. All he did was talk to her.'

'Yeah. *Talk*.'

'Deano says he only wanted to see his kid. Got a right, hasn't he? No reason to send the cops round on him.'

'What? Don't be daft, I've not been near no cops.'

'You know they'll be after you too, if you say stuff.'

She gave him a dirty look. 'Look, I gotta go. Moving out today.' Better let Chris know she wasn't going to be here, just in case he felt like dropping by with any of his other lovely mates.

'Oh yeah? Where you going?'

She shrugged. 'Away. Far away. Mind your own.' That was a good question though, wasn't it? The lad wasn't as dumb as he looked. Where the fuck *was* she going?

'You been ringing anyone recently?' Jonny asked innocently.

'How the fuck would I do that? He's cut my phone off, the twat.'

'Deano reckons you might've seen that blonde chick. The one whose fella got banged up for Anto Johnson.'

'What? I don't even know her.' She thought of the blonde girl's purse with her address, inside the house in her 'keep' bag. 'I'm busy. Fuck off, Jonny. Tell "Deano" I don't have no more eyes for him to black.'

Jonny shook his head as if Chris had accidentally drunk

her last can of Coke or something. 'He never meant it, Keesh. Just stressed, you know? Times are hard. He misses you. Said you might've had a misunderstanding, like about that club night.'

She looked at him. Did this mean she'd been right – Chris *had* gone back to help Anthony Johnson that night after all? Why did he beat her up then, if all he'd done was get blood on him trying to save the man's life? 'Don't know what you mean.'

'You gonna visit the kiddie then? Your little Ruby?' Jonny cracked his knuckles like he was just passing the time of day. 'Deano was wondering where she was.'

There was no way she was talking about Ruby with this twat. 'I don't know where she is. And he won't find her either. She's not here.'

He smiled again. It was horrible. 'Found *you*, didn't he?'

Her heart was thudding. 'Listen to this, Jonny. You can fuck off. And you tell him he can fuck off too. Leave me alone, leave Ruby alone. Or else I'll tell what I saw. You tell him that. He'll know what it means.'

Confusion was spreading over Jonny's face. She set off walking, refusing to look back. But before she opened the door she paused; she didn't want him to see what house she went into. He'd gone.

In the quiet gloom of the house, she put her back to the door, breathing heavily. Fuck. Fuck. Jonny had hands like a gorilla. Thank fuck it was the middle of the day. She had goosebumps all up her arms. What was Chris playing at? He wanted her back now, after he'd thumped her about? She wasn't that girl – was she?

'He's after me, Mum,' she whispered to the empty house. 'What do I do?'

There was no answer from the oily shadows. Well, there was no need, she knew what Mercy would have said. Keisha picked up the bag of things to keep, then closed the door and posted the keys back through the letter box. Keeping a good eye out for six-foot-four loonies in Umbro tracksuits, she got on the train and took it up to West Hampstead. Without really knowing why, she was going to Belsize Park.

Charlotte

Charlotte practically ran down the last street to her house. She hated being outside in that area now. There was the memory of the red gloop sliding over her eyelids, and maybe she was getting paranoid, but she felt people were looking at her, the gang of kids by the chicken shop, the black woman wheeling her baby. Everyone who was black, she felt they were staring at her and thinking, *That's the one, the racist one. That's her.*

Finally she was on her own, and almost in a fever she pulled Dan's jumper round her, shivering in the emptiness of the flat. It wasn't cold; it was just that he wasn't there. Then she took the tea-stained letter out of the bin and sank down on the floor. It seemed better somehow, more suited to the depth of her feelings than just sitting down on the sofa. She remembered one time coming home from work with flu, sinking down like this, and Dan had picked her up and carried her to bed. No one was there to carry her now.

What an idiot she was! Of course she hadn't been ready to go back to work. She couldn't pretend to care about tampons and cereal now. But God, how embarrassing! She banged her head lightly against the door. Chloe and Tory and Fliss would be having a good old giggle at her. It was a mistake she'd never have made before. But when she came out of the ladies' the Snax people had arrived, a greying corporate man, his wedding band eating into his pudgy finger, and a hard-faced blonde girl all shiny with lacquer and gloss.

'Here's Charlotte,' Simon said with that fake heartiness of his, showing her he was nervous about this one. It was a big new account for them and the recession hadn't been kind to PR firms.

'Tea? Little café au lait?' Ugh. Simon was so full of bullshit. They were making murmurs about transport. 'Oh, tell me about it, that Northern Line's making me prematurely grey! No, don't look.' Gales of fake laughter.

Charlotte hauled the corners of her mouth up into a smile, wiping damp hands on her dress. Before, she'd have known exactly what fluff to say to them. 'Hiii! Have you come far? Love your shoes. Oh, it's such an honour to work on this brand, I eat them all the time . . .'

Now, smiling blankly at them, all she could think was, *My boyfriend's in prison. Did you know? My boyfriend's in prison. I have to get him out! He's locked up in there!* She swallowed her hysteria and wobbled into the meeting room on her uncomfortable heels.

The problem started when the blonde began leafing disdainfully through the documents Charlotte should have assembled in advance. Instead, running late, she'd pulled them off the copier in passing.

Simon was in full flow with his jargon-generator: 'Social media platforms . . . Digital SEO strategies . . . Pushing the envelope on this one . . .' when the girl curled up her mouth and said, 'Er, what's this?'

'Paradigm shift in snacking behaviour . . . I'm sorry?'

'This.' She waved one of the bits of paper. 'Why is this here?'

Charlotte's heart thrust up her throat and into her mouth. 'Oh God, that's mine! Sorry! Wait, wait.' She tried to grab it, but Simon had already picked it up. Printed on the paper was INNOCENT – *have you been a victim of rough justice?* She'd printed out the wrong screen. Shit shit shit.

Charlotte flushed a horrible colour, like rotten beets. For a second she wondered madly could she relate miscarriages of justice to low-calorie snacks. *It's a crime that snacks have so many calories.* No, no. God, that was a terrible idea. 'I'm so sorry. I've printed the wrong thing.' And to her horror, the tears she'd been fighting all day rose up to her mouth in a sort of shrieking sob. 'I'm sorry!' She clapped her hands over her mouth. 'Oh God, I'm so sorry.'

Blonde Girl, Corporate Man, Fliss, and Simon all stared at her as she tried desperately to hold back the tears, twisting and blinking and sniffing. Corporate Man cleared his throat and said, 'Ahem. Do you have an actual sales plan for us?'

'Of course. Of course.' Tripping over her feet, wiping at her face, she went to print out the right thing, and the meeting continued, but it was already too late. Blonde Girl looked at her watch several times, and at the end of Simon's presentation Corporate Man cleared his throat and said, 'Well. We'll be in touch.'

Everyone knew that meant: *Fuck off, you bunch of rank amateurs.* And once he'd shown them out, laughing and back-touching all the while, Simon turned to Charlotte. His expression changed like a shutter coming down. 'A word?'

Alone in her kitchen, Charlotte moaned softly and banged her head again. The faint pain she felt on the outside was

almost a relief from the twisted mess inside. It was unbelievable. She'd never even got less than seventy per cent in any
test or exam ever, never missed a day of work, and now she
was fired!

Or, she assumed she was fired. Simon would never say
anything so direct, not when there were words to lard around
it like plastering a wall. Clear she wasn't ready to be back, he
said. Not ready for client-facing opportunities. Needed to
trim some fat. Take some time for herself.

She thought it meant she was fired. Certainly it meant she
wasn't going back tomorrow, and she wasn't getting paid.

Try to keep working, Dan's letter said, crumpled in her
hand. *You'll need the money.* Already she was failing him.
Charlotte hugged herself, balled up against the door. She'd
thought it was rock bottom before, when Dan was taken
away and her tooth was lying bloody in her hand, but she
hadn't realised then just how many things she had to lose.
And now they were all gone. This was worse. This was worse
than the worst. What the hell was she going to do?

Hegarty

It was easy in the end to locate an address for one Mercy
Collins in Gospel Oak, and just as easy to find out she'd died
the week before. The neighbour seemed delighted to see
Hegarty and wanted to tell him all about the youths in the
area. 'Eggs, they are throwing at my door! What kind of
children do this?'

'Yes, I'm very sorry, Mrs – Suntharalingam, is it? Listen,
I'm trying to locate Mrs Collins. Her house appears to be
shut up.'

'She has gone, God bless her, my poor friend.'

'Gone?'

'Passed away.'

So the mysterious Keisha Collins wasn't to be found in her mum's house, either. He was sure she knew something, that stroppy girl. But where was she?

When he'd assured the neighbour he would look into the incidence of egg-related crime in the area, and she'd re-latched her door, Hegarty stood on the street tapping his pen on his notebook. So, Chris Dean would have scarpered by now, warned off by his mate Jonny. Keisha Collins wasn't at her mum's, she wasn't at her old flat, and there was no record of her in any hostel in the area. He didn't blame her if she was trying to hide.

The kid, he'd found out, was in foster care in Kilburn, and hadn't seen either of her parents for weeks. The social worker, Sandra something, had said rather sniffily, 'We encourage them to keep up contact, of course, but we do think it's best for the little one if she's removed from parental influence right now. Unless they radically change their lifestyles, it's unlikely the parents will gain custody again.'

'Even the mother?'

Sandra had sighed. 'Keisha has tried, Officer. But Christopher's influence is too strong. I'm afraid she's quite likely to tell him where the child is, and in the circumstances, we can't allow it. We have to protect Ruby. Unless Keisha stays in touch with us, arranges visits, there's a good chance we'll move the child to permanent adoption.'

So where had she gone, Keisha Collins? Her mother was dead, her child gone, her boyfriend who knew where. As Hegarty stood on the street, turning it all over in his head, his phone began to ring. When he heard that sound, it was usually something bad, someone else dead or beaten or raped. He'd have no time to follow up this case. Well, it seemed he'd come to the end of the trail anyway.

The phone rang; once, twice, three times. He answered. 'Hegarty.'

Keisha

It was getting fucking ridiculous now. She'd been outside the blonde girl's house for at least twenty minutes, sitting on the low wall. She couldn't ring the bell for flat three – what would she even say? *Yeah, it's me, the girl who nicked your wallet.* She'd thought somehow Charlotte would come out of the house and she could warn the girl that Chris was after her – though she'd no idea why. Had she seen something, that dappy-looking blonde girl? What did she know?

That was the plan, anyway. But she'd been here for ages now, and people kept walking past her on the pavement with little ratty dogs on leads, or old couples in matching brown coats. Keisha ducked her head and scuffed her trainers on the cracks in the paving stones. But she could see them looking. Who's that pikey girl, they were thinking. Maybe I'll put in a little call to the friendly local cop-shop. A woman with a toddler on a scooter nearly swivelled her neck right round to look at Keisha, and that was it, she was getting up to go, when the big front door of the house opened and a man came out. He was like someone in a catalogue with his stripy scarf, glasses, baby strapped to his chest.

'Can I help you?' He was polite, but she heard it in his voice: *You don't belong here.*

'Eh, does Charlotte live here? Charlotte Miller?'

'Are you a friend of hers?'

Keisha thrust up the wallet with the dog on it. 'Her purse – she lost it. I found her name in it.'

He smiled uncertainly. 'That's kind of you. I'll get her.' He buzzed the little button she'd been staring at for hours. 'Charlotte?'

Keisha heard a wavering voice on the intercom. 'Who is it?'

'It's Mike from downstairs. There's a lady here says she has your purse. Did you lose it or something?'

'Yeah, I did. Thank God.' The door buzzed and the man stood back to let Keisha into the solid old building, pizza flyers scattered in the hallway. It was that easy. Keisha hoisted up her bags and touched the baby's covered foot just for a second – he kicked his legs just like Ruby had when she was little. 'Thanks,' she said quietly.

Charlotte was on the second floor up the carpeted staircase, and she had the door open. 'Oh you found it, how amazing.'

She was so bloody trusting, this girl. Even after her lip had been bust and her eye blacked, for fuck's sake, her tooth had been knocked out falling on a sink, she was still opening the door to any old stranger. Keisha mounted the stairs and the daylight fell on her and she saw Charlotte frown, recognising her from somewhere.

In a second she would slam the door shut. Keisha held the purse out. Her voice had gone. She coughed. 'I can help. Please. I can help you. I can help him – your fella. I can help Dan.'

Part Three

Charlotte

Afterwards, Charlotte was never really sure what had happened to mean Keisha was suddenly staying at her flat. It seemed as if a sort of fog filled those first days, and during that time she did things and said things she would later have no real memory of, as if the coke she had taken was still silting up her brain. All she could recall was Keisha coming to the door, and her thinking for a split second something she would always be ashamed of: *Is she selling something, is she begging?* And then Keisha's mad story about being at the club – she was the black girl who didn't look black, of course, the angry one – and how she'd been with her boyfriend, and how he'd gone home without her, and his clothes were in a bag, and she was sure – she could swear to God – there'd been blood on the rug. Then Keisha would burst out with, 'The bastard! I'll fucking kill him!' and bang on the table, and it turned out her daughter had been taken away and it was something to do with this Chris, who was after Charlotte too.

'I mean, what would he want with you?' Keisha kept saying. 'You must of seen something. Why'd he care about you otherwise?'

'I don't know. I've no idea. Are you saying – you're saying you think Dan didn't do it?' Charlotte tried to swallow all this information in a dull cold lump, like ice cream sliding down her throat.

'You said it yourself, yeah? There was no blood on your fella. He'd blood all over himself, I'd swear on the Bible – Chris, I mean.' She seemed reluctant to say her boyfriend's name.

Charlotte stood up. Her head swam. 'He didn't do it. I knew he didn't do it – oh, Christ.' And she'd fainted on the Axminster rug that had been a present from Dan's parents, hitting her head on the table as she fell.

Keisha had woken her by throwing a glass of water in her face. 'Sorry. You gave me a scare.'

Charlotte woke up hearing music. Not music she would ever play, but something loud and tinny with radio fuzz. She padded into the kitchen in her T-shirt, the carpet warm under her bare feet. Morning light came in the window with the sound of traffic.

The girl was sitting with her bare feet up on the coffee-table. She had *Friends* on as well as the radio, and Charlotte went over and turned the music off.

'All right?' said the girl warily. 'Still alive, then?'

'Yeah – oh.' Charlotte remembered hitting her head and put up her hand; there was dried blood on her forehead.

'Went down like a ton of bricks, you did. Thought you might have that, what's the name, concussion. Someone had to stay with you.' She was defensive. Her things were strewn round the room, huge clumpy shoes by the door, sleeping bag unrolled, catching the light on its silky surface. On the kitchen table was a cereal bowl swimming in milk, a few Bran Flakes floating in it. Charlotte started tidying it away automatically, and the girl rose to her feet.

Charlotte said, 'Look – Keisha, right? Sorry, I'm a bit hazy. You said last night you knew something, that you could help Dan?'

Keisha nodded, keeping her eyes on Charlotte. 'Yep. Then you went down, arse over tits. Hit your head off that there.' She gestured to the table.

No wonder she felt woozy. Charlotte pinched the bridge of her nose. 'You said that your boyfriend – ex-boyfriend – was there that night, at the club? He was the other man?'

She didn't want to say it, but then Keisha said, 'Yeah, the other white guy.' Then Charlotte felt stupid because what was wrong with saying it? It was the most obvious thing.

'I saw him, I think. In the club that night . . . I can't remember. He ran off?' She'd seen Keisha too, but didn't mention their run-in in the toilets.

'That's right, buggered off. Bastard. Then I get home and he's in bed, and I'm thinking, *This is well off. And* he takes his clothes down the laundrette next day – as if he ever washed his clothes in his fucking life!'

'Right . . .' Jesus, they went to *laundrettes*. 'And the shoes, what were you saying about them?'

'Stains on 'em, all over. All red, the soles was. Said he stepped on a kebab! Ha!' Keisha made a cynical noise and Charlotte winced.

She looked over by the phone, where that policeman had left his sticky footprint. 'I suppose it doesn't prove he did it, even if he was there.'

'Get this though. Why's he after you? Why'd he set those girls on you?'

'The ones who hit me?' Charlotte put her fingers to her mouth. 'It was planned?'

Keisha seemed to think she was thick. 'Course it was. That

was Anthony Johnson's sister, one of 'em – she's a right stroppy cow. He wanted your purse, so's he could find out where you lived.'

'But – he must have got it! I don't understand. What happened to the purse?' Her head was spinning.

'I got it, didn't I? Hid it off him. He got in a right mood, that's why he did this.' Keisha showed off her own black eye, less obvious than on Charlotte's milky skin but still brutal. 'And then I see Jonny yesterday, down near me mum's, and he says Chris is looking for you, knows you live round here.'

'Christ. I had some graffiti on my step the other day, these kids – and I could have sworn someone followed me yesterday.' Charlotte felt cold and sweaty down her back.

Keisha nodded grimly. 'That's how it is. Word gets round, for a racial thing.'

'And you came to tell me. But you don't even know me. Why?'

The girl shrugged. 'Not fair on you, is it, even if your fella did knock off that dude. Bet no one ever lifted a hand to you in your life, eh? And if he thinks he's going after Ruby – well, he can go fuck himself. I've had enough.'

'So, you just left like that? You left him?' Charlotte didn't know if she could trust this girl who came so out of the blue, and stood across the living room in the morning sun.

'You don't believe me?'

'I'm sorry, no, no – Keisha, it's not that. It's just – it's such a shock, you turning up. And I think, well, you don't know me at all. Why would you help me?'

Keisha seemed to think about it for a long time, then she bit her lip and looked at her feet. 'Me mum – she had a heart attack, after he went round her house.'

'God, and is she—'

'No. I fucking buried her the other day, OK?' She stared even harder at the ground.

'I'm so sorry. Christ. And the little girl?'

'She's OK. Never mind that,' Keisha said hurriedly. 'Look, I can go. Just thought you should know. Keep your eyes peeled for him. Never know what he might do, and that psycho Jonny. Bastards.'

'No! You don't have to go. I'm sorry, it's just been a difficult time.'

'You're fucking telling me,' said Keisha grimly. 'Seriously, I won't hang about if you want me outta your hair.' She started picking things up, her phone, one large shoe.

Charlotte sighed. 'I'm sorry, I've messed it all up. And you came all the way here. Listen, would you like some tea?'

Keisha stared her out, holding one shoe in her hand. 'Three sugars, then. Please.'

Later, after many, many cups of tea, and many, many retellings of the story of That Night and the week after, purple shadows were creeping in the windows. Keisha stirred. 'Gettin' late.'

For a moment neither of them spoke.

'So I best . . .'

'Sorry.'

'Don't be bloody sorry,' said Keisha. 'I was gonna say, I'll go now.'

Charlotte turned her face away, tidying up the crumbs from her last packet of Jaffa Cakes, now destroyed. 'Where will you go? Didn't you say you had to leave your mum's house?'

'Yeah. S'OK.'

'Ah, look. You're not going back to that hostel.' Did she even have the money? Charlotte thought not. She wondered how to say it, how to talk to this girl who was so different to her, so proud, so defensive. 'Dan said I should get someone to move in,' she said, opening the swingbin. 'And to be honest, I'm getting bloody scared at night now, since the paint, and . . . all that.'

'Yeah?' Keisha was fiddling with her bag.

Charlotte came out and said it. 'You should stay a while. Please. I'm not good by myself – I don't sleep, I don't eat, hardly.'

'Yeah, well, you can afford it, skinny thing like you.' Keisha made motions to get up.

'Oh, I can't say it right. Listen, I know it must have been hard to come here, when he's your boyfriend and all, and I'm just some – random girl from a club. But you did it, because it was the right thing to do – yes?' She tried to think how to say it. 'If you would stay for a few days, maybe we could write all this down. Go back to the police.'

'Dunno about that.' Keisha looked alarmed.

'That's why you told me, isn't it? So we can do something about it?'

Keisha smiled a bit, maybe at the *we*. 'Mostly so you could know that maybe he wasn't bad. Your fella.'

Charlotte felt this for the gift it was, how much it took for Keisha to say it. 'I'll never be able to thank you enough.'

'Aw, come off it.'

Charlotte was nearly tearful again, she so much didn't want this girl to walk out the door, even though she was a stranger and she wiped smeary handprints all over the glass table. 'Just for a few days. Till you get settled, maybe?'

Keisha sighed deeply, and set her bag down. 'Put the kettle on, then.'

*

And so Keisha was installed in the box room, a girl with the rangy build of an East African runner, hostile eyes, hair straightened and treated into a substance as far from natural as Teflon. She ate bags of Wotsits, the lurid dust gritting itself into the cream wool of the sofa. She left her size nine trainers, cheesy as the crisps, always in places where Charlotte would trip over them. She seemed to have access to no money but the few pound coins in her market-stall purse, saying there was an envelope waiting for her at the nursing home where she did nights – apparently this was how she got paid and thought it was *normal*. But she couldn't go to collect this envelope yet because *he* might find her there. She was absolutely insistent on this point. He would know if she went anywhere she normally went. Look what had happened to her mum, after all.

Sometimes she would burst out laughing. On the second night, after another day of rehashing their mashed-up stories and eating biscuits, Charlotte was standing outside the bathroom waiting to brush her teeth, as Keisha gurgled and hocked up minty spit everywhere. Both their faces were reflected in the cabinet mirror.

'What's so funny?' Charlotte was getting irritated having someone so strange in her house, even though she'd begged her to stay.

'Look at the fucking state of us, Char. Black eyes, busted teeth. It's like fucking Women's Aid round here.'

Charlotte surprised herself by letting out a huge belly-laugh. She covered her mouth. How could she laugh when everything was so unbelievably fucked up?

'S'OK,' said Keisha, rinsing her toothbrush. 'You gotta laugh, don't you.'

*

That night Charlotte woke up again, tense as a board in her bed, heart thudding. Voices, again, outside. They were back.

She opened the door to the living room and nearly jumped out of her skin, before realising the long pale shadow by the window was Keisha.

'They're back.'

'Mm. You got a torch, like a big one?'

'A torch? Er, I think so.' Trying to breathe and slow her heart, Charlotte rummaged in the kitchen drawers till she found Dan's big camping torch. Remembered in a flash cold nights, wrapping him round her like a blanket, seeing the dawn through sweaty canvas. He'd been happy, camping. But not for a long time. 'Here.'

Keisha flicked it on, nodding as if she approved. Then she flung open the window and shone it down. 'Fuck off, you little fuckers. Who's that? Michael Rutonwe, that you? Don't think I won't tell your mum what you're up to.'

'And who the fuck're you?' one called up.

A stone hit the wall but Keisha didn't flinch. 'Can't see me, can ya? But I see you little shits and I know you all. So you better fuck off sharpish.'

There was a moment when they squared up to her. Then the black shadows peeled off from the dark and, miraculously, they started to leave. 'Stupid cunt,' one shouted back.

Charlotte was shaking. 'Oh, God. You did it. Did you really know them all?'

'Nah, just that one kid. Everyone knows him round my way, little fucker.' Keisha switched off the torch and looked at Charlotte, pale in Dan's rugby shirt. 'You look like you need a cuppa.'

*

How was she to talk to this girl, so different to her, so full of angry energy that she hummed with it? They'd gone over their stories until holes were worn in them.

Charlotte would say – 'And then they just bust in and they took him away, and I was so upset, I couldn't believe it when they said no bail, I was about to be sick, and then they whacked my head into the sink . . .'

Keisha – 'Then I see his shoes all red, and I say, What's going on? and next thing I know there's his fist coming up, and when I wake up he's locked me in . . .'

Charlotte – 'So my mum just up and arrived and all she could talk about was cancelling the florist, like I don't feel bad enough, and there were reporters on my doorstep, and it was meant to be my wedding but my dad thinks I need a lecture on the banking system . . .'

Keisha – 'My mum, she always hated Chris, since day one. Drove me mad. Couldn't believe it, I just went in the ward and she's not there, and I'm like, where the fuck is she . . .'

It was as if they both had a suitcase full of troubles that had to be upended. There were things Charlotte was afraid to ask, too. 'But what I don't get, right,' she was saying later over microwaved supernoodles from the corner shop, full of salt and soy sauce and strange, powdery residue that rang with flavour. 'Why was Ruby in care in the first place? I mean, it's always on the news that Social Services won't take kids away, then they end up dead and . . . Oh, sorry.'

Keisha got a look on her face between shame and fury. 'Mum took her, didn't she. After – what happened – she called the Social on him. Chris.' She said the name in a tiny voice. 'And they asked Ruby – kid said she always went to Nana's at nights anyway.' She fiddled with her fork. 'See, I been doing nights at the nursing home, and he couldn't stay home with her, could he. He had business and . . . stuff.'

Charlotte couldn't look at her. She'd never known anyone as proud as Keisha, and here she was explaining how she'd lost her child, loving a bad man. It could happen to anyone.

Everything Charlotte bought in the corner shop had to have a receipt to be added to the IOU pile for when Keisha got her envelope, and if she forgot, Keisha would badger her for the price of everything. How much were Pot Noodles? Doritos? When Charlotte admitted she had no idea, she could see herself slide down even further in Keisha's estimation. You had to know the price of things. How else could you know the value of anything? How else would you know what you'd gained, and what you'd lost?

The third day slid round, sleeping and eating, talking themselves hoarse, the coffee table littered with crisp dust, slimy spilled noodles, stained mugs.

'We were supposed to be in Jamaica now,' Charlotte half-laughed, rattling the dregs of a bag of Doritos. 'I keep thinking about it. I had this image, you know, all candlelit dinners on the sand, and the sun going down, cocktails . . .' She tailed off, seeing Keisha's expression. 'You know how it is with holidays. I always have, like, this picture in my head of what it'll be like, all blue water, white sand. Then in real life it's too hot or I get mosquito bites or something.'

'Never been on holiday.' Keisha shrugged, digging at a knot in her hair.

Charlotte was so shocked she blurted out, 'What? I mean, really never?'

'No.' Keisha eyeballed her. 'My mum was from Jamaica, you know. Came on the boat, but after that she wouldn't travel, not even on the tube. The school were gonna take us down Southend one time but I got kicked out, didn't I?'

'Oh.' Once again Charlotte felt she was in at the deep end, scrabbling to get a hold on some common ground between her and the other girl.

'Guess we're in the same boat now,' Keisha said, hoisting her large feet onto the sofa, toenails poking out. 'No boat at all, ha ha.'

It was true, Charlotte thought. It wasn't what she had expected, but for the moment there was nothing else on offer.

Eventually, all the adding up of receipts and dividing by two was getting right on Charlotte's nerves. 'Why don't you just go to the nursing home, get your pay?'

Keisha stiffened. 'Dunno.'

'Come on, he won't be there. What, you think he can be everywhere at once?' When she said it she worried she'd gone too far. Even though she barely knew Keisha, the other girl's cynical bantering style had set her off talking like that too.

Keisha muttered, 'I know that. Not thick, am I?'

'I know, I know. I'm sorry. But – don't you think we should go? You said he'd been evicted, didn't you?'

'That's what Jonny said. Can't trust him s'far as you can throw him.'

'Look, I'll come with you. Won't you be pleased to get the money?' She knew by then how proud Keisha was.

'All right, leave it out.'

So now they were on a clanking, puffing bus – Christ, before all this Charlotte hadn't been on a bus since she was at school – and lurching slowly up Finchley Road. Charlotte fidgeted with her Ugg boots; too hot. An awkward silence had settled between them. 'Far, isn't it?'

Keisha was snapping her chewing gum. 'Normally walk this every night. And back, four in the morning.'

Once again Charlotte was silenced.

As they got near they both became nervous. Charlotte was getting a bit freaked about going into the Home, and she noticed that Keisha was fidgety, looking about her as if Chris might be hiding in the bushes. Inside, Charlotte was hit in the face by the smell of bleach and what it was covering – human crap. She must have gagged because Keisha gave her that look that was fast becoming annoying.

Keisha barged her way in through swing doors, her trainers squeaking off the floor. 'Wait here a sec, will ya.'

Charlotte waited awkwardly in the hall. Through an open door she could see old people in chairs, vacant faces, and a whole room full of beige, beige cardigans, beige slacks, beige skin. She saw a woman loose a long stream of drool onto her chest, and shuddered. What was she doing here? She barely even knew places like this existed, just up the road from where she and Dan had been buying the *Guardian* and eating fresh croissants. The floor, she noticed, was exactly that same speckled blue plastic as the toilets she'd passed out in at the courthouse. She shuddered, remembering.

The door slammed back again and Keisha came out. She looked pissed off but Charlotte knew by now that didn't mean much. 'Well?'

'Come on.' Still looking round themselves, they headed back to the bus stop. Keisha sighed and fiddled with the pocket of her denim jacket.

'Did you – you got it?'

Keisha inclined her shoulders; *yes*. 'He gave it me, but he said don't come back, 'cos I never showed up this week. Bastard.'

'Oh.'

'Don't care. S'a shit job anyway. I'll see about something else, agency work, waitressin'. Whatever.'

Charlotte sighed. 'I'd better look for something too. We spent so much on the wedding.' It still hurt so much she could hardly think about it. 'I had a look round the PR firms but there's nothing about, with the recession. Christ, I was lucky to have that job. What a dumbass. I really, really am in no fit state to job-hunt. I'm still crying at least ten times a day.'

As the bus drew in, they pulled out their Oyster cards and Keisha squinted at her. 'You want this job here?'

'Huh? Me?'

She shrugged. 'S'easy work, just make the tea and that. He can't be arsed advertising, tight-arse that he is.'

Charlotte almost laughed. To go from PR in Soho, all shiny hair and statement shoes, to a nursing home full of blank-faced old people! 'Do you have to like . . . wipe them, or anything?'

'Their arses? Sometimes, if they're short-staffed. But everyone shits, Char.'

'Oh.'

Keisha swung herself up into the bus by the pole. 'Things are different now, yeah? You gotta do what you can. Sign up to my agency too. Bunch of bastards, but they pay OK. Not cash in hand like that bloody home.'

When they got home, Charlotte had to have a shower to wash away the smell of poo and bleach, and when she came out Keisha was watching TV. There was a pile of money on the table, notes and coins. Beside it was a sheet of printer paper with a long column of figures scrawled onto it. 'You added the receipts up?'

'Yeah, I can do sums.'

Again she was embarrassed. 'I didn't mean . . . Thanks. You didn't have to do that.'

Keisha got up and came over to the kitchen table. 'Listen, Char, we need to talk money. How much is the mortgage on this here place?'

Charlotte wasn't used to being so upfront about money. Vulgar, her mother always said. 'I'm not sure.' Keisha gave her that look again. 'Oh wait, it was in Dan's letter.' She fished it out from the fruit bowl. 'Here. Two thousand a month.'

'Two grand, fucking hell.'

'Well, it's classed as a two-bed, and, you know, the area . . . And then there's the bills, and the gym, and the cleaning lady usually comes – she thinks we're in Jamaica now.' And now that Charlotte looked around her, the place was already a tip in just two weeks without Maria's expert touch, cooking spatter up the wall, the bin overflowing. Charlotte didn't dare look at Keisha when she said about the cleaner.

'Listen, I do a week of nights in that place, and I get two hundred and fifty quid. So, if you want me to share this place for a bit, I can't pay half. See?'

'Neither can I, not even on my old salary. Dan paid it.' Dan earned over two hundred pounds for just an hour at his work.

'And now you've nothing coming in. Plus, you've all that wedding shit to pay off.'

Charlotte bristled: what was so shit about her wedding? 'So you're saying I need to take the nursing-home job?' Or something else crap.

'That won't be enough, even. You could move.'

As if she hadn't thought of that. 'Well, I can't, actually.

It'd never sell, not in this market. And Dan loves this flat; I have to keep it for him. Imagine, he gets out, and I've lost our home as well as everything else. He *will* get out – I know he will.'

Keisha paused. 'OK. But then you need more cash. His work – they sacked him already, yeah?'

'Yes.' Charlotte slumped forward on her elbows. 'It's probably their fault anyway, making him so stressed. I mean, Christ, did they have to stop his card? I know he lost his temper, but they really screwed him over.'

Keisha was scribbling on the piece of paper. 'In the news all the time, innit, these City twats get fired, sue for stress or whatever. Get millions, sometimes.'

'You think I should do that?' And did that mean Keisha thought Dan was a twat too?

'S'an idea. Or ask his folks – they're loaded, right?'

Charlotte squirmed. 'I can't.' Keisha gave her a look. She tried to explain. 'They're kind of scary, his parents. They didn't give us anything towards the wedding – they don't believe in making a fuss – and they won't come to see him. They just sent my letters back, said we should get a lawyer but they couldn't help.'

She could see the other girl wasn't convinced. 'I'd still hit them up if they're good for it, tight-arses. Chris's ones were the same, never gave us a penny for Ruby. Rather spend it on Special Brew, they would.'

It wasn't unlike her own dad, Charlotte thought – if you replaced the Special Brew with Courvoisier.

'There's another thing, too.' Keisha started fiddling with the pen. 'If you got anything to sell, that could tide you over.'

'You mean like furniture?'

'Could be, but did you think about, well . . .' Charlotte

saw Keisha was staring down at her hand, and the flawless diamond that glittered there.

'You think I should sell my *ring*? Jesus Christ, no.'

'What? S'only jewellery, isn't it?'

Only jewellery! Charlotte just stared at her hand, the ring Dan had put there, the happiness of that night when he asked. She heard herself say, 'It's all I have left from him. What would he think if I just sold it, like some crappy old watch or something?'

Keisha got up, but Charlotte was sure she'd heard her snort in contempt.

The next day was Sunday again, and Charlotte got up early, blinking in the strange quiet light. Outside her window the street was empty, the odd car swishing past in the silence, and she had that same sad feeling remembering croissants, papers, talking in lazy half-sentences. No. None of that. She was going to prison again. She blocked out the thought of what he'd said. Of course he needed her to visit. It was ridiculous. Of course she had to go. This time she chose her most downmarket clothes, jeans cut below the knee, worn with trainers and a hoody – not the Oxford one, God no. Still she knew she wouldn't fit in, didn't have the right fuck-you attitude, the right shiny cheap fabrics, the hoop earrings. She stopped a quick thought that she should borrow some of Keisha's things if she wanted to look right.

Keisha. The girl was asleep, her snores reverberating out from the spare room. Charlotte knocked on the door, thinking it was strange to do that in her own flat. Small as it was, every crevice of that place was as known to her as Dan's body had been. Before. 'Keisha?'

A long pause, then a snorting groan. 'It's early, man.'

'Yeah, I have to go. You know, Pentonville.' She hesitated. But one of the good things about Keisha was she didn't get freaked out at all by the prison stuff.

Keisha opened the door, her hair sticking up like she'd touched one of those generators in science class. The room behind her was already a mess of clothes and dirty dishes. 'You want me out for the day?'

Charlotte was ashamed; was that what she wanted? 'Where would you go?'

'Cinema, shops . . . wherever.'

'No, no, don't be daft. I'll be back later.'

'OK. I'll stop round here, then.' They stared away from each other, embarrassed.

The trip up to the prison wasn't quite so bad this time. She knew her way, and didn't feel so nervous wondering what the place would be like. How it would look and smell, if people would eye her over. She started watching people in the carriage – the woman in the pink tracksuit seemed to be going the same way. Charlotte stole glances at her all the way, but when they got off the woman walked in the other direction, and Charlotte set off alone to the prison, lugging with her the bag of clothes for Dan. She'd put in his nicest things, good wool jumpers, jeans faded to softness. As if she could wrap him round in love.

Queuing up, she was thinking whether it was, in fact, a good idea for Keisha to be there on her own. After all, she barely knew the girl. Was it wise to leave her there with all their good things, just because she might know something that could help Dan? Charlotte wasn't even thinking about where she was. That was how quickly you got used to things.

The woman behind the desk, a sullen-faced prison officer

in slacks, looked up into Charlotte's face and then got out her radio, static crackling.

'Something wrong?' It was just like when you went to a restaurant and they couldn't find your booking, and they looked at you like it was your fault.

The woman's eyes shifted away. 'Sarge'll be with you now.'

As the queue behind her grew impatient in the heat of the close little room, the guard from last time came lumbering over, walking as if his shoes hurt him. Again she had that ice-cream feeling in her chest. 'Is something wrong? Is he OK?'

The guard scratched behind his ear. 'Sorry, miss, he don't want a visit today.'

She stared at him. Couldn't speak.

'Says he won't see you. Told him, it's a crying shame, lovely young lady like that waiting, but no, he won't see you.'

Charlotte was standing there in her 'prison visit' outfit, clutching her Mulberry bag. Behind her she heard one of the women in the queue mutter to get a bleeding move on.

The guard was embarrassed. 'I'm ever so sorry, miss. Don't even want a lawyer, he says.'

'But – he won't even see *me*?'

He shrugged. So it was really true. The stale smell of the room was all about her, sickening. She looked down at the glimmer of the ring on her finger, worth more than all the clothes on all the women waiting to get in and see their men. What did this mean, if he wouldn't see her when she went to him?

When she got back, Keisha was up and watching TV again. Her shoes were lying in the hallway; Charlotte tidied them aside. She tried not to get annoyed about them, or the large glass of Coke Keisha had sitting un-coastered on the coffee table.

'All right?' Keisha didn't look up; she was picking at her hair again.

'Not really, no.' Charlotte went into the kitchen and tidied some more. 'He wouldn't see me.'

'Shit.'

'I don't know what to do.'

'Well, sit down, have a cuppa. I'll make it.'

She collapsed onto the chair. 'I mean, have you ever heard of it? Someone in prison, turning away visitors? I brought him his own clothes and all. He must be wearing the prison stuff, even though he doesn't have to.'

Keisha was spooning sugar into a mug. 'Happens. They don't wanna be seen inside. You know, the shame.'

'But he's only on remand! By the way, I don't take sugar.'

'Course you don't, skinny minnie like you. Had a bad morning though, yeah?'

Charlotte put her hands over her face and then she was crying, her nose burning with it. Keisha put the dark sweet tea in front of her, slopping a bit out. 'Aw, it'll be OK. Just a big shock for him, innit?'

'Yes.' She wiped her eyes on the back of her hand. 'He thinks – he told me last time that he thinks he did it. I wanted to tell him what you said, so maybe he'd fight, he'd see it wasn't him. Or, there's a chance at least that it wasn't.' She mopped at the spilled tea with the piece of paper Keisha's addition was on.

Keisha shrugged. 'Might not believe you. Thinks he's all guilty and stuff, don't he? He wants to be in prison, sounds like.'

Keisha could be so astute. Charlotte just stared. 'That's

exactly right. He does.' She slumped even more. 'I need to get him out. He's going under. Do you know what I mean? He doesn't belong there.'

'You think other fellas do?' Keisha bristled.

'No – I don't know. Christ, please, Keisha. Help us. You said you would help, when you came. So can we go to the police?'

Keisha froze with her own cup of tea in her hand.

'Oh for God's sake, what? Why did you come here if you won't help me?' After Charlotte had said it, the silence in the kitchen seemed huge, the traffic outside, a bird in the tree by the window.

Keisha stared at her feet. 'I will help ya.'

'I know, I'm sorry, you have helped, really you have. But you see – I'm afraid I'll never get him back again. Not the way he was.'

'Yeah, but—'

'But what? You're scared about Chris, is that it?'

'No!' Keisha flared up. 'You don't get it, do you? Round my way, you don't go to the police. They're the ones you run away from, see? Why would they even believe me? I was there too, yeah? And I got no proof, not one fucking thing.'

Charlotte sighed, wiping her hands over her face. It was true, she had to admit. She didn't think the police had listened to anything she said once they'd decided Dan was their suspect.

'There must be something,' she said. 'You know, it's a public place, the club. There must be something, if they would just go back and look.'

'You mean like CCTV or what have you?'

'Yes, but they had that already, the police. It showed Dan

going out the back.' She winced; she hated remembering all the things they'd amassed to make him look guilty.

'Unless there's another one,' said Keisha absently, gulping her tea.

Charlotte furrowed her brow. 'You know, I never thought of that.' She was trying so hard to remember, grasping at it, like a slippery fish darting out of her hands. 'That night,' she said, struggling, 'I think there was something – I can see this yellow sign in my head – you know, for when there's CCTV. Can't remember properly. The problem is that no one else went out the back. That's why they sent him down, I'm sure.' She felt hopeless. 'But there must be something they've missed. Maybe we should go back there, to the club.'

Keisha was looking at her curiously. 'You really not got any idea why Chris'd be after you? Sure you didn't see something?'

A memory came up from the depths of her fuddled brain, bobbing to the surface as if suddenly inflated. The man pushing past her. The white man shoving her, his smell of sweat and cologne. His annoyed breath as she got in his way, and he ran – where? 'I can't think. I can't remember.'

Keisha was fiddling with the bag in her tea; Charlotte had given up asking her to take them out first and put them straight in the bin. Keisha said, 'Me mum knew the family, you know. The Johnsons – they own the place now, I guess. You know that bitch with the afro, the one who . . . yeah?'

'Yes.' Charlotte's tongue crept to the hole where her tooth used to be, before the girl had knocked it out.

'Well, she's Anthony's sister. And the other girl that time, she was his bit of stuff. But he was married too, got two little kids about Ruby's age . . . What? What'd I say?'

Charlotte's face was numb, but now it was wet again too

as tears spilled out of her eyes. 'Sorry. It's just I somehow keep forgetting he was a person, and those poor kids.' She wiped her face with shaky hands. 'You really think Dan didn't do it? Because, you know, it's the only thing keeping me going.'

There was silence for a while. 'I told you. I've no proof.'

'I need it not to be true. And you need Chris to be gone, don't you?'

Keisha squirmed. 'Yeah, but—'

'You'll never get Ruby back if he's about.' The words rang out in the kitchen. Had she really said them? Charlotte's hands shook.

The other girl's head went up. 'What the fuck do *you* know?'

Charlotte snapped, 'Because, duh, he's the reason you lost her! Remember what he did to her? Your little girl. Bloody hell, wake up!'

Keisha blinked. 'I know that, don't I? It's just hard.'

'I know it's hard. God, I'm sorry for snapping. I'm so sorry. We just can't go on like this. Maybe you could talk to them, the family, see if they know anything. And I can talk to the police guy again. Don't worry, I won't say your name. And I'll write to Dan's parents like I said, promise. Maybe they'll come round. What do you say? Can we try, at least?'

Keisha gave a big burdened sigh. 'Whatever. If you say so.'

The jeweller had a poky, dusty shop behind the flashier stores on Hatton Garden. It hurt her like a needle to come to this street, where they'd chosen wedding rings not two months before, but she needed in a way to feel that pain, to hold her head up and walk into the shop and offer her diamond for sale.

He kept a professional cool as he looked in his little eyepiece, but she saw his bushy eyebrows go up. He had the black hat and curls of a Hasidic Jew. 'Four thousand.'

She didn't have any idea what it was worth. She'd never before had to haggle and had no strength to start. As he made out a cheque she imagined writing a letter to Dan, that he would probably never read – how she'd sold the ring he'd given her.

Charlotte had put on her running shoes, with the vague thought she might jog back. She'd eaten so much rubbish over the past week that her wedding diet was all gone to pot. But was there any point now in foregoing Jaffa Cakes to try and be a size eight? No. Life was bad enough, she may as well eat the bloody biscuits. After the jewellery shop she tucked the cheque into her bag and tried jogging up towards Camden past Euston station. Although weeks before she'd been running 5k with ease, she had a stitch already by the time she reached the station. She stopped, feeling the weakness in her legs and chest. It must be the shock. Instead she slowed to a plodding walk for the rest of the way down Eversholt Street, towards home.

She was just walking, with a vague sense of sadness about how she used to breeze in and out of these shops, when like a blow to the stomach, there it was. The restaurant tucked away on the side street, discreetly shuttered. Inside she remembered exactly the dark Oriental interior, the elaborate cocktails they had drunk, steeped in rich booze and excitement, eyeballing Dan over the huge menus, knowing somewhere in the pit of her stomach that it was going to happen, imagining already the celebratory phone calls; her nails painted, her ring finger bare.

Now Charlotte blinked as if she saw herself dancing from

the restaurant on that frosty December night, her hand glittering with the ice-hearted stone. She'd worn a red dress, a tight Hervé Léger copy from Reiss that meant she could barely eat her chocolate pudding. But in the darkened windows she saw who she was now, a pale girl with scraped-back hair, roots showing, a sloppy jumper. Because what was the point now? Of any of it?

Charlotte shook her head to chase away the ghost of the laughing polished girl, encircled with love. That girl was gone now, and she wasn't coming back.

As she went home she remembered the kids outside her house, and tensed up with fear. But Keisha was there. She'd see them off. Walking on, she felt a deep relief in the knotted ball of her stomach that this strange girl had come to help her.

Keisha

The kids streaming out of school didn't notice much. It was three o'clock and they were done for the day, time to visit the sweetshop or watch telly. They definitely didn't see Keisha standing there, sliding back against some bushes on the other side of the road. She tried not to be nervous. She'd a right to be there, hadn't she? Her eyes were swivelling round. He wouldn't come here. Of course he wouldn't. He probably didn't even know what school the kid went to. No, he wouldn't come for her here.

Most of the kids were out now, a whole stream of them in their red jerseys, the noise of them like birds when you wake up really early and everything else is quiet. Keisha used to hear that noise as she walked back from the nursing home, that high chattering sound, no meaning in it. Every time a girl with black hair walked by, Keisha's heart jumped up in her like a frog. No, that wasn't her either, too tall. Christ, there were a lot of little black girls at this school. Not that she was really black. That was the trouble.

Then, just as she was drumming her foot up and down in impatience, there was Ruby, her glasses slanting on her nose. They'd been fixed up with tape – what had happened? Why didn't they take her down bloody Specsavers? Her hair was corn-rowed, something Keisha had never done, since she didn't know how. Ruby was holding hands with a bigger girl, a black kid with bunches in her hair, and they crossed the road further down from Keisha. A woman was waiting for them, young, skinny, a pretty sparkly scarf round her hair. Black, of course. Was this the foster-mother? No, she was too young. Who were these people taking Ruby home?

Keisha pressed herself further into the bushes as they crossed. As crap as it was to be this close to Ruby and not talk to her, it would be even crapper if the kid knew she was there. Not fair on her, was it? At their closest they were just metres away, and she saw the woman reach around to close up Ruby's huge schoolbag. Ruby toddled off, the bag nearly as big as she was. Keisha wondered did the kid smell different already, of some strange person's house. Not like hers anymore.

As the girls and woman walked away, Keisha peeled herself out of the damp bushes, looked all around her two or three times, and went the other way.

It was weird how things turned out. Her mum would have said it was God moving in mysterious ways, or some such crap. When Keisha went to Charlotte's that first time, it was one of those things you just do without thinking. Even though she didn't know her, and what she did know made her think Charlotte was a posh bitch, she went. To help her, to warn her. To find out what she'd seen. Fucked if she knew why.

She'd never expected to end up staying there, and if someone had told her she'd be living there she'd have said, yeah right, stop fucking about. Even though, let's be honest, she'd nowhere else to go. But when she'd spilled her story out, all mixed-up and breathless, sounding like a loony, and Charlotte finally got what she was trying to say, that maybe, probably, her fella *hadn't* been the one to whack off old Anthony Johnson after all, she'd gone all white like her face was being wiped over, and then she went, bam, whacking her head off the table. After that it didn't seem right to go and leave her, all confused and crying, and anyway, where was Keisha going? She'd no money left for the hostel and couldn't face those showers full of pubes again. Plus, and she didn't like to think about this too much, there was definitely some reason Chris was after this girl. She'd seen something – but she obviously didn't know what yet. So now, somehow, Keisha was living with the blonde bitch. It was mad. But there was nothing else for either of them to do.

After she'd hung round Ruby's school for a bit like a nutter, Keisha set off back down to Gospel Oak. It was raining again, and she hunched her shoulders up against it. Getting a bus would have been quicker, but this way took her past the Church of Holy Hope, and freaky-ass as that place was, she was going there for the third time.

It was all bloody Charlotte's fault. The day they'd got that crappy envelope off the nursing home was the same day Keisha realised they'd never pay all the bills, working in homes and hostels for strung-out druggies. No, they'd have to get better jobs if Charlotte had her heart set on keeping that overpriced flat.

But Charlotte wasn't ready, a blind man could see that. Christ, it was a good day if she only cried two or three times, watching the news (story about prisons came on), doing the washing (Dan's sock in the basket), or getting an email (some snooty mate of hers didn't invite her to a cheese and wine night or whatever). It was like being around a leaky tap, her tears never all the way off.

So it was down to Keisha to help her, the poor little rich girl. But the daft thing was, even though Keisha had been dumped and punched and lost her mum and her kid and had to think about maybe putting that kid's father in the nick, she really did feel sorry for Charlotte. She was like a kid whose puppy got run over by the ice-cream van. Like she didn't fucking know, like no one had ever *told* her life could be shit. So Keisha was helping. She was going to see Pastor bloody Samuel.

She stood in the porch again trying not to feel nervous. It was just a church, wasn't it? She could go in if she wanted. They weren't going to make her be a bloody Christian just like them. In the porch were posters for normal things like cake sales and fair trade, as well as stuff like talks on witches and meetings about how not to get shagged before marriage (that's what it meant, anyway). This was what her mum had believed in. This was the place Mercy had come every week for ten years. Keisha went in. It was quiet inside, the noise of traffic muffled. Her feet made a squelching noise on the rubber floor.

'Welcome!'

Christ! She jumped, luckily not swearing out loud in church. Pastor Samuel was there in his tank top, carrying a mug in his good hand.

'Yes?' He peered at her through the dark of the church.

'It's Keisha, Mercy's daughter. Mercy Collins.'

'Of course, welcome, child. My old eyes.' He came padding across the quiet floor, no hand free to shake hers, but grasping her round the shoulder with his arm. She tried not to look at the *nothing* coming out of his cuff. He smelled like a charity shop, of old clothes, but his eyes were kind. 'What brings you back to us, Keisha? Are you troubled?'

Bloody hell, he didn't know the half of it. She hadn't stopped being troubled since that Friday night. 'Wanted to say thanks for sorting the funeral and all. I wasn't, like, I didn't know what to do.'

'That's our job, here, and our blessing. We miss her greatly, but God has taken her to Him.'

Keisha dipped her head so he couldn't see how much she didn't believe this. It felt to her like Mercy was behind some kind of brick wall where she couldn't hear or see or feel her.

He was looking at Keisha. 'Your mother used to speak of her worries for you.'

'I left him,' Keisha said suddenly. 'She didn't get time to tell you, but I left him, Ruby's dad. Mum never liked him, not even when we was at school.' Crap, she was close to crying again. She screwed up her face.

'You miss her very much, I think.'

'Who? Me mum or Ruby? I miss them both.' Stupid churchman.

'You have difficult choices ahead, Keisha.' He smiled at her again. It was annoying, what did he know about her choices?

'Thing is, Pastor, I wanted to see that Mrs Johnson. She was kind, at Mum's funeral. She made all them sandwiches, didn't she? And she lost her boy.' She spoke quickly, sure that God and Pastor Samuel would see through her.

'Oh, well, her son is here now.'

Keisha must have looked shocked, because he explained, 'Her other son, my child. I will call him. Ronald! Are you here, brother?'

He called and the door opened into the back part of the church, and a man came in. And in. He was fucking huge, muscles up and down his arms. There was a gym bag over his shoulder, and his black T-shirt was darker in patches with sweat. 'Finishing up now, Pastor. Sent the boys to change.' He looked at Keisha, and she looked at him, the muscles tight under his T-shirt. He had an earring in one ear.

'Ronald, this young lady would like to see your good mother. Sister Collins's child, do you remember? Mercy who helped with the flowers?'

'Yeah.' His accent was hard to pin down, London by way of Jamaica, and he was still looking at her. 'Sorry for your loss.'

She blushed, her stupid light skin turning red. 'You, too. I was here – I mean, I came to your brother's funeral.'

His face was blank, smooth like polished wood. 'S'good of you. You want to see Mum?'

She stared at her feet. 'Yeah, er, just wanted to say thanks, like. She was dead kind when my mum . . . you know.'

Pastor Samuel was smiling away between them as if he was Cilla Black on *Blind Date* or something. Ronald – crap name for such a hot guy – shifted his bag. From outside in the yard behind the church, Keisha started to hear a noise like twenty boys shouting and running and slurping down Fanta.

Then she saw the first ones come streaming through, tall and short and pudgy boys, chins dribbling with soft drinks. They were all black, the boys. The noise was mad as they crowded round Ronald and the Pastor, almost swamping the smaller man, who held up his bad arm laughing. 'Boys, boys, this is the House of our Lord, hush now.'

Ronald cleared his throat. Growled, 'Oi, shut it.' Instantly the kids shut up, some giggling a bit. 'Now, get on home,' he said, like a teacher at school, strict but with a bit of a smile that said he was nice, really, he watched *EastEnders* in the evening like you did. 'Don't be getting in no trouble on the way, you hear?'

'Yeah, Ronald,' they all shouted, and streamed out to the street like a bunch of balloons let go, giving Keisha a good old look on the way.

'Ronald takes our class, Football for Life,' said the Pastor, when he could be heard. 'It teaches them to avoid crime. So much violence here, now.'

And Ronald had lost his own brother to it, stabbed in the neck. Keisha couldn't look at him, thinking about it, thinking what she knew. It was the same as when she thought about Dan sitting in that prison up the road. 'Er – you done it long, helping?'

He gave her another look. 'A while. Go back home a lot, Jamaica.'

'Ronald has many businesses.' The pastor patted him with his bad arm. 'He's the rich man going through the eye of the needle, ha ha!'

Ronald hauled his bag up again. 'Ain't rich. Off to me mum's now, if you wanna see her. S'round the corner.'

'Now?' Shit.

He shrugged. 'She'll be there now.'

'Yes, yes, do go, child.' The pastor waved them off with his stump, smiling like a retard. 'Come again – this is your home too, as it was your mother's.'

Something about the way he said *home* brought that feeling back to her, that she might cry. She swallowed it down. 'Maybe. Thanks.'

Outside on the street in the noise and dust of traffic, Ronald walked so fast she had to half-run after him. 'What sort of business?'

'Eh?'

'He said you had businesses . . . Is it the same as your brother?' She'd no idea why she said that. Maybe she wanted him to know she'd seen his brother, she knew something about him.

But Ronald turned round, stopped. 'My brother's dead, yeah?'

'I know! Sorry, I just – he owned a bar, didn't he? Thought maybe you did too.'

He sighed. 'Come on.' They started walking again. 'Anthony ran the club. I got a few out in Jamaica, beach bars, restaurants. But now I gotta sort out all his shit, since he died.'

'Sure, sure.' She was such a dumb-ass.

They'd reached a small terraced house a few streets away. From the open window was the sound of music and voices. It was just like her mum's house, even the same smell of spices and oil.

'Hang about.' Ronald stopped her gently with his arm; it was like a beam. 'You knew him – Anthony?'

She stared down. 'Nah, just went to the club, one time.' She didn't say it was *that* night, the night he'd died.

Ronald looked at her hard, like her mum used to when she

bunked off school. 'Me mum, he's her angel boy now, yeah? Like he never done a thing wrong. She needs to think that now, right?'

'I didn't even know him, honest.'

'OK.' He let his arm down. 'What's your name?'

'Eh?'

'You never said your name.'

'Oh.' Shit, she was dumb. 'Keisha. Keisha Collins.'

He nodded and led her into the house.

The Johnson house was full of noise, and really hot, as if the oven had been going for hours. Over the noise of the TV and shouting in the back kitchen, Ronald yelled, 'Ma! Someone to see you.'

More shouting. A thundering on the stairs and two little kids came running down, grabbing Ronald's neck and legs. 'Lift us! Lift us!'

'Throw me over your shoulder! Uncle Ronald, throw me!'

'All right, all right, keep it down, yeah? There's a lady here.'

They stared at Keisha, the 'lady', with their round dark eyes. She was backing away to the door without realising; God, they were so like Ruby to look at. But Ruby was so quiet, creeping about like a little mouse. Not like these kids.

Ronald picked up one under each arm as if they weighed less than cushions, and jerked his head at Keisha to follow him into the sitting room and through to the back kitchen. An old man, old as the ones in the nursing home, sat watching telly, and out the back smelled of chicken and ginger.

'Put those children down, Ronald,' said Mrs Johnson. 'Where have you been? All this time I am waiting for you to lift my rice cooker down.'

'I'm here now, yeah? This here girl wants to see you.' Now she was a 'girl'. They all looked at her, fat wobbly Mrs Johnson, and a woman she'd seen at Anthony Johnson's funeral, who seemed to be the mum of the kids, and there was the skinny sister too, with the afro. Her hair was tied under a patterned scarf now, and she was leaning up against the cooker in tight jeans.

She gave Keisha a dirty look. 'Ma, it's getting late. Do I have to go, like?'

Mrs Johnson gave her daughter a look that Keisha knew. It was the same one her own mum used to do. 'I don't want to hear another argument! Now put on some decent clothes – the world can see your bottom in those trousers, shameful!'

Rachel went out in a huff and Keisha backed away a bit more. 'Sorry, didn't mean to interrupt. Just wanted to say thanks, like, for your help with me mum.'

'Oh my darling, such a small thing to do.' Mrs Johnson came close, taking Keisha's hands in her floury ones. She smelled like milk. 'Starved you are, look at you. Tanika will make extra.'

'Er, no, sorry, don't want to put you out.' But wait, they were asking her to dinner. Was this not what she wanted?

'Come now, no arguments. Your poor mummy will see I take good care of you.' She touched Keisha lightly on the cheek, leaving flour dust that Keisha didn't wipe away. 'Tanika, make more of those.'

Tanika, the kids' mother, was forming a huge line of little patties and crimping them with a fork. She gave Keisha a little smile, sad and tired. She was darker than the Johnsons – Rachel was nearly as pale as Keisha, a gorgeous caramel colour, the bitch – but you could see the red rims and dark circles round her eyes. Under all the noise and talking, this house was sad, you could feel it. And the reason they were sad, well, Keisha wasn't going to think about that now.

When Keisha and Mercy used to eat in the evenings it was usually on their knees, in front on the telly, and they hadn't even done that for years. The Johnsons ate round the table, pulled out as far as it would go in the sitting room. There was the mum and daughter, Ronald, the daughter-in-law Tanika and her two kids – Anthony's kids – and the gummy old man who, it turned out, was called Pappy. He was the father of the Johnsons' dad, who'd died four years before. Keisha found out a lot about the Johnsons during this meal.

'All those gangs, it was, coming round the club. Mr Johnson, he just dropped down dead with a heart attack.' Mrs Johnson banged on her own chest.

'Ma-a,' said Ronald, irritated. 'The doctor said it was his cholesterol. You're obsessed with the bloody gangs.'

'Cholestr'ol,' huffed Mrs Johnson. 'We never had this in my day.' The same as Mercy, and like her mum's house the table here was about to bust under all the stews, patties, bread, dumplings. Trying to control herself, Keisha ate more than she had since she could remember. Every mouthful of juicy meat and crispy plantain was just like being with her mum. It was as if Mercy was right there with her.

'Pappy, wipe your chin,' said Mrs Johnson. Her name was Asanta, Keisha would later find out, but everyone called her Mum or Granny. Pappy smiled all the time but didn't talk at all. You didn't know if he knew what you said or not. Rachel reached over and wiped the gravy off his face for him, making Keisha think about her nursing home and how he could almost fit in there, with his shuffling slippers and old tank top. But he was here, with his family.

'Keisha, darling, have more rice. Thin as a shadow, you

are – what would dear Mercy say? God bless her.' Mrs Johnson raised her eyes to heaven.

'Who is that lady?' The little girl had been staring at Keisha, and her mother scolded her, holding up a spoonful of patty to the little boy, who was younger. 'Tia, shush now. Come on, Ricky, eat up.' Ricky – named after his dead grandad – was quieter than his sister, peeping out from behind his Sponge Bob Square Pants bib.

'Who is she, eh?' Mrs Johnson pushed more bread towards Keisha. She barely seemed to eat at all herself, between loading her family up with treats. 'She is our friend. Her mummy is gone to Jesus, so she needs to eat her dinner with us.'

Tia stared. 'Does she have a baby?'

They all stared at Keisha then, and she swallowed down her food. 'Er . . . yeah, Tia. I've a baby girl, she's five. What age are you?'

Tia stuck her nose up. 'Five and a half.' Everyone smiled. Pappy patted the little girl on her braided hair. 'Where is your baby?' Tia was still curious, liking the attention.

Crap. Keisha put down her fork. 'She's, well, some people are looking after her, now.' She heard herself say, 'She'll be home with me soon.' When she looked up, Ronald was watching her. Why did these nice people have to find out she'd lost her kid?

The kids' mum was quiet, gentle. 'What's her name, your girl?'

'Ruby.'

'Pretty.' She smiled.

Tia wanted attention. 'Uncle Ronald, look what I can do.' She flicked rice off her spoon and it spattered onto the table.

'Oh, Tia,' said her mum, tired. 'You have to behave at the table.'

Ronald put down his fork. 'Come on, up.'

'Nooo!'

'Come on.' He picked Tia up over his shoulder, kicking and shouting, 'No, no! I'll be good!'

'I'm sorry,' Tanika said quietly. 'Her daddy died, you see. She misses him.' She looked at the huge photo of Anthony Johnson that was on the dresser. 'I don't know how to tell her he's not coming back.'

'Oh, *Mum*,' Rachel sighed, because Mrs Johnson was crying, dabbing her eyes with a tea towel that had a picture of the Queen on it. Rachel rolled her own eyes as she patted her mum's hand. 'You'd think we could go one dinner without crying, yeah?'

Keisha stared hard at her plate. What right had she to be here, with all her problems? They were good people. The only thing wrong with the Johnsons was that Anthony was dead. And here she was, in it up to her skinny neck, sitting at their table. 'I should go, sorry.' She tried to get up, banging her knees on the leg of the table.

'No, no, you must have cake first.' Mrs Johnson sniffed back her tears. 'Rachel, get the cake.'

'Aw, I have to go now! Since you're making me work there, I should be on time, at least.' Rachel was also what Mrs Suntharalingam would call a *cheeky miss*.

'Your brother will take you. Ronald! Ronald! You will take Rachel to the club?'

Ronald reappeared, Tia trotting happily in front of him. 'What? Say sorry, Tia.'

'Sowee!' The little girl was beaming. 'Cake for me?' Her little brother already had sticky crumbs over his face and hands, and Keisha fought the urge to wipe them off. Just then Tanika leaned over and did it. It was the same, Keisha thought, for mums. Somehow you were the same.

'I'm going down the gym first,' Ronald was saying. 'She can get the tube like all the other staff.'

'Always in the gym, what about your family?'

Rachel shouted, 'Oh, so I'm staff, and you can run the place? How's that fair? I don't even wanna work there. I'm at university, duh!'

'Technical college.' Ronald crammed cake in his mouth.

'Muuum!'

'Oh my goodness, worse than the children, you two, fighting. Keisha, are you working now?'

All eyes on her again. 'I was. Looking for some waitressing now, maybe.'

Then, as if it had been planned out, Mrs Johnson said, 'You should give Keisha a job in the club.'

'For God's sake, Ma!' Ronald exploded. 'Can't give a job to everyone just 'cos you met their mum down Tesco's or something, can I?'

'The Lord's name in vain, oh!'

'Sorry, Ma.'

'And her poor mother passed on! And Rachel has her studies, and she fights with your customers, you said.'

'They piss me off!'

Keisha looked between them, Ronald and his sister and his mum. If she worked in the club she'd be able to look everywhere, go into the office where someone had stuck a bottle into Anthony Johnson's neck. But they were nice people. 'Thanks,' she said. 'I'm sure you've enough staff, though. Better go.'

'Ronald will give you a lift home.' Mrs Johnson never gave up.

'S'OK, I'll get the tube.' She grabbed her denim jacket. 'Thanks, thanks for dinner, thanks, see you soon.' Christ, it was hard to be polite. Easier when everyone was pissed off at you all the time.

'Will we see you at church?' Mrs Johnson called, but Keisha was out the door.

Ronald was standing on the doorstep with his car keys and gym bag. 'Going now. Rachel's not ready.'

'Oh.' She misunderstood him. 'See you then.'

He pointed to his car. 'Come on. I'll drop you.'

'But—'

'It's dark now, look.'

Getting into his little car, Keisha actually felt shocked. Imagine a man caring that she had to walk to the tube in the dark. And he hardly even knew her. She remembered Chris on That Night, leaving her to walk all the way from Camden in her stupid high heels.

'Put your belt on.' Ronald had his hand over her seat back, reversing.

'Oh, sorry.' She hadn't been in a car for so long. Nervous, she babbled at him. 'You don't have to drop me, you know. My mum, she was the same, always saying, Oh, yeah, Keisha'll babysit your kid or walk your dog or something. Like, without even asking me. She sent me to your brother's funeral, 'cos she was sick then. Don't know if you saw me there.' He said nothing. They'd arrived at the station so she undid her belt. 'Right, eh, say thanks to your mum for me.' She got out onto the pavement, again looking round her swiftly. Just in case.

He leaned over and wound the window down. 'Listen, if you want a job, come in next week sometime. No promises.'

'No shit?'

He shrugged. 'Just a trial. Rachel, she's crap at it. You worked in a bar before?'

'Done catering near ten years, and silver service, event bars.' What hadn't she done? As long as the pay was shit and the hours crap, there she was.

'Give us a bell at the club then.' He rolled the window up again.

'Oh, thanks—'

He was gone.

So it was easy, this spying lark – if your mum happened to have had interfering Caribbean ladies as friends, who'd make their sons do anything they wanted. Keisha had gone home with a pound of ginger cake in Mercy's embroidered bag, wrapped up in tinfoil. She put it on the table as she went into Charlotte's. 'Cake there, s'nice,' she called. Then she saw something else on the table, a cheque. Looking at the amount, her eyebrows went up. 'Char? Where you at?'

Muffled, from the bedroom. 'In here.'

Keisha went in. She'd not seen inside Charlotte's room before, but was fairly sure it didn't always look like this. There were clothes all over the bed and floor. 'Jesus, you moving out?'

Charlotte blew hair off her red face. 'Selling stuff, like you said.'

That was Charlotte's wedding dress there, in the long white wrapper. 'How'd you get that cheque?'

Charlotte turned, a skirt draped over her arm, and she held out her hands. They were totally bare, the nails clipped short.

'Fuck! Your ring! Are you OK?'

'Yeah, sure. Like you said, it's only jewellery.' Charlotte rummaged in the cupboard, flinging things out behind her, jeans and jumpers and T-shirts.

'Char?'

'I'm fine!' From inside the wardrobe came a little choked sound.

'Come on, leave it out.'

She came out. Her face was shiny all over, wet and slick with tears. 'It's OK. I just can't stop crying.'

'Listen, I got a job. In the club, like you said. I can go there for a trial, they said.'

'You did?' That worked, and she was smiling through her tears. 'That's amazing!'

'I met the brother, Anthony Johnson's brother. He's running it now. He's . . . well, seems like a nice guy.' She thought about how his muscles rippled, how he'd turned on her when she mentioned his brother.

'He had a brother? No, don't tell me, I can't bear it. I have to focus on Dan.'

'Yeah, well, I had it all today, didn't I. His mum, sister, brother, grandpa . . .'

'Stop.' Charlotte wiped her face on a T-shirt. 'I can't think about it. So you'll go and see what you can find out?' A wavering smile was on her face. 'This could be it, then. We might be able to show Dan didn't do it?'

Keisha remembered the look on Ronald's face, the anger and pain at whoever had killed his brother, but hadn't the heart to crush Charlotte. 'Could be, could be. Come on, let's get the kettle on. There's enough cake there to bust your guts.'

Things were moving on. It was summer already, and Dan had been in prison for nearly a month. Ruby had been away from Keisha, properly away, for a month. Her mum was dead and buried, so was Anthony Johnson. In just a few weeks everything had changed so much, it was like a picture turned upside down and shaken.

Ruby would be off school soon for the summer holidays, so Keisha wouldn't have her sly little trips to hang out by the school gate. Maybe Ruby'd look back and this would be the first summer she really remembered, the summer when she was five-nearly-six, and her mum had left her with strange people. Sometimes, though Keisha tried not to, she thought about what Sandra had said. Adoption. Was it true? If she stayed away from Ruby to keep the kid safe, could she lose her for good?

If you only knew your mum until you were five, would you remember her? Ruby wouldn't remember her granny much, despite all the hours of love and TV and sweets and kisses. There were times Keisha lay and thought all these things, waking up in Charlotte's little room, all her stuff cramped up in one corner around Charlotte's ironing board and box-files and a set of weights that must be Dan's. Charlotte had so much stuff, it must feel like lugging round a massive suitcase all day long. Like you could never just walk away and leave it all, the Laura Ashley sofa and the machine that cut pasta for you, for fuck's sake. For people like Charlotte and Dan and their friends, Keisha thought it must be like they literally got to a point where they couldn't think what to spend their money on any more, so on came the pasta-machines and coffee-makers and what have you.

Those friends, they weren't around much. When she wasn't writing to Dan and getting the letters sent back, or arguing with her mum on the phone, Charlotte kept trying to call her mates and they just blew her off, seemed like. One time she'd gone to a party and she came home early and went in her room and cried for like three hours.

'They all think he did it,' she'd said, red and puffy. Charlotte was practically keeping Boots in business with all her tissues and eye-masks and Rescue Remedy. 'They think he's, you know, racist. And they don't think I should stick by him, because of what he did. This guy asked me tonight how I could live with myself!' She fiddled with her hands all the time too, drove you mad, it did. The white strip where the ring had been stuck out a mile. 'But then I don't know what to say. *Am* I even sticking by him? I sold my ring, I haven't seen him in ages now. Am I even engaged?' And the tears, then, the sobbing and snuffling and gulping in big gasps of air, blowing her nose on Kleenex Ultra-Balm tissues, not cheap at all.

Keisha couldn't afford to cry like this so she didn't cry at all. She went to work at six most nights, came home at four, slept till lunchtime. If Charlotte wasn't in she felt as if she'd no right to be there, as if she had to creep about. Sometimes the phone rang, making her jump. Usually she ignored it, but one day it rang and rang until she had to pick it up just to get some peace. 'Yeah?'

A posh woman's voice. 'Who's that? That's not you, Charlotte?'

'No, er, she's out.'

'And with whom am I speaking?'

'Eh – just a friend.'

'You don't have a name? Don't you know how to answer a telephone?'

Keisha said nothing; she wasn't sure how to respond to that.

'Well, are you hard of hearing? Where is my daughter?' Shit, it was Charlotte's mum.

'She'll be back later, yeah?'

'For goodness' sake.' The phone clattered down. Snooty bitch!

After that, Keisha just left it alone. You never knew who'd be on the other end. In the afternoons she'd just lie there and think about her mum and Ruby – and Chris, wondering where he was. That's who she would have said was her family, those three people, and everyone else could go screw themselves. But they were all gone now, in their own ways.

The first night Keisha had turned up at the club, she was in her usual work mode, i.e. just waiting for them to give her grief. Tapping her foot for trouble, almost.

The manager was called Dario, a skinny black guy with a real Cockney accent. How the hell he was called Dario when he was from Dagenham she didn't know. It was probably Darren. The first time he saw her, 'Dario' gave her this big look up and down. 'Yeah, darlin'?' She was fairly sure he was gay. Mercy would have been shocked.

She squared up to Dario, with his falling-down jeans and tight T-shirt. All the staff wore black work tops, but Dario seemed to have one of the girl ones. 'Here to see Ronald,' she said. The arched eyebrows went up. Did he pluck them? So she was put to work, stacking dirty glasses, shovelling ice until her hand froze, opening about sixty thousand bottles. They didn't let her talk to customers the first night – mostly a black crowd there for the pounding reggae music, but the occasional white wanker with fistfuls of cash. She wasn't allowed to work the big flashing till yet either. Everyone talked like you needed a bloody degree to go on that thing.

At the end of the night she was knackered, and she could see Dario looking at her with a bit of a smile. 'Too much for you, darlin'?'

She slammed the fridge door shut. 'Nope. Been cleaning up actual shit for months, so this is nothing.'

'Hmm. Well, you'll have to see if Ronald wants you to stay, babes.'

Babes. He could fuck right off. It was the most annoying thing when people called you 'darling' and 'sweetheart', and you could see all the time they were hating you inside. Like lying, it was.

Ronald was walking across the club, rolling on his feet, as if he was thinking hard. He towered over everyone else and seemed surprised to see her. 'How's takings, mate?' he asked Dario.

'Not bad, picking up.' She'd overheard that the club had been quiet since Anthony died, except for some weirdos who asked where 'it' was found. 'Fucking coffin-chasers,' Dario called them.

'So?' She looked at Ronald. 'I did me trial, like you said.'

'Oh.' He scratched his shaved head. 'She do OK, Dar mate?'

Dario/Darren smiled a bit. 'Better than wiping shitty arses, I bet.'

'Eh?'

He dumped a bag of ice in the sink. 'She'll do. Not as stroppy as your sister.' That was what he thought then, anyway. Because pretty much everyone hated Rachel. She was always late, swanning in like Paris Hilton or someone, just 'cos her family owned the place. 'Little Miss World-owes-me-a-living,' Dario called her, though to her face he called her 'gorgeous'. 'All right, gorgeous? Looking a treat.' And kissy-kissy on the cheek. Yuck.

Meanwhile Charlotte was getting up every day around about when *This Morning* came on, and going out to work in jobs Keisha's agency found her. They didn't really like Keisha there, not since she'd spilled gravy all over the bare shoulders of some posh bitch at a silver-service do. And shouted out, 'MotherFUCKER!' at the same time (well, some of it got on Keisha's hand too). They must like Charlotte though, with her nice ways and blonde hair, because she seemed to be out most days at the nursing home or in staff canteens in big branches of Sainsbury's or Tesco's. What was surprising was how behind closed doors there was a whole city of crap jobs out there, and most of them meant you came home stinking of old burned coffee. It was a smell like vomit that you could never wash out of your hands; Keisha never drank coffee because of it.

The first night Charlotte worked a shift, Keisha heard her come in about five in the morning, and opened the door to see if she was OK. Charlotte had eyes like a zombie and her white shirt was stained all over with baked beans. 'You survived?'

Charlotte was half-staggering. 'Tired.'

'But you did it? Served the toast and made tea and stuff? S'easy, yeah?'

Charlotte shook her head. 'Dunno. I couldn't find anything. Didn't know how to work the urn. I felt like a div, to be honest. Have to sleep now.' She went to bed and slept in her underwear, chucking the dirty shirt and trousers straight onto the floor. But fair play to her, next day she got up and went out again. Who'd have thought she had it in her, to serve up eggs for hours, surrounded by the smell of crap? The posh girl wasn't as weak as she looked, in fact.

Once Keisha was settled in to work it was easy to find her way around. She hated being the new girl, always did in her jobs, people giving you funny looks and going, Oh no, we don't do it *that* way. How was she meant to know? She worked hard, no one could say she didn't, whipping the tops off bottles and crushing up the ice and chopping the lemons so everything was ready at their elbows for the bar staff. Rachel was very slow, she noticed, looking round her as if the bottles and glasses would magically dance up to her on their own.

'Here,' Keisha muttered sometimes, shoving mint at her, as Rachel stood gaping at a man who'd asked for three mojitos (wanker). The white customers always wanted stuff like that.

'A mo-whato?' Rachel said. Dumb cow. Keisha wondered what this university was like, where she was meant to be studying Business Management. 'Cos as far as she could see, Rachel was as thick as Bailey's Irish Cream.

All the time Keisha worked, Dario/Darren was watching her with his eyebrows and his little smile. Noticing. 'We chop the limes in wedges, not slices,' he said. 'We give the change on saucers – make sure there's enough.' Always something. She thought he was testing her, seeing if she'd blow up, so she did what he said. Even if sometimes she chopped the limes so hard it left big scores in the board.

She kept going. After a while it got better, Dario eased off, she saw him watching her still, nodding sometimes. But Rachel didn't seem to get any better. When Dario spoke to her about giving the wrong change or putting in the wrong mixer, she threw a strop, shouting, 'I'm trying!' One night she flipped. She'd given some arrogant tosser Sprite instead of tonic, and he kicked up such a massive fuss Dario had to come over and say he could have more drinks for free. 'Sorry, mate, so sorry, yeah?' Under his breath he said, 'Wanker. Rachel, babes, we need to talk. I'll go over the buttons again with you.'

'For fuck's sake, I learned it like five times.' Rachel looked tearful.

'Yeah, but you still don't know it, babes.'

Another customer came over, a black guy with dreadlocks, and he asked for two Coronas. That was easy – Keisha had them open and the lime wedges in before Rachel even went to the till. That was when the trouble started. Rachel put in the wrong price, and the till was making a beeping sound. 'Oh, shit. What'd I do? Where's the Coronas?'

'Under "bottled drinks",' Keisha shouted, mopping up melted ice. Even though she wasn't 'till-trained' (what a ponce) she knew that.

'What? Where?' Rachel was poking random buttons. 'Shit.'

'Hey, can ya get a move on?' The customers were getting fed up.

'Here.' There wasn't time to be nice. Keisha shoved Rachel aside and pressed some keys on the till. 'Right. Seven-eighty, please, mate.' She put his twenty-pence change on the plate with the napkin and he took it. Fair play, she'd have done the same herself. Seven-eighty for two beers was criminal.

Dario had been watching. 'OK, Miss Keisha know-it-all, you're on the till. Rachel, babes, go out back and clean your face.'

Once her break came up, Keisha went out to the staffroom. Rachel was curled up on the sofa clutching a tissue.

'Hard work, that.' Keisha was sweating. 'You OK?'

Rachel sniffed loudly. 'I hate it, you know. I wanted to be a student, like, and live in a flat, not serve beer all night. Some of them customers are wankers.'

'Yep, they are that.'

'It's just . . . I'm so crap at it, and I hate it, then you come and you're all good and shit and you just started.'

Keisha felt like being kind. 'Well, I been doing shit jobs since I was fourteen. Working in the corner shop, Maccy D's, the old folk's home – after a while you just know how to do stuff.' She saw Rachel was crying again. 'If you don't like it, can you not pack it in? Your mum wouldn't mind, would she?'

'No.' Rachel gulped. 'Ronald would. God, I miss our Anthony.'

So that was it. Sitting beside her, Keisha looked at the clock; her break wasn't long. 'Been about a month now, has it?'

Rachel nodded, mashing the manky tissue up in her fingers. 'You met him that one time? He was always the life and soul, our Anthony. When he was young, Mum was so afraid for him she'd lock him in the house. 'Cos of gangs and stuff, you know? Mum used to say, That boy, he'll come home in a coffin one day and break my heart in pieces.' She blew her nose. 'But then we thought he'd be OK. He meets Tanika, has the kids, gets this place . . . But look!' She cried again a bit. 'Got himself fucking killed after all.'

Keisha didn't know what to say. This was dangerous. 'I thought it was just like some banker dude lost his temper? Random, like.'

Rachel dabbed her eyes and looked round, lowering her voice. 'Don't say nothing, yeah, but Anthony, he sorta borrowed cash for this place. Losing money, see. So he needs cash, he goes back to his old mates in the gang, don't he?'

Keisha pressed her nails into her hands. She knew more than she wished she did that once or twice, Chris had been involved in getting debts back. And not exactly for legitimate bailiffs. 'What're you saying?'

'Oh, I dunno. Shit, they never told me nothing, Anthony and our Ronald. I'm just the little baby sister, aren't I? But Ronald's in there every night with the accounts, never lets anyone else near the computer, whatever's on there. I know he was worried, Anthony. I know I was worried for him.'

'But – you told the police it was the banker. He said racist shit, didn't he?'

Rachel sniffed. 'Mel said he did, and I thought I remembered . . . I dunno. I was upset, wasn't I?'

Upset enough to knock Charlotte's tooth out, yeah. Keisha decided Rachel might be annoying and up herself, but she knew a lot more than you'd think. 'I'm sorry. Sucks, what happened.'

'Ta.' Rachel sniffled some more. 'Thanks for doing the till. I'm crap at it.'

That was when Dario threw open the door and said it was nice they had time to chat and brush their hair or whatever, but he had a bar to run and could they get their arses out into it? Rachel gave Keisha a roll of the eyes as they got up, and after that they were sort of OK with each other.

People got used to her at the bar. When they did, it was easy to slip about and no one'd pay you a blind bit of notice. The door out to the back of the club opened with a code that all the staff knew. It led into a corridor that had the staffroom, the storeroom full of barrels and stuff, and at the other end, the office where Anthony Johnson had died choking on his own blood. At the end of the corridor was a fire exit, and that opened out into an alley where the bins and things were. Keisha'd seen it open when they got deliveries, and she couldn't hear any alarm. You could hardly see the door when it was closed.

After watching for a few nights as people took in barrels

and took out rubbish and stepped out for fags, she decided to test it out. Sneaking down past the office with a load of dirty glasses, she gave the back door a nudge with her foot and it opened. Nothing happened. But maybe it went off somewhere else?

She went into the staffroom, where Dario was smoothing down his hair. 'Er, hiya? I knocked the back door open by accident.' Accidentally on purpose, more like.

'So?'

'So, says it's on an alarm. Did I set it off?'

He was looking in the mirror. 'Nah, it don't work. We lock it up last thing. S'OK.'

Well, that was a bit of a find, wasn't it? She wondered had the police, so sure they'd got the right guy, figured out that any random person could get in from the *outside*. The side of the door facing into the alley had no handles, but she'd been around Chris long enough to know you could open that in a second with a knife or something. Keisha stood in the corridor, thinking hard. She thought of Chris leaving the club that night. Going home. What was he up to in between? She thought of Charlotte, standing outside waiting for Dan. What had she seen? There had to be something.

'Not busy?' She jumped. Fuck! Ronald was standing in the doorway of the office. He looked tired, like always, and pissed off.

'Oh yeah, just doing the glasses.'

'Are you done? 'Cos it's rammed out there, you know.'

Her heart was racing. 'OK, OK. Christ, you can be really arsey, you know that?' Shit, she hadn't meant to say that. He was her boss. She'd get sacked.

He looked sad for a moment. 'You're right. I am arsey. Wish I didn't have to be.' He went back in and she saw him sit down at the computer and put his head in his hands. His feet were right near where his brother's head had fallen back, dead.

Keisha would have said to him, 'What's up with you, then?' But she knew. Even without Rachel's story of lost money and old gang connections, she knew. And Ronald thought, everyone thought – the police, the Johnsons, Dan's family, even Dan, for Christ's sake – they all thought they knew who did it. The only people who thought something else were herself – and what did she know, really? – and Charlotte, keeping her faith, not able to believe she'd been about to marry a killer.

Keisha went back into the noise and dark of the bar.

Dario shouted over the racket, 'Where's your head at tonight?'

Her head was everywhere. She was thinking, you never knew anyone, not really. You never knew what someone would do, or how many ways they would let you down. And in that moment, without knowing why, she had already decided not to tell Charlotte about the door. Not yet, anyway.

Memories. Bits of the past. She lay in the room in the long mornings and they were all she had. The day she found out about Ruby – not really that much of a surprise, since she hadn't taken her pill in months.

Chris's face when she showed him the stupid little stick, shy, nervous to her stomach. 'Fuck.' He'd gone white as a sheet. 'How the fuck?'

She'd got angry. 'How d'you think? Never used nothing to stop it, did you?'

'Thought you did.'

'Well, looks like you thought wrong.' This wasn't how it was meant to be. He was meant to hold her in his arms and spin her round and all that shit.

His face when he looked up. 'Christ, Keisha, I never wanted this. My dad . . .'

Chris's dad, father of eight kids (that they knew about), was an Irish drunk, falling out of Kilburn Wetherspoons any day of the week you wanted to walk past.

'Thought you'd be pleased.' Her eyes filled up when she said it. 'It's your kid, you know.'

'Shit. Shit. I need to think.' And he'd got up and gone, and she'd sat there on the grotty sofa with her little wee-stained stick in her hand. Fuck, what an idiot. Up the duff, as bad as her mum, and now she'd probably get fired from Maccy D's, and he'd most likely give her the elbow. That was when he'd started up with the gangs, for the easy money, the bling. And he didn't really want some pregnant, grumpy, mixed-race girlfriend cramping his style. As she sat there and waited, she'd known how it would be. But he came back that night, with a bunch of crappy carnations, the yellow discount sticker from Tesco's on the side. And it was OK, at least for a while. Until what happened to Ruby, of course.

There was a noise outside the room. Keisha looked at her phone and saw it was getting late, nearly time for *Loose Women*. She got up in her 'sleepwear', as Charlotte would call it, sports shorts and a man's T-shirt. 'All right?' When Charlotte came in she always felt like she should be cleaning something, doing something.

Charlotte was opening and shutting cupboard doors; she'd done a load of proper shopping, in Waitrose, no less. That was a first. There were bananas, bread, carrots. Proper things, not just Pot Noodles. 'What's all this?'

Charlotte shrugged. 'Don't you just feel we've been eating rubbish for weeks?'

That was all Keisha ever ate. 'Where was you today?'

'In that canteen again. But they've got me a new place next, homeless shelter. I'm not sure I'll like that.'

'They're OK, those. Pay's better.'

'Yeah.' Charlotte turned round to her, holding a packet of biscuits. 'Listen. I called DC Hegarty today. You know, the policeman who arrested Dan.'

'Oh.' Shit, the police. She'd been wondering when this would come.

'He's coming round tomorrow. I told him some of the stuff you found out, about the club's money troubles and all that.'

That explained the shopping then, and Charlotte looked different somehow too. Keisha peered at her. She'd put make-up on, that was it. Mascara, lip gloss.

Come to think of it, what with all the working nights, she hadn't seen Charlotte much that week. So, this was for the policeman, that bloody annoying one who'd hauled Keisha in after the girls beat Charlotte up. She didn't like him, his green eyes sharp like he could see all the way through you. Nosy bugger. 'He's coming tomorrow night?'

Charlotte was staring into her cupboard. Maybe she was thinking, Viennese sandwich or chocolate chip? Make Keisha dob Chris in before or after the cucumber sandwiches? 'Hmm? Yes, in the evening.'

'Oh, right.' Keisha could play this game too. 'Probably be at work then, won't I.' She sat down and turned on the telly, put her feet on the coffee table. She knew that drove Charlotte mad.

Charlotte snapped out of her thoughts. 'What? No, you need to be here.'

'What d'you need me for? You and him can have all those nice biccies together.'

Charlotte came over and stood in front of the telly. 'That's what you call helping?'

'I found out all about the gangs and that. Told you what I know, didn't I.'

'Did you?' Charlotte's face was getting red. 'Look at me, will you? Is there something else?'

'No! For fuck's sake, I'm trying to watch *Loose Women*. Anyway, if anyone knows something, it's you.'

'What's that supposed to mean?' Charlotte looked furious.

'You must have seen something, why else'd Chris be after you? Stands to reason. If you'd just tell me – well, maybe it'd make him keep away. Leave us alone.' And Ruby.

'I don't remember anything, I already said. I don't know what he wants with me. And if you've told me everything, why won't you make a statement? I mean, do you think the law doesn't apply to you or something?'

Keisha stood up stiffly. 'I'm not fucking stupid.'

Charlotte sighed, running her hands through her hair. 'I know. That's what's so annoying. Are you scared Chris'll find out? Because I hate to tell you, I think it's a bit late for that.'

It wasn't fair. Keisha didn't need this shit. 'You sprung it on me! I get up and there's you taking out biscuits for him! "Oh Officer, would you like some more tea?" Anyone'd think you fancied him.' Shit, she couldn't talk to the cops. What if they lifted her? Then who would stop Chris getting to the kid?

Charlotte took in a deep sucking breath. 'Oh, fuck off, will you?'

Silence. Neither of them said anything. Charlotte slumped

down on the sofa, wringing her hands together. 'I didn't mean to say that. I'm just – I can't go on like this. I haven't heard from Dan for weeks. I don't even know if he's . . . Look. That came a few days back.' She slapped a letter down on the table. 'He's going under in there, just so you know. Look at it – someone beat him up.'

Keisha wouldn't look at the letter. 'Well, whatever. I have to go. You wanted me to work in the club, remember? Trying to find out shit for you?'

Charlotte put her head in her hands. 'Whatever. Do what you want.'

Keisha bashed about in the bathroom getting ready, making as much noise as she could. She made a point of using Charlotte's bottle of that perfumey Jo Malone stuff, cost, like, twenty-five quid. Criminal. Then, ignoring Charlotte who was still sitting at the table, she went out, banging the door behind her, so angry she almost forgot to peer into the bushes just in case someone was hiding. As she stomped along to the bus stop, she was getting more and more pissed off. Bloody Charlotte! She'd *told* her, she'd said she didn't want to talk to the police, when they wouldn't believe her anyway, when she had no proof, when Chris was still round somewhere, and hello, he wouldn't exactly be loving it if she told the fucking cops on him! Charlotte was so stupid some-times, like she came from another planet where the police were your chums. Keisha was glad she hadn't told her about the door. Why should she? She had to look out for herself, her kid.

The bus came and Keisha got on, giving the driver a look that just dared him to make trouble. Yeah? Yeah? He didn't even look at her. Well, fuck him. She swung into a seat at the back of the bus and turned the music on her phone up high, swivelling round to see if any old biddies wanted to tap her on the shoulder and say they could hear it through her headphones and could she turn it down please, it was meant to be a *personal* stereo, wasn't it?

She was still pissed off when she got into the club, banging the door into the staffroom and chucking her denim jacket over a chair.

'Afternoon to you too, Keisha.' Ronald was in already as well, in his office across the corridor, computer on again.

She stomped out again in her staff T-shirt. 'Well? What'm I on tonight? You want me out back hauling bottles, in case I upset the poor little punters? Oh poor them, so sad if they want diet tonic and they get normal instead, it's a tragedy . . .' She was storming off as she ranted, about to go and find Dario so he'd tell her what to do, but Ronald said, 'Hey, come in here.'

'In there?' She hovered in the doorway. Although it had been cleaned and repainted, she couldn't go near it without thinking about the blood all over the floor.

'Yeah. Shut the door.'

Was she fired? 'Listen, right, I didn't mean it, I'll be nicer, honest I will.'

Ronald didn't look up from the screen. 'Good to know, Keisha. You won't be calling the punters *fucking arseholes* any more then?'

She didn't think he'd heard her ranting in the staffroom. 'Ah. No.'

Ronald looked up. 'Rachel said you was here that night. When my brother got killed. Says you came with some white fella who wanted business with him.'

Keisha hung back against the filing cabinet. 'Yeah, so? Lots of people were.'

He just looked at her. 'You gonna tell me who he was?'

Shit, what was the point? Rachel would've told him. 'Chris. He was with me. My, you know, my boyfriend.'

'Your kid's dad?'

'Yeah, but like, we're split now.' She stared at the newly painted floor, not wanting Ronald to look at her and see somehow that she'd left Chris after he mashed her face up.

'Why'd you come that night?'

'Dunno. Chris was a bouncer, like, before all the credit-crunch shit. Thought he wanted to talk to your Anthony about work.'

Still Ronald looked. He said, 'Police talk to you? Rachel told me about the court, and the girl, that fella's missus. She's sorry for that now. She was upset.'

'Yeah, the police talked to me after it.'

'And?'

'And what?'

'What'd you tell them? What'd you do that night?'

She was tired. 'I went home, didn't I?'

'And your fella went too? Chris?'

Shit. SHIT. 'Er, dunno. Nah, think he went ahead, said he felt sick.' Her heart was beating so fast he could probably hear it in the small room.

'Keisha. Darlin'.'

'What? I told you all I know.' She might cry at the way he said *darlin'*.

For a long time Ronald said nothing. 'You can trust me. Maybe I'm arsey, like you said, but I look after my family, yeah?'

'I'm not your family.' She was just some girl who could fuck up his life and everyone else's too. But when he said it, she looked up at him, heart thudding. *Family.*

'You'd tell me if you knew something?'

'I don't.'

Slowly, he sighed. 'Right. OK. Go on, then.'

Outside in the corridor she let out a shaky breath, like a balloon coming down.

'Got you too, did he?'

'Fuck!' She jumped. 'What're you doing?'

'Getting ready, duh.' Rachel was in the staffroom with the door wide open, pulling her T-shirt on.

'What's up with your Ronald? Gave me a right grilling.'

'Yeah, sorry.' Rachel patted out the halo of her hair. 'I told him you was here that night. Didn't mean no harm by it. He's been over us all, me, Dario too.'

'Why? What's got up his arse?'

Rachel gave herself a last look in the mirror, probably thinking, *Oh wow, I am so gorgeous, who can resist?* 'Had a visitor, didn't he. About that cash our Anthony owed.'

'What?' Keisha leaned back against the wall as if someone had punched her in the stomach.

'Yeah, some fella came round. I weren't here and Ron didn't know him. I thought maybe it was that Chris, your boyfriend. You split, didn't ya?'

She couldn't breathe. 'W-why would *he* be here?'

Rachel rolled her eyes. 'Our Ant might be Mum's golden boy now, but he weren't no saint. I told you he was in a gang years ago? The Parky Boys – they lent him some dosh. So they're gonna send someone round to get it back, aren't they. So maybe it's the same fella what was here the night our Anthony—' She looked at Keisha. 'Hey, you OK? You gone all white. More than usual, like.'

Hegarty

'Get that down you, then. None of your soft London drinks here.'

Hegarty looked with distaste at the pint of 'real ale' his Uncle Sean had put down in front of him. 'Er – ta.'

They were watching to see did he drink it or ask for a lager instead, or worse, a spritzer. A Smirnoff Ice. Nothing would surprise his Barrow family now about Matthew Hegarty and his southern city ways. He swallowed a big gulp and tried not to gag at the bitterness.

His uncles – Sean, Paddy, Seamus – let out big spews of laughter. Sean slapped him on the back. 'You don't get that down south, eh?'

'Nope.' There were lots of things he didn't get down south. Like buffets of warm sausage rolls out of Tesco's. Like three solid days talking about why immigration needs to end before there's a mosque on every corner. Like bored off his tits as God-awful pop music played on a loop. The Vengaboys, for fuck's sake! As he watched from the bar, where the men of the family huddled for protection against dancing, his Auntie Sheila shimmied past, waving her arms in the air. 'Come on, lads, doo-doo doo-doo do dooo-do . . .'

'Pissed off her face,' said Uncle Paddy, himself on his tenth pint.

'Excuse us.' Hegarty made a break for freedom, his uncles shouting, 'Aye, goes through them southern bladders, lad,' and avoided being dragged onto the dance-floor by his mother. 'Come on, our Matty, dance with your mam!'

'Need a slash,' he shouted over the music – if you could call it that. A slash, Christ, he'd better get back to

London soon before he started saying 'asylumseekersbenefits-scroungers' all in one word like his Uncle Seamus did.

He slipped out of the hotel's French windows onto their 'lakeview terrace'. The air was cool and clear out there; he gulped it in like water after the reek of perfume and BO inside. The lake glittered like spilled milk just yards away, the dark hills peaceful except for the din of the Hegartys and their crap taste in music. 'Our Nicola' was the first girl in the family to get hitched – although her five-year-old daughter was flower girl – and the Hegartys were making a big do of it. He hadn't wanted to come, not just because it would be boring, with crap food and worse music (all so far true), but because his family had no problem asking, So, when's it your turn? Nicola, the bride, was twenty-three. Hegarty had five years on her, and his two older brothers had been married for years, four kids between them. But for Matthew Hegarty, nothing, no one. He tried not to think about *her* again, wishing he had a cigarette.

'Hiya, Matty.' Matty. Oh no. Apart from his mother, only one person called him that. He turned away from the lake's moonlit beauty. 'Hiya, Danni.'

Danielle, his first girlfriend. Last girlfriend, if you didn't count anything under a month. Her face was pasty in the dark. 'All right?'

'Yeah, how're you?' Crap, he'd better hug her. Her feathery hair thing tickled his face. She smelled the same, of Peach Schnapps and sweat. 'You look nice.' You had to say that to women at weddings, even if they were poured into a pink strapless dress a size too small for them.

Danielle smiled a bit. 'Ta. You too. Hoped you'd be here.'

He said nothing.

'Your mam said you was doing well for yourself, down

there.' She spoke of London like it was another country. 'You don't miss it here?' Her nod took it all in, the glittering lake, the mountains, the stars in a dark, orange-free sky, and also the Girls Aloud and the recycled *Sun* opinions of his family.

'Sometimes. The fresh air, at least.'

'And your family? Your mates?' She stepped closer. Crap.

'How're you, Danni? Any, er, romance on the scene?'

'Was seeing Paul – you know, Paul Gregg from school. He had that Star Wars bag?'

'Oh, yeah.'

'But I finished it. Didn't feel it, you know. The spark. Like in *Sex and the City*.'

'Sure.' He'd rather stick pins in his eyes than watch *Sex and the City*.

'Hear you're going out to Tom's wedding in Australia.'

'I am, yep. You?'

'No. Didn't really keep up with him after you and me split.'

The music had changed. Robbie Williams, 'Angels.' Enough to make you vomit, but Danni's face had softened. 'You want to dance, Matty? For old times' sake?'

Crap. This was what cigarettes were for. Why had he quit? 'Sure, in a minute.'

She gave him sort of a half-smile over her shoulder. 'Well, find me.'

He watched her walk away, remembering her slim back under her T-shirt, that first disco they went to at fifteen. What was wrong with him? Danielle was a lovely girl, if a bit heftier than she had been. There were lots of girls here, pals of Nicola's, girls he'd known for years. But all he could think was how that one was too big, that one too skinny, that one's blonde hair too fake. None of them were *her*. That was the problem.

It wasn't the sort of thing he'd expected to happen. Normally the women he saw on arrests were rough as, stringy hair, missing teeth, shouting at him and sometimes throwing things. So when he burst into the flat that morning, and she was there with her silk nightie, all that hair round her bare shoulders, it was a shock. He'd tried not to look but it wasn't easy. And then later, he'd interviewed her and seen her name written down in front of him: Charlotte Miller. *Charlotte*. Even in her jeans and her face tired and confused, she'd been lovely, just so lovely he had to force himself to look at his notes and remember it was her fiancé who'd most likely stuck the guy in the club like you might slice up a juicy steak. He remembered how she'd fiddled and twisted the diamond flashing on her thin finger, as if she'd lost weight and it was too big for her.

Inside, the families were making a circle round Nicola, her strapless dress falling down to show her tattoos, and her lumpish new husband busting out of his hired waistcoat. What would Charlotte's wedding have been like? If he hadn't turned up at her door, she'd have been married for a while now, and happy, most like.

The glass doors opened and it was his dad, smaller and wirier than Hegarty's loud uncles. 'Your mam's looking for you. What you at out here, lad?'

He looked at his father, Mike Hegarty, aka Maverick Mike, ex of the Cumbrian Police Service. A suit that was too big for him and, underneath, muscles now softening with age.

'Dad? Can I ask you something?'

'Make it quick, lad, buffet's out.'

'Did you ever . . . Did you ever worry that you'd got the wrong guy for a case?' It came out in a rush.

His dad peered at him. 'You in some kind of trouble at work?'

'No, nothing like that.' At least, he hoped not. He'd tried to follow it up, hadn't he? But the trail had gone cold, and anyway everything pointed to Stockbridge. Didn't it?

'Let me tell you something, lad. You will get the wrong fella. Even if it's not now, you will. And you'll wonder, did I bang up some innocent man? But it's not your decision, is it? You just bring them in, son. Let the courts decide.'

But it was his life, Dan Stockbridge's. And hers. 'Dad? You met Mam on the job, didn't you?'

'I did that. Lifted her fella for drunk and disorderly, took your mam out the next night.'

'Oh.'

Hegarty Senior laughed a tobacco-stained rattle. 'You're only human, lad. Now come on in before the sausage rolls get cold.'

He could never tell his father anything, never tell anyone that he was out here thinking about a suspect's girl. A man he'd put away, his biggest case, and he couldn't stop thinking about his girlfriend's hair and her mouth and the tears drying on her face.

He cleared his throat. 'Coming, Dad.'

In his pocket was his phone and on it the message Charlotte had sent him earlier, five weeks to the day since he'd first seen her. *Hi*, it said. *It's Charlotte Miller. Wondering if I could call you when you're free? I really need your help.*

So there it was, her text.

All typed right, spelled right, none of that *dat de u* stuff from her. Hegarty didn't write much. He spent hours on his police reports, using a dictionary, even a thesaurus sometimes, just trying to get the words right. 'Rainman', they called him, which was sort of unfair 'cos the point of Rainman was he was a natural genius. He wouldn't need to use a dictionary, would he? But the only thing harder than stopping a nickname was trying to start your own.

Hegarty was back at his desk in London, still aching and hungover from the wedding and the nearly worse trip back on Virgin Trains. Now he was picking his way through a packet of Nurofen and drinking his fifth cup of rank station coffee, and in his head turning over and over Charlotte's short text. What did it mean? What could he help her with?

'Back from the north, Rainman?' Susan was so close he could smell her cheesy breakfast roll.

He winced. 'Shit, don't sneak up on me like that.'

Not much put Susan off. 'Gorra hangover?' She leaned in. 'You wanna try my supplements, you do.'

Susan believed firmly in the power of herbal healing – that and Jesus Christ. Hegarty wasn't convinced about either.

'Yeah, yeah. You want me for something?'

'Boss wants to see you.'

That couldn't be good. But there was no way the boss could know about Charlotte's text, could he?

DI Bill Barton was rubbing his stomach when Hegarty went in, staring at the huge pile of paper in front of him. Hegarty noticed an open pack of Rennies on the desk.

'You wanted me, sir?' Although the boss did his best to be friendly and informal, it was still a sir and last name kind of place, and there was no changing that.

'Matthew. Hi.' Genuine warmth. 'Everything ticking over, any problems?'

'Nossir.' Apart from a ranging hangover and a developing obsession with a suspect's missus, that was.

'There's been another incident. Like the one at Kingston Town.'

Hegarty's mouth fell open. 'A bottle stabbing?'

'No, a knife this time.' The boss clutched his stomach and winced. 'Same as before, guy in a bar, in the neck, though. Word is he owed money. But someone got to him in time, lucky sod.'

'Not dead?'

'No. Can't make an ID though. Forensics is in.'

'So – what's it mean, sir?'

'You never found that other witness, did you? The white guy in the photo?'

'From Kingston Town? No. No, he scarpered.' Hegarty sighed – he couldn't explain he'd got an ID on the guy, working on the side, and then lost the trail. 'You think . . . you think there's maybe a chance it wasn't Stockbridge?' Saying out loud what he'd been thinking for so long almost made him gasp.

'Now, I didn't say that, Matthew. The evidence, as your report put it so well, was weighty and compelling.' Hegarty blushed at this reference to his wordy flourishes. The boss spoke slowly. 'There are, how can I say it . . . a lot of people who want this Kingston Town case wrapped up. Race relations, class struggle. Not good for London.'

'Nossir. Did we ever get that other CCTV I mentioned? You know, from the dry-cleaner's across from the Kingston Town club?'

The DI looked blank. 'I'm sure we followed up every angle, Matthew. While always being mindful of resources.'

'Yessir.'

'But look into this other one, will you?'

'You want me on it?'

'Want you leading it, Matthew.' The boss beamed like he'd just given Hegarty a Christmas present. And it was true, it was a good sign to be asked to lead an investigation.

'Thank you, sir.' Bloody hell. He was well on his way to that promotion. His own team! No more Susan and her Bible, her breath! Hegarty went back to his desk and dialled Charlotte's number.

She looked like she was about to cry again, he thought, when he met her in the café on Mornington Crescent. He'd dodged buses to run across the road from the station, then ducked in to the greasy spoon looking for other officers; this was the place for them. 'Charlotte?' It was the first time he'd called her that and not Miss Miller.

She had a cup of soupy tea in front of her, and the plastic table was gritty and sparkling with sugar. 'Was it bad to contact you? I didn't know if I should.'

'It's OK.' He'd decided it was a witness interview, nothing wrong in that. Even if the case was officially closed. 'What was the problem?'

'This.' Sighing, she laid a thin piece of paper on the table. 'It went to Dan's parents, but they won't help – they say they're too far away to come. He didn't even ask for me.' She looked miserable.

Hegarty examined the paper, a letter from the prison. 'He's been ill, then.'

She nodded. 'More blackouts, they said. He's been moved to solitary.' She looked up, her eyes red-rimmed. 'That means he's been in trouble, doesn't it? People have been hurting him.'

She was staring at her hands like she might cry any minute. He was shocked at the change in her. She'd put on some weight, and her clothes were drab, her hair dull. But still. Didn't make a blind bit of difference. He put his hand under the table to stop from touching hers. 'He'll be OK. It's not like you see on telly, prison. They look after them.'

'But I don't know that! That's what's so hard – I haven't seen him in weeks. I've no idea how he is . . . I can't get through to him at all. I suppose you've seen the papers. All that Banker Butcher stuff, it's awful.'

Hegarty didn't know what to say. 'Must be hard, and you on your own.'

'I'm not really on my own. That's the other thing.'

For a second he thought, oh crap, she has a new man. But why'd she be here, then, trying not to cry?

'Long story. A friend sort of moved in. She – well, it doesn't really matter how. But she knows stuff. Keisha? I think you interviewed her once. After the court.'

Hegarty stared at her. The angry girl from the hearing, Chris Dean's missus! All this time she'd been up in Hampstead with Charlotte? 'Didn't know you knew her.'

'No, I didn't. It's kind of a long story, like I said. But I do now, and she knows stuff. That's what I wanted to tell you. She really knows, but she won't come forward.'

Hegarty sat back. He'd heard of this happening before, a family member or spouse of someone you arrested would come to you weeks or months or even years later with some 'new' evidence showing that the person they loved could never have done this terrible thing. They'd set up websites, they'd send huge packets of documents without enough postage and you'd have to pay the difference. He should walk away, he should take his manky tea and leave. 'What is it you want from me?' He said it as kindly as he could.

'I thought – would you come and see her? She thinks you're all out to get her. But I promise you, she really does know things.'

Hegarty was leaving. He really was. But he thought of the new stabbing, and the picture of Chris Dean he still had in his desk. 'You think there's new evidence?'

She nodded earnestly. 'I honestly wouldn't waste your time if I didn't.' She paused. 'After you came round that day, I just felt . . . Well, I knew you would help me. I just sort of felt it.' She stared down at her tea, embarrassed.

So somehow he found himself agreeing to go to her house the next night. He didn't tell anyone at the station, they'd only laugh.

Hegarty'd had a bad day. First he had to go and interview the cleaner who'd found his boss gurgling blood all over the floor of a pub in Hammersmith. This one also had predictable gang connections, and money owed. The boss himself was still in hospital and too weak to talk, and Hegarty got nowhere with the cleaner, who didn't know much English and was clearly terrified of the police.

'I no see,' he kept saying, swivelling his eyes back and forth. One of those 'asylumseekersbenefitsscroungers' as his uncles would have said.

Hegarty tried again. 'You found the owner on the office floor, bleeding. What happened then?'

'Yes.'

'What happened? Did you see anyone else come out?'

'Yes. Yes.'

Hegarty sighed. 'Listen to me, Mr, er . . .' Crap, he could see the surname written down but it had too many letters in it. 'Er, Mr. Did you see anyone?'

'Bloods. Much bloods.'

'Yes, blood, but was there a person? Did you see the assailant – eh, the person who did it?'

'Yes, bloods. Yes.'

So he gave that up as a bad job. It would take them ages to find a translator who could speak whatever African language it was, even if they could scrape up the funds, and it turned out the bar CCTV was just for show and hadn't worked in months. Typical. He looked at his watch; time to follow up the other angles. Was that even what he was doing? Hegarty wondered about these little side trips of his – the club, Charlotte's house. Why do that when he had his suspect nicely locked up on remand? He told himself it was the legendary policeman's hunch his dad had always talked about, and not just because Charlotte Miller had asked him for help. With that he headed up to leafier Belsize Park, and Charlotte herself.

But now he was there and talking to this Keisha girl was like pulling teeth. She was flashing him evils, as his girl cousins would have said, and when he sat down at the table she got up and went to the sofa, flicking channels on the muted TV.

He was a little shocked at the flat too. A lot dirtier than when he'd made the arrest. It looked like his place, unwashed dishes, pizza boxes in the recycling. And where was the Eames chair, and that nice painting from the wall?

Charlotte looked back and forth between them, tea slopping out of the cups in her shaking hands. 'Keesh, are you sure you don't want tea? It's Tetley.'

'No, thank you.'

'There's biscuits, nice ones . . .' She trailed off. Hegarty took a biscuit, chocolate chip with a chocolate coating, very nice. Could have done with those at the station.

Charlotte cleared her throat. 'So, DC – er, sorry, what should I call you?'

'So long as it's not Matty, I don't mind.' She looked confused. 'Matthew, Matt, whatever you like.' They were about the same age, him and her.

She looked up at him from under her lashes. 'Like I told you the other day, Keisha came round to see me a bit after – everything. It was really kind of her, because she sort of like came to warn me.'

He thought he heard the other girl snort.

'Warn you?'

'Basically Keisha was there that night, in the club, with her boyfriend.'

'Wait.' He fumbled in his satchel for the picture printout. 'That him?'

Charlotte stared at it for a while, her brow furrowed. She shook her head. 'I never saw him, not really. Keesh, is that Chris?'

Keisha ignored her as long as she could, then got up with a sigh. 'Give us it.' She peered at the grainy print for a long time.

Charlotte was gripping the table. 'Well?'

'Course it's him. So? It's just some picture.'

Hegarty folded it away. 'I asked you before if you knew him, didn't I?'

She scowled. 'Dunno. Still with him then, wasn't I? Anyway, you'd arrested your fella – or that's what you told the court.'

He decided to play nice. 'You're right, Keisha. We thought all the evidence pointed to Dan, but maybe we missed something, and you spotted it.'

'All right,' she said, after a pause. And she told her convoluted story about this boyfriend, this Chris, and how he'd left the club and her 'freezing my arse off at the bus stop,

I was' – so she'd gone home and there he was in bed, his clothes in a bag and shoes all covered in something sticky and red.

'Blood?' he asked, pen hovering.

'I dunno, not on bloody *CSI*, am I?'

Charlotte sighed. Hegarty shut his book. 'What you've told me is a bit shaky, to be honest. It was weeks ago, and you didn't come forward at the time.'

'He was my fella! I'm not lying.'

'He knows you're not lying, Keesh, but is there anything else, anything at all?' Charlotte leaned forward but Keisha shook her away.

'I said everything I know. What else am I meant to tell you? You can't come after me, it's not fair.'

Hegarty raised his eyebrows. 'I'm not coming after you, miss. You're just a possible witness. You haven't seen Chris since?'

Was it his imagination, or did she hesitate before shaking her head?

Charlotte tried again. 'You didn't say Chris was after me, for some reason. That's why she came, DC, er, Matthew. She saw this friend of Chris's and he said he was after me, and the reason she left in the first place was because he beat her up when he found out she had my purse. With my address, you see?'

'Leave it, Char,' said Keisha, full of steel.

Hegarty looked between the two, the one earnest girl with her fair hair falling into her eyes, the other sulky, arms folded. He could almost hear his dad in his head, the voice of the copper forty years on the job: *Walk off, son. Walk off.* He opened his notebook again. 'Any reason this Chris'd be after you?'

Charlotte frowned. 'I don't know, but I do seem to have this memory where someone pushed past me at the club – maybe outside, maybe inside, I don't know. I can't really remember, it's so frustrating.'

When Charlotte said this, the Keisha girl stiffened. He caught her eye and she looked away. He sighed. 'And how would Chris have got home before you, Keisha, if he went back to the club? You got the bus?'

'Musta got a taxi. Wouldn't get one for me, tight bastard.'

He clicked on his pen and scribbled it down. 'Might be able to find the driver. I'll look into it, no guarantees though.'

'Oh, thank you.' Charlotte nearly knocked over her tea. 'Oh God, I can't tell you, it means so much, just to think maybe it wasn't Dan.'

'Keisha, you'll need to make a sworn statement on this.'

'What?' Her head shot up. 'I'm not swearing nothing.'

'He can't admit it as evidence if you don't make a statement, duh!' Charlotte seemed to be losing patience.

'Yeah, yeah, who died and made you Legally Blonde? Chris'll kill me if he finds out, like actually kill me.'

'But they'll arrest him, for God's sake!'

'And you believe that, same coppers what came round here and lifted Dan?'

That shut Charlotte up. 'I have to trust them.' She turned her big blue eyes to Hegarty. 'Can she have a bit of time to think?'

'I can arrest you, you know,' said Hegarty, just to rattle the grumpy girl. She had enough attitude to bury a small building.

'I can plead the fifth.' Keisha crossed her arms.

Hegarty stood up. 'Think you'll find that's America, miss,

and sadly for you there's no such thing in the UK. Criminal Justice and Public Order Act 1984.'

Keisha muttered something that sounded like *wanker*. Giving the other girl a dirty look, Charlotte got up to see him to the door. 'I'm sorry to spring all this on you. You must think I'm an idiot, trying to be all *Murder She Wrote*.'

He shrugged his jacket on. 'Nah. Although I did have a thing for Angela Lansbury in *Bedknobs and Broomsticks*.'

Her face lit up. 'I love that film, I've got it on DVD.'

Of course she did. He looked at her for a second too long, her hands wringing together.

'And the other thing, the letter about Dan? Will you . . . ?' She dropped her voice and he saw she didn't want Keisha to know she'd asked him to help Stockbridge. Maybe she didn't totally trust the other girl.

'I'll see what I can do. No promises.'

Hegarty's dad, Maverick Mike, knew a lot of people. Before he married and settled in Cumbria, he'd been all round the country, and it was getting to be a bit of a joke how often a court clerk or officer or even a judge would say, 'Oh, you're Maverick Mike's lad?'

As it happened, Hegarty Senior also knew one of the POs at Pentonville, where Daniel Stockbridge was currently being held awaiting trial. Hegarty'd already decided, even apart from his earlier impressions of a cold bastard, that Stockbridge was a twat. Imagine being stuck in there with three hundred men and turning down a visit from the lovely Charlotte. But when he got into the interview room and smelled the stale air, he understood better. Maybe it was just too much, to be in here and see her or smell the outside rising off her hair.

The door opened and Stockbridge was brought in.

Although he was a remand prisoner he was wearing the same grey prison tracksuit as the other men. There was a healing cut over his eye, yellowing on the edges. He looked awful, Hegarty thought, pale and blinking in the orange light of the interview room. The man must have lost two stone since his arrest.

Stockbridge sat down slowly. 'You want to arrest me for anything else?'

'How are you, Daniel?'

Stockbridge gave him a dirty look. 'How do you think? Waiting for a trial date.'

'Shouldn't be long now. I hear you might be pleading Guilty.' That was the advantage of being Maverick Mike's boy – you heard things, you knew ways to wind them up.

'What's it to you? That's what you think, isn't it?'

'But when we first met, you didn't exactly agree, did you?'

Stockbridge looked angry. 'You had all that evidence, showing I'm a racist, my prints on the bottle. You found it all.'

Hegarty leaned forward. 'Do you remember what happened, Dan? Do you remember that night?'

A long pause. Hegarty saw the man was shaking. 'Well?'

'No.' His voice was a whisper.

'So, why would you plead Guilty?'

'You said – you had all that evidence. The bottle, the CCTV. No one else could have done it. That's what you said. And the lawyer said, maybe they'd go easier on me if I admitted it.'

'Are you sure no one else could have done it?' Hegarty pushed his chair back.

'What the hell is this? You said no one else went in, but he was dead. And I don't remember, you know that? I don't remember a fucking thing. So what am I supposed to . . . ? *Fuck.*'

Hegarty let the echoes of the man's voice fade away. 'So you're pleading Guilty because you don't *remember*?'

'I don't know. The man's dead, isn't he? Someone has to be punished for it.'

Christ, the man was in a bad way. 'You had another blackout, I hear.' He nodded at the cut over Stockbridge's eye.

The man clammed up. 'Accident.'

'Someone lamped you, I hear tell. Think you're a racist, don't they?'

'And who the fuck did that come from? You were the one who dug up all that old stuff.'

Another pause. 'Dan,' Hegarty said quietly. 'You didn't say anything racist to Anthony Johnson, did you? She was lying, wasn't she, that girl?'

Stockbridge hung his head. 'I don't know. I just don't know any more.'

'You had a blackout.'

'Yes.'

'Wasn't the first time.'

'No. I've had them a few times. I didn't know what was happening to me.' Stockbridge was whispering, staring at his restless hands. 'I was so stressed. All that stuff at work – God, you wouldn't believe what was going on there. I could tell you some things . . .'

'Yeah? Tell me then.'

He slumped. 'What's the point? It's me that's in prison, not them.'

'If you spot an irregularity, you have to report it. Isn't that the law on banking?'

Stockbridge laughed. 'And if I don't – what? You'll arrest me again? I think that ship has sailed, Officer.'

'Who gave you the coke, Dan?'

'Why, you want him in here too?'

'What if I do? Did any of that banking lot stand by you when you needed them? You know how much stuff they gave me on you, Dan? Mountains of it. Handed it over on a plate. Why'd they do that, eh?'

The man shook his head. 'There's no point in saying.' His voice was dead.

'Did you know something? Was that it? You had something on them?'

Daniel Stockbridge's face was shining with tears. Had he even noticed? Hegarty relented, sat back. 'Someone called Alex, wasn't it, who had the coke? Charlotte remembered the name.'

A whisper. 'Carter. Alex Carter. He's head of my division. He's my boss. Was my boss.'

Hegarty scribbled it down. 'Thanks, Dan.'

'Don't call me Dan.' He rubbed at his face with the back of his hands, like a kid.

Hegarty cleared his throat. 'So it says here you've been diagnosed with epileptic blackouts, Mr Stockbridge. You know what that means?'

'That I'm totally fucked?'

'Means you can't remember what happened. You're an unreliable witness.'

Stockbridge looked up. His eyes were red and haunted. 'What?'

'Dan, you're not a reliable judge of what happened.'

'But – no one else could have killed him. You said.'

Hegarty got up. 'We'll let the jury decide that, shall we? In the meantime there's someone waiting to hear from you, and she wishes you'd at least make an effort.'

Dan said quietly, 'I don't want her to see me like this. She's better off without me.'

Hegarty turned away in impatience. 'She's waiting for you – you realise that? She's out there, every day, waiting for you to start fighting.'

Stockbridge stared at his hands again, still trembling. 'You seem to know a lot about my fiancée, Officer.'

Hegarty signalled to the PO that he'd finished. 'Get a lawyer, Stockbridge, will you? Make her see she's got a reason to wait for you.'

The other man thought about it for a moment. 'And what if I don't want her to?'

There's plenty who'll pick up the pieces. Hegarty bit down the thought. 'See you in court, Dan.'

The door clanged shut as he left Stockbridge in the small, windowless room.

Part Four

Charlotte

The next thing that happened was a trial date came through. Of course Dan didn't tell her, wouldn't even accept her letters, so Charlotte only found out when Hegarty phoned to let her know.

She was on her way to work, walking down Tottenham Court Road. 'Pardon? Oh, sorry, the traffic is so loud. What did you say?'

'The trial date. Just heard it on the grapevine. CPS'll let you know, but I reckoned you'd want to hear soonest.'

She stopped walking. 'When?'

'October. They don't like to hold big trials in summer.'

The traffic was deafening, and for a second Charlotte felt she might choke on the dust and fumes. 'Does he know? Did they tell him?'

'Well, sure, he's meant to have time to prepare his defence.'

'He needs a lawyer. Did he say he would get one?'

His voice was gentle down the line. 'I only saw him for ten minutes, like. Didn't really get on to that.'

Christ. She'd had such a sharp stab of hope when Matthew – DC Hegarty – agreed to go and see Dan in prison. But nothing had changed. No one talked about Dan. No one thought of him. It was as if he'd vanished from the world, and nobody even cared. Except her.

'Charlotte? Get ready for your witness summons. Prosecution'll almost definitely call you.'

Charlotte pictured them suddenly, waiting to testify, side by side in court and Dan across the room in a wooden box. 'And Keisha?'

'Not unless she makes a statement. I did look into her story, but . . .'

'But?'

He sighed. 'I couldn't find anything. No taxi records, nothing.'

'Oh. Listen, I'm so sorry about how rude she was when you came round. She's just not ready. Could I – could we meet up again, not at my place? Another coffee or something?'

He didn't ask why she wanted to see him again, and in the long pause she could hear her own heart beating.

'Thing is, I'm about to go away for a while. Mate of mine's getting married out in Australia.' She heard him sigh. 'Or dinner?' he said finally. 'If we can do it before I go – tomorrow, maybe? I know somewhere not far from you.'

She couldn't breathe. 'That would be lovely. Will you text me the place?'

No one in London made last-minute plans like that. But he'd offered and she'd said yes. She started walking again, on shaky legs.

Charlotte's latest job was in a homeless shelter, and she was nervous. Odd to think of this place being here, just behind all the nice shops and the shiny company offices. It wasn't far from her old office, in fact. Imagine seeing Chloe or Tory or someone on her way into a homeless shelter.

Then there it was. Just as it had hit her when she'd passed the engagement restaurant, she'd turned a corner and the bar was there. That was the problem with always working and going out in the same area – soon the streets became almost haunted, crawling with the ghosts of old lovers and friends, old nights out. Old kisses. And she'd forgotten, in all her worries, she'd forgotten that she had to avoid this street.

Although the morning was muggy, Charlotte shivered in her white work shirt. Let's go to Q, he'd said. I've got a card. We can have a nice quiet chat there. And she, God help her, only a week in her first big PR job and still excited at having a desk and an in-tray and an email address, she'd thought he was gay – if she'd even thought of it at all. He wore cardigans, for God's sake. He drank Vodkatinis and called everyone 'sweetheart'. And then when she realised she was wrong, well, it was too late, and she was staggering to the tube the next day in her heels and dress, making up some lie to Dan about having to stay at Chloe's.

Oh God. There it was, shuttered and closed, and the space in her mind was as raw as ever, like the soft bit in her jaw where the tooth was missing. Oh God, bloody hell. But she was already late, so she had to swallow the shock of the memory and walk on, thinking, *The bastard, the fucking bastard.*

Outside the homeless shelter people were gathered, a group of men and women with cans of Stella in plastic bags. She kept her head down, walking fast, and heard one of the woman saying something like, 'Can I borrow your Visa card?' and they all laughed. Blushing, she buzzed in, wishing she could lose whatever it was about her that so screamed middle-class. Whatever she wore and even if she tried not to say things like 'Pardon', they could always spot it a mile off.

The woman who came to meet her, 'Just call me Trina', clearly thought Charlotte was middle-class too. Like many of the clientèle she had dreadlocks, even though she was white, and tattoos on her arms. 'What happened to Irina? We always get Irina.'

'Er, she went back to Poland, I think.'

'Oh.' Trina looked Charlotte up and down. 'Well, come on.'

She'd moved into the dining room and the noise was so loud Charlotte couldn't hear her. 'Pardon?' Oh, crap.

Trina glared at her. 'You're on lunches, I said. Ever been in a homeless shelter?'

'Course,' Charlotte lied, following her into the bleach-smelling kitchen. She was a bit sick of people like Trina disapproving of her, to be honest. It wasn't her fault she'd gone to nice schools, was it?

Lunch was beans, of course, it was always beans, the better to ruin your good Oasis shirt with. It was like any other job, really, putting out bread rolls, ladling gloop, emptying and washing all the massive pots till her hands were raw and stinking of detergent. She tried to be nice, like on every job, smiling and saying, 'Would you like beans? Bread roll?'

Also like on every job, she was doing everything wrong, apparently. They weren't allowed butter *and* jam, Trina said. She shouldn't smile at them. 'It'll create attachment. They need boundaries, yeah?'

A great queue of people passed her ladle of beans, skinny shaking men (drugs, abuse), loud women with dirty hair and no teeth (drink, family breakdown). After an hour her hand ached and her face was sweating. All in all, a long way from happy Charlotte Miller, the girl who'd gone to the club that night just a few months ago. About to be married, so happy she was sure the world ought to spin round on her axis. So it wouldn't be surprising if someone who'd seen her before didn't recognise her. But then, she didn't know him either, not really. After all, she'd only seen him in a blurred picture from a phone, and maybe, once, pushing past her into an alley.

He was far down the end of a long straggling line, when Charlotte was long past gagging at the smells of bad breath and unwashed clothes, and had already lost all feeling in her hand from ladling. 'Beans or sweetcorn?' She wasn't even looking up. 'Beans or sweetcorn?' A bit more impatient this time, since there were still about twenty people waiting.

The man on the other side was thin, and had a shaved head, but he didn't have that engrained grime of the streets, the teeth rotting and falling out. Trina had said not everyone who came to eat was on the streets; sometimes they were 'experiencing negative financial situations'. She really did say things like that.

'So . . . beans?' She tried again. The guy's hands were trembling, maybe he was a druggie. He was staring at her and she began to feel uncomfortable. Maybe Trina was right about not being too nice. His eyes were very blue, she noticed. Had she seen them before somewhere?

'Naw . . . naw. Sorry.' Muttering, he pushed out of the line, spilling some of his tea onto the floor.

Charlotte looked round at the hovering Trina, who was tutting at the spillage. 'Someone'll have to clean that up, it's against health and safety.'

'What was all that about?'

'Who knows?' Trina was dialling for cleaners. 'Had a guy once who thought I was his mother. Convinced of it, he was. Never mind, just get the rest served.'

The thing was, she thought she'd seen him somewhere before. That smell, like sweat but something sweeter, a type of cologne. She'd smelled it before. It stood out among the reek of boiled food and unwashed clothes like a streak of glitter in the air. When she'd finished serving and went to clear the dirty plates, she searched the room for the guy with blue eyes. But there was no sign of him at all.

The next thing that happened was Sarah came.

Charlotte was exhausted after her shift at the homeless shelter. On top of the usual bodily tiredness she had from every job, aching right down her back and into her feet, there was something else. She had never understood just how much hopelessness there was in the world. So many people with hands shaking, eyes staring, teeth falling out. And what was she even doing in that place? She'd been to a good university. Her father worked in banking. Just two months ago she'd had a job in shiny offices a stone's throw from the shelter. From the place where all hope had drained away like fat down the sink.

Charlotte dragged herself off the tube, then stopped. It was afternoon, the days long and gentle, summer at its height. Had she heard something? She paused at the turning to her street and looked over her shoulder. She could have sworn she'd heard footsteps.

The road was empty behind her, a summer breeze rustling in the trees. But she thought of the man with the blue eyes, and walked quickly away. There was something about his smell – why couldn't she remember?

She reached her flat bone-weary and scrabbled around in her bag for the keys. She noticed that the strap on her Mulberry bag, so lovely when new, was fraying from being scuffed around on kitchen floors and bundled into staff lockers. Was it hopeless for her too? Or did having a trial date mean hope of Dan's release? Ten years at least, he'd said. And although DC Hegarty hadn't told her much about his visit, she guessed Dan hadn't been in a good way then either.

Keisha was in the kitchen when she went in, yawning and boiling the kettle. Charlotte registered that she was still in her work T-shirt.

'You're late back,' Charlotte said. 'It's three o'clock.'

Keisha didn't meet her eyes. 'You wanted me to hang about, didn't you? The boss, he's showing me cooking.'

'That's this Ronald guy? The brother?'

'Huh? Yeah.' Keisha fiddled with the tea bags.

Charlotte thought of the man with blue eyes, and considered for a moment telling Keisha. But what was the point in scaring her? It was no one, just some loser, just her imagination. 'Listen. Dan's trial date's through. It's in October.'

Keisha stopped with a mug in her hand. 'So what now?'

Charlotte sat down on the sofa, struggling under the weight of it all. The hopelessness. It was like she'd carried it home on her skin. 'Need to find a lawyer, persuade Dan to plead Not Guilty . . . And your statement.'

The kettle shut off with a snap and Keisha poured the water out, ignoring Charlotte. 'You want one of your smelly perfume teas?'

Christ, it was never going to end. She'd be forty and still here in this flat, with Keisha moaning about the tea bags. 'I need your statement.'

'Eh?'

'Keisha – will you just stop for a second? It's been months

now. Are you going to help or not? Can you not even just write it down, to have like a dossier?'

'A what-ier?'

Charlotte glared at her – she knew by now that Keisha was about ten times quicker than she acted. 'You want Ruby back, don't you?'

'You know I do. For fuck's sake. S'complicated.'

'Well, then you have to tell your side. Explain about Chris. We should both write down everything we know, before we forget. Look, they won't want to keep Ruby, will they? Not if they think it's OK to turf her back to you. Cheaper, isn't it?'

Keisha narrowed her eyes. 'She's safe where she is,' she muttered. 'Anyway, you still didn't tell me what you saw that night.'

Charlotte pushed away the thought of the man. 'I told you, it's hazy.'

'Just seems weird, you still wouldn't remember, after all this time.'

'Well, that's how it is. Come on. PR them a bit,' said Charlotte, handing her a pen. 'I don't know much, but I know how to do this.'

That was when Sarah arrived. They weren't expecting anyone – obviously, no one ever dropped in on you in London. So when the buzzer went, Charlotte's heart thumped, thinking of the paint on her step, the footsteps behind her . . .

Keisha froze too. 'Who's that?'

'I don't know.'

'Well, get it.'

'Hello? Hello?' Charlotte's heart slowed when she heard Sarah's bossy tones on the intercom. Then she thought, *Oh crap, Mum's sent her to check up on me.* She buzzed the door open and peered down as Sarah climbed the stairs. 'What are you doing here? What a surprise.'

Her step-sister stomped up and hugged her efficiently. She was in her cycling gear and carrying her ugly helmet under one arm. 'Gail said she called here and some girl answered. You know, she worries.'

Keisha was managing to blend into the cupboards. 'Er, yeah. That was me.'

'Keesh, this is my step-sister,' Charlotte said. 'Sarah, Keisha's staying with me. She's like, a friend.' A friend? Flatmate? How the hell would you explain what it was that brought them together? Sarah was looking at Keisha in an imperious way that was about five seconds from pissing her right off, Charlotte could see. 'Keisha just made some tea.'

Sarah was peering round the flat. 'I'll take mint, thanks. Did you get rid of your cleaner or something, Char?'

'Sarah – sit down, will you? I just heard that Dan's trial date's come through.'

'I know. That's why I came.' Sarah plonked down her helmet and Keisha brought the mint tea, at arm's length.

Of course, Sarah always knew everything through work, that was her thing. And bloody annoying it was too. 'How was Bangladesh?'

'Hot. Smelly.' Sarah kept staring at Keisha, blowing on the tea to cool it. She swallowed, and made a face. 'Hard to go back after real mint tea.'

Charlotte didn't dare look at Keisha. 'Work's OK?' That was usually good for a half-hour rant.

'Don't have time to draw breath, as per. One a.m. I got home last night.'

Once Charlotte had tried to play this game with Sarah, totting up how many extra hours she did and how busy and important she was. Now, through Keisha's eyes, she saw how stupid it was. She raised her eyebrows at Keisha in a silent apology. 'Listen, now you're here, Sarah, I had an idea. The trial's coming up, and there'll probably be a lot of media interest, yeah?'

'Yep. It's on our calendar.'

'So, I was thinking about doing some counter-PR. To tell my side. I know you're not allowed to be biased about the case, but you could interview me, couldn't you?'

Sarah put down her cup barely touched. 'Is that such a good idea? Dan'll be crucified by the press. Everyone hates bankers just now. They blame them for the recession. Even us – we laid off twenty reporters last month. And for God's sake, he killed a black guy. You must see. Gail said you already got fired over it, and most of your friends won't talk to you.'

'I didn't get fired. And he's not been convicted, so can you please not say he killed someone?'

Sarah was giving her a pitying look. 'They have his prints, and the CCTV. I'm sorry, but you need to face it. Didn't he tell you himself to let him go?'

With difficulty, Charlotte kept her voice calm. 'Keisha was there that night. She's got evidence. Really, we don't think Dan did it.'

'Hmm. So that's why she's here.'

'What's that supposed to mean?' Finally Keisha spoke, from where she was backed into the kitchen corner.

Sarah laughed. 'Nothing. Just that Gail may have been right for once.'

Charlotte said, 'Sarah, please . . . I need your help. Please help me. It's Dan, for God's sake. You know Dan.'

'OK.' Sarah sighed. 'Bloody hell. Send me what you have

and I'll see. But I can't go out on a limb, OK? Even for you, I can't.'

Charlotte felt awful. 'I know. I know. But I have to at least try, do you not see that?'

'I suppose.' Sarah patted her shoulder awkwardly. 'We just hate to see you do all this for him, when he might be a killer. Your job, Charlotte! Doesn't that matter to you? I mean, are you really working as a waitress now?'

'It's just a blip.' Charlotte was staring at her work-roughened hands, trying hard not to cry.

'Listen, I can't stay. Call Gail, will you? Even your dad's been on to her.'

'He has?' Charlotte hadn't contacted her father since their disastrous dinner. As far as she was concerned, he was just some other person who'd let her down.

'And you need a lawyer. Jamie might know someone – he's worried too. I went to see them last week.'

'You did? Oh. I didn't know.' Jamie was Charlotte's brother, not Sarah's, but she hadn't seen him in months.

'Yeah, well, don't take it the wrong way, but everyone's very upset by what happened.' Sarah was getting up and starting the laborious task of donning her cycle gear. 'So you'll call them? Everyone's worried about you. I'm working flat-out and I still came round.'

Worried about you. It sounded nice but it was just another way to say they thought you'd ruined your life, wasn't it?

'Guess you're right,' said Keisha, after Sarah had clumped down the stairs.

'Hmm?' Charlotte was still sitting there, a little shell-shocked.

'We need to write it down. No one believes stuff if it's not written down, do they?'

'No.' She dragged herself up. 'Sarah's right, sort of. I'm going to ring my parents.'

Gail was in full flow. 'Oh darling, you know you've always been just a bit naïve. Dan did take care of you, but now I worry. Some of these people are just waiting to take advantage of a girl like you.'

A pause. 'What do you mean, like me?'

'Well, darling, you have that big flat, and I imagine his parents will see you right, even if your father won't. And, well, you've never been so good at looking after yourself, have you? Remember at college, when you had all that mould in your kitchen, and I had to come down and clean it?'

'For God's sake, Mum, I was eighteen!' This was rich coming from a woman who wouldn't even drive on her own when her husband left her. They'd taken buses for a year until Phil came along, Charlotte and her mother and Jamie.

'You know what I mean. Sarah says he won't even see you at that place.' She could hear her mum's pursed lips. Bloody Sarah! She deserved to break another toe, if not all of them.

'He's ill, Mum. They think he might have epilepsy. It's just not right, him being in there.'

Gail hesitated. 'It just seems, darling, that if he doesn't want you to go—'

'What?'

'Maybe you shouldn't.'

'And just leave him there?'

'Oh, I know, it's so hard! I thought he was wonderful too, dear, at the start anyway – although last time we saw you he was odd, wasn't he, quite cold and jumpy. I actually said to Phil . . . Well, anyone can be wrong, sweetie. Look at me and your father.'

Charlotte gritted her teeth. OK, a lot of what Gail said was true, but he was still her dad.

'And then this strange girl just moving in with you. Sarah already told me. What is she anyway, half-caste?'

'MUM! You can't say that!'

'I don't know anyone like that, do I? What should I say? Coloured?'

'No, for God's sake. She's mixed-race. Why do you have to call her anything?'

'Because, darling, it's what she is.' It was blindingly obvious to Gail, and Charlotte suddenly wondered, was she the same? Was part of her desperately aware that Keisha was different to her, and handling the fact as carefully as a porcelain vase? But you couldn't help how you thought, surely. It was what you did and said that mattered. Wasn't it?

Although Charlotte rang off from her mother dazed and confused, Gail's final comment had struck home: 'Call your father, why don't you? It's about time he did something for you.' And she was right. It was.

Charlotte had never been good at working out time differences. She'd always asked Dan before, and now she got it wrong, phoning her father's apartment at what was about four in the morning, Singapore-time.

'*Wei?*' A woman's voice. Did she have the wrong number?

'Hello? Is Jonathan there? Sorry, I don't speak . . .'

The woman switched to English, with an accent. 'Charlotte?'

'Yes! Er – Stephanie?'

'Yes.' There was a long pause. 'How are you? I'm sorry about your wedding.'

'Thank you. It was bad, yes.' Stephanie hadn't been

invited, since Gail had flat-out refused to go if 'that Dutch woman' came. 'Actually, things aren't great, Stephanie. Dan, he, well, he won't see me. He won't get a lawyer, and his trial date's just come up.'

'Ah. You want your father.'

'Please. I'm sorry, is it early there? I never know.'

'Yes. But we get up early.' Stephanie set the phone down and spoke a different language – Dutch? Did her father know Dutch? She tried to picture him in this flat she'd never seen, with this woman only dimly remembered from when she was ten. Charlotte had spent the whole of their dinner at the Hard Rock Café leaning in to catch her perfume smell, deciding that when she was grown up she'd also walk round in a cloud of lovely scent.

'Hello?' Her father always sounded gruff on the phone. 'It's the middle of the night.'

'I'm sorry, Dad. I messed up the time difference.'

'Never mind, we're up now. Are you all right?'

She hesitated. 'Not really, no. Can you help me?' She remembered how she'd called him *Daddy* when he came to her house that day, and felt she might cry again. 'I need to find a lawyer for Dan. He won't get one himself – and I can't afford to pay for it.'

'All right, let's not get upset.'

'S-sorry.' Her father hated crying. 'Do you know anyone, any lawyers?'

'It would have to be a good criminal barrister, preferably with appeal experience. You've left it rather late, I'm afraid.'

'I'd have to trust them too. I mean, the way the evidence looks . . . they'd have to believe me.'

She heard her father hold the phone away and speak the other language again. She waited. 'All right. Stephanie knows someone here. Australian girl, qualified in the UK, she says. Not a full QC yet, on the young side, but in your financial situation, well . . . And I suppose we can discuss some help with fees, too.' He said it grudgingly. 'Although I should warn you I can't cover it all.'

'But how would I meet her?'

'You'd come out here, of course.'

Had her father ever asked her to visit before? 'Really? But I can't . . .'

'I'll help out with the fare. You can get away? Your mother said you weren't working any more.'

'I am, actually, but I can get off. When?'

'You'd need to instruct as soon as you can. It's quite late already.'

'Oh, OK.' They made more small talk – something her father was truly awful at – and she hung up and went back into the kitchen, feeling dazed.

Keisha was back on the sofa with *Friends* on, her feet up on the table again, an open bottle of Coke leaking rings onto the cream carpet beside her. Charlotte thought about what her mother had said: *People are just waiting to take advantage, darling.* On the table was another sheet of printer paper. It looked as if Keisha had started on her statement, this most vital document, and given up after a few lines.

'Listen, Keisha, I think I might have to sell the flat, when I get back.' She was surprised to hear herself say it. But how else would she help Dan, without making sacrifices?

Keisha didn't seem to take it in. 'Oh yeah? Back from where?'

'I'm going to Singapore,' Charlotte said, marvelling to herself that it was true.

Keisha didn't look up. 'What's that, a takeaway?'

Did she say them on purpose, these things? Was she really going to let this girl stay here in her house, with all her things, while she was gone? And what about the man? But no, it was nothing. Her imagination. Charlotte looked down at the scrawled-on piece of paper again. 'It's a country. I'm going away for a while.'

Charlotte had decided to make an effort for her meeting with DC Hegarty the next day. Maybe because she was tired of looking at her own face, worn and sullen, tired of pulling on and off the same frayed pair of jeans. It was sort of nice to get dressed up again.

Keisha watched Charlotte drying her hair into loose curls. 'You fancy him or something?'

Charlotte shot her a look. 'He might be able to help.' But suddenly she was embarrassed by the black slingbacks she'd paid so much for, and the mist of perfume drying on her neck. What was she doing? 'It's rude not to dress up for dinner,' she said snootily, and saw Keisha raise a cynical eyebrow. Sighing, Charlotte tousled her hair one last time and ran down the stairs to meet him at Kentish Town. No cabs now; she laced on her trainers and carried her heels wrapped up in a Tesco's bag. It was starting to rain so she held her bag over her head. When she got to the bus stop near the restaurant she leaned awkwardly on the slanted bench and pulled on the heels – the first time she'd worn them since That Night. The night when everything went wrong.

He was waiting in the place he'd chosen, checking his watch and looking nervous. It was a small and cheap Malaysian restaurant with fairy lights on the wall, and it was BYO so she wondered if he'd picked it because it wouldn't cost much and he would try to pay.

He was anxious. 'It looks a bit, you know, I know, but the food's good, I promise.'

She flipped open her menu. 'It's fine. I like it.'

'I'm sure you're used to something fancier.'

'Honestly, I like it.' Suddenly she wasn't at all bothered what she ate. She looked up at him. He met her eyes and looked quickly away.

'Drink? I got wine, beer . . . Whatever you like.'

They didn't talk about the case, as it turned out. A tea-light was placed on their small table, panpipe music in the background. They were almost the only people there in the quiet of the rainy night. The food when it came was sweet and hot on her tongue. Charlotte ate as if starved, sweet potato and coconut and fluffy roti bread. It was spicy, but damned if she'd let him see, she sipped her drink discreetly. He'd brought red and white wine as well as beer. 'I didn't know what you'd want.'

Afterwards she could never remember what they talked about for so long, just the soft roll of his Cumbrian accent, smudged round the edges with London, and how his wiry forearms sat on the table, shirtsleeves pushed up, the chink of his metal watch against his beer bottle. Looking up and looking away, each time with a lurching certainty in the pit of her stomach that she hadn't just come about Dan. She almost didn't even want, in the drowse of the beer and candlelight, to bring it up. What kind of person was she? She tried to focus. 'Listen, my dad just asked me to go to Singapore, to meet this lawyer he knows.'

'That's good. Will he see them?' Neither of them seemed to want to say Dan's name.

'Who knows?' She laughed thinly. 'I have to try. I think I'm going to have to sell the flat to pay for it.'

'Well, getting away for a bit, that'll do you good.' He sounded like her mother.

'Sure. You said you were off to Australia soon?'

'In a few days.'

'Well, I was thinking . . . do you come back by Singapore?'

His voice was casual. 'Haven't decided yet. There, or Hong Kong.'

'Well, if you do – maybe I'll be there too.' God, he was making it hard. 'I could show you about.'

'I don't know if it'd be that easy.' He looked wary.

'Why not, if we're both there?'

'Well, if we are. I dunno.' He laughed. 'You rich girls. Let's meet up halfway round the world, just like, all right, let's meet up for coffee.'

'I can't see why not.'

He thought about it. 'Suppose I can't either, now you put me on the spot.'

'OK then.' They applied themselves to the food for a while.

'Why did you go into the police?' she asked, chewing.

He tore off a piece of bread and offered it to her. He said, 'I worked in an office first, for a year. When I left school. We don't go to uni in my family. Waste of money, my dad said.'

'My dad would've killed me if I *hadn't* gone.'

'I'll bet. So this office, it was selling toilet seats. Bathroom fittings, you know. "Hello, Bathroom World." That was me. Solitaire, soggy sandwiches, crap coffee – mind you, I still get that now. But I thought, Sod this, I can't spend the rest of my life smelling Alan in Accounts and his pickled onions.'

'My office was like that,' she said, thinking how young he seemed, compared to Dan. 'Everyone was sort of really shiny and never ate anything, never mind pickled onions, but it's still other people all day long, clearing their throats and going on Facebook – you know.'

He nudged the chicken closer to her, cooling in its thick coconut and coriander. 'Have a bit more there.'

'I'm stuffed, thanks.'

'You don't miss it then – your work?'

She thought about it. 'Maybe just having to look nice every day, having somewhere to get up for.'

'You look lovely now,' he said, and blushed violently. 'I'll get the bill.' She took out her little designer purse, and he said, 'Please, don't.'

'But—'

'No. Please, Charlotte. I invited you.'

Touched by his pride, she let him pay. 'Thanks. It was nice, wasn't it? I ate tons.'

'You need it,' he said. When the bill was paid he crunched one of the hard white mints left on the saucer. 'So. You didn't want to see me to get my thrilling life story.'

She was almost sorry he'd brought it up. 'The thing is, I think I've found out a few new things.' She could see his face change. 'I know it must be annoying, but you see, this is his life – Dan's.' It felt so bad to say Dan's name between them, at the table they'd sat at for two hours gone.

'Tell me,' Hegarty sighed.

'Well.' Charlotte didn't know how to begin. 'After you came last time, and Keisha was sort of . . . you know. Well, she found out a few more things.' And she told him about the gang rumours and the club owing money and the blue-eyed man at the shelter, how she thought maybe she'd been followed. 'I don't know for sure, but I thought . . . I sort of thought I'd seen him that night. At the club. I didn't tell

Keisha. She'll never make her statement if she thinks he's back. God, that sounds awful, doesn't it?'

He said nothing for a while. 'This is very dangerous, what you're doing. You and your friend.'

'She's not my friend – I mean, she's involved. She came to me. It's her life too, you see. He killed her mum, you know that?'

'Sorry, I didn't know that, not at all.' He folded up his wallet with maddening calm. 'I'm telling you, it's very dangerous to sniff around men like Chris Dean.'

'But we're not. Keisha just works at the club. She's allowed to *work* there.'

Again he stayed so calm, as she was becoming increasingly petulant.

'Of course. But please, both of you, be careful. If it's like you say, he's very violent, this man.'

'I told you what he did to their little girl?'

'Yes. So you see, you need to be careful.'

'You believe me then? You'll look into it?'

He was quiet for a long time. 'I put him away – Dan. It was my case.'

'So? You want him in jail even if he's innocent?' Something burst up in her, anger, terrible fear, and she stood up to go.

'Wait!' He held up his hands. 'That's not what I meant. I can't use anything you got by deceit or trespassing.'

'She works there! There's this guy, Ronald, he's the brother of the man who died.' She still couldn't say *who was killed*. 'Ronald will give you a statement, I'm sure of it. So – anyway . . . You should call him.' She fumbled in her bag for Ronald's business card, swiped by Keisha off his desk. 'Please, just ask if he's found out anything. He won't come forward, it'd be like betraying his community. You see?'

'You don't wear your ring any more,' he said, catching up her hand, the cuticles ragged from biting.

Immediately she was angry. 'It's none of your business. You're the police, aren't you? I'm asking you to look at new evidence, real evidence, and you just – I don't know why I pay taxes.'

He almost laughed at this, as she threw on her raincoat and jangled furiously out of the door.

'Wait, Charlotte – come back!'

Charlotte marched to the bus stop, ears ringing with anger. How dare he – how incredibly rude. After a few steps she realised it wasn't just chill rain running over her face – she was crying. Screw him. Screw them all, as Keisha would say. Fuck 'em.

'Wait! Charlotte!' She turned. The candy colours of the traffic-lights were shiny with rain, the gutters rushing with it, and DC Matthew Hegarty was chasing her down the street in Camden, in just his shirt. 'Please wait.' He caught her sleeve, breathless. He smelled of strong mint, and schoolboy aftershave, the heavy drenched smell of the rain.

He was so different from Dan, this policeman. He looked so young, with his Adam's apple working over his collar and eyes so intense, as if they couldn't look at anything but her. His hand was still holding the arm of her raincoat and his shirt was getting soaked in the rain, a cheap shirt, his thin body showing pink underneath. How long was it since someone had run after her down the street, since someone had looked at her like this? Years. Maybe never.

'Wait,' he said again. She put her hand to his chilled face, cold as bone, and he shivered. She was so very cold, she realised, and so very lonely, so very tired.

Hegarty

All the way on the plane from Australia, Hegarty couldn't settle. He kept thinking everyone knew what he was up to, that it was only his second time flying, like that stewardess with all the make-up who kept smiling at him. 'Everything all right, sir?'

'Grand.' In fact, he couldn't sit still. The cramped seat wasn't kind on his six-foot-one frame; he felt like a piece of paper stuck in a too-small envelope. He ate all the foil-packaged meal they brought on a tray, beads of moisture clinging to the butter, joggling his bony elbows into the fat bloke on the other side. Then he put on the eyemask and the socks and blew up his travel pillow and tried to sleep, but his body didn't understand what time it was, and anyway he was too excited about it all, his first proper foreign holiday, Tom's wedding behind him, and then as if that wasn't enough – Singapore. Singapore and her. He must have slept then because he was woken up some time later by the shades going up on a harshly pure light, and the stewardess handing him another foiled-wrapped tray of almost identical food; breakfast.

Staggering off the plane, Hegarty breathed in new air that was free of recycled farts. There was a smell that was nothing like England, a hot and wet frying smell like the end of a sizzling day. He was here, and so was she.

After the night of the rain, he'd known he had to tell someone. It was against regulations, it must be, and if there was anything he was good at, it was sticking to regulations. He wasn't Maverick Mike, doing it old-school, sharing cigs and punches with suspects on the way to the station.

As discreetly as he could, he looked into it. Was there

anything in the rules about not meeting up with a girl in an exotic foreign country, if it just so happened you'd booked her fella a few months back for murder? If chances were you'd have to testify against him come the trial, was there any guidance on it being OK to take his missus out for dinner and then chase her down the street in the rain like something out of fucking *Notting Hill*? And he would have kissed her then, he knew it, if she hadn't pulled away.

He couldn't find anything specific. Maybe because no officer'd even been so stupid before. He was sure they all knew, too. The lads in the station stopping a laugh just when he walked up to make himself a drink. Of maybe he was paranoid. He tried asking the boss during their 'chats' if there'd been any talk about the daft DC and the killer's missus, but the boss, missing the point, just told him earnestly what a 'valued member of the team' he was. Hegarty couldn't think how else to bring it up.

There were other worries on his mind, too, especially after what Charlotte had said. 'Sir? You ever have any doubts on this Kingston Town case?'

The boss looked worried. 'Why? Have the press been about?'

'No, not that.' As if the press were the worst thing that could happen. 'You know, there was that other case, same MO. And you know the other witness from Kingston Town?'

The Inspector looked like he was struggling to remember. 'The white fella?'

'Yeah. I, er, might have some intell on him. Off the record.' He couldn't meet the boss's eyes.

'The name?'

'Christopher Dean.' He felt like he was betraying Charlotte, saying it.

'Hmm. Can you get it on record?'

'Dunno. Maybe.'

'You're doing a great job, Matthew,' said the boss heartily. 'Carry on.'

'You like Stockbridge for it, then?'

Bill Barton hadn't risen so far without choosing his words carefully. 'That's who we've got, isn't it? You made a case.'

Yes, he'd made it. That was the problem. Hegarty cleared his throat. 'OK, sir. Getting nowhere on that second stabbing. The victim's recovering though, so we could try him again with E-fit. You know I'm off on Friday.'

'Oh, yes. The Land of Oz. Well, chuck some steaks on the barbie for us, eh?'

'Yessir.' The guy had no idea. Sometimes Hegarty was jealous of that.

Now here he was again, at the end of a week of barbies and crocodile watching and whatever else Tom's new missus had set up. He'd barely slept, spaced-out with jet lag and drinking. His second wedding in less than a month and what was he doing? There'd been girls at the wedding, of course, a never-ending stream of them chucked out by Lizzy and Tom. On the way to the airport they'd even said, 'So, nobody catch your eye then?'

'Thanks, I'm sorted,' he heard himself say. And that was the truth of it. He wasn't interested in any of these Marys or Kellys or whoever, because there was just no room left. That position had already been filled.

Hegarty put up with the slowness of the passport queue and the trundle-trundle of the baggage wheel. He nearly grabbed his passport back off the immigration man, and then finally he was out into the big glassy airport, and there was a girl waiting by the fountain. She was standing with her back to him, wearing a denim dress, red belt. Sunglasses on top of her fair head, curls damp on her neck.

Hegarty'd never understood it when people said that their heart skipped a beat or that their heart stood still or any of that crap. But when he walked into Singapore airport arrivals hall, sweaty and crumpled in his shorts and Burton T-shirt, and he saw Charlotte waiting for him, he sort of got it. God, it was sad.

'That's the Raffles Hotel. Stephanie took me there the other day. We'll go for a Singapore Sling, it's the best.' Charlotte was so different. She talked all the way in the taxi she made him get – 'Honest, the bus takes forever.' Not a hint of tears or that sad, strung-out look she'd had in London.

'You look well,' he said awkwardly. 'Got a good colour.'

'Oh, thanks.' She examined her rosy arms. 'There's a pool at Dad's apartment block.' She pointed out of the window. 'There's the zoo, if you have time. Can you really only stay one night?'

Christ, she wanted him to stay. 'Depends.' He was running out of cash, truth be told. He'd had to pay in the end to stop over in Singapore. But she didn't need to know that.

She paid for the taxi with a big wad of notes. 'Come on, let's get a drink.' They were getting out at the harbour area, the sea shiny. 'Isn't it gorgeous?'

'Glad you came over, then?' He felt different too, out of his depth. He'd no badge here, no notebook, no authority. She seemed to fit right in, leading him through the hot streets to an outdoor market where you bought satay chicken on sticks and ate at plastic tables in the spicy air.

'Hmm? Oh yeah, really I wish I'd come sooner. Daddy

and Stephanie are so good to me – well, she is. He's working as usual. But she's really nice! She really understands about everything. And it's been so good to get away.' She leaned back, sucking hard on some kind of pink drink she'd made him get from a vendor. It tasted like sugared roses, so sweet it made him gag. It was so different from the last time he saw her, in the chilly rain of London. They were both acting as if that night had never happened. 'You know, I was so unhappy before. I was, wasn't I? I was a wreck. I can only see it now I'm away.'

'Found a lawyer yet?'

She nodded, slurping. 'Stephanie's got a meeting set up with some Australian barrister. Supposed to be very good at this kind of case. I'm sure she'll be nice, if she's friends with Stephanie.'

'Well – that's good then, isn't it?'

'Yes.' A pause, and she looked up at him, and turned away. Was she thinking of the same thing as him, of the rain, and him running after her down the street?

He made a face, and she noticed. 'What is it, the pink stuff? Too girly?'

'A bit, yeah.'

'I'll get you a *chai* – it's spicy tea, you'll like it.'

He watched her go to the stall, ducking between the tables in her wedge heels. Everything was different here, the air, the smells, her, him. In London he was the copper who followed the evidence and arrested her man. She was the witness looking for a way out, probably pointless, the whole thing. But here? Who were they?

Charlotte was coming back with a steaming plastic cup. She was smiling as she came towards him and he was smiling back, couldn't help it.

'Here.'

He gulped it down – like over-sweet PG Tips with curry powder in.

'Nice?'

'Yeah,' he lied. 'Grand.'

Charlotte was unstoppable. The creeping tropical heat felt to him like carrying a wet blanket round your shoulders; he could hardly move. But she was fine, apart from the curly wildness the humidity brought to her blonde hair.

The day was packed, the Indian quarter, the sea-front and shops, lunch, on to the Changi Prison museum. Here Hegarty went silent before the displays. His grandfather, Big Mick, had been a prisoner in Burma, and although he came home, he never spoke a word of what happened out there. Sort of put it all in perspective, the worries he had in London.

A fan was whispering overhead, stirring the heavy air. Charlotte came back from the bookshop, springing on her cork shoes. 'All right?' She pulled her hair away from her neck, fanning her flushed face with the visitors' guide.

No, he wasn't all right. He was all at sea.

As the day went on, he noticed once or twice how she would brush against him when they walked along, or stand so close when reading a display that he could smell the clean sweat of her forehead. In the Botanical Gardens she asked a woman to take their picture, and put her arm over his shoulder. For the ten seconds it took to snap the picture, Hegarty was dizzy with the heat and flowers and her.

Then, over lunch, she pulled her chair in close to his as they ate fried noodles in a cheap canteen, and he felt her bare feet scuff over his legs. The hairs stood on end.

'Sorry,' she said, pulling them away. 'My feet were too

hot. Here, want to try mine?' She held out a chopstick-full of noodles.

Finally it was dusk. The taxi was idling through the crowded streets of the Indian quarter, music and light spilling out from the shops, as they went to drop Hegarty at his hotel.

'So, what for dinner?' Still she was full of energy, while he felt like a wrung-out sponge.

'My flight's at eight a.m, you know. Maybe I should get an early night.' He had the money ready in his hand in case she tried to pay again. It felt greasy to the touch, different to UK money.

She fiddled with her hair, drawing it up in her hand. 'I was going to say we could get Dim Sum. It's sort of like Chinese tapas.'

'I know,' he said, even though he didn't. 'You want me to stay out then? You think there's stuff in Singapore still to do?'

She met his eyes. 'Maybe.'

'Yeah?'

'Well, it's a big place.' She looked out of the window and he thought she was blushing. 'Look, we're here.'

He opened the door. 'Meet you in the same place at seven?'

She smiled; it lit up her face. 'Brilliant.'

Hegarty got into his windowless cupboard of a room and had a shower, washing off all the tropical sweat of the day. He couldn't help smiling at himself in the steamed-up mirror. She wanted him to stay. And right that minute she was probably in the shower too, getting ready to come and see him, picking out a dress, combing out her wet hair over her bare shoulders.

Christ. Still with the daft smile, he drank one of the warm beers he'd bought in the shop next door. He tried to control his hair with wax, and he put on jeans and a clean, if crumpled, white shirt. He slapped on some of the Acqua Di Giò he'd got in duty free. Then, just as he was about to head out, already imagining he might try to hold her hand as they walked along, his mobile rang.

Charlotte was already there when he finally got out of a taxi at the pier. She had her phone out as if she'd been waiting, and God she looked amazing, her hair piled up and sparkly earrings brushing her neck.

Shit, Hegarty thought, waving over as he paid. *Shitting hell. Why me?* 'Sorry,' he called as he jogged over. 'Got a phone call.'

'OK.' She was nervous, he could tell. She looked up and away, fiddling with a silver bangle on her arm. 'Anything serious?'

'Yeah.' Crap, why now? 'Listen – they've arrested Chris Dean.'

'Oh, I see.'

'There was a bar stabbing a while back, and the victim just made an ID. I think I should try to get an earlier flight. Sorry.'

'No, it's . . . Does this mean they'll interview him about Dan's case?'

'Maybe. I'll try to make them, if I get back in time.'

'Right. Thank you.'

'Charlotte? Can I ask you something?'

She paused before she said, 'OK.'

'Do you really think he didn't do it? Dan, I mean. You believe that?'

Again a pause. 'I have to.'

Hegarty couldn't stop himself. He reached out and pushed

back a strand of the hair that fell over her face. He looked hard at her. 'Well, then. Make sure you get a lawyer who believes it too, yeah?'

'Wait.' She put up a hand to stop him, it rested on his arm. He was tense as a bow and arrow. 'You're just leaving me?'

'You'll thank me for it, if I can get them to question him.'

She took her hand away, nodding as if she understood what he was doing for her. 'Thank you.' She leaned up and kissed him on the cheek, a quick kiss, sticky with lipgloss. For a second he breathed in the perfume of her hair.

'Safe journey,' she said, stepping away.

Keisha

'What's that, then?'

'I dunno, I told you.'

'Come on, woman. Try and guess.'

'I dunno, ginger?'

'Ginger!' He burst out laughing.

'I told you, I don't know.'

'But still, you mix up ginger and cumin, your curry'll taste like cake, innit.'

'Shut it.' Keisha elbowed Ronald, sending up a cloud of the spice.

'Watch it. Come on, mix it in. Oi, not that much.'

Ronald was teaching her to make curry – slowly, messily, with lots of making fun of her. The empty club kitchen, scrubbed bright and silver, was full of hot frying spices.

'Right, you watching? This is curry paste.'

The last time it was jerk chicken. Before that, fried plantain – starting her off easy. Ronald's first jobs had been cooking in bars and restaurants and now that he owned them he hadn't forgotten how.

She shoved him again. 'You don't need curry, mate. WeightWatchers, that's what you need.'

'Aw, what're you chatting about? At least I got an arse.'

Her stupid pale skin turned red. 'I've an arse. Fuck off.'

'Come on, chop up that beef.'

Yuck, meat was horrible raw, all pink and wobbly like what came out of her when she had Ruby. Ronald scooped the beef up and added it to the pan, then when it had cooked a bit he threw in a tin of coconut milk. 'Smell that, eh?'

Keisha breathed in. 'Not bad. Maybe I'll make it for Char when she gets back. She'll drop down dead if it's not Pot Noodle.'

'That's your mate you live with?'

'Yeah.' She didn't normally say much about herself to people she worked with, especially not now when she had so much to hide. But he was easy to talk to.

'She's away?' Ronald stirred the good-smelling mixture.

'She went to Singapore. Her dad lives out there, see.' Ronald wasn't really listening, he was just being kind, but she carried on. 'Yeah, her dad moved there when she was like eight or something.'

There was no reason for her to tell him all this stuff. But she had to say something about Charlotte's dad, or else she would say what was really on her mind – that she'd been looking for hers, too.

When Charlotte went away Keisha had started to feel weird in the flat. Like she had no right to be there. She waited for ages before going out in case the old woman or the couple from downstairs would be there and give her a look. She hadn't forgotten it was the man who let her in the day she first came, clutching onto the purse as though it was a magic bloody key or something.

She tiptoed round the flat, listening to the noise of far traffic. Sometimes the phone rang again, on and on, but if she ever picked it up to stop it, no one was there. There were gaps in the furniture now Charlotte had sold the best things, some chair that was worth loads apparently, a painting that Ruby could've done better, bits of jewellery. It had helped keep the flat for those months, but Keisha had always known it wouldn't last. Sometimes she heard Charlotte on the phone to the bank, pleading in that sad voice of hers. So, the place would be sold, and she'd be moving on. Where to?

To get away from all the quiet, the feeling that maybe someone was watching, she'd started spending lots of time at the club, where Ronald also seemed to practically live. It was easy, just hanging out with him, not having to go out on the street and worry she'd be followed. After the news that Chris had turned up at the club, she'd considered quitting the job. Making a run for it. But where to? And besides, Ronald somehow made her feel safe. You couldn't imagine anything bad happening with him around. And anyway, there'd been no sign of Chris since. Maybe it wasn't even him. Rachel could have been wrong.

Every day she left the flat and the first job was to check her bank balance, which was coming along nicely from her club wages. Enough to think that maybe, one day, a flat . . . Ruby . . . They could move away, and Chris wouldn't get them, and there'd be no need to find out what Charlotte knew or tell the police about the door and – everything else. Maybe.

Sometimes she walked about as she had when Chris had first hit her. Always looking over her shoulder in case he was about. Around Camden, as far as Russell Square, sometimes. She didn't ask herself why she went to that particular place so much. She'd sit on the benches under the trees in that little square near the fountain, wondering if anyone would think she was a student. If someone looked at her and said, 'What are you doing here?' she'd tell them anyone was allowed to sit on a bench, for fuck's sake. Then when it was time for work, she'd go to the club, and Ronald would be there waiting for her. She sort of knew he'd always be there, even if they hadn't arranged it.

As the summer ended the people changed and the square got busier, new people hanging about, students still at school by the looks of some of them, wet behind the ears. Down for 'open day', she overheard, whatever that was. One day Keisha was sat watching a little kid on the other side of the grass. It seemed like a million years before Ruby would be back to school and she could watch her coming out again. During the summer it was like she'd gone to the moon or something.

The student sitting next to her – a boy in clothes his mum must've bought – went over to the group calling his name ('Hey, Jasper!'). He left behind a sort of booklet, colourful, nice shiny paper. Keisha picked it up, turning it over in her hands. It was a brochure of all the things going on at the university, talks, seminars, all kinds of stuff. Imagine being a student, nothing to do all day but sit and listen to people talk! She was flipping through and there it was – the name. Ian Stone.

She sat up and looked at it again. *Ian Stone*, it said. *Professor of Legal Studies. Emeritus Fellow of Civil Liberties.* There was a small picture of a man with a ponytail. An earring, for Christ's sake. Ian Stone – her dad, probably – was someone who had long hair and wore an earring. And he was speaking on a public panel in just a few weeks. Keisha got up, stuffed the flyer away in her bag, then set off to work.

On the bus she started thinking about the brochure. There was a quote on top of the bit that said what the lecture was about. A quote from Ian Stone: *Even if you're not a law student, we can all fight for justice. Every one of us has to stand up for it.* Then at the bottom another quote from someone famous: *For evil to triumph, all it takes is for good people to do nothing.* Keisha looked at that for a long time, as the bus pushed towards Camden through the summer streets, people outside bars, laughing, drinking. Kids on bikes. The canal all shiny in the late afternoon sun. No one trapped like her, running away from everything but still stuck. Looking over her shoulder before every step she took.

Write it down, Charlotte had said. For Ruby. To try to explain. How could she, how could she show them she'd been staying away for the kid's own good, to keep the bad people away from her? Would Ruby understand, if she told her one day?

She thought about everything she knew. The blood. The shoes. Sometimes she thought it was all going to crush her.

When Keisha got into work, and saw the office empty, and the computer sitting unused, it seemed like everything was just coming together perfectly. She sat down and started to type as quickly as she could, making lots of mistakes. She just wrote the words straight onto the screen, what had happened, what she remembered. Everything she'd never said. And it was good, it was good for once to spill it all out, let out everything she'd been carrying round in her head like a too-full suitcase.

She was so taken up with what she was doing she forgot about cooking with Ronald. The door of the office clicked, and she looked up. Froze.

Ronald was standing in the door. 'What you doing?'

She looked down at her fingers on the keyboard, the computer no one was supposed to use. 'I was just—'

'You can't be on there. No one's meant to be . . . Fuck.' He was striding across the room at her, and she was fumbling with the mouse trying to save what she'd done and click out of the screen.

'Wait, hang on! I was just—'

'You can't be in here, Jesus Christ, what are you . . .' He yanked the keyboard from her hands and she was suddenly afraid, because it was just like before, in the kitchen with Chris, and then he'd—

Keisha didn't know she'd screamed until she saw Ronald's face. 'Hey, I'm sorry. I'm sorry, Keesh. I wasn't gonna – I just can't let you see stuff.' He looked so ashamed. 'I swear, I'd never hurt you.'

She was breathing again. 'I know you wouldn't.' And she did, she realised. He'd never knock someone out, never break a bottle, never . . . He was standing over her. Light was glinting off his dark skin. 'I'm sorry, Ron. I was just – eh, doing a course application, s'all. I never looked at nothing, honest.'

She saw him try to calm down. 'S'OK, s'OK. It's just got private stuff on there. But that's good, applying for a course, good to study.'

He was so bloody nice all the time. That was the trouble. She went to get up. 'I'm in your seat.'

'Wait. Keesh.' He put out his hand and stopped her by the desk. He was half a foot taller than her. 'You didn't show for cooking today. I waited. I was worried, I guess.'

'Sorry. Just busy.'

'I missed you, you know.' He was bending down. 'You don't trust me, is that it?'

'Course I do.' It was herself she didn't trust.

'Well, what's wrong? I never meant to shout at you. I'm sorry, yeah?'

'It's not that.' She opened her mouth to tell him what a liar she was, but before she could speak, his face was coming at her and his rock-hard arms were round her, and he was kissing her.

She pulled away eventually, breathless.

Ronald looked a bit shocked at what he'd done. 'I . . . er . . . Sorry.'

She stared at her shoes, trying to stop a smile breaking out over her face. She couldn't help it. 'That was a surprise.'

'Yeah. Yeah. Me too.'

She pulled herself together. 'Better go . . . my shift's starting.'

'Yeah. OK.' Still looking shell-shocked, Ronald stood back to let her go out.

When she came home after her shift, Keisha was so much on a cloud she didn't realise for a moment that Charlotte was back. She was so taken up with remembering every second of the kiss, every breath, every move. Then she saw the passport on the table and the trail of clothes leading to Charlotte's bedroom. New things, tags on them. Charlotte was in the room unpacking. Her face looked burned and raw.

'You're back?'

'Yeah.'

'Have a good time?'

'Yeah.' Charlotte didn't look round from her suitcase.

Hmm, and fuck you very much too. Something had

happened. 'Listen, I been doing my statement like you said. Started it anyway. I was thinking, you know, I'd give it a go.' Keisha was walking out to the kitchen again and Charlotte followed behind. She came into the room and leaned rigidly against the doorway, shoulders hunched.

Keisha met her eyes. 'What?'

'I have to tell you something.' Charlotte looked miserable.

'Fuck. What've you done?'

'Nothing – well. It's Chris. They're arrested him. While I was away. And I think . . . I think I saw him, before I went. At the shelter, when I was working. And I think maybe . . . he knows you're here.'

Keisha thought for a minute she might faint.

'I'm sorry! I didn't know for sure, and I didn't know if – if you'd change your mind about helping. Look!' Charlotte grabbed the prison letter from where it was shoved in the fruit bowl. 'Look – Dan's ill. It's killing him in there! I need to get him out.'

Keisha felt it in her blood, roaring through her veins, the anger back again. She had to smash something or break something or hit someone. The never-used wooden fruit bowl was right in front of her. She knocked it off the table, and it bounced off the kitchen cupboard, and rattled to a slow stop, like one of those kids' toys, those tops that go round and round.

'I can't believe you did this. You saw him, and you never told me? Fuck, all this time I been here on my own, and . . . You don't even trust me one fucking bit, after all this.'

'I do!'

'Don't fucking patronise me.'

'I didn't know if you'd go to him! I see you still looking out for him, every time you leave the house. I had to help Dan.'

'Dan? Dan doesn't give a shit about you any more and you know it. Dunno why you don't just give up and go off with your fucking copper.'

Charlotte was going to cry again. 'I love Dan.'

'Sure you do,' Keisha sneered.

Charlotte gave a little sob and dropped her shoulders. 'I'm so sorry. I didn't – oh!'

Keisha marched into the little room and started throwing things into her mum's embroidered bag. The stuff from Mercy's house, some clothes, whatever. She could hardly see straight. 'You can just put my stuff out. I'll come back and get it later.'

'But you can't – Keesh, no! I'm sorry!'

'Well, you should have thought of that before you fucked me over.' She went out, slamming the door so hard it rattled.

She'd meant to leave. Really she had. The bang of the heavy door shutting in Charlotte's face had been a good sound. She'd be off, back to her life before Miss Meddling Cow here, with her blonde hair and innocent face. But halfway to the tube Keisha stopped. Ronald had kissed her last night, tasting like ginger cake. If she turned up now at the club, what'd he think?

Write it down, Charlotte had said – interfering cow. Tell the story, you'll get Ruby back. Was it fair to be cross at Charlotte for keeping secrets, when there was so much Keisha knew herself – so much she had never said?

A breeze went through the trees on Belsize Crescent, and Keisha shivered. This weird time, it was going to end soon. Chris was in jail. Ronald had kissed her. There'd be a trial. And somewhere not far away, Ruby would soon be going back to school.

Ruby.

Keisha picked up her bag and started to walk back. Charlotte was standing on the pavement outside the house, shivering in her shorts and T-shirt.

She started to cry as Keisha came round the corner. 'I knew you'd come back. Oh God, I'm sorry, I never should have done it, I'm so sorry.'

Keisha put the bag down again. 'You gotta trust me. Me too – dunno if I can trust you now. You never told me you saw him, and you know he's after me. He's after my kid.'

'You *can* trust me. Oh Christ, I'm so sorry.' She threw her thin arms round Keisha, the first time they'd hugged – and Keisha could hear the girl's breath catching like she was trying to stop crying. She stiffened up at the feel of someone so close, but then she patted Charlotte gently on her shoulder. 'Come on, it's freezing.'

Part Five

Hegarty

'About me,' Kylie said, blinking her eyes behind her glasses. She looked round the table at the men seated there, and told her story as if she'd done it many times before. 'So when I was ten my kid brother was killed by a paedo. Big case in Oz. But they got the wrong guy; he was let out after five years, and in the meantime the real perp killed two other kids. So I do miscarriages of justice. Dodgy trials. Screwed-up evidence. No one should have to go through all that twice, that's what I think.' She opened her file, businesslike. 'You can find all this out online so I'm just telling you now. Least over here not everyone knows. Oh, his name was Matthew, by the way, Officer.'

She looked up at Hegarty's shocked face and said, laughing, 'I know, and I got Kylie. You'd think it would have been Brad or Jason or something, right? Now, let's get on with it. OK to proceed, Mr Hunt? Inspector? Now if I can turn your attention to page three . . .'

Around the table in the police station meeting room, the prosecution barrister, Hegarty's boss, and assorted people from HR and the press office, all turned to the dossier Dan's new lawyer had put together.

Hegarty wasn't having a good week. There'd already been

that awful 'chat' with the boss. The day after Singapore he'd knocked sheepishly on DI Barton's door.

'Ah, Matthew.' The boss was watering his (dying) rubber plant. 'Good trip? See you caught the sun.'

'Yes, sir. Er – can I talk to you?'

'Of course, of course – you heard about Chris Dean then? Lifted him during a drugs bust, believe it or not. We've charged him with this Hammersmith assault for now, have to see if he gets remanded.'

'And the Kingston Town case? The MO's so similar, and if we can tie Dean to the scene . . .'

The boss winced. 'Bit of a pickle, Matthew. We're under a lot of pressure to get a conviction there – community tensions, you know. And all your witnesses said Dean left the club *before* the attack, didn't they?'

'Yes.' The ones who'd spoken up had, at least. And there was no record of the taxi Dean might have got home. But. But but but.

'Last thing we want is the press in. You up to looking into it? On the QT, so to speak?'

Hegarty decided not to say he already had been. 'Well, sir, thing is – I need to take myself off the case.'

The boss's eyebrows shot up. Hegarty ploughed on. 'I need to declare an interest.'

'On what grounds?' The poor plant was drowning under a flood of water.

'Er, personal, sir. Being personally compromised. In the PACE codes – you know.' He tailed off.

The eyebrows nearly disappeared into the sandy hair. 'Is there something you need to tell me, Matthew? Has something happened?'

'Nossir.' He remembered her lips on his face at the harbour

in Singapore, the slight catch from her gloss as she pulled away. 'Nothing yet.'

Even though he was off the investigation, Hegarty had to testify in Dan's case, as arresting officer, and so he'd been hauled in by this – this bloody Aussie woman, the lawyer Charlotte had found in Singapore. Tiny, she sat behind the desk like a little kid and went through the evidence over and over. Usually the police wouldn't give the defence the time of day, but after Hegarty's ill-timed confession, the powers-that-be had decided to play nice. So here they were, along with the prosecution guy, this Adam Hunt QC. Poker up his arse and fond of himself, you could tell.

Kylie said, 'So talk me through the procedure, Officer. What led you to Daniel Stockbridge on the morning of May tenth?'

'I told you,' Hegarty said impatiently. 'We found his employee credit card on the desk in the office, and we checked with his workplace and got the address. It was very simple.' In fact, Haussmann's had been only too keen to give up all they had on Daniel Stockbridge. That was one of Hegarty's dad's famous warning signs: *Ask yourself why they want to help so bad, son.* But he hadn't asked, had been so keen to crack his first big case.

'Other than the card, did anything tie him to the incident?'

'It was a murder, actually. He'd been seen by many witnesses going out back with the victim.'

'The alleged victim . . .'

'. . . with the *dead man*, and a taxi driver identified him as a pick-up he made at the club shortly after.'

'How could you be sure it was him?'

'Two witnesses picked him out of a parade, and he

subsequently admitted to assaulting Mr Johnson at the scene. We then decided to proceed with the charge.'

She clicked her pen on and off for a while. 'That was Johnson's sister, and his girlfriend, yeah, your witnesses? Bet they were upset.'

Hegarty had been in court before. 'Hearsay. I'm not answering that.'

'No matter. Anyhoo, Mr Stockbridge confessed to what exactly?'

'A light punch. He said in his statement that the victim was fine. You can read it yourself.'

'The *alleged* victim. Right. And Forensics found only a small trace of blood on the defendant's shirt, right?'

'Right, but—'

'Just answer the question, Officer.' She winked at him, and he looked away, grinding his teeth. 'So there was no blood to speak of on the shirt.'

Hegarty glanced at his boss, who nodded slightly. 'No. But his prints were on the bottle. We felt it was enough to bring a charge.'

'Yes, the alleged weapon had the defendant's print on it, and it was identified as a bottle of Red Stripe sold to him – or rather, not sold, as his card was declined. Oh-kay. Foot imprints. Talk me through what happened there.'

He'd been a bit worried about that. The crime scene had been stamped all over with prints, but none could be found that matched Stockbridge's. 'There were a number of footprints in the blood – it was a mess, really, no one stopped staff going in to help. They tried CPR, of course. Stockbridge's could have been obscured, or maybe he just didn't step in it.'

'You yourself stepped in the blood, in fact, did you not?'

Hegarty took a deep breath. 'Unfortunately, as I was first

on the scene, I proceeded straight in to ascertain if the victim's life could be saved. Sadly, it could not, but in the process, my, er, my footwear became contaminated.' How did lawyers talk like this every day? His tongue felt tangled in knots.

He tried to focus on what Kylie was saying. 'Not usual, is it, that you'd make the arrest if you'd been at the scene?'

Again he looked at the boss, who wore an expression of deep pain. Whether at his bowels or Hegarty's incompetence wasn't clear. 'Unfortunately, as it was a Friday night, the Force was rather overstretched at this point,' Hegarty ploughed on. 'It was felt that – to avoid the risk of the defendant fleeing . . .' He'd just gone, was what he meant. Tearing off, bad as Maverick Mike himself. Friday night in Camden wasn't the best time to get murdered. He tried not to think about what he'd seen when he crashed into the office, the blood leaking from the guy's neck, the sprays and splashes up and down the walls.

'Didn't the perpetrator stand on the victim's hand, crushing it? You released that to the media.'

That was another sticky point. 'Someone did. No way to know who.'

'R-i-i-ght.' She flipped over the paper. 'Tell me how you approached the defendant's workplace. You didn't get a court order to release.'

'Well, they were quite open. There was a complaint on file about racist bullying in the team, from a young female intern.'

'And this intern, she got a payout of a hundred thousand pounds in compensation, right?'

Peevishly, Adam Hunt QC said, 'Miss McCausland, how is this relevant?'

'She did, you know. Oh-kay. Find any evidence about Mr Stockbridge's blackouts?'

'HR said he'd had memory lapses at work.'

'Were you aware that the defendant has been diagnosed with stress-related epilepsy?'

'I wasn't at the time, but now, yes.'

'R-i-i-ght.'

'I was also aware he'd taken a large quantity of cocaine.' Hegarty saw the boss wince, and shut his mouth before he could say more.

'Oh, yeah.' Kylie smiled. 'Charlotte gave the game away on that, didn't she.' She read from the transcript. '"I don't even do drugs." And speaking of Miss Miller, you stepped down from the case recently. Why?'

Around the room, the men stiffened. Hegarty swallowed. 'I felt I was too involved.'

'R-i-i-ght. You met with Miss Miller several times? Coffee, dinner, and on holiday?'

He gaped at her. 'Er, is that relevant?'

Adam Hunt sighed. 'It will probably come up, Officer.'

'I . . . thought the case was closed. She was upset.' His Irish skin was flushing like a Belisha beacon, as his mum would say.

'I'll make sure it comes up,' Kylie said cheerfully, making notes. 'May as well know what you'll say.'

'Right.' He stared at the table.

'OK, mate,' Kylie said, all smiles. 'That'll do for now. See ya in court.'

Outside the door Charlotte was waiting, pretending to read the *Law Gazette*. She looked tired and anxious, and when she saw him she flushed red. 'Hi.'

'Hi.' He held his coat awkwardly in his hands.

'You OK?'

'Yep.' He realised after a while he should say it back. 'Er, you?'

She bit her lip, but then Kylie opened the door, her long cardigan draped round her small compact body. 'Come on in, Charlie. Time for your grillin'.'

This Kylie was just so irritating! Everything about her – that she wore flip-flops with a designer suit, that her baby-soft hair fell over her face all the time and she blew it away. That she scrunched up her eyes as if she needed glasses, and she chewed her pen all the time – even chewed his pen when she borrowed it off him. That she seemed to know everything – every time she mentioned Charlotte she gave him this big smile, as if to say, *I'm onto you, mate!* See you in court, she'd said. That would be the next thing. He would also be seeing Charlotte in court. And Stockbridge, of course. Her fiancé, still.

Charlotte

Charlotte was a bit flummoxed by Kylie, if she was honest. When they'd met in Singapore she'd seemed so nice. A short girl with hair falling over her face, making scribbled notes on napkins in Starbucks. But now this barrage of questions, it wasn't what she expected. She'd expected fireworks between Kylie and Keisha if anything, when she finally persuaded her reluctant flatmate to talk to the lawyer. But Keisha had come out of her interview in a good mood, for her. 'She's not bad, that Kylie. Not full of shit and long words like most lawyers.' And when Charlotte had phoned her after, Kylie was still laughing.

'She's a riot, your mate. Mouth like a sailor on shore leave.'

A bit put out, Charlotte asked, 'She say if she'd testify?'

'We-ell, no. She still won't let me put her on my list. But we'll see. Never say die, eh, Charlie?'

'They could arrest her, couldn't they? If she won't do it?'

Kylie sounded surprised. 'I don't think they'll do that. No need to worry.'

But that wasn't quite what Charlotte had meant. It didn't exactly worry her. She wasn't sure what she'd meant, in fact.

Today when she'd gone into the station for her interview, supervised by the CPS and police, Hegarty was coming out, and Charlotte had gone shaky and red. She was sure Kylie noticed. She'd smiled at Charlotte and said, 'Don't worry, I'm just grilling you.'

She felt like a burger, flipped and dropped. The girl who came out of the questions wasn't someone she recognised. Someone who'd take drugs, and shout at detectives, and doggedly stand by a man everyone else thought was a murderer. Who'd engineer a meeting with the arresting officer just because that man wouldn't let her visit him in prison.

The prosecution had a whole row of lawyers, all suits and designer glasses. All Dan had was Kylie, five foot nothing and ink all over her hands. Surely it was meant to be the other way round? The evil defendant with all the money, and the plucky prosecution bringing them down?

'And Officer Hegarty, what's the story there?' Kylie had said, tapping her pen on her blotter.

It was like she could read minds, Charlotte thought. 'Nothing! He's been nice to me. I've been struggling.' She looked down at her bare hand, avoiding the eyes of the suited men in the room. 'It was meant to be my wedding day, you know, just after.'

'Yeah. And you said he met you in Singapore for an exotic holiday?'

Charlotte's mouth fell open. 'I . . . no! I was there to meet you, actually, and he was just passing through. I didn't think it was wrong to meet up for a drink. Was it?'

'The arresting officer on your fiancé's case? Bit strange, maybe. Anything happen?'

'Of course not.' Blushing, she looked away from the men. But she was remembering waiting for him on the pier, all dressed up and perfumed, and how her heart had hammered every time she saw a tall man walking towards her. And then that time when he'd chased her down the street in the rain and held her while she cried, shivering in his thin wet shirt. When he'd let go his eyes had locked into hers and he'd said, 'You need seeing home?'

That was it, she knew. That could have been the moment when she moved on with her life. When she did what everyone was telling her to do, even Dan himself, and forgot her fiancé, gave it up as a bad job. But she'd held on this far. She'd pulled away from DC Hegarty, the air chill after the heat of his body. No, she'd shaken her head. No. And she'd trudged home alone through the puddles collecting on Prince of Wales Road.

'OK.' Kylie suddenly moved on. 'Let's talk about your first statement . . .'

Afterwards Charlotte slumped on the bus, replaying it. At the end of her interview she'd stood up, late for her waitressing job. The men in suits had left the room and Kylie was shoving papers randomly into a Tesco's carrier bag. 'I never thought of him in that way.' She'd felt the need to explain to Kylie. 'DC Hegarty, I mean. I didn't.'

'Oh?' Kylie was cracking a pen lid in her mouth. 'Maybe you should start. I'm pretty sure he does.'

And she remembered seeing him before she went in, and

how she'd watched him walk out until Kylie had to touch her arm to get her attention. 'He's just a friend,' she'd said again.

'R-i-i-ght.'

Charlotte had other problems. When the news came about Chris Dean's arrest, she'd girded her loins and called Dan's parents again, the first time in months, since she'd given up on them ever helping.

The phone rang for a long time, and when Dan's father answered it was in the wavering voice of an old man. 'He . . . llooo?'

'Mr Stockbridge? It's Charlotte. Er . . . Dan's Charlotte?'

'Is something the matter?'

Of course it was, his son was in prison. 'Well, the thing is, I've found some more evidence in Dan's case.'

He was silent. 'I don't think we can help.'

'Listen, please! It's not what you think.'

'What are you saying, dear? We can't cope with much more of this.'

'I'm saying he didn't do it.' She enunciated clearly; no way would he 'pardon' her on this occasion. 'I think it was a MISCARRIAGE OF JUSTICE.'

Like a lab rat, she could almost hear Justice Stockbridge's ears prick up at the words. 'Do you honestly believe that?' he said after a while.

'I have proof,' she said, stretching the truth just a little. 'We think someone else did it. It wasn't Dan.' There was a long scuffling in the background, whispers, the phone dropped. 'Ex-CUSE me?' she said loudly, with a small stab of satisfaction.

'Yes,' said Edward Stockbridge. 'I'd like to know a bit more about this, dear.'

'I've got a lawyer, a good one. Will you please let her explain it? Just talk to her?'

She could only imagine what the Stockbridges would make of Antipodean Kylie in her flip-flops, but it seemed to have worked. Now they were on their way, and she had to meet their train and escort them to a hotel. It had always annoyed her how Dan, the only child of old parents, treated them like they might keel over if they had to so much as hail a taxi. London wasn't the jungle, for God's sake. Even her own flapping mother could probably use the tube, if she'd written down the colours of the lines first. Still, at least they were on board now and willing to help with the legal fees. Something about that niggled at Charlotte. Why would they suddenly believe what Kylie said, while Charlotte herself had been fighting for months with no one to help? She was so sick of it, all the different angles, the million different impressions from that one night, those ten minutes inside the club and then outside, the man pushing past . . . Well. It would all be over soon.

At the same time Kylie was also meeting Dan at the prison. Charlotte had expected a fight over this, but there was none. 'So he saw you? He was OK?'

Kylie was surprised by the question. 'Yeah, think so. He's not in great shape, but OK once I got him going. Had a good natter, we did.'

This was the same Dan who'd refused to see his own fiancée for months. 'Did he look all right? Different?'

'I never saw him before, Charlie.'

'Did he show an interest, like, does he actually want to win?'

'Course he does!' On the phone, Charlotte had heard her shuffling papers. 'We're gonna, too. No worries.'

So she'd have to wait, it seemed, till she faced him across a courtroom like any other member of the public. Charlotte felt very, very tired. With his parents as intermediaries, Dan had signed the papers, and the flat was going on the market in the next few weeks. Then it would just be a matter of time before everything changed for ever. The last link to the old life gone. She'd fought for him so long, through all she'd lost – friends, job, home, life – and he would still talk to this loud-voiced Australian over her. A thought crept in like tumbleweed: if she'd sold her ring, was she even engaged any more? Or was she single?

But before picking up the dreaded in-laws, or nearly-in-laws, or whatever they were, she had one even worse thing to do. Charlotte left the police station and took the Northern Line back to Tottenham Court Road. From there it was a short walk down the back streets of Soho, and to her old office building.

From the moment she stepped into the lift it all felt wrong. In the reflected metal she could see her face, flushed from the hot tube. She didn't look like she belonged here at all, not any more. In fact, Kelly the receptionist didn't recognise her at first. She gave her a sneering up-and-down look that was usually reserved for couriers. 'Can I help you?'

'It's me. Charlotte.' She made herself smile, and actually it was sort of funny how surprised Kelly was to see glossy Charlotte Miller with the ghosts of bean stains on her shirt.

'Oh! Are you back, then?'

'Just to see Simon. And no, I don't have an appointment, before you ask.'

Kelly's mouth was a lipglossed 'o'. 'Right . . . would you like to take a seat?'

'Not really.' Charlotte was kind of enjoying this, in a way.

Sure enough, Simon was out there in seconds after Kelly's muttered call. He too looked surprised and even a bit scared. 'Hello, darling! What a surprise!'

'Just in the area. Do you have a moment?'

'Well, it's a bit last-minute, love.'

'It's urgent.' She started walking and after a worried look at Kelly, Simon followed.

'Meeting room?' She nodded towards it. Ah, the same office smell of toner and slightly rotted fruit. Odd how you forgot it, the air you had breathed. She kept her eyes fixed forward – last thing she needed now was Chloe or Fliss to come over all gushy and insincere.

Simon shut the door into the airless meeting room, sealing them off. He had on his grey cardigan and skinny tie, and he was carrying the coffee mug he'd had in his hand at Reception. 'Listen, Charlotte, you can't really just turn up like this.'

She sat down. 'I need you to help me. Please, would you sit down?'

He sat grudgingly. 'You want to sort your contract, is that it? Well, I didn't want it to come to this, but I do have certain rights, if you go down that route—'

She cut him off. 'I said I needed you to help me. I need PR help.'

'What?'

She sat back, trying to remember the speech she'd been rehearsing on the tube. 'As you know, my fiancé is going on trial soon, for murder.' Simon looked pale. 'I believe he didn't do it. Since I left here I've found out quite a lot, actually, that makes me think I'm right.'

'What, you think he's *innocent*?'

'That's right. I think they got it wrong – it does happen. So I need you to PR him. Get me some interviews, exposés, whatever. I know you can do it.'

Simon now looked furious. 'Look, I've tried to be understanding, but even if that's true, I'm not a bloody charity. PR for a murderer, for Christ's sake.'

Blood was thundering in her ears. 'But you know people, you could help.'

'But why the hell would I? I like you and all, love, but come on.'

This was it. She licked her dry mouth. 'Because – I was thinking, you sort of owe me.'

'What?'

'Because, because . . . you used to like me a lot, at first. Remember?'

'I don't know what you—' He was half-laughing at her cheek.

She cut him off. 'That bar. Q. My first week? You forget? I haven't.' Her voice wavered and it was all flashing round and round her mind, waking up and smelling straight away that she wasn't in her own bed. The fear – *Oh God, what happened to me?* The terrible fear.

Simon sneered, 'You think I should help you because, what, you were drunk one time, and . . .' He tailed off.

Charlotte gulped. 'I think you should help me because it's the right thing to do.'

'But I can't guarantee anything, it's PR, for Christ's sake, not advertising. And the case is *sub judice*, or don't you understand that?'

She had to laugh at that, a gasping dry laugh. 'I did work here for six years, Simon. I know how it goes. You can get me some interviews, can't you?'

He picked at the lettering on his Oxford mug, sulky. 'I suppose I could talk to some people.'

She sagged with relief. 'OK.' She forced herself not to thank him. He didn't deserve it. 'And I think you ought to pay me some redundancy money, you know. If you want me to quietly disappear.'

'Whatever.' He slumped in his chair, pissed off. 'You know you can't prove . . . Oh, what the hell. Fine.'

'Bye then.' She exited the office in a flash, to avoid seeing anyone she would once have counted a friend. They weren't her friends any more. Maybe they never were.

Once Simon was on board, it was easier to sway Sarah and her editor into printing a story.

'This had better be true,' her step-sister kept saying, all the way in the taxi to the photo-shoot. 'I'm going to be really pissed off if he's convicted after all. My reputation'll be shot.'

'It won't be.' Charlotte didn't say that she too, and not to mention Dan, would be more than a little pissed off if he went to prison.

Sarah tapped at the driver through the glass partition. 'Here, thanks.' She turned back to Charlotte. 'Now, you've approved the copy I sent over? I had to be very careful not to say anything about the case details.'

'I suppose.' The article was very sentimental, all about Charlotte's pain waiting for her lost love, but Sarah worked for a paper that valued sentiment far above legal process. 'Do you need to have all that stuff about the police being crap? I don't know if it's fair.'

Sarah rolled her eyes. 'Didn't you work in PR? It needed to have an angle. The police being crap is what our readers want to hear.'

'But I think they did their best – I mean, the evidence did look bad. Couldn't you just stick to that stuff about how bad the banks are, driving people to stress?'

Sarah just sighed. 'God, you're naïve. We're getting out here.'

Charlotte spent the next hour standing on the grimy pavement opposite the walls of Pentonville Prison, in front of a fried chicken shop. Sarah had said to dress in her poshest clothes, so the readers could see she was safe, middle-class. It was a dry, windy sort of London day, blowing grit and pollen into her eyes until they watered.

'That's good.' Sarah pounced on the photographer. 'Did you get that? Looked like tears.'

'I got it.' The photographer was a patient, cynical East End geezer used to hanging round nightclubs waiting for *Hollyoaks* actresses to fall out. He gave Charlotte such a sardonic look behind Sarah's back that she started giggling, and had trouble afterwards rearranging her face into a suitably sad expression. She had to make herself think of Dan behind those walls, alone and ill, to look heartbroken enough for Sarah.

'For God's sake, you're meant to look sad! Your wedding got cancelled!'

'I know.' Charlotte giggled again. 'Sorry.'

Much, much later, it was finally done.

'That's the one,' Gary said, showing her a shot on the digital camera. She was standing by an overflowing bin in a gust of wind that swirled her hair and Burberry mac. Her eyes looked wet and sorrowful, as she gazed over at the prison. In her hand – a fake engagement ring on it – was a picture of her and Dan on holiday in Turkey, tanned and smiling, colourful drinks in front of them.

'Gorgeous,' said Gary, matter-of-factly. He was packing his gear with tattooed arms. 'You should use that one.'

'I'll decide, said Sarah snootily. 'It is good, though.'

'Picture Editor'll decide,' Gary said, but Sarah wasn't listening. 'I might get an award for this, if he's acquitted.' She glared at Charlotte as if she would be personally responsible for the trial outcome. 'Anyway, got to run, bye.' She bustled off to hail a cab, already on her phone.

'Hope he appreciates all this.' Gary was lugging his gear to his car. 'Not every girl'd do that for her fella.'

That was a good point, Charlotte thought, trudging off to the tube. She leaned on a lamppost to swap her high heels for trainers. Did Dan appreciate how much she'd fought, and lost, and given up for him? She'd even gone to Simon, for God's sake. Not that Dan knew what had happened with Simon. Because he'd never noticed, had he? Not noticed she'd stayed out all night and couldn't meet his eyes for weeks.

What kind of person would confess to a crime they hadn't done, turn away all their friends and family? She thought about this for a while, standing on the dusty pavement. She cast a look behind her to the prison, then turned, and walked off. Tomorrow she had yet another difficult thing to do. She was losing track of them all.

Charlotte had only the vaguest idea where her brother worked. They'd not been close since she was nine and Jamie twelve, and he went off to boarding school. It was the year after their father left and just before their mother married Phil. She was remembering that as she stood on the marble steps of his office building, all twenty floors of glass and steel. She'd thought about calling in advance, but didn't know what to say. Jamie had sent an email just after Dan's arrest, asking would they get the deposits back on their hotel rooms for the wedding. After that she hadn't really wanted to see him or his nervy wife Amy, who'd given up her own law career to achieve perfection in home and family instead. She didn't even want to see Tilly, her four-year-old niece. So in the end she'd decided on a surprise attack; it had worked with Simon.

The lobby was empty, a cavern of shiny marble, and behind a desk an equally shiny receptionist. She didn't have an appointment. She hadn't considered that it might be hard to see her own brother without one. Eventually, after several phone calls upstairs and arguing that she really *was* his sister – even showing her driving licence – she was given a plastic visitor tag and allowed into the space-age lifts, all touch-screen buttons and computerised voices.

As another shiny girl showed her to Jamie's office, Charlotte saw him through the glass walls. His hair was thinning on top and his face was going jowly. She watched him talk on the phone, tearing off lumps from a Prêt à Manger sandwich and stuffing them in his mouth. When they were very little, when they went on long car journeys to their grandparents', he'd let her fall asleep on his shoulder. Later, when Phil appeared, they'd been briefly united against the bluff man and his bossy daughter. But that was a long time ago.

He saw her, and she went into the glass cubicle. 'Nice office.' She felt dizzied by the soaring views of the city.

Jamie wiped avocado off his hands. 'I thought I might be seeing you. Sarah called.'

'Yes. I heard you two were talking.' She sat down, self-conscious in her jeans and vest top. You needed some kind of armour on, to walk into places like this.

'So, you're thinking of suing the bank.'

She felt embarrassed. 'It's just that money's been so tight. And what they did, it wasn't right. They stitched him up, Jamie. Right from the start, he hadn't a chance.'

He twiddled a pen. 'This is how I earn my crust, it's nothing to be ashamed of. His HR record is a matter of public record now, so we can show he was stressed, and I'm sure there are experts to say his outburst was caused by work. Your trial lawyer will be looking at that angle, I suppose.'

She bit her lip. Did Jamie also think Dan was guilty? Like everyone, except her. She didn't, did she? 'I don't know.'

Her brother was making notes. 'I think there's a good chance they'll want to settle. From what I hear, Haussmann's is under a lot of fire right now. And there's a precedent for stress-related payouts.'

'But what if he's . . .' She couldn't say it.

'Even if the claimant's convicted of a crime, they sometimes pay out.'

It sounded too good to be true. 'You think we should do it?'

He tapped his pen. 'Is he on board?'

'He will be.' If she said it, maybe it would be true.

'I heard he was going to plead Guilty.'

'He's not. He's working with Kylie right now.'

'Oh yes, Kylie.'

Charlotte's hackles rose. 'She's very good. Dad recommended her.'

'I heard about your little holiday out East. Enjoy it?'

Was he jealous? 'I wished I'd gone sooner, to be honest. They're happy. You should go sometime. He'd love to see the new baby.'

Jamie's face changed. 'Amy's been very upset by all this, you know.'

'All what?'

'Knowing she had a killer round for Sunday roast, that sort of thing.'

'Really? I was a bit upset myself when my wedding got cancelled. Hope you got the hotel deposit back, though.' She started to stand up. 'You know, you haven't even said his name once. You remember Dan, don't you? He was the one who drove your daughter to hospital when she fell off her bloody trampoline. I guess you don't remember any of that.'

'Wait.' He spread his hands on the table. 'It's been hard for all of us. People know me in the City, they know he was engaged to you. And Mum can hardly hold her head up in the village. But I'm sure it's been hardest on you.'

'On Dan, actually. Seeing as he's the one in prison.'

Jamie made a sort of face, as if to say Dan deserved what he got.

'Look.' She felt very tired. 'I don't need more hassle. I don't really care if you think he did it or not. I don't think he did, and I need to help him as much as I can. So, you can help, or I'll just go away, and I'm sure I'll see you at Christmas or whenever.'

Jamie looked sad. Maybe he also remembered the days before Phil, and divorce, and boarding school. 'I want to help, if I can. But you do need to get Dan on board. And I'd need a complete deposition on what happened to him there. Will he see me?'

Charlotte said, 'Probably. Anyone but me seems to be fine.'

Keisha

The week before the trial, things went a bit mad. Dan's folks arrived, a posh couple with pokers up their arses. Keisha was staying well away. Then the article about Charlotte appeared on page five of her step-sister's paper, in full colour and beside one about Cheryl Cole. In the picture Charlotte looked like she was about to cry, all cold and alone with her fella's picture outside the prison. It started, *Charlotte Miller should have been married by now. Instead she waits outside prison walls. Fiancé Daniel Stockbridge, 31, was a stockbroker with Haussmann's Bank, recently besieged by rumours of dodgy deals and insider trading. In May, Daniel was arrested for the murder of nightclub owner . . .*

She didn't read the rest, it was lots of guff about Charlotte being 'fragile and pretty' and having to sell her engagement ring, blah, blah. Then all this about the stress people were under in the City, poor diddums getting paid millions to fiddle about with computers, and the 'culture of aggressive bullying and old school tie'. Keisha wasn't sure what that meant. Some guy called Gary had sent a big photo print, same as the one in the paper, only Charlotte was laughing in it at something. It was nice – she looked happy.

'Look,' said Charlotte, turning over the papers. 'Dan's in *Private Eye*.' By the sound of her voice, that must be a big deal. 'Dan hates *Private Eye*. Says it reminds him of his old school newssheet.' Charlotte laughed. 'Jesus, he's going to be so pissed off.'

Keisha couldn't figure out what was so funny about it.

After the article appeared, things started to happen quite fast. There were phone calls from other journalists – Keisha learned to tell, because they were always women and they started out so friendly. 'Hi there! Is that Charlotte?'

Charlotte would take the call and ask quick, short questions: What page? How many words? Picture or not? What was their angle? And with Charlotte buying just about every paper there was, Keisha noticed lots of new stuff about bankers was appearing, this time a bit different. Seemed now everyone was jumping on the bandwagon of, 'Hey, maybe they weren't all bastards after all!'

Also calling were Charlotte's mates, the ones who'd dissed her at that party and not answered her emails. When Keisha answered these – Gemma or Holly or whoever, calling 'just to see if I can help, I saw the paper' – she would mouth the name to Charlotte, and nearly every time Charlotte just shook her head. 'Say I'm out. Wasn't much help when I needed her, was she?' On top of this, Charlotte was fielding offers on the flat. She'd priced it low so it was sure to go, even in that market, she said, as if she knew what she was talking about.

Keisha was sort of impressed with this new Charlotte. She'd hardly cried once since she came back from Singapore, and in among all the newspapers and legal stuff, Keisha'd seen other things – printouts about studying, course booklets, that sort of thing. She was different.

Charlotte wasn't the only one moving forward. A few days before the trial, Keisha went back to London University. That was where Ian Stone would be on a panel about his pet peeve – the 'erosion of civil liberties'. Keisha thought this was something to do with being able to stop people on the street to see if they had knives or whatever. She agreed vaguely this was bad – she didn't want some policeman being able to stop her when she was just minding her own business.

She tried not to be too stupidly early, and ended up hemmed in at the back with all these eager student types taking notes and nodding madly every time Ian Stone said something about 'construction of a surveillance state' or 'destruction of centuries of liberty'. The other people on the panel were some stuffy man with a red face, who was an MP, and a black woman they'd chucked on to say things like 'As an ethnic female . . .' What a load of balls.

She tried to follow it. It was strange to be in such a packed room, everyone hanging on the words of the panel, nodding or shaking their heads like they were angry. They really cared! To her shock, right in the middle of it, she heard a name she recognised.

Ian Stone was saying, 'If you look at many current cases going through the courts, the rush to conviction is worrying. Many of you will have seen in the papers about the case against Daniel Stockbridge – one of the so-called "Banker Butchers". Despite the mostly circumstantial evidence, this case is still being pushed through to trial. We must ask ourselves why this is.'

Afterwards she waited for bloody hours, it seemed, while Ian Stone was grabbed by all these left-wing students. 'Do you agree Tony Blair should be tried as a war criminal?' 'Wouldn't you say kettling violates the Human Rights Act?' God, they were sucking up to him so much it was embarrassing. Listening to his answers, she thought maybe Ian Stone felt the same.

Finally she was left. He gave her an irritated glance, saying, 'I really must go, I'm sorry.'

'You mentioned that Stockbridge case.'

'Yes?' He was fiddling with his iPhone. He had a knitted waistcoat, little ponytail, grey hair. Good Christ.

'I might be in that case. I'm a witness, like.'

'Oh?' That made him look up.

'You think I should I do it – testify, like? If I know something?'

'I don't know, er – what's your name?'

'Keisha.'

'Well, I don't know, Keisha. Why wouldn't you?'

'Say I knew something, but if I told, someone else might get hurt. Someone important to me, like.'

His eyes were flicking from her to the door. 'It's an ethics question, really. I don't have the time, I'm afraid—'

'Can they arrest me, if I don't want to do it? Are they allowed?'

'I'm sure they won't arrest you.' Fuck, this wasn't working. He was edging to the door, still poking at his phone.

'Did you know someone called Mercy Collins years ago?'

'What? No, I don't think so. I must go. There's drinks . . .'

'She was my mum. You taught her.'

'Well, I teach a lot of people.'

What could she do? What could she say to make him not walk out of that door? She scrabbled round in the embroidered bag – Mercy's bag. 'Look!' Her voice was too loud. She shoved her birth certificate at him. 'Look, is that you?'

He took it, frowning, in a hurry. He opened his mouth and then closed it again. He folded it up and passed it back to her, carefully, like a bomb. 'Come with me,' he said.

The place he took her to was up on a deserted floor of classrooms. It was some kind of staffroom, where he switched on the kettle and made her coffee with old powdery Nescafé. 'There's only instant, I'm afraid.'

'S'OK,' she said, as if she ever drank coffee, yuck.

'So. This Mercy is your mother?'

'She died.'

'I'm sorry.' He blinked as if he really hoped she wouldn't start crying.

'Do you remember her?' For some reason she really wanted him to say yes.

'Er . . . I'm not sure. It was a long time ago, and I have so many students, you see.'

'You shag your students a lot, then?' She took a gulp and burned her tongue – how in the hell did people pay three pounds fifty for this stuff?

Ian Stone looked miserable. 'I, er, no. Of course not.'

'But you did with my mum.'

'I don't know. The thing is, er, Keisha, I've had a vasectomy. So I don't know if I can be . . . You know, that means . . .'

'Jesus, I know what it means, I'm not thick. When?'

'Oh. Maybe twenty years ago?'

She took a tiny sip. 'Why'd you do it?'

'I suppose I felt the world was full enough, and it would be a selfish act, reproducing.'

He was the selfish one, she thought. 'Thing is, I'm twenty-five, aren't I?'

'Oh. Are you?'

'Yep. So you'd have taught me mum in what – like, 1984?'

He looked so depressed. 'I don't know. She was black, I take it?'

'Er, yeah.' Duh!

'But you're not, are you? Not really?'

He was looking at her pale skin, her flat hair. 'Not really.' God, and this dude was a professor.

He fiddled with his mug. 'Ah, Keisha, this is a bit of a

shock to me. I never – well, I had a vasectomy, so you can see, I never wanted children.'

'S'OK. Never wanted a dad neither.' Miss Cheeky! Was it even true? *Keisha, you bull-shitter.*

'Did you really want to ask me about this trial?'

'Sorta. I dunno if I can do it or not. They'll ask me questions, won't they? What if I don't know the answer? Or like what if they make it look like I'm lying? People'd get hurt for no reason.' She sighed. 'See, I had a plan. I was saving money. I was gonna go . . . well, I was gonna try again. But now it's all different. This trial – I don't know what to do.' Chris was in prison. Ruby maybe lost for ever, if she didn't get her soon. But she couldn't explain any of this to Ian bloody Stone.

He paused. 'Would you like me to help you? I could read your statement – you do have a statement? Sometimes I help people prepare for trials, if they aren't . . . if they're not exactly familiar with the legal system.'

'Maybe.' She narrowed her eyes. She didn't need anything off him.

'Are you a student here? You said you were twenty-five.'

'Nah – finished already.' Finished school at sixteen, that was, with three GCSEs. And her dad was a professor!

'And are you – you have a boyfriend, or anything?' It was painful, watching him stumble over the words.

'Nah.' She thought of Chris – bloody, awful, unforgettable Chris. 'Got a little girl. Ruby.'

'Oh! Goodness.' He smiled weakly. 'I could be – well, a grandfather, then. What's she like?'

'Ruby? She's gorgeous. Lovely, special kid. And all she's ever had is crap.'

It was too much. Her fat old mum dying on the kid, that

violent bastard for a dad, this pony-tailed hippy for a possible grandad, and worst of all, half-and-half Miss Keisha Collins for a mum. Not black, not white. Too scared to go into court and tell the truth, even if an innocent man was banged up because of it. 'Shit.' She was crying. For the first time since everything, and in front of Ian bloody Stone. He'd not know she never cried, not even when her mum died, not even when she lost Ruby. He'd think she was one of those sappy girls like Charlotte, who cried at adverts for BT.

'Oh, God.' Ian Stone slumped. 'I'm sorry, I'm no good at this. Please – don't cry. I don't mean to reject you . . . it's just a lot to take in. How do I know if I really am . . . Oh, please.'

He sounded so scared that she took a huge breath in and willed her eyes to stop running. *Do not fucking cry, Keisha, you sap.*

'I'm so sorry,' he said again. 'I promise I'll do what I can to help with this trial and – well, with whatever I can. But please don't expect much. I don't have it to give.' He looked tired, in his silly waistcoat. A silly man, getting old.

'I don't never expect much,' she said, wiping her face. 'Only gets you disappointed, expecting.'

'Wait – here.' He hunted through his pockets for a bit of napkin. 'You have a pen? This is my email and phone.' He scribbled. 'Will you contact me, please? At least with your trial. I could help with that.'

'Dunno if I'll do it or not yet.' She didn't want to tell him that she'd not even finished the statement she'd started writing. But she took the corner of napkin and folded it in the pocket of her denim jacket. On her way out of the empty building, past rooms with ghostly writing on the boards, lights and computers breathing like people sleeping, Keisha stopped in Reception and picked up a few course brochures. Because, you never knew, did you?

The next day she woke up and realised she'd decided something. Charlotte was up already and had been for a run; her trainers were lined up neatly by the door and her running clothes already spinning in the washing machine. Keisha could hear her on the phone.

Charlotte's voice was low. 'Can I come round?' she was saying. Who'd she be talking to in that voice? Not any of her girl mates. No, it was a fella, and Keisha'd bet everything she had (not much) that it was a certain copper.

Chris had been arrested in a different part of London, over west, and so he was being held in Wormwood Scrubs Prison. Took bloody ages to get there on the crappy overland trains. She went up to the desk and said, 'Chris Dean.'

He looked like shit. That was the first thing she thought. He looked like he'd been sleeping rough – maybe he had. His hair was grown out in patches, and his face you could hardly see under the fuzz of his gingery Irish beard. He looked so different that for a second she didn't know him. For a minute she was going to say, 'Is that you?' But who else could it be?

He sat down, staring at her the whole time with his blue eyes. They hadn't changed. 'Didn't think you'd come. Put your name down, just on the off-chance, like.'

'Yeah, well.' She broke the look, stared down at the chipped table.

'You OK?'

'Yeah.' *Since you busted my face up, yeah*, she thought. The last time she'd seen him, his fist was coming at her nose.

'They got me on this assault thing,' he said, licking his chapped lips. 'Didn't have no one to post bail.'

'They want me for that Kingston Town trial,' she blurted out. She saw his fingers were all raggedy and cut, like he'd been biting them.

'Prosecution lot?'

'Defence.'

He said nothing. They were just sitting there in that big hot room with only the small table between them. Might as well have been miles. 'When we had that row,' he began, and she stiffened.

'You mean when you knocked me out, more like.'

He mumbled, 'Never meant to hurt you.'

'You gave me a fucking black eye.'

'Just got mad – I never meant to hurt you, Keesh.'

She'd seen him like this once before. After Ruby. After what he did to her. 'They took her,' she said. 'You know that? Mum died, so they took Ruby away.'

His hands shook. 'Sorry.'

'Don't know if I'll ever see her again, thanks to you. My own little girl.'

'I know.'

'You're a dickhead, do you know that?' She was saying it just because he seemed so beaten, with his head bowed.

'Yeah.' He took it, like he might cry. Oh shit, she thought, don't cry. Somehow she wouldn't be able to sit there if he cried, not Chris Dean, not the boy she'd seen walking into the classroom that day years ago.

'Keesh,' he said quietly, looking up with those blue eyes. 'You tell them anything about that night? At the club?'

'Maybe I did.'

'Listen.' He leaned over the table. 'They got me on this assault, babe. That's two years, maybe. If you tell them the

307

rest – I'm screwed, Keesh. I'll be in here years. Ruby, she won't know me. But if you just said we left at the same time, you and me . . .'

She wanted to say so many things, like, *You deserve all this, you shit*, or *Why the fuck would I help you?* But there were his eyes in his pale face, and his thin shoulders under the sweatshirt that looked too big for him.

'Time's up,' said the guard, two metres away.

She leaned over and whispered hard. 'You went there to get the money, I know you did. For those guys – that gang. I know you know them. You went to get it off Anthony Johnson, didn't ya?'

He mumbled. 'I wasn't gonna hurt him – it was just business!'

'Sure. Business.'

'I wouldn't do nothing like that. You know I wouldn't.'

'But Ruby—'

'That was an accident. Lost me temper. That kid means the world to me, you know it.'

'What about your shoes? Fuck, I know it wasn't ketchup.'

He met her gaze, blue and steady. 'I went to help. Thought I oughta go back – but he was there all blood, and I stepped in it. I freaked, Keesh.'

She swallowed. 'The back door. That's how you got in?'

'Yeah. But I never hurt him, Swear to God, Keesh. I just freaked. I thought, with my record, and blood all on my shoes . . . Never meant to hit you. Just got so freaked.'

'I don't believe you,' she said, but her voice was wavering. 'Why'd you send Jonny after me, then?'

'Just, just . . . I didn't trust you. Thought you'd go against me. Tell the cops.'

'I don't trust you either.'

'We gotta.' He put his face close to hers. 'We got to trust each other, babe. You're the only one for me, you know? Since we was twelve or whatever. They might arrest you too, babe, the cops. If you saw stuff, and you never said. We could both go down. Then what'd happen to our girl?' Chris grabbed her hand. It was hot in the room but his skin was cold. He gripped her. 'I'll make it up to you. Swear to God. We'll get our girl back. We'll get past this.'

How many times had she imagined him saying that before, when she still thought things could still work out OK, just maybe?

'Come on.' The guard was making him get up, but Chris didn't take his blue eyes off her. 'I'll do it, babes. Just help me. Do it for me.' He was led out, and she was the last woman left in the sweaty room. She couldn't get up.

'You'll have to move, love,' said the guard, locking the door to where they took the prisoners. Keisha tried to get up, gathering her jacket. *Shit*, she was thinking. *What am I going to do now?*

Hegarty

Hegarty was knocking off the night-shift when she called. It had been a crap night, busting into a series of awful flats to enforce arrest warrants. Men, nearly all men, young and middle-aged, fat and skinny, tattooed or hairy. There was one woman they lifted out of a squat at four a.m., on drug charges, bleary, tired, fighting like a cat; the arresting sergeant got a whack across the cheek with one long leopard-skin painted nail. 'Mad cow,' he muttered, making notes.

'I didn't fucking do nothing,' the woman was screaming as the WPC bundled her into the car. She reminded him of Charlotte's mate, that grumpy Keisha.

Charlotte. He sighed, noting down the details – chair overturned, bong chucked at head of arresting officer – no need to search this place, it was riddled with drug stuff. Charlotte had been off with him since they got back from Singapore, since he left her on the pier. There was that awkward meeting at the station, then nothing. He didn't text or call – she'd always come to him before, and somehow that was OK. But for him to call her – well, he was still on the Force. And then, a few days ago, the paper with her article. Someone had thoughtfully left it open on his desk. There she was, sad by the prison – beautiful. She was so bloody beautiful. Then his phone rang and it was the boss saying could they have a little chat, please? And he had to walk in there with all the officers sniggering behind their screens, to meet with the boss and the Risk Officer and the Press Head about 'minimising the negative PR'.

So when he'd dragged himself home to his tiny flat, rattling with the noise of buses up and down Kentish Town Road, he wasn't expecting to hear from her. He was damp all over with sweat and stripping off to go straight to the shower when his mobile rang and he looked at the name flashing up. *Charlotte*. Shit.

He held it for a long time, five or six rings, before stabbing the button. 'Yeah?'

'Oh, hi, Matthew?'

'Yes, it's me.' *You called me, of course it is.* What the hell did she want now?

'Are you busy?'

'I just got off work.'

'Oh!' She was so hesitant. Then she said, in a rush, 'I wanted to see you. I need to talk to you.'

'Is this about the article?'

'You saw it?'

'Had a full team-briefing on it.' During which some nasty mutters had come Hegarty's way, and the boss made a number of pointed comments about keeping ourselves emotionally removed from cases, while looking straight at him with the same look his mam used to do when he kicked footballs into her washing. *Matty, I'm disappointed in you.*

Charlotte said, 'I did ask her not to slate the police. But you know, they always have an agenda.'

'I know now.' He hadn't realised how pissed off he was until he heard her voice.

'So can I see you? Are you at home?'

'Yeah, but . . .'

He heard her move. 'I can be there in twenty. Kentish Town, right?'

'But—' Crap. 'OK. I just got in, though.' Then he had a mad dash round to clean up his bachelor's shithole, jumping in the shower then throwing on jeans and his Man City shirt, kicking dirty kecks under the bed, shoving all the dishes in the sink and running hot water over them. There was a sort of cheesy unlived-in smell in the flat, so he opened the living-room windows, and the room filled with traffic noise, fumes coming in.

The doorbell buzzed when he was rubbing his hair with a towel – no time for wax. He'd look like one of the Jackson Five. She was standing there with her fair hair drawn up into some kind of twist, in the same smart trench-coat he recognised from the paper. High heels. Her legs were bare, since it was a warm, windy day.

'You better come in, then.'

'Thanks.' She looked round his small living room and even smaller kitchen, the dust an inch thick on his Xbox and CDs, cups he'd missed clustered round the one armchair, an empty pizza box on the also-empty bookshelf. She said nothing.

'It's a bit of a tip – I've been working a lot.'

She ignored it. 'I came to say I'm sorry about the paper. It wasn't fair. I just needed to do something to stop all that Banker Butcher stuff.'

'It was a good picture of you. You looked – good. Yeah.'

'Oh! Thank you.' She went a bit red. 'I just thought it might help.'

He nodded. She fiddled with her twist of hair. 'Kylie told me you took yourself off Dan's case.'

He ducked his head. 'Yeah. I thought, since Singapore . . . I had to, really.'

She said, calmly, 'I've really fucked things up for you, haven't I?'

'No. Well. Doesn't matter.' She had, but it wasn't really her fault.

'It was meant to be your big case, wasn't it – catching him.'

'I don't want to make it on the back of a mistake. If I was wrong – if he gets out . . .'

'You think he will? 'Cos I just don't know any more. I thought he would, with everything we found, but now I don't know. Kylie's got all this stuff they'll be throwing at me, twisting everything. And Keisha still won't say if she'll even testify. I think she went to see Chris the other day, too. She was crying.'

'Oh.'

She paced a few steps. 'You could arrest her. Couldn't you?'

'Is that really what you want?'

'I don't know! And I'm not even sure what happened now. All this evidence . . .' She stood in the middle of his smelly living room, her bright hair falling down at the back. 'Matt? What do you think?' She never called him this.

'I don't know either.'

'Then I start thinking, What if he does get off? You know I haven't spoken to him in months. He still won't see me. His parents, yeah, Kylie, yeah, but not me.'

What did she want from him? Did she think he'd be sad that Stockbridge wasn't getting in touch? 'Well, I dunno. That's for you to work out.'

She laughed, breathing in quickly. 'You say it like it's nothing to do with you.'

He waited, listening to the noise of traffic from the open window. 'It's not.'

She took a step towards him; the room was very small. 'You say that, but you took yourself off the case for a reason. Didn't you?'

He said nothing.

'Come on, Matt.'

'Don't make me say it.'

'OK,' she said, and she took the last two steps over to him and put her arms round his neck and kissed him.

It seemed to go on for a long time, but also be over in seconds. He'd imagined it as long as he'd known her, since he'd seen her that first morning half-asleep and scared, to feel her body against his as her coat fell open on her light summer dress, to hear her breath catch in her throat. When he kissed her neck, she tasted faintly of salt. Her mouth was soft. Her hands went into his damp hair and he felt her sag against him. 'Oh.'

He pulled away, pushed her back, and they stared at each other. 'Why did you do that?' he asked, when he could speak.

'I wanted to. For a long time. Didn't you?'

He sighed: a deep, deep sigh. 'We can't. Not now.'

'But I thought you—'

'Christ, of course I do. Every minute, when I see you. But the trial's next week. You don't want to do this, not while he still needs you.'

'He doesn't seem to think he needs me,' she said, folding her arms. 'I mean, he doesn't love me any more, does he? It's pretty clear. He won't even try. He won't even say he didn't do it.' Her voice wobbled.

'I know. But still. It's not right.'

'God, you're obsessed with what's right, aren't you?' She pulled her coat round her. 'I really am sorry about your case, and you know, messing up everything for you.'

'It's OK.' She'd never know how much she had messed things up, and exactly how little he would ever change, if it meant she was here, kissing him.

She turned at the door and kissed him again on the side of his mouth. It was a kiss that made offers, a kiss that was just millimetres from the truth. His hand crept round to the back of her neck as if it had a mind of its own. He pulled away. 'Don't. Come on.'

'OK, OK. Jesus, what is it with men and not knowing what you want?'

As he listened to her clatter down his bare staircase in her high heels, he thought it wasn't that at all. He knew exactly what he wanted. He also knew all the reasons why he couldn't have it, not now. Maybe this was how that bastard Stockbridge felt, too.

Part Six

Charlotte

Dan's trial started on a Monday in October. Reporters gathered early at the Crown Court, setting up camp on the wet morning streets, among the hum of street-cleaners pushing machines. There were TV, radio and newspaper reporters, everyone agog for this one case of a wealthy banker who'd slipped, and fallen. Charlotte, trembling and white, arrived in a taxi at the back entrance, all pipes and concrete, and was led through bleach-smelling corridors to the witness room. As she sat there with her empty stomach churning over and over, she could hear the next-door room begin to fill. She heard the clatter and stamp of feet and dry coughs and murmurs. Still she sat, head down, staring at her feet. The floor was the same, the speckled plastic, the little islands. Charlotte closed her eyes, breathing deeply, trying not to pass out.

She heard a swell of shouting that rose and died away. Now they would be bringing in Daniel Stockbridge, possible murderer, disgraced banker, and her fiancé. If he was even that any more. So long since she had seen him. She shut down the memory of kissing Matthew Hegarty, of pressing herself in so close she could breathe him. She hadn't spoken to him since then. Not now. This wasn't the time.

She knew Kylie was planning to start right off with a plea

for a mistrial, based on the huge amount of media speculation into the case. How could it be a fair trial when they were calling him a Banker Butcher? But as she waited, nothing happened. It must have been turned down.

She waited. Right now, she knew, they'd be doing the plea. And if he said he was guilty – if he did what he'd threatened to do – they would all be going home and that would be that. Charlotte held her breath: *Oh, please, no.*

The door opened and in came one of the guards, hair combed over his bald skull. She looked up, her heart in her mouth. 'Is it . . .'

He shook his head. 'They've called you, miss.' She breathed out. Thank God. He'd pleaded Not Guilty. She stood up and her legs buckled.

'OK, miss?'

'Yeah. Yes, I'll manage.' She willed herself to walk.

As Charlotte went in, a murmur went up. Scarlet, she kept her eyes on the floor. One step, then another, like Dan had said.

She looked up at the dizzying heights, the seats where the spectators sat, the seal of law on the wall. Into this room Dan had come to receive an idea of justice. These people, the row of faces in the jury box, would look only at the facts as they were packaged by Kylie and the prosecuting lawyer. They'd choose which package they liked best. They'd judge.

Dan had on his five-thousand-pound Prada suit, which his mother had delivered to him in prison. He stood up straight in the dock, but the difference in him was shocking. His tanned skin had turned yellow from months inside, like an old dried-out tea bag. She could see what looked like a healing bruise over his eye, and his hair had been cut severely short. Dan was vain about his hair and this shocked her more than the rest, that he could let it be cut so badly, all tufts and patches. He looked like someone else. His eyes roamed, dazed, and found her sitting there. What she saw hurt her so much she was the first to look down.

There was the judge, a white-haired cliché of a man, brisk and no-nonsense. He had a wig over his own white hair. Then there was a whole lot of preamble, Kylie standing up in her robes and white wig and the prosecuting lawyer, Adam Hunt QC.

There was a pause. Then Adam Hunt QC was looking right at her. She swallowed hard; it was like being caught in class. 'The Crown calls Miss Charlotte Miller.'

That was her. She got up, feeling her hot legs stick to the seat in nervous sweat. She walked over the floor in her clip-clopping heels. She sat down in the box, did her swearing on the Bible, confirmed her name and address. It was like being on the stage, a sea of heads swimming before her. Her hands felt slick and cold.

Adam Hunt was waiting to question her. 'How do you know Mr Stockbridge?'

She cleared her throat. 'I was his fiancée. I am, I mean.'

'You still are?'

She scanned the crowd; there were Dan's parents, and Sarah, but no Matthew Hegarty. 'Yes,' she said, licking her lips. She didn't look at Dan but heard him sigh across the space of polished wood.

'Can you explain what happened on the night in question?'

'Dan and I went out to a club in Camden. It was some kind of Jamaican place . . . we were meant to go there on our honeymoon.' She explained how she'd come home that day, and Dan was there, and what he'd told her, their decision to go out. Dan didn't look up once as she spoke.

'So you went with your fiancé to the Kingston Town club, is that correct?'

She nodded, then, remembering she had to speak out loud, said, 'Yes.'

'How would you describe his behaviour?'

She glanced over; Dan's head was bowed. 'He was very upset at first. But after that he seemed better, I thought.'

'Was anything else influencing your behaviour that night?'

She cringed. 'We – Dan brought home some cocaine.'

'You took illegal drugs, is that correct?'

'Well, yes, but—' She looked at Kylie – *Just answer the questions*. 'Yes.'

'Do you regularly take drugs, Miss Miller?'

'No. I don't.' Don't sound defensive, Kylie had said, but honestly, it was hard.

'Tell the court what happened with Mr Johnson. Did you witness anything out of the ordinary?'

'Well,' she hesitated. 'Not really. I went to the ladies', and when I came back I saw Dan talking to him. Then they went off – to the office, I think.'

'What did you do then?'

'I got our coats, and went to wait outside. Then Dan came, and we went home. He seemed fine. I didn't notice anything strange.'

'How long was he gone?'

'Not long at all. Just a few minutes.'

Adam Hunt narrowed his eyes at her. 'You're sure about that? The court has seen taxi records and CCTV, which indicate it was more than ten minutes, Miss Miller.'

'I don't know.'

'Can you tell us, Miss Miller, about your journey home?'

She said nothing.

'Miss Miller?'

'No. I . . . I don't really remember it, you see.'

'You said in your first statement: "It's a bit hazy, I wasn't used to drugs." Is that correct?'

She blushed. This was awful, your drunken ramblings dragged out for all to hear. 'Yes. But I remember the rest of it. The rest of the night. I remember he was fine.'

'Hmm. All right, Miss Miller, that's all for now.'

The judge raised his head. 'Miss McCausland, your witness.'

Kylie got up, not making much difference in her height, since she was barely five feet tall. 'Miss Miller.' She gave Charlotte a quick flickering wink, almost unnoticeable, and Charlotte had to bite down a sudden nervous laugh. 'At the time of Mr Johnson's death, you were about to be married to Mr Stockbridge?'

'It was meant to be a week later, yes.'

'And this was cancelled after the arrest?'

'Postponed.' She lifted her chin, trying to believe it was true.

'Miss Miller, you've commented in papers recently about this case. Why did you do that?'

'I felt I had to. I don't believe Dan could ever have done something like this – not kill someone. I'm so afraid a mistake's been made.'

'Yet Mr Stockbridge admitted to throwing a punch at the victim. Could you imagine that?'

'Well, maybe. He was very upset that night, very humiliated.'

Kylie let that sink in, not commenting either way. 'While you waited for Mr Stockbridge outside, did anything happen?' She kept the question bland, not leading.

'A man pushed past me. I think he was running.' She said it firmly, because it was true, wasn't it? She remembered – mostly.

'Did you get a good look at this man?'

'Not really. It was a white man. He had a shaved head, I think.'

'Well.' Kylie's eyes opened wide and blue at the jury. Here was a new angle. 'Let's proceed. Miss Miller, you have since lost your job, I believe – can you say why?'

'I was very upset over Dan,' she said. She couldn't help but look at him, yellow and hunched. He didn't know she'd been fired.

'And what have you done for money?'

'I'm working as a waitress,' Charlotte said defiantly. Let them judge her. 'And I sold my engagement ring.'

'So it's fair to say you lost your wedding, your ring, your job, and you were also followed, harassed at home. Yes?'

'Yes.'

'Let me ask you, Miss Miller. After all this, do you still want to marry Mr Stockbridge?' She was deliberately not calling him 'the defendant'.

'How is this relevant, my Lord?' said Adam Hunt QC.

Kylie's eyes went wide again. 'Love? I'd say that's always relevant, my Lord.'

There were titters of laughter round the room.

'Get on with it, Miss McCausland,' said the judge drily.

'Miss Miller, do you?'

Charlotte scanned the room again, and there he was, down the back near the door. His green eyes found her and she felt hot and cold. *Oh, I'm sorry. I'm so sorry.*

'Of course,' she said, not looking at Hegarty. 'Of course I do.'

Adam Hunt QC rose again, irritated. 'This man you say pushed you, Miss Miller. You were, were you not, in an intoxicated state at the time?'

'I said I was. Yes.'

'So you can't be sure.'

Charlotte made herself smile. 'As sure as I can be about anything I'm saying.'

'Hmm. That's all. Thank you.'

Hegarty

Hegarty didn't take much to this Adam Hunt. The lawyer was nice, as if he wanted to show he respected the police, but it wasn't real respect, because he was a lawyer and Hegarty just a DC.

'Good morning, Officer,' he said, with his lizardy smile. It was the second day of the trial, and the courtroom was hushed. 'You were the arresting officer on the Kingston Town case, is that correct?'

'I was.' Christ, Stockbridge looked even worse than before. In the gallery sat Charlotte, pale and worried. Opposite, Adam Hunt and Kylie, watching.

'Can you talk us through what happened that night?'

Hegarty went through it, the call to the station that sent him rushing down to the club, the office with the man, wondering for a second was he still alive, blundering in. All the blood spattered on the floor in little round drops.

'So, to summarise, you answered an emergency call as you were in the area.'

'Yes.'

'And when you went in, what did you see?'

'Blood. Lots of blood.' He remembered how the red of it had shocked him. It was so red it looked fake, like ketchup. 'We ascertained that the victim had been stabbed in the neck, most likely with a broken bottle, severing his c . . .' shit, he'd forgotten the right word '. . . the artery in the neck, and he bled to death within minutes.'

'Did you find the bottle in question?'

'We recovered a Red Stripe beer bottle from the scene.'

'And did you fingerprint it?'

'Yes.'

'And?' Hunt looked impatient.

'The prints matched the defendant's.'

A murmur went up; Hegarty saw Charlotte flinch.

'I see.' Up went Hunt's eyebrows. 'Was there anything else to link the defendant to the scene?'

'The CCTV, several witnesses, and his credit card was found actually in the office, on the desk.'

Hunt turned to the judge. 'My Lord, statements were taken from a Miss Rachel Johnson, the victim's sister, who was present on the night. Miss Johnson was too upset to appear before the court, but you will find her statement in your dossier about the row over the credit card in question, and how the defendant made racist comments to the victim.'

Hegarty was increasingly doubting what Rachel had said, but he kept quiet.

'Then what happened?'

'I proceeded to the defendant's residence, cautioned him, and made the arrest.'

'Did the defendant reply to the charge?'

'Mr Stockbridge said, "It's that guy from the club."' Hegarty read from his notebook.

'Was anyone else there?'

'Yes. Miss Miller – his, er, his fiancée. She was upset. She said, "I don't even do drugs".' He held his tongue to keep from defending Charlotte, and did his best not to look over to where she sat. 'Mr Stockbridge was taken to the station where he gave fingerprints, and was questioned. He admitted punching Mr Johnson, but said he then left. I then showed him pictures taken at the scene of the death.'

'And what was his reaction?'

Hegarty cleared his throat. 'It was my opinion that he was genuinely shocked to learn the victim was dead. He said, "But it was only a light punch".'

'Interview transcripts are available in your packs, my Lord, ladies and gentlemen. At this time, Officer, was the defendant protesting his innocence?'

'Yes. He appeared to be very surprised by the arrest.'

'And did he continue to protest so?'

'Er, not entirely. He said he might have had some kind of blackout.'

Here the judge interrupted. 'Mr Hunt, it would be useful here to clarify what is medically meant by "blacking out". As I understand it, this term is rather meaningless.'

There was then a lot of talking and shuffling of papers. Hegarty stopped listening, looking the whole time at Charlotte's bent fair head. She looked miserable; so did Stockbridge. The man stared at his feet but his hands were visibly trembling.

The judge was still talking. 'So we can enter that the defendant had some kind of stress-induced memory loss, can we describe it so? Miss McCausland?'

He was speaking to Kylie. She blinked calmly. 'That is acceptable to the defence, my Lord.'

Hunt finally came back to Hegarty. 'You took statements from the defendant's former place of work, I believe. Could you please summarise these for us, Officer?'

Bloody hell, he wished he couldn't. 'Well, there was a complaint on record from a former colleague.'

'And the nature?'

'Bullying,' said Hegarty reluctantly. 'Racist bullying, was the claim. But it was the team, not—'

'Just a brief summary, please, Officer. No further questions. Thank you.'

Fuck. Charlotte must hate him. He looked around for her, but couldn't see her face.

Next Kylie stood up, pulling her too-big robes round her like a little girl on Bring-your-daughter-to-work Day. 'Officer Hegarty,' she said softly, and tipped him her quick wink. 'You found prints on the bottle. This was the drink that Mr Stockbridge was trying to pay for with his declined credit card, was it?'

'I believe so, yes.'

'Wouldn't his prints be on it from that, then?'

'Yes, of course they would be.'

'My client was at the scene, obviously, that is not in dispute. He touched the bottle, obviously – it was his drink. He got into a row, picked up the drink, and followed Mr Johnson to his office. He then came out several minutes later, and was captured on CCTV exiting and meeting his fiancée. Taxi records show they then went home. Is that an accurate summary of the facts?'

'I suppose so.'

'You said there was a lot of blood, Officer.' Her voice was soft. 'Would you expect the perpetrator then to be sprayed with it?'

Hunt stood up. 'My Lord, the witness is not forensically trained.'

Kylie looked innocent. 'He is an experienced police officer, my Lord.'

'Proceed.' The judge didn't look up.

Hegarty said, 'In my experience, yes. Usually.'

'Did you find any on my client's clothes?'

'A small drip on his sleeve.'

'Which might be consistent with the sort of light punch my client admitted to?'

'Objection! This is not the witness's area of expertise!'

Kylie just smiled. 'Withdrawn. You yourself contaminated the defendant's home, did you not, Officer?'

'Yes, I inadvertently tracked in some blood during the arrest, but it was catalogued and disregarded.'

'My Lord, you will find in your pack a statement from the taxi driver who took the couple home. Like Miss Miller, he also noticed nothing odd, certainly not the copious sprays of blood that the scene shows came from the victim.'

'Get on with it, Counsel.' The judge was tetchy.

She smiled. 'R-i-i-ght. The HR report you found, Officer. Was this against my client only?'

'No, it was more about the atmosphere in the bank generally.'

'Where is this report you refer to?' The judge was leafing through his papers.

Oh,' said Kylie, mock-innocent. 'Did the prosecution fail to include this paper?'

'I will see that the report is submitted, my Lord,' said Hunt quickly.

'Do so. And in future kindly do not call on a report which the court has not seen.'

Slight titters. Hegarty smiled, but lost it quickly when he caught a glimpse of Stockbridge out of the corner of his eye. The man was swaying; he looked as if he might collapse at any moment.

Keisha

The last kid had already come streaming out of the primary school, but there was no sign of Ruby. The bushes were dry, half-dead compared to when Keisha had hidden in them back in June. Covered in the dust of a long London summer.

Well, the kid wasn't there today. Was she sick? Had they moved her? Keisha had no idea. She pushed her way out from the wall and walked away from the school. Where to go now? She didn't want to go home – there was too much she was hiding from Charlotte. The club door, and – well, other things.

Where else? She couldn't go to work; in fact, she'd rung in sick the last few days. Afraid to see Ron and have to explain what she couldn't even understand herself. Afraid he'd kiss her again, afraid he never would if he knew what she'd done.

Shit, coppers! Keisha flattened herself into a shop doorway as on the other side of the road two officers went by. Yellow vests. Community Support, but still. She was staying well away. They could get you too, Chris had said. She didn't want to think about that, or anything he'd said. Best to lie low.

Keisha walked on, and after a while, she wasn't really surprised to find herself opposite the Church of Holy Hope. Maybe it was the last place that reminded her of Mercy, with the house gone. She slipped in the open doors – they left churches open, it seemed – and sat down at the back on one of the plastic chairs. The building hummed round her, empty and quiet, homemade God-bothering posters peeling off the wall.

She thought about Charlotte, how she was spending all her time rushing round with Dan's parents, doing interviews, swotting up on what happened at court each day. Keisha hadn't even gone yet. She'd stopped asking how it was going. She heard Charlotte crying at night; that told her pretty much everything she needed to know. Meanwhile all the shit in the papers went on, even though the judge had told them to stop. They didn't stop.

'Mum,' she whispered. 'I need some help.' Of course, nothing. Then she heard a noise and nearly jumped out of her skin. 'Jesus!'

'No, only myself, I fear.' It was the pastor. He had slippers on his feet. 'It's young Keisha, is it? Sister Mercy's child.'

'Yeah, that's me.' She wanted to explain what she was doing there, but realised she couldn't.

He sat down beside her, joints creaking. She stared up at the altar, glowing slightly with security lighting. 'What's it for?' she said out loud. 'Why do people come here?'

He rearranged his empty sleeve. 'Many reasons – comfort, company. Why have you come?'

'Dunno.'

'For answers, perhaps? For help?'

'I want to know what I should do.' She was speaking quietly in the silent room. 'You see, there's this thing – a thing people want me to do. But I don't know if I should do it or not.'

'But I think you already know what the right thing is. We always do.'

She stared hard ahead. 'I'm scared.'

'It's normal.' He held up the sleeve. 'You have seen this? This hand was taken from me because I did what I thought I should. Yes, I said, not, No. I was scared then, when they brought the machete.'

She wanted to say, Yeah, but, you were probably in a war or something, not North London. 'I can't be brave like that.'

'You don't know if you can be brave until you have to. I promise you, there is no way to know.'

'Oh, *great.*'

He laughed quietly and got up, laying his good hand on her shoulder. She smelled his fusty smell.

Keisha sat for a while in the cool dark of the church, then got up and ventured out to the noise of the thundering traffic. If she got there before six it would be OK, she thought.

The library was still open when she arrived, the windows glowing warm and orange. She'd been worried Julie mightn't be in, but there she was, stamping books behind the desk. It was a sign, if you believed in things like that. 'Ah, it's you! "Shondra." '

'Yep. Back again.' Keisha grinned nervously.

'Don't tell me, you wanted to read Jordan's next autobiography. How you doing?

'I'm all right.' She realised that she still had no real home, no proper job, and no Ruby, but somehow she was better than when she'd last seen Julie. She wasn't sure how, but she was. 'Surviving.'

Julie peered over her glasses. 'Course you are. What can I do you for?'

'Well.' Keisha leaned over the counter on her elbows. 'You got any legal books?'

Julie pushed back her wheely chair. 'Finally! I told you life was exciting here.'

Charlotte

Jamie checked his watch for the third time. 'We should just make it. These people don't hang about, you know.' The heel of Charlotte's stiletto caught in the lift door as she got in, it was so long since she'd worn them. Her brother caught her arm. 'Careful.'

As the lift soared silently up, out of the glass walls Charlotte could see palaces of steel and light, reflected in the rough grey water of the docks. Down below, small figures hurried, tapping into phones, oblivious. Had Dan really been one of them just months ago?

'You ready?' Jamie cast a critical eye over her, red-faced from rushing from court, roots growing through. We're so far away from what we were, she thought, the two of them zooming up this tunnel of light. Dan had always said the higher you went in Haussmann's, the more important you were. On the very top floor were the executives, god-like, alighting in helicopters. She fidgeted with her hair in the mirrored door.

'Calm down. You can't show fear.'

'But I'm scared.'

'Well, don't be. This happens all the time here. It's routine.' He was twiddling with his own BlackBerry.

Routine. The rapid collapse of her life and Dan's, being forced to sue the place where he'd worked for eight years, that was routine? No wonder Dan had gone into shock when he thought all this was falling down: it was like a small city, she thought, as they swished past floors and floors of plush carpet and glass. A city with its own laws. Its own punishments.

The lift voice said, 'Thirty-second floor.' If not quite top-floor material, they were certainly up there. Jamie put his hand out to hold the door. 'This is it. Sure you want to do it?'

'Of course. Why?'

'It's just – it doesn't sound like the trial's going so well. And when I saw him at the prison, well, I told you. He's not looking too good.'

She pushed out. 'It'll be fine. He hasn't had a chance to speak yet. You'll see. Come on.'

They were ushered into a hushed boardroom by one of the sleek smiling women who seemed to run these places. Charlotte gaped at the floor-to-ceiling views of the city, the sun sinking over the O_2 dome.

'Don't fidget,' said Jamie, taking out his files.

But she was worried. These people had ruled Dan's life. Through the glass walls she saw a bald man with a moustache look their way, talking to the receptionist. 'Oh my God, Jamie, look.'

'Yeah,' Jamie whispered. 'I know. He does look exactly like Phil.'

She couldn't help but let out a nervous trill of laughter, and Jamie's tired face creased, and they had to smother their giggles as the man who looked so much like their step-father came towards them.

Just like in court, Charlotte couldn't follow much of what was being said in the meeting. Yes, she told them, Dan had appeared stressed for months, sleeping badly, snapping easily.

The suits looked unmoved. They'd already talked about the responsibility of employees to 'manage their own stress'.

'We don't require anyone to work more than EU laws state,' said Moustache Man, pompously. He had the stale breath of the corporate luncher.

'That's rubbish,' Charlotte burst out. 'Dan knew he'd be fired if he didn't do at least sixty hours a week.'

'You will find nowhere that's stated, Miss Miller.'

'You don't have to write it down to make it true.'

Jamie gave her a warning look. 'Why don't you go and grab a coffee, Charlotte? We'll go over some figures here.'

'Well, OK.' Glad to get out of the stuffy room, she flounced to the ladies' and splashed cold water carefully over her make-up. She kept imagining how Dan would have felt, stuck inside this steel box all day, watching clouds dissolve into the water. Maybe prison wouldn't seem so strange if you'd been locked up here for years. She tried to remember why she was here. Dan needed something from these people, and she had to get it for him. She had to help him.

In the reception area there was a familiar face, leaning over the desk at the girl. 'Hello, Alex,' she heard herself say. It was almost funny, how he looked. As if he'd seen a ghost.

'Charlotte! How are you?'

She stepped back in case he tried to kiss her cheek. 'Not great, my fiancé's in jail.'

'Yes – um, how's he doing?' Alex Carter, Dan's former boss, fiddled with the knot on his tie.

'How do you think? You can always go and visit, if you want to know.'

'Yes, well. I must get back.'

She raised her voice. 'You don't blame yourself then, Alex?'

'Me?'

'I know you gave him the coke in the first place. I know

you gave stuff to the police – his HR record, told them all about his blackouts. I know why you did it, too.'

His head swivelled frantically. 'Er, I'm not sure—'

'He had stuff on you, right?'

'Charlotte!' he hissed. 'Stop this.'

She spoke quietly. 'I'll keep my voice down if you help him.'

'But how? I can't . . .'

'In there.' She nodded at the boardroom. 'I know you can influence it. Don't you think Dan deserves something, since you all hung him out to dry?'

'I—'

'He told me what goes on here,' she risked. Her heart was pounding. 'I've got his documents and everything. I can tell the police, you know.'

'I've no idea what you mean. Of course it's against our terms of employment to take confidential papers from the office . . .'

'Good job you already fired him, then.'

The man's mouth twisted. There was a film of oil over his forehead. 'I don't know what you mean. Charlotte, I can see you're upset.'

'Of course I'm bloody upset!' Her whisper was vicious. 'You set him up. You leaked all that stuff to the papers, that racism stuff. I know you did.'

He dipped his eyes, professional cool coming down like a curtain. 'Of course we want to help Dan. We'll do what we can – of course we will. But you must see we're under no obligation.'

Charlotte stood looking at this corporate man, his rumpled pink shirt, his face sagging. It was like looking at what Dan might have been in five years, if he hadn't fallen so far. It was a long way down from the top floor. A long way to fall.

As she turned to go back to the boardroom, she wondered if DC Hegarty might like to take a look at the papers she'd found hidden in Dan's desk.

Hegarty

The judge looked sternly down on the courtroom. 'It is unfortunate that I must once again remind members of the press to remember their obligations in reporting this case. If this carries on, it would not be the first time I have held one of your members in contempt.'

Then there was a lot of chat with the jury about whether they'd heard some TV report the day before. Hegarty shifted in his seat. It was a warm and muggy day, and already the atmosphere in the courtroom was like Golden Syrup.

They were still bogged down in a long array of Forensics witnesses. Today's was an Asian woman (deliberate, of course), who wore a short skirt that got the male members of the jury paying attention. Dr Amit gave evidence about the death of Anthony Johnson, which had been quick but perhaps not quick enough. She had a handy PowerPoint diagram and a laser-pointer. 'The bottle penetrated here, severing the carotid artery. That's the artery carrying blood and oxygen to the brain. It pumps at a very high pressure, and so if severed it's extremely messy.' She shook back her glossy hair, eyeing the jury. 'You can see from these crime-scene photos that the splashback was considerable.'

As the pictures flashed up, several people groaned and turned away. Hegarty himself closed his eyes slightly. He'd seen it first-hand, after all, the spatters up the walls and door and the dark pool oozing over the floor. Dr Amit then concisely outlined how they'd found a broken bottle, matched it to the shards in Anthony Johnson's neck, and identified Daniel Stockbridge's prints. 'We can also tell,' she said with a flourish, 'that the direction of the wounds suggest the attacker was some inches taller than the victim, perhaps six feet tall or more.' All eyes swivelled to Stockbridge, who even with his head bowed in the dock clearly fitted this description.

During this testimony Adam Hunt said little, nodding with a tiny smile on his face. When Kylie got up Hegarty could almost hear her take a deep breath. This wouldn't be easy to recover from.

'Dr Amit,' she began. 'Your lab analysed the clothes Mr Stockbridge wore that night, is that correct? Did you find blood on them?'

'Just a small drop on his sleeve.'

Kylie eyeballed the jury as she asked, 'But in your model a large amount of blood came from the victim?'

But Dr Amit had her own theories on why Daniel Stockbridge could have got away without being splashed in blood. 'In one scenario, the victim was left with a shard in his neck, effectively plugging the wound. This would have given the defendant time to leave the room. The victim then most likely attempted to remove the shard – and tragically, this would have been what killed him. We see evidence of this kind of "plugging" in many trauma cases . . .'

Kylie did her best, but it was clear this round was lost.

As the court adjourned, Hegarty was about to race off, late for his night-shift. Then he saw Charlotte standing in the lobby, pale as milk. They hadn't spoken in weeks, not since that day at his house. 'Hiya.'

She looked at her shoes. 'Hi.'

'I . . . er, I went to see that Alex Carter, like you said. Bit of a twat, eh?'

'I never liked him. He tried to grope me once. Never told Dan.' She still didn't look at him. Hegarty waited to see would she say anything else, about the kiss, about him. Anything. She rubbed at her bare arms in the evening air. Nothing.

'So anyway, I've passed the papers on to the Fraud Squad for now, to look into.'

'Thanks.'

'See you, then,' he said.

'See you.'

He watched her walk away.

After the night-shift – the usual round of drunks and fights and screaming women – Hegarty went round the corner to the pub that opened at six, catering for those dregs of humanity who couldn't wait till lunchtime for a drink. Them, and off-duty policemen. Because what did you do when you were so full of doubts you could hardly think? Drowned them, to start off with.

The morning rain washed vomit off the pavements as Hegarty sat hunched by the bar, hoping the other sad-eyed punters also wanted to get drunk alone.

'You're a hard man to find.' Kylie was standing in the door, shaking drops off her umbrella. There was rain in her hair, curled damply on the shoulders of her coat.

'That's the idea.' He took a sip. Whisky wasn't really his drink.

'Liquid breakfast, huh? Not a good sign, Officer.'

'It's evening to me.' He looked solidly ahead; maybe if he ignored her she'd go away.

In the bar mirror he saw her struggle on to the high stool. Her feet didn't touch the floor. 'I'll have what he's having,' she said to the barman.

Hegarty looked at her in the mirror, curious despite himself. Who was this strange woman, tiny as a child, drinking whisky at seven a.m.?

She gulped hers without grimacing. 'So, how come you're hiding out in this dive?'

He looked round him, the harsh wet light showing up the shabby seats, dirty carpet, fruit machines. 'Not hiding.'

'Still upset about the papers getting into you? I'm sure Charlie didn't mean it to turn out like that. You know the press.' She met his eyes in the mirror. 'She'll call you, I'd put money on it. After all this is over.'

He shrugged. 'You came to tell me that?'

'No.' She put down her glass. 'Hate to say it, but I need your help.'

'Really.'

'Yep. Look, I know you're not exactly my biggest fan—'

'You could say that.'

'But I got to tell you, I'm getting worried.'

He turned to her, surprised. He'd never heard her be anything but annoyingly upbeat about Dan's case. 'You think he'll go down?'

'All the evidence, it sounds pretty bad when they read it out. And he's a banker . . . he sounds posh. No one likes a banker right now. I need our Keisha to testify, really. But so far, she won't. And if you arrested her, say, she'd probably lie, let's be honest.'

He sighed. It wasn't his problem. He just brought them in. Didn't he?

Kylie was watching him very closely. 'There's something else, isn't there? Something I'm missing. I know you didn't check the CCTV across the street in time – it's wiped now. I know you couldn't find the taxi that took Chris Dean home – if it ever existed. What else?'

He drank more whisky. 'Should you not be – well, looking more closely at the evidence in favour of your client?'

'You got a problem with this approach?'

'Yes, actually. Seems you're going for police incompetence instead of acquittal.'

She took a gulp of her drink, smiling that annoying smile. 'That, diminished responsibility due to blackout – I'll try what I can.'

'But I thought your case was that he didn't do it.'

She scraped back her wet hair. 'You believe in the truth, Officer?'

'Dunno what you mean.'

'I mean, I see one thing, you see another. You know that story about the elephant in the dark? One person says it's a wall, one says it's a snake. Our Charlie, she thinks he didn't do it. Why? 'Cos he's her man. I believe her, or I wouldn't be here. But you and me and the judge and jury, we'll never know for sure, will we? So, I have to go down every road that might be the right one. That's my job. It's the jury who have to decide, not us, yeah?'

He remembered what his dad had said: *You just bring 'em in, lad.* Not his job to decide on what really happened. He sighed. Wished for a moment he'd never had to meet this annoying Australian, never stepped into that office full of blood, never set eyes on Charlotte Miller.

'Hegarty – come on! Did you do anything wrong? If you did, now's the time to admit it – before it's too late.'

Hegarty took another mouthful of whisky and pushed it away; he wasn't going to finish it. 'It's my career, you know.'

'I know. I know it is, but . . .'

He thought of Charlotte in his flat, stepping up to him, the smell of her hair. His mouth on the warmth of her throat. He said, 'There was a back door.'

'Hmm?' He'd spoken so quietly, she hadn't heard.

He said it louder. 'There's a back door to the club. It's in an alley behind the place. We never checked if it was locked that night.'

'So you're saying someone could have got in that way?'

'I dunno. If it was open, maybe.'

Kylie seized her bag, grabbing tissues and mints and lip balm as they fell out. 'You're a life-saver, you know that?' She saw his face and paused. 'I'm sorry. But it's the right thing. You know it is.'

She went, and Hegarty was left alone with his whisky, and his own eyes in the bar mirror that he couldn't quite meet.

Keisha

Keisha took a very deep breath as the door to the Wormwood Scrubs visitors' centre buzzed open. A clanging sound. Very final. *Breathe, breathe*, she reminded herself, walking across the floor. *You aren't arrested. You can leave any time you want.*

When she woke up that morning, she had known what to do. A peaceful feeling. A way out of all this shit, these months of being frightened, hiding, turning things over and over in her head till she didn't even know what she'd seen or what she knew any more. In the early dawn, she had quietly opened Charlotte's desk and taken out stamps and paper – her stash from all those letters sent to Dan, wasted, never read most likely. Then she'd reached into the bottom of her bag and taken out the pages of the statement she'd started. Started and never finished.

It took her an hour to complete it. She'd never been much good with words, but she put down what she knew, what she remembered. What she needed to say. Then she folded it up, wrote an unfamiliar address on the front. Letting herself out of the flat before Charlotte stirred, she put on her shoes in the corridor, shut the front door quietly behind her, and went down the stairs.

Now here she was again at the prison, and there he was too. She almost turned and ran when she saw his face. Hopeful. He hadn't looked at her like that for a long time.

'Wasn't sure you'd come back.' He tried to take her hand across the table but she put it in her lap.

'You OK?' He was looking at her closely. 'You don't look so good, Keesh. You all right?'

She almost laughed at that. He was in jail and her kid was in care and she could be arrested any second, and he asked was she all right? 'You don't look too good either.' And he didn't. His skin was sort of grey, eyes bloodshot. She saw his knuckles were torn.

Chris saw her looking and folded his arms. 'I'm not good. Need you to help me. You think any more about it?'

'I thought about it, yeah. Didn't think about much else.'

'So?'

She sighed. 'So, maybe I'll help you. You're Ruby's dad. And you and me – well.' She shrugged to indicate all their long history, more than half her life in love with him. 'But I need you to tell me something first.'

'Anything, babe.' His hand was snaking across the table again, reaching for hers. She let him take it and she leaned in close.

'Did you?' She whispered it. He knew what she was asking; of course he did. 'Just tell me. That's all I ask. Tell me if you did it.'

There was a long silence between them, stretching out as if for years, and in it she could see all their time together, all the good, all the bad.

After a while he said, 'He was a bit of a wanker, Anthony Johnson, did you know that?'

She waited.

'He disrespected me. Said I could fuck off back to the little boys. He was a man now, he'd left all that behind. Said to tell them they could go and piss for their money.'

She was surprised by how calm her voice was. 'It was them, then, that Gospel Oak lot? They sent you?' A stupid gang of overgrown teenagers, trying to frighten Anthony Johnson into paying back the money with a visit from Chris. He nodded.

'And you went back, after you left me. You picked up the bottle he dropped, is that it? The banker. And then you . . .'

Another nod. Slow.

'So – just 'cos he *laughed* at you?'

Chris rubbed at his knuckles. 'I never meant it. He aggravated me.'

She was trying to take it in. 'And so . . . you'd let this other fella do time for it?'

'He punched him, that Stockbridge guy, didn't he? He was

just lucky. Could have hurt him more, couldn't he? I never meant it. Just lost my temper.'

She heard herself say, 'That's what you said before. When Ruby – after what you did. You "lost your temper".'

He hissed, 'Keesh! It was an accident, both times were! I never meant it, then he was – all blood everywhere, and he was like choking in it and I just panicked. I ran and . . . and these guys, the Parky Boys, they don't fuck about. They said if I went to the cops they'd go after everyone – me, you, the kid.'

Ice slid down her throat. 'Ruby?'

He said slowly, 'I didn't know what else to do. Then the cops got that banker fella – well, he's had a good life, why shouldn't he go down? He was just lucky it wasn't him. It was an accident. I fucked up.' He was rubbing furiously at his shaved head. 'You gotta help me. They'll go after you too, the cops.'

Keisha pushed her chair out. He raised his voice. 'You gotta help me! You knew all this time, and you never said nothing!'

She was standing up.

'Think about your kid!' he yelled. 'Both of us locked up! Think about it!'

She was going. She wasn't looking back. As she left the prison she dropped her letter into the first postbox she passed, and walked away.

Charlotte

As the trial went on, eventually even Charlotte was lost among the endless back and forward of facts, interpretations, suggestions. Finally it was time for Dan to speak in his own defence. He took the stand to a huge swell of interest, the whole courtroom of reporters and family and jeerers and well-wishers all waiting to hear what he was going to say.

Adam Hunt had managed to build up quite a picture of Dan with the prosecution witnesses. A privileged young man, sent to Westminster and Oxford, continuing his sense of entitlement into his banking career. (She thought that was a bit rich, considering Adam Hunt QC had almost certainly gone to public school and Oxbridge too.) A man who used drugs, bullied interns, lashed out when his platinum card was declined. Who could have been responsible for the vicious sprays of blood all over the walls of that office. She hoped Kylie would manage to change this picture. Because as it stood, even Charlotte didn't much like the person who'd emerged.

Then it was Kylie's turn. She stood up, giving Dan a big smile. Charlotte loved her for it, at that moment. Everyone else in the room was staring at him as if he was dirt on their shoes.

'Mr Stockbridge. You are accused here of a very serious crime; the most serious, of taking a life. What did it feel like when you were first arrested?'

Dan looked surprised; this was a very different tack to the endless rehashing about prints and blood and CCTV. 'I was shocked, I suppose. I thought it must be a mistake. I knew that we'd fought – I just got angry, I'd had such a bad day. But I thought . . . I thought he was OK, the – Anthony Johnson. He even laughed at me, after I – after I hit him.'

'Can you tell the court what you remember about the night?'

Dan was quiet for a moment, staring at his hands.

Everyone watched, breath drawn in. 'There's bits that are gone. I'd had a few – blackouts, I suppose. At work, a few times. It was so stressful. I really don't think I could have coped much longer.'

'Can you tell us why that was?' She was quiet, probing, more like a therapist than a barrister.

Dan thought for a moment. 'The bank was going under. I was so stressed out, and, well, there were things going on that we knew to be – in some cases – illegal. We knew that if we didn't toe the line we'd be fired, but if we did these things, we could go to prison.' He smiled briefly, bitterly. 'I didn't know then I'd end up there anyway.'

'Can you tell us what put you under so much stress?'

'I was thinking of – I was trying to put evidence together. Whistle-blow, I suppose you'd call it, but it wasn't as dramatic as that. I just . . . I knew I could be arrested any day, and there was my wedding coming up – yes. So there was a huge amount of pressure, yes.' He looked at his hands.

Kylie was gentle with Dan. She took him through his version of that night, the worry and the drugs, the club, the row, the brief time he had been in the office, the taxi home.

'Was there anything unusual when you got home?'

'My knuckle was a bit sore, and I had a small spot of blood on my sleeve. That was all. I was so tired, I just threw my clothes on the floor, and then next thing I knew, the police were at the door.'

She smiled at him. 'Thank you, Mr Stockbridge. That's all.'

Adam Hunt QC was ready with his big guns. 'Is it fair to say, Mr Stockbridge, that on the tenth of May this year, you had one of the worst days of your life? Your bank was collapsing – source of all that wealth and status. You knew you might lose the luxury flat, the lavish wedding you planned with your fiancée.' Charlotte cringed. Her neck was burning as hundreds of eyes bored into her.

'It was a bad day,' said Dan evenly.

'To ease your tension, you decided to indulge in a binge of cocaine and alcohol, is that correct?'

Charlotte made a very small 'huh' sound; Adam Hunt QC was laying it on a bit thick. As if *he* wouldn't drink, if someone told him he was getting fired.

'Isn't it true, Mr Stockbridge, that in the magistrates' court you said, "I'm so sorry, God, I'm sorry"?'

'I did, yes.' Dan gritted his teeth.

'May we ask why you would do this, if, as you profess, you are innocent?'

Sweat stood out on his forehead. 'Because I'd heard the evidence. I thought – I just wasn't sure. Those people – they were all shouting. I don't know what I thought.'

Up went the eyebrows. 'Surely you would know whether you were guilty?'

'But that's the thing. I've tried and I just don't remember. It's – well, it's sort of like a big black hole where the memory should be.'

'Had you suffered from memory loss before?'

Dan's brow was sweating. 'Not really. I mean, yes, it had happened a few times. Work was extremely stressful during that time. Extremely.'

'Just answer the question, please. Record that Mr Stockbridge said yes.' The lawyer shuffled his papers. 'Would you call yourself a racist, Mr Stockbridge?'

Dan looked away. 'I'm really sick of that question.'

'Just answer it, please.'

Dan's thin face was set in hard lines. 'No, I am not a

racist. I'm not. Just because he was black, you can't assume that.'

'Mr Johnson was, as you say, *black*.' Hunt managed to make it sound as if Dan had made a racial slur. What else were you supposed to say? 'The court has seen a number of statements to the effect that you subjected the victim to racial abuse before the murder, is that correct?'

Dan just shook his head. 'No. It's not true.'

'But you have previously said you do not remember everything?'

'I – I don't know. But I know I wouldn't do that.'

'Does the name Rumila Chakri mean anything to you, Mr Stockbridge?'

'No.' Dan barely opened his mouth.

'You didn't work with her at Haussmann's last year?'

He looked confused. 'Oh, yes. Rumila. I forgot her name.'

Charlotte put her head in her hands. What was wrong with him? Was he trying to come across as an arsehole?'

'Ms Chakri was hired from university as a junior analyst, but she left after just three months, alleging serious racial and sexual harassment from the team at Haussmann's. That team included you, did it not?'

'Yeah, but – it's always like that. You banter with people. Shows you can rely on them, when your ass is on the line.'

'Mr Stockbridge, please watch your language,' said the judge sternly.

The lawyer frowned at his paper again. 'Would you say calling someone a "terrorist Paki" was banter?'

Dan looked irritated. 'I never called her that.'

'She didn't accuse specific people. But the fact remains, a young Asian woman was forced from her post due to sustained racial harassment by your team, was she not?'

'I suppose. Whatever.' His hands were shaking again.

'To go back to the night of the murder. You became embroiled in a row with the victim, is that correct?'

'We had words.'

'And when these "words" became heated, you went to the victim's office to settle the score?'

'Not settle the score, I mean, yes, we went, but—'

Adam Hunt QC stared round the courtroom to make a dramatic point. 'And was it not in this office that Mr Johnson was found dead just ten minutes later? Bled to death from a neck wound inflicted with a broken beer bottle – a bottle, Mr Stockbridge, covered in your fingerprints?'

Dan was shaking his head. 'No. I mean, yes, they were on it, but I didn't—'

'And after you lashed out, I put it to you that you fled the scene, leaving the victim to bleed to death, and you went home to your luxury flat with your fiancée. Is that correct?'

Again Charlotte made a tiny incredulous noise. He hadn't exactly been there, had he, to know all this? This time Adam Hunt QC glanced over and she flushed tomato-red.

Dan said, 'I went home, yes, but he was fine. I swear he was fine.'

'But you don't remember, do you? As you have previously stated?'

'No.' His voice was very small.

And on it went, through the racist accusations and the bullying and the workplace blackouts and the prints on the bottle and the fight he'd had with Anthony Johnson, and once again that big killer, that no one else had been seen going in or coming out until the man was found, dead, his blood already leaked out all over the floor. Dan had nothing to say to these facts, inarguable as they were. He sat with his head down and Charlotte's heart sank with every word.

At the end Adam Hunt said, 'Let me ask you this, Mr Stockbridge. Did you feel that you, as a wealthy, privileged young man, could act with impunity? That you could attack a black man, and go unpunished?'

At this several people clapped, and the judge glared. Adam Hunt looked officially disapproving but wildly pleased, the twat.

Dan's face was shining with sweat. He twisted his hands together. 'No. I don't think that. I didn't. Of course not. But you see, I didn't—'

'Thank you. No further questions.'

The courtroom sat in stunned silence as Kylie got up again. 'Can you describe exactly what happened with the intern, Ms Chakri?'

Dan seemed to be struggling. 'The atmosphere was – I could describe it as kill or be killed. If you couldn't cope, you were no use to us. So I suppose we tested people.'

'Tested them how?'

'You could call it bullying, I suppose, but it wasn't that really. It was seen as totally normal for that environment. With her, the girl, it was maybe because she was Asian, but it could be anything. Your sore points.'

'To summarise, you're saying that bullying was normal for the way your team functioned?'

'Yes. The reason I don't remember her that well, it was because people started every week and then they left. Couldn't hack it.'

'Why did *you* stay?'

His eyes found Charlotte's; she looked away. 'I felt I needed the money. I felt trapped into that life. And what I'd done, I knew some of it wasn't legal. You see, they had you by the . . . they had you where they wanted you.'

Very quietly, Kylie asked, 'How do you feel now about what happened?'

He leaned forward and put his hands to his face. 'I'm so sorry. It must be so awful, to have someone just die like that.'

She nodded gently; go on.

'But now – I don't know if I did it. I've been in prison for months. I've lost my job, my wedding – my life. If it wasn't me, well, I shouldn't be punished any more. I've had enough.'

The judge had to call for order four times before the noise died down. Dan was led out again, and this time he looked back, and for the first time Charlotte caught his eye and held it. He met hers, strong and steady, and for a long moment they just looked at each other across the courtroom, as if no one else was there. Then he was gone, and she felt her knees almost give way at the tidal wave of feeling that swamped her.

Hegarty

The trial went on, experts and Forensics from both sides wrangling over the details, evidence piled up and then just as quickly whipped away, like a magic trick. Kylie pushing all her facts – the scene had been contaminated, no one had checked the other CCTV, and the irrefutable fact that Daniel Stockbridge's clothes and most importantly his shoes had not been covered in Anthony Johnson's blood. The prosecution hammering home their own points – the prints on the bottle, the overheard row, the fact that no one else was seen going in or out of the office before the body was found.

Days of argument went by on whether or not Dan would

have been spattered with blood. The expert Kylie had wheeled out was a big noise in the government and he felt, although he wouldn't commit fully, of course, that on balance the defendant would have had 'substantial spatter of bodily fluids, most notably on the soles of his shoes'. Kylie dwelled for a long time over a computer model the expert had done for her that showed blood had gone all over the walls of the office, as high as the top of the door.

'Would someone standing there have been in the trajectory?' Her questions were so sweet, like she was amazed at the expertise before her.

The old guy liked her, you could tell. 'I would expect to see that, yes.'

'From the CCTV when he emerged, did the defendant have any visible blood on him at all?'

'No, he didn't.'

'And from the forensic reports you were able to review, was there any blood on the shoes Mr Stockbridge wore that night?'

'There wasn't, no.'

'Thank you, Dr Smith.' She smiled at him with her wide blue eyes. Damn, Hegarty had to admit, she was good at what she did, even if this sweet-as-pie act was fake as Adam Hunt's hair. The court watched the CCTV to prove the lack of bloodstains, and noted how Dan was shown weaving and swaying on his way out, bumping into the door as if drunk – or blacking out. It was also clear there was no bottle in his hand when he came out.

But then it all changed again. Adam Hunt tore into the witness, asking over and over whether the wound could have been plugged until the defendant had left the room. Dr Smith had to admit it was possible.

And on and on with the studies and the models and the arguing over what direction blood had spilled. God, they could really make a gory murder into a snooze-fest. Half the courtroom looked to be asleep. Charlotte was propping herself up on her hands. She saw Hegarty looking and smiled as if caught out; it was so boring, what could you do? More forensics experts were wheeled out – he could just imagine how much this was costing the Stockbridges, but then they could probably afford it.

Kylie then re-questioned Dr Smith and was now worrying at another detail like a dog with a bone. 'Doctor, you re-examined the police findings, I believe. The glass bottle – in the prosecution's theory, in order to be used as a weapon, it would have been smashed somewhere in the office, we assume? Aside from the shattering that occurred after the bottle had been used, was any glass found in the room?'

'It wasn't,' said the doctor. 'But it could have been disturbed, of course. There was considerable disarray at the scene, suggesting several people had been in and out. I believe the staff had tried to help the victim when they discovered him.'

Kylie let that sink in; she knew they wouldn't win by avoiding the sad central fact of this case, that a man was dead. 'And was broken glass found anywhere else in the building?'

'Yes, outside in the corridor. The defendant could have smashed it going in. It could also be that Daniel Stockbridge simply dropped the bottle outside the room – on his way *out*, crucially – and some other person picked it up and used it on the victim.'

Someone gasped. The doctor continued, 'We just can't tell from the forensic evidence.'

'Meaning we can't tell if Daniel Stockbridge struck the fatal blow?'

'Not for certain, no.'

The room exploded into murmurs, the judge called for order, and Hegarty caught Kylie's eye, and the flicker of her almost unnoticeable wink. 'My Lord,' she said. 'The defence calls DC Matthew Hegarty again.'

Bloody hell. This was it.

Kylie shifted on her feet at her desk, her robes almost trailing on the floor. 'Officer Hegarty, as we know, no one else went into the corridor *from the club*. Can you tell the court how many exits there are from this corridor?'

Oh, crap. But he'd agreed to it, hadn't he? No going back now. He cleared his throat. 'There's the main door, and there's also a back door, to an alley.'

She let this sink in. 'To confirm, there are *two* main doors leading into and out of the corridor? Could you indicate on the diagram, please?' She even had a floorplan of the club, the office marked in a red cross, the staffroom and storeroom there, and at the back the fateful door. 'Please describe this door to us, DC Hegarty.'

What a daft question. It was door-shaped? In the wall? 'An iron door,' he said carefully. 'A fire escape sign on it, and an alarm warning.'

'The door was alarmed, to be clear?'

He hung his head. 'I don't know if we checked.'

'I'm sorry, can you repeat that?' Kylie, who had perfectly good hearing, was all sweetness and light.

'I don't know if we checked if it was definitely on an alarm or not, that night. The sign said it was.'

She let that one sink in, too, a little smile playing round her mouth. There was Charlotte, behind a fat man. She was pale. Her eyes locked on Hegarty.

Kylie said, 'So, to confirm, Officer, there is a back door,

which may or may not have been alarmed on the night in question.'

He stammered, 'I think I made a mistake. Yes. I didn't check.'

Murmurs spread out through the room and the judge tutted again.

'Thank you. That's all.' Kylie sat down abruptly.

Hunt got up. 'You recently took yourself off this case, did you not, Officer?'

'Yes.'

'Why?'

Shit. *Shit*. 'I, er . . . I felt I was not as impartial as I should be.'

'How would you describe your relationship with Miss Miller, Mr Stockbridge's fiancée?'

Hegarty glanced at Kylie to see would she yell out, 'Objection!' like they did on telly, but she just sat there calmly. 'We got to be friends, I suppose.'

Hunt turned over his papers. 'Isn't it true, Officer, that, according to your own statement, you visited her in Singapore over a month back?'

'Well, I was in transit, but . . .'

'Yes or no, Officer?'

'Yes, I did.'

Hunt pointed. 'I put it to you, DC Hegarty, that you have fallen for Miss Miller, to the serious detriment of this case and your investigation. Is that correct?'

'I . . . I . . .'

'Is that correct, Officer? You have developed unprofessional feelings for Miss Miller?'

'I . . .'

'Answer the question!'

There was a sliding sound, a chink of metal off wood, and all heads turned. Daniel Stockbridge had fallen forward, hitting his head on the glass of the dock. His eyes rolled, a bubble of spit foamed at his mouth. The courtroom exploded in noise.

'Can someone call a doctor?' said Kylie in clear tones, over the hubbub. 'Mr Stockbridge is having a seizure.'

Keisha

'There you are!' Ron was in the office when she showed up, staring at his computer again. It made her sad to see how he looked up when she went in. Like he'd missed her. 'Haven't seen you for ages, missus. Where you been?'

'Had to go to prison.' She was standing in the doorway, still in her jacket.

He smiled. 'Been doing armed robbery again?'

She didn't laugh. 'Had to visit my ex. Chris, you know.'

'Oh. What's he done?'

She had to tell him. There was no more time left. 'Stabbed someone in a bar.' She saw his open face slide into confusion. She had to tell him. Had to tell him now.

Keisha took a deep breath. The filing cabinet was digging into her back. 'You know I was here that night, yeah? When your brother . . . Chris, he had some business with your Anthony. Dunno what it was. Anyway, when it all kicks off, Chris scarpers, leaves me at the club on my own. And when I get home, he's there in bed. So I'm thinking, That's a bit weird. Then I see his shoes. All covered in red. Stepped on a kebab, he says, but I'm thinking, That don't look like ketchup to me.'

She could see his hands, gripping the desk. She went on. 'So then Monday comes, he wants to go to court – this bail hearing. That's when your Rachel gave Dan's girl a kicking – Charlotte, that was.'

'Charlotte?' His face creased in confusion.

'Yeah, so I says to Chris, Why'd we go, why'd you set those girls on Charlotte? He asked that Mel to steal her purse, you know. And when I ask him, he hits me – see?' She pointed at the faint scar over her eye. 'Then he puts me out, and next I hear he's after me and Charlotte. So I went to Char's, to warn her, like. And, you know, I ended up staying. Didn't have nowhere else to go.'

Ronald was staring at the computer like it was a really hard Sudoku. 'You're saying you think your fella, this Chris, had something to do with our Anthony? But – they got the guy for it.'

'I dunno, do I? I'm not on the bloody police, am I?'

She saw it spread through him, the shock, until he was rigid. 'You been here all this time, and you never told me? They maybe got the wrong fella and you never said?'

'I dunno! How'm I meant to know?'

'You should of told me.' He looked up at her. 'Thought you was different, Keesh.'

'I'm sorry! What was I meant to say? "I saw my ex and his shoes were red all over"? Doesn't prove anything, does it?'

'You should of said something.'

She was still standing at the door. Last time she'd been there he'd kissed her. When she was finished with what she had to say, he'd never want to see her again. She was sure of that, but she had to say it anyway. 'They want me in court,' she said desperately. May as well tell him everything. 'They want me to say about Chris, but I went to see him, and he asked me not to, he said we can start again and we'll get Ruby back . . . You ever wonder why the kid doesn't live with me, eh? You wonder why? Well, it's 'cos he broke her arm. Comes home one day, he's been fired 'cos of the recession, and she's just trying to give him a hug, make him feel better, but she spills his beer. So her own dad broke her little arm, and this guy, this guy still asks me to help him after that. So what'm I meant to do? How do I know they won't come after me too, and then what'll happen to my Ruby?' She was crying. 'What'll I do, Ron? Tell me and I'll do it.'

'You're asking me? For fuck's sake.' Ronald hardly ever swore. He went to church, for God's sake.

'Yeah, you tell me. He was your brother. I don't know nothing any more. You tell me. Will I do it?'

He was staring at his hands, saying nothing. She felt it all rising up in her, desperate, spilling over, like she was going to scream or something. 'I never even told anyone everything. There's more.'

He looked up. His face was terrible but she kept going. 'I *saw*. You see? I was in the loos that night, when they had that row – your brother, and that banker. When I come out I see Chris is gone, left me, the twat, and there's still shouting. So I just wait there by the loos.' She pointed through the wall to where she'd waited in the dark, that night when everything had gone so wrong. 'And I see him come back out, Dan Stockbridge. You saw it on the CCTV – all swaying, like he's drunk, yeah. No blood on him. I wrote it all on this here computer, when I was here.'

Ronald made a quick movement like he was going to lash out, and she backed away. 'Listen, wait. Everyone saw that, I know, but I saw down the corridor, from where I was. You know? I was right beside the door, and it swings open, and I see Dan Stockbridge drop the bottle and smash it there in the corridor. Not in the office.' She pointed again. 'Out there, in the corridor. *After* he comes out. You see? I saw it.'

There was a long pause. His voice was awful, choked. 'Did you see my brother? Did you see him, still alive?'

Keisha tried to remember, the dark of the club, the flashing lights, someone glimpsed down a corridor in the time it took for a door to swing shut. How could she know then how important it was going to be, how many lives would depend on that split second?

'I – I think so,' she said in a small voice. 'I never knew for sure – didn't know what I was looking at, did I? I didn't know it'd matter. But I think so. There was someone standing there . . . You know, I might go to prison too, Ron. And Ruby – what'll happen to her? Who'll look after her? She's got no one. So you tell me now, Ronald Johnson, you tell me, will I do it?'

He got up, scraping his chair back. 'What, tell the fucking truth for once? Yeah, you do it, Keisha. But don't come back here after, yeah?'

'I'm sorry!'

He shook his head. 'Just go.'

She backed out. 'You're the one with the bloody computer. What you got on it? You never gave that to the police, did you?'

Ronald froze.

'Yeah, Rachel told me. Said he was into everything, your brother, up to his bloody guts in the gangs. You really think it was some City banker knocked him off?'

He sagged. It was awful to see, such a tall, strong man. 'He was my brother.'

'Yeah, well, Chris was my boyfriend.'

Ronald looked at her. Neither of them said anything for a long time. 'Oh, fuck it.' She went out and slammed the door behind her.

She couldn't help it any more, not since she'd cried that night over stupid Ian Stone. The tears were running over her face and into her mouth as she packed up her staff locker, taking out an empty can of Impulse, a picture of Ruby.

'What's this then?' Dario burst in, preening at his cropped hair in the mirror. 'You're late.'

'Been fucking fired, haven't I? You'll have to get Rachel back on tills.'

'Crap,' he muttered. 'You OK?' He looked at her full on, no sympathy.

She swallowed down the tears but they didn't stop. A week ago it'd have killed her to cry in front of Dario, but now it didn't seem to matter. Nothing did. 'I'll be fine, OK? Just sick of this – always moving on, leaving people. Even when it's a rubbish job. You get used to people, don't you?'

Dario looked in the mirror again, rubbed down one of his eyebrows. 'There's always more people, babes. You don't need the ones you think you do, not always.'

But Ronald. How did you find another Ronald? A six-foot-four brick shithouse who made curry, was nice to his mum.

'Look at me,' Dario pointed to himself. 'Whole family kicked me out, said I was an offence to God.' He turned to go, clapping her on the arm with more real feeling than any of his air-kisses. 'There's always more people. You'll be OK, Keisha Collins.'

For a second she wanted to ask him if his name was really Dario. But maybe it was better not to know. As she went out into the early dusk of London streets, bars crowded on the warm autumn night, buses rumbling, it was a funny thought to know that Chris couldn't be near. For once she knew exactly where he was, and there was no need to look around and look back again as she set off home.

Keisha went to Charlotte's. No one was there; Charlotte had gone out for dinner with Dan's folks. That was pretty much all they did, eat out, and the mother was always complaining things were 'too rich'.

In the quiet flat, Keisha picked up the phone and listened to the dialling tone, before keying in the number on a scrap of napkin she'd dug out of her purse. She stood there with her tongue out, listening to it ring for a long time. 'Hi,' she said, clearing her throat. 'This is Keisha here. Keisha Collins. You said you'd help me, if I needed it. Well, I do need it. I really need some help.'

Charlotte

Then suddenly, it was all coming to an end. After Dan had a seizure in court, there was an adjournment. There were meetings between the prosecution and defence. There were mutterings, rumours in the press. There'd be a mistrial. There was new evidence. No one had a clue what was going on. In the few days of adjournment, she waited. She tried to call Kylie, didn't get through. She stayed inside and watched. Finally, there was a call from Hegarty.

All he said was, 'There's a new witness.'

'Who's that?'

'I don't know, couldn't find out. They're still wrangling over it.'

'Must be some new Forensics person.' But what was the

point? They'd already had so many, and it was just like chucking wet paper at the brick wall of the facts. The camera. The prints. The row. Even the door, it hadn't been enough. There was a heavy weight in her stomach.

'Aye. Most likely.' His voice was very tired. 'I'll see you, Charlotte.' He hadn't called her by her name much. The sound of it made her sad. She didn't know why.

The day before the trial started again, Charlotte woke up very early. She sat in her window watching the light come up pink and grey over Parliament Hill. Keisha hadn't come home the night before, and Charlotte no longer knew where she was or what she was doing. The certainty she had, that the girl knew more than she'd said, it would probably never go away. It lodged in Charlotte's chest like a ball of lead. She'd done her best for Dan, she'd given up everything she could. But maybe it just hadn't been enough. Because whatever she did, those facts weren't going away.

Then the doorbell was buzzing and, puzzled, she went to it and pressed the button. 'Hello? Oh, hello. What are you – is everything all right? He's not—?' Her heart began to pound.

'Nothing like that,' said Edward Stockbridge stiffly over the intercom. 'Elaine and I are downstairs. Could you come somewhere with us, please, dear?'

Charlotte sat nervously in the taxi as Dan's father helped his wife out of the car and slowly onto the pavement. 'I don't think I should do this,' she said.

'We believe it's necessary. It might be the last time.'

She looked up at the walls of the prison. 'But he won't – he doesn't want to see me.' A wave of shame hit her as she said it. The man she'd lived with for four years, been about to marry, and he didn't even want her to visit.

She felt a soft pressure on her arm; Elaine Stockbridge was offering a laundered cotton hankie. Her face was kind, neutral.

'Th-thank you.' Charlotte mopped at her face. 'I'm sorry, it's just – I can't believe he would want me to come.'

Elaine bit her lip, and Edward spoke. 'He's in a bad way. Very bad. We didn't realise. The time he's had . . .'

Charlotte didn't say she'd tried to tell them. There was no point.

Elaine spoke in a wavering voice. 'We feel it would be a good idea, Charlotte. Just to see him, before.'

She swallowed hard. Looked round her at the quiet morning streets. Every detail seemed to etch itself onto her, the shuttered shops, the smell of early-morning bin-bags, the clatter of trucks. London waking up. This might be the last time she ever saw the city with the same eyes. Tomorrow it could all change. She might have to leave, go somewhere she wouldn't be known as the Banker Butcher's missus. This might be the end of everything. Or the start.

'All right,' she said, and let herself be led into the dark solid building for the last time.

Oh God. Edward and Elaine had left her at the gate, gently urging her to go in alone. She was walking into the room, the same old dirty smell, and there he was, sitting at the table. Dan. It was all she could do to cross the floor and sit down and try not to cry, try to breathe. She took her seat, and looked up at him.

Neither of them said anything for several minutes. Dan in his grey tracksuit, thin and pale, eyes bloodshot, Charlotte in the expensive jeans she'd bought in her former life, nails bitten, hair falling over her face.

'Why?' she said simply, after a while.

He thought about it. 'I just realised some things, I suppose. I found out – well, it doesn't matter how – but I know how much you've been doing for me.'

She just looked at him.

'Charlotte, when I – when I asked you to go away, I thought it was for the best, you know that?'

'You don't know what's best for me.'

'I suppose not.' His voice was quiet. 'Charlotte. I think I'm losing this case.'

She felt burning tears behind her eyes, but fought to hold them back. 'It didn't work, did it? What I did.'

He reached over the table and very slowly took her hand. 'Don't blame yourself. It was just bad luck, the worst – like falling, or something, like an accident. You were the only one who . . . Listen, I tried to say this before, but please listen to me now. You're not even thirty. And you're beautiful. I don't know if you even realise that, how beautiful you are.'

'Don't—'

'Let me. Please.' He looked at her steadily. 'Please don't let this define your life, what happened here. If there's a way you can move on, then you should take it.'

A long silence. She thought about how he'd fainted in court when Hegarty was being questioned, and she made herself meet Dan's eyes. 'You really mean that.'

Softly, he said, 'I have to try. Do you remember when we met?'

Of course she did. Swimming against the current of London in her mid-twenties. Drowning, almost. And then, at a party of Jamie's, there was Dan. Like a rock she could cling to. Someone so strong she was sure he could never crumble, or fall. Like finding a treasure in your back garden, there all the time. She heard herself say, 'Did you ever love me, Dan?'

'I loved you so much. If I didn't always know how to say it, well – I'm sorry. I suppose when this happened, when I asked you to leave me, it had always been in my mind. That maybe you didn't love me as much.'

'You were wrong,' she said. 'I did. I really did.' It was a relief, finally, to realise it. Everything she'd lost, everything she'd sacrificed, at least she knew that some things were real. For what it was worth, she had loved this man in front of her, broken, sick, defeated. 'It wasn't enough, was it?' she said.

'No.' His voice was almost inaudible. 'I'm sorry, sweetheart. I don't think it was.'

When she got outside, Dan's parents were still standing awkwardly on the pavement, Elaine clutching her alligator-skin handbag in front of her. They couldn't have looked more out of place if they'd tried. They saw her coming and nudged each other.

Dan's father cleared his throat. 'We want to say, Charlotte, that whatever should happen tomorrow, we know you did your best for Daniel. And we hope – well, we hope you'll come to us, should you ever need anything.'

'He's our only child,' said Elaine Stockbridge, struggling to control herself. 'Please consider yourself – part of that.'

'Thank you.' Charlotte was surprised, touched by their dignity. Maybe in some ways they'd be losing more than her. 'My father asked me to go out to Singapore, you know. So – well. We'll see.'

They were talking of what they'd do if he was convicted. As if they all knew there wasn't much hope.

'Let's take you home then, dear.' Dan's father extended his arm, and Charlotte realised what was happening. In their own stiff way, they were trying to thank her.

Hegarty

Hegarty was drinking another cup of very bad coffee, this time from the courthouse coffee bar. He'd had to put one of those sachets of powdered milk in, and it had ripped and spilled all over his trousers. One day, he swore, he'd be drinking good coffee. If he got that promotion he'd buy a machine for his office, but it didn't seem likely now, not with all the bad feeling from this case, not with him on record as fancying a suspect's missus. He gulped down some of the dishwater liquid and grimaced. Either way, this wasn't going to end well for him. A failed conviction, or possibly sending the wrong man to jail. As his father said, he would always wonder, if Daniel Stockbridge was put behind bars – did he mess up? Was it his fault?

The angry skinny girl was hovering by the door, he noticed. Keisha. He hadn't seen her there before – had she come to hear it all wrapped up? 'I hear your friend got a visitor the other day,' he said, moving over to her with his cup of grainy coffee.

'Eh?'

'Your friend in Wormwood.'

'You know people, do you?' She hated him, he could tell. Nothing to do with him, just for what he did.

'I do, as it happens. He wasn't too pleased after this visit, I hear, our Chris. Chucked a chair through the window.'

'Oh.' She sounded bored but she was squeezing her hands

together so that her bitten nails left crescents in the skin. 'Will he get in trouble?'

'Yep. He's in solitary. Broke a guard's nose – won't go well for him in court, that.'

She raised her dark eyes to look at him. 'Will he go down, then? For that assault?'

'He'll be gone a while, I'd say.'

'Oh.' She crossed her arms over herself and breathed in deeply. 'Do we have that witness protection in this country?'

He was surprised. 'We can take steps to help you stay anonymous, if that's what you want.'

She laughed. 'Bit bloody late for that, d'you not think? What about going away?'

'You want to go away?'

'I'm not asking for me. I'm just asking, like, what if.'

'Hypothetical.'

She glared at him. 'Whatever.'

'I'd see what we can do. Why, you making a decision?'

'None of your fucking business. Officer.'

The door to the little room opened and Charlotte came in on her high ankle boots, that she wore with a grey shift dress and her hair pulled up again into a sort of bun. She looked them over, Keisha, who held so much between her bitten ragged hands, and him, who'd given evidence against her fiancé. Him, who she'd kissed like that, and you couldn't do it like that unless you meant it, could you?

'They're going in,' she said.

It had been a strange week. The day before, he'd been in the station after court, trying to keep up with his paperwork, when Susan came over. She had biscuit crumbs clinging to her shirt. 'People to see you,' she said, with one of her meaningful looks.

'Who's that, then?' He was sorting through his post, hoping for no more of Susan's church flyers – *Prayer bbq, free soft drinks!* That sort of thing.

'You'd better take a look.'

In the waiting room sat a tall, broad, black man, with his arm round a crying, toffee-skinned girl. Without her make-up and afro it took Hegarty a few seconds to recognise Rachel Johnson, and when he did he realised that the other guy was the brother. The living brother, that was. Ronald, who'd avoided him at the club.

He held out his hand. 'DC Hegarty. You must be Miss Johnson's brother.'

Rachel made a snivelling noise. 'You tell him, Ron. I can't.'

Ronald stood up to his full height; Hegarty took a step back. Over six foot tall himself, he didn't often have to look up to people. 'Our Rachel's got a few things she needs to straighten out.'

'Her statement?'

The guy nodded. 'Maybe a few things she got confused on, like.'

'OK. Let's go into the room, then.'

'There's another thing.' Ronald was holding out his hand and in it was a small black box. It looked like a computer hard drive. 'Seems our Anthony had a few secrets,' said the dead man's brother, and then Hegarty understood.

But now it was back to the trial. He'd submitted what he'd learned from Ronald Johnson, and his dead brother's computer had been sent for analysis. Rachel Johnson's statement had been retracted and Kylie was moving for a mistrial, but so far the CPS weren't dropping it. They might have to wait for the appeal to present the new evidence, Kylie said, and that could take years.

There was an even bigger turn-out on that day, thanks to all the stories in the papers about the bank and the police mistakes. Hegarty could hardly get into court as the hearing began. He could see Anthony Johnson's mother and Rachel, newly made-up, who shot him a look, taking her mother's arm, and Ronald, looming over everyone. There were Stockbridge's parents, talking to Charlotte. He could feel the strain coming off them and ducked back into the coffee-room to hide. Kylie was there now, he noticed, making notes on a messy pile of paper in the corner.

'Hiya.' She took off her glasses and rubbed her little eyes, nodded towards the door. 'Oh dear, trouble?'

'No.'

Kylie gave him a look; kind, level. 'She was never really free, was she?'

'I know.' He stared at the door where Charlotte had been. 'So. You're ready?'

'As I can be.'

In his heart, Hegarty just didn't know. Either he was going to lose Charlotte for good, or he was going to send a possibly innocent man to jail. He'd fucked up the one big case of his career. No promotion, now. Another year of busting warrants at three a.m., women throwing tins of beans at his head. 'Well, you tried.'

Kylie gave him a tired smile. 'Don't give up yet, mate. I might just have something up the sleeve of these here robes.'

'Eh? There's nothing left to do, is there?'

'Maybe.' Kylie came up beside him, gathering her papers into her shabby leather bag. 'Hey, when this is over, we won't be working together any more.'

'No.'

'Thank God,' she said, and laughed. He laughed too.

Then Kylie did something he wouldn't have expected in a million years. She stepped right up on the tiptoes of her flat shoes and kissed him on the chin, as far as she could reach. It was a very gentle kiss, like maybe a sister would give. 'Take it easy, Matty.'

'What did you call me?'

'Matty? Oh, that's what I called my brother. Remember, his name was Matthew.'

She walked out, tipping him that annoying little wink of hers. Hegarty stood there. She'd smelled of some very fresh flower, like grass or daisies or something. Like innocence. In every way you could mean it.

'Going in?' The court officer, a wizened little man in uniform, was dangling his bunch of keys.

'Yep.' Hegarty gathered his thoughts and went in.

'All rise,' said the clerk, and the judge came out for the end of everything. He shuffled his papers and glanced round the courtroom. 'I have received an application from the defence to allow one final witness. Despite objections by the prosecution, I have been convinced that this last-minute testimony will relate information crucial to the case, and therefore, following the adjournment, I have allowed it. Silence, please.' He looked up irritably as the murmuring grew up again and died away.

Charlotte was so pale, Hegarty thought she might faint. Dan in the dock was looking around him, terrified. Who the hell was the last witness? Hegarty had no idea. Then, all at once, he did.

Keisha was sitting in front of him, and he saw her gripping the edge of her chair. Then Kylie said, 'The defence calls Miss Keisha Collins,' and she stood up. Charlotte made a little strangled noise. As Keisha walked up in her soft-soled shoes, Charlotte caught her hand. Hegarty saw Keisha look down at her, and squeeze it just for a second. Then she walked on.

She took her seat in the witness box, and the clerk came forward, and she took the affirmation, the non-religious one.

'Could you state your name and address for the record?'

Keisha sat forward. For a second the strip-lighting laid shadows over her pale face. Then she cleared her throat and spoke. 'My name's Keisha Collins. Not got an address just now. But I'm gonna tell you what really happened.'

Epilogue

Six months later

A mile before the church, they started – little wooden signs tied onto the trees, waving slightly in the afternoon breeze. They said: *Wedding this way*.

'Must be the right place.'

'Bloody well hope so.' They'd had a long drive from London to Dorset, and now the roads were so narrow, two cars couldn't pass, and the trees grew together above them, so it seemed nearly dark despite the sunny day. It was the country – she hated the country. It was a warm spring day, the sun making long gold shadows in the trees. There were cows in the fields, and the village had red-brick cottages and people playing cricket on the green. She'd expected it to be exactly like this: the cows, the bloody cricketers, the cutesy little signs.

'Think it's here,' he said, drawing into a field beside the little village church. Cars were parked there already, but not so many as she would have thought. It was a much smaller wedding than the other one would have been. Too many people had just not been there when it mattered, and wouldn't be forgiven now. So the wedding was this, a small country church, reception in the pub, nothing else. You had to respect that.

Suddenly she was jumpy. 'What if they've started?'

'They've not – look.' A white wedding car was pulling up,

and inside you could see someone all surrounded by lace. 'Nice set of wheels there.'

She looked at him.

'Jesus, woman, go on. Do it.'

'You'll mind her?'

'Course.' Ruby had fallen asleep before they even left London, her head dropping onto her shoulder in the back seat. Keisha looked at her daughter for a good few seconds, little legs dangling from the booster seat. She was still getting used to it, that she could let Ruby out of her sight, and the kid would still be there when she came back. 'OK. Give her a juicebox if she wakes up.'

She took off her seatbelt and grabbed the package from the back, opened the car door. Lucky for her she was wearing her usual jeans and trainers, 'cos the fucking ground was like quicksand with spring mud. She'd bet ladies in stilettos would get caught in that.

When she got to the church door the guests had been chased inside and there was just one little girl in pink and a bigger one standing among the crooked gravestones and waving trees. And there, in a different white wedding dress, this one bought in Monsoon, just one flower tucked into her pile of fair curls, was Charlotte. She looked pale with nerves, her step-sister fussing round with the bouquet of pink roses.

'Honestly, I said she hadn't dried them right. They'll leave marks.'

'All right, Sarah, it doesn't matter. Take Tilly inside.'

'I need a wee-wee.' The little girl was whining already. This was Charlotte's niece, Keisha thought. Ruby was much better-behaved.

'For God's sake.' Sarah was pissed off. 'I told her to go at the house.'

'Will you please just—' That was when Charlotte saw her, standing at the corner of the church in her jeans and denim jacket. 'Go in, Sarah, will you?'

'What? You mean walk down?'

'Just go, OK?'

'All right, all right.'

Once the church door had shut, Charlotte turned to Keisha. 'Didn't think you'd come.'

'I'm not staying.'

'You're not? Oh. Where's Ruby?'

'In the car. Ron drove us. Your dad not walking you in?'

Charlotte shrugged. 'I sort of wanted to do it by myself.'

Keisha understood that; better to prove to yourself that you didn't need anyone to walk with you. You had to show that you could stand alone, if you needed to. Just in case. She cleared her throat. 'Sorry about the flat. Sale went through, then?'

'Yeah.' Charlotte sighed. 'It's OK. I think it's been good for us. No mortgage, less money, less stuff – does that make sense? You must think I'm daft.'

Keisha shook her head. She'd given up trying to understand what it was like to be someone like Charlotte. She never would. They were too different, but that was OK. 'You're living down here now?'

'Yes. His dad found me a training post, in his old practice. Can you believe I decided to retrain in law? That's ironic, huh?'

Keisha was never really sure what 'ironic' meant. 'You're a student again, then?'

'Yeah. The money off Dan's firm, you know. It won't last for ever, but – it helps. Since Dan can't work yet – he's not up to it – yeah, it helps.' She was blushing and Keisha wasn't surprised. Three hundred grand must be a help, for sure. That was how much Haussmann's had paid to make Charlotte's brother go away with everything he'd found out about the bullying and stress at Dan's workplace. She'd seen on the morning news that the police were investigating the bank for dodgy dealing now. Couldn't happen to a nicer bunch, she was sure.

'He's still bad, then? Dan?'

Charlotte winced. 'He still can't sleep all night in bed. I find him outside, just sitting in the garden . . .' Something went over her face. 'But we'll manage. He'll get better. He needs me now, his epilepsy's been bad too. We're getting into a routine with the meds. It'll be OK.'

'Yeah. You heard from anyone else at all?'

Charlotte flushed. 'If you mean DC Hegarty, yes. He sent a card.'

'That's nice. Not in trouble then.'

'We-ell. A bit. He'll be all right. Just a reprimand, I think. I suppose they wanted to hush it up, they made so many mistakes.' She wouldn't meet Keisha's eyes.

'Right.'

Charlotte fiddled with the roses, which were indeed dripping water. 'You didn't answer any of my texts.'

'Didn't know what to say, after everything.' Keisha shrugged, taking in the trial, and her surprise testifying, and everything that happened after.

Charlotte nodded stiffly. 'Congratulations, anyway. I didn't have your address to send a card.'

'Oh, no, don't.' Keisha looked down at the diamond on her finger. It wasn't as big as Charlotte's had been, but it was big enough.

'You'll do it over there, in Jamaica?'

'Think so. We're going next week, the three of us. Ron thought it was best to get away. You know, people aren't so happy with us after . . . everything.'

'No. I suppose not.' Charlotte shivered a bit in her dress, probably thinking of the stones thrown at her house and the paint on her step. 'Be careful, will you?'

'S'OK. Anyway, I just came to see you, wish you all the best. Got you this. It's not much.' She shoved the parcel at Charlotte, the tissue paper already falling off. It was the photo of Charlotte that had come from Gary the photographer. The same as the one in the paper, but in this one she was smiling. She looked happy. She looked like she could do things. Keisha had taken it after all the hoo-ha with the trial and she'd put it in a nice silver frame.

Charlotte looked at it for a long time. 'Hard to think I did all that.'

'You did. Better remember it.'

'You definitely won't stay? I want you to be here.'

'Aw, no, Char. I'm in my jeans, aren't I.'

'But it's not fancy – just the pub. Honest, it's not like last time.'

'Char. No. I'm sorry.'

'All right.' She looked sad. This was wrong, Keisha hadn't meant to make her sad, not on her wedding day.

Inside, there was the sound of music starting up, that one, what was it called, something Canon.

'Come *on*, Charlotte,' they heard Sarah hiss from behind the door.

'Go on. You look gorgeous. Told ya you don't need designer shit.' Keisha scuffed her feet, embarrassed.

'Keesh . . .'

'Oh, come on. It's your wedding day!'

'I know.'

'Don't cry. You'll ruin your make-up.'

'OK.' Charlotte sniffed.

Keisha moved towards her and Charlotte threw her arms round the other girl, stifling a little crying sound in her throat. The flower in her hair scratched Keisha's face. She smelled of very strong, very nice perfume. 'I wish – I wish . . . You know, without you, I—' Charlotte was trying to say something. 'I know you sent the letter to Dan. He told me. He said that was why he started to fight, and I never knew, I never thanked you.'

'Don't. It's OK.'

Charlotte tried to smile. Even her tears looked pretty today. 'You'll keep in touch, when you go to Jamaica? Promise?'

'Sure I will.' She said it even though she didn't think she would. She just didn't know how they could, her and Charlotte, after everything. After all that water under the bridge. That was the truth.

The music was starting to falter. 'Go on, they're waiting.'

Charlotte gathered up her skirt and took a deep breath. 'OK. I'm going.'

And she went in, and Keisha peeked in the church door as she walked down in her simple dress, the small crowd smiling and snapping away on their phones and cameras, music swelling. Flashes going off, the smell of flowers. At the end of the aisle was Dan, in a plain suit, his eyes fixed nervously on his bride. One foot in front of the other, that was all it would take. And as she walked to him one step at a time, Charlotte didn't look back once.

Acknowledgements

Sometimes, ideas come from nowhere; sometimes, you know exactly where. The idea for *The Fall* came from a dream I had sometime in 2009. If that hadn't happened, it's unlikely I would have set out to write a novel about a police investigation and a trial, when I know pretty much nothing about these things. Therefore, I have to thank everyone who helped with the research, especially writer Elizabeth Haynes, my cousin Niall McCarron, and my friend Kelly 'Efficiency' Hagedorn, who certainly lived up to her name on this one. Any lingering mistakes are of course my own.

I'd like to thank everyone who contributed to this book's journey from my subconscious to the object you see today. This includes: Sony for launching the new writers' competition; my agent Francesca Barrie for finding me through that; and Ali Hope and everyone at Headline for being so enthusiastic about the book. Being a new writer is a bit bewildering, and so for guidance, welcome, and many, many drinks, I'd like to thank the Crime Writers' Association and all the lovely crime writers I've met so far. They know how to party (and kill you in inventive ways).

Finally, I doubt I'd have got to this stage without the support of everyone who read the book and said they liked it. Especial thanks go to Oliver, who, although it is not a book about management theory, read it first and said, 'Actually, *do* give up the day job.'

If you've read this book, I would love to hear from you. Please visit my website at http://clairemcgowan.net or find me on Twitter, where I am @inkstainsclaire.